Praise for Cara Putman

"Putman skillfully illustrates the individual pain and heartache behind stories of abuse in this captivating third Hidden Justice novel . . . [and] threads a believable layer of faith into the characters' development and offers spiritual asides that enhance rather than crowd the narrative. This character-driven inspirational thriller is an honest look into the hard work of addressing past harms."

—*Publishers Weekly* on *Delayed Justice*

"*Delayed Justice* will hold you to the end . . . A very timely story!"

—Susan Page Davis, author of
the Maine Justice series

"*Delayed Justice* is a timely and compelling legal thriller that will have you turning the pages in search for justice. Putman packs an emotional punch and tackles tough issues head on while demonstrating God's redeeming love."

—Rachel Dylan, bestselling
author of *Deadly Proof*

"This is the way legal thrillers are meant to be—compelling, intelligent, and deeply satisfying."

—Randy Singer, author of
Rule of Law, on *Imperfect Justice*

". . . a frightening yet compulsive reading experience."

—*Library Journal* STARRED
review on *Imperfect Justice*

"The second book in Putman's Hidden Justice series is intricately plotted and thoroughly engrossing . . . This page-turner is smart, thoughtful, and appealing to readers who enjoy legal thrillers and solid mysteries."

—RT BOOK REVIEWS, 4 STARS,
ON IMPERFECT JUSTICE

"The hopeful ending will satisfy fans of romantic suspense."
—PUBLISHERS WEEKLY ON IMPERFECT JUSTICE

"*Imperfect Justice* is solidly written with great tension and a feminine-yet-tough heroine."

—CBA MARKET

"A legal thriller that takes on a burning social issue and the role of faith and strength in meeting that challenge. Like all good storytellers, Cara Putman makes you care. She is at the top of her game with *Imperfect Justice*."

—JAMES SCOTT BELL, BESTSELLING
AUTHOR OF ROMEO'S RULES

"*Imperfect Justice* tackles a gritty subject, and Cara Putman writes with finesse and delicate sensitivity. This legal thriller had me turning pages long after even lawyers have retired for the night, and the fine threads of romance and faith brought hope where often there is none. With a superior story of law and crime, the verdict is in: *Imperfect Justice* will stick with you long after you've devoured the last gripping page."

—JAIME JO WRIGHT, AUTHOR OF
THE HOUSE ON FOSTER HILL

"With its menacing mood, crisp dialog, and quick pace, Putman's action-packed legal thriller highlights a complex political scene. Starring a determined female attorney who will stop at nothing to resolve her case, this title will please fans of Joel C. Rosenberg and John Grisham."

—LIBRARY JOURNAL ON BEYOND JUSTICE

"Putman's new legal thriller is exciting from start to finish. The author builds suspense throughout and, just like real life, it's not easy to distinguish the good people from the bad. This story is well thought-out and incredibly detailed. The author's expertise shines through and adds a tremendous amount of credibility to the story. Danger, adventure and intrigue pour from every chapter."

—RT BOOK REVIEWS, 4 STARS, ON BEYOND JUSTICE

". . . a relatable and fascinating story . . . Remarkably akin to today's news headlines . . . a legal thriller that is intricately written to keep readers on edge."

—CHRISTIAN MARKET, ON BEYOND JUSTICE

"John Grisham, move over for attorney Cara Putman! *Beyond Justice* showcases Putman's deft hand with pacing and authenticity to create an unputdownable novel that kept me on the edge of my seat. I loved the peek into the workings of Washington's political scene as well. *Beyond Justice* is a spectacular novel, and I highly recommend it!"

—COLLEEN COBLE, *USA TODAY*
BESTSELLING AUTHOR

"Cara Putman's legal background has definitely been put to good use in this nail-biter of a romantic suspense/legal thriller. The tension is gripping and the suspense rarely lets up. The story should come with a warning label: Expect high blood pressure and no sleep if you start this book. You won't be able to put this one down until the very end."

—LYNETTE EASON, BESTSELLING, AWARD-WINNING
AUTHOR OF THE ELITE GUARDIANS SERIES

"Cara Putman's expert legal mind shines in *Beyond Justice* as she weaves a gripping, suspenseful tale of intrigue that takes on one of the hardest issues of our time. Hayden McCarthy is one feisty heroine who doesn't let anything get between her and the truth—no matter the cost—even if it's her own life. John Grisham should watch his back!"

—JORDYN REDWOOD, AUTHOR OF THE BLOODLINE
TRILOGY AND *FRACTURED MEMORY*

"*Beyond Justice* is a page-turning mix of action, mystery, and romance that wrestles with real-life issues. Cara Putman packs twists and turns into every chapter. I dare you to put this book down before you reach the end."

—RICK ACKER, BESTSELLING AUTHOR
OF *DEATH IN THE MIND'S EYE*

"Cara Putman's *Beyond Justice* is a great read featuring crisp writing, page-turning suspense, and a deeply satisfying ending. **Highly Recommended.**"

—CARRIE STUART PARKS, AUTHOR OF
A CRY FROM THE DUST AND
WHEN DEATH DRAWS NEAR

IMPERFECT JUSTICE

Cara Putman

THOMAS NELSON
Since 1798

Imperfect Justice

© 2017 by Cara Putman

Published in Nashville, Tennessee, by Thomas Nelson. Thomas Nelson is a registered trademark of HarperCollins Christian Publishing, Inc.

Thomas Nelson titles may be purchased in bulk for educational, business, fund-raising, or sales promotional use. For information, please email SpecialMarkets@ThomasNelson.com.

Scripture quotations marked NIV are taken from the Holy Bible, New International Version®, NIV®. Copyright © 1973, 1978, 1984, 2011 by Biblica, Inc.™ Used by permission of Zondervan. All rights reserved worldwide. www.zondervan.com. The "NIV" and "New International Version" are trademarks registered in the United States Patent and Trademark Office by Biblica, Inc.™

Other Scripture quotations are taken from *The Message*. Copyright © by Eugene H. Peterson 1993, 1994, 1995, 1996, 2000, 2001, 2002. Used by permission of NavPress. All rights reserved. Represented by Tyndale House Publishers, Inc.

Publisher's Note: This novel is a work of fiction. Names, characters, places, and incidents are either products of the author's imagination or used fictitiously. All characters are fictional, and any similarity to people living or dead is purely coincidental.

ISBN: 978-0-7852-2463-1 (mass market)
ISBN: 978-0-7180-8348-9 (trade paper)
ISBN: 978-0-7180-8350-2 (e-book)

Library of Congress Cataloging-in-Publication Data
CIP data is available upon request.

Printed in the United States of America

19 20 21 22 23 QG 5 4 3 2 1

To My Readers:

Thank you for reading these stories. I can't tell you how many times an email, tweet, Facebook post, or other contact with you spurs me on with each story. Thank you for taking what are mere words and breathing life into them by reading my novels.

To Amanda Bostic & LB Norton:

We had to dig deep to pull this story out. Thank you so much for your care and investment in Emilie and Reid's story and in me. It is a true privilege to write with you!

PROLOGUE

As he reviewed the logs from Kaylene's car, he was impressed. She was venturing beyond the short leash he had given her. So long as she remembered he was in charge, all would be well. But he sensed a growing resistance.

He stroked his chin as he leaned into the computer screen. There was a pattern here. Once he uncovered it he would know how to rein her in and remind her that she lived for his pleasure. He could bring her back into compliance. One moment was all it would take.

But first he had to know where she strayed.

The combination of the tracker and her phone log gave him a perfect picture of her comings and goings. Grocery stores, library, that church she used as a crutch. All were locations he approved.

But this repeated stop at a strip mall that held a CPA's office, a dry cleaner, a coffee shop, and a women's resource center . . .

Kaylene's stops were too long to be dropping off or picking up clothing. He handled their finances; she wouldn't be visiting an accountant. And Kaylene didn't drink coffee.

So what was she doing at the center? He snorted. Women's resource center. What a joke. He'd looked it up.

While cloaked in benign words, its purpose was more invasive. It existed to rip families apart.

It was time to up his surveillance. She always went on Thursdays when the girls had piano.

She'd underestimated him, something she wouldn't do twice. He'd make sure of it.

Maybe he'd create something else for her to do this Thursday. An errand perfectly timed to disrupt her plans. A grim smile grew across his face as he cracked his knuckles. That was perfect. If she protested, he'd know he'd been too lenient.

It was time to remind her who was in control.

CHAPTER 1

E milie Wesley glanced at her watch and frowned. In fifteen minutes her client would take a critical step toward freedom. It was a step that had taken months of preparation and more than a little bit of counseling and backbone stiffening. Now all that work, time, and effort would culminate in a protective order. Emilie would step to the background, her role in helping Kaylene Adams alter her abusive present finished.

When she'd finally received the text saying her client was ready to file, Emilie had jumped into action. She wanted to file it before Kaylene changed her mind. Emilie knew from hard experience that could happen in a moment.

But before the judge would grant a protective order, Kaylene had to appear in court.

Without her testimony, the motion was a complete no go.

Emilie stopped pacing and tapped the face of her watch, then pressed it to her ear. The steady *tick, tick* affirmed it was working. What wasn't working was Kaylene's promise to meet her forty-five minutes before the hearing at the Haven, the nonprofit that served women who wanted to escape difficult domestic situations.

She had waited in her office as long as she could before calling Kaylene's cell phone, a call that went directly to voicemail. She'd left a message and then told Taylor Adele, her paralegal, that she was headed to court. Maybe Kaylene had misunderstood where they were meeting. She could be a nervous wreck, waiting outside the courtroom for Emilie to arrive.

Emilie had almost convinced herself that was exactly what had happened until she reached the broad hallway outside the courtroom and couldn't find her client. She pulled her cell phone from her briefcase and called Taylor.

"Any sign of Kaylene?"

"None."

"You're sure? She's got to be somewhere." There was a churning in her gut that left Emilie unsettled, fearing what could have happened.

In the practice of law, clients were people you served during normal business hours and then forgot about when you left the office. Somewhere in her three years at the Haven that had stopped working. She sometimes woke up in the middle of the night panicking over a client's situation—and this was such a case. Kaylene's situation bordered on tenuous even after all the detailed planning and careful work. Her home life was one spark away from erupting, and there was so little Emilie could do to prevent it or protect Kaylene and her girls.

"Want me to keep calling?" Taylor's words penetrated her worried mind.

"Yes. I need to know she's okay."

"She probably got snagged in traffic somewhere. You know how 66 is."

"Stop-and-go all hours of the day." That was exactly why she'd bought a town house that was ridiculously expensive but also incredibly close to where she worked. Vehicles were made to move, not sit in lanes of traffic. "You're likely right. Let me know if you reach her."

Meanwhile, Emilie would check the courtroom just in case Kaylene had slipped around her. An unlikely scenario, but she felt ripples of desperation.

The courtroom was quiet, the dark wood lining the walls somber and weighty. It was surprisingly empty for a Monday morning, a circumstance that would change in the coming minutes unless the judge had canceled the general motion hour. That happened if the court had a jury trial or series of hearings calendared. This morning the only people in the courtroom were a court reporter seated at a computer near the front of the room and the judge.

Judge Emma Franklin had served the people of Alexandria City for fifteen years. She glanced up from the file resting on the large desk in front of her and acknowledged Emilie. "You ready, Miss Wesley?"

"Not quite, Your Honor. My client is on her way." She hoped. "Can we have a few more minutes?"

"The hearing is slated to begin in five, and I have ten minutes after that."

"This won't take long. I'm sure she's looking for parking."

The judge slid reading glasses down her nose and eyed Emilie, her gaze direct and not without warmth.

"You understand your client has to be here to receive a temporary protective order."

"Yes, Your Honor." Emilie fought to keep her tone respectful—the judge knew she understood that. "I'll check the hallway for her again. The courthouse can be intimidating."

"It's easy to forget that when one works here. Good luck." Judge Franklin turned back to her files, and Emilie hurried to the doors leading to the hall.

The moment she exited the courtroom, she stepped to the side and pulled out her cell. A text from Taylor flashed on her screen. Still no answer

Emilie frowned and pulled up Kaylene's number. She hit call and waited for what felt like forever for anyone to pick up. Something was wrong. She hit redial and still no one picked up. The call finally went to voicemail, and she left a brief message: "Kaylene, tell me you're okay."

When she'd started working with domestic violence victims, Emilie had naively believed she could fix their lives—or at least take her skill with words and use it to help these women navigate their turbulent lives.

She'd learned the hard way it wasn't that simple.

If she wanted hope, she should have focused on adoptions.

Instead, she dealt with the real-world dysfunction that kept two people from sustaining a relationship. Where one or the other, sometimes both, fed off a destructive cycle of control and pain.

Did any of Kaylene's neighbors have any idea what happened behind her closed doors?

Probably not.

One or two might suspect, but it wouldn't have risen to the level of intervention.

That was one tragedy of relationship violence. If you didn't see the bruise, you could pretend it didn't exist. If you never thought about the disproportionate number of broken bones, you could believe someone simply had a string of bad luck. Happens to the best of us. After all, a grown woman could always flee if her situation got dangerous, unlike a child trapped in the power of someone bigger and stronger.

It was a fiction, but a fiction people chose to embrace.

Emilie walked down the side staircase to the first floor and checked with security. Then she searched the bathrooms on each floor. Still no sign of Kaylene.

She glanced at her watch as she hurried back to the courtroom. They were out of time, and she'd have to beg Judge Franklin for leniency in the hope Kaylene would eventually appear.

Had Robert, her husband, somehow found out what she was doing?

That was a worst-case scenario, one that could lead only to even worse scenarios. Emilie dislodged the thought as she reentered the courtroom.

"There you are, Ms. Wesley. Did you find your client?"

"No, Your Honor. I'm afraid we'll have to ask for a continuance."

Judge Franklin watched her for a moment, but Emilie refused to shift or fidget. "All right. You can handle that with my clerk."

"Thank you." She hurried from the room and scanned the hallway again as she walked around the corner to the judge's office. It only took a moment to reschedule for the next morning, and then she called Taylor. "I'm going to search the courthouse one more time, then head back."

"All right. I'll call you the moment I hear from her."

"Thanks." Emilie slipped her phone into the side pocket of her Italian leather briefcase. For a moment her thoughts flitted to her graduation trip to Florence and the open-air market where her mom had insisted she buy the briefcase so she'd look the part of an attorney. She shook her head. The memory of her hope and optimism that day disappeared in a wave of fear.

There were a few more people about as Emilie looked into courtrooms and checked the bathrooms one more time. Kaylene wouldn't be the first client who'd had the courage to start the process only to have it fail when she most needed it.

As Emilie walked down the first floor toward the exit, a detective strode toward her. She didn't know Detective Gaines well, but the man had been around a long time and might be able to help. She hurried to him, her heels clicking against the stone floor.

"Detective Gaines, do you have a moment?"

"Not really." His gaze was intent, if slightly unfocused, as if he was preoccupied with whatever matter had brought him to the courthouse.

"My client was supposed to meet me here to get a protective order in front of Judge Franklin. She didn't show."

"I'm sorry, but how can I help? Your client has to want the protection."

"Yes, I know." She blew out a breath, stemming a

wave of annoyance. "I'm worried her husband found out and did something."

"Has he been violent before?"

"Yes." Kaylene had caught her husband in an affair, which had been the proverbial straw that destroyed her ability to carry on as though nothing were wrong. When he beat her for confronting him, she knew she must escape and had shown up at the Haven.

"Give me her name, and I'll check after I take care of something else."

"Thank you." She gave him Kaylene's name and headed outside. In fifteen minutes she was back in her office at the Haven comparing notes with Taylor. "I don't understand."

"That makes two of us." Taylor's usually smiling face wore a mask of concern as she meet Emilie's gaze. "Kaylene was as committed as any of our clients."

It was true, and that was what had Emilie tied up in knots. She moved to her desk and tried to focus on other case files, but her thoughts continued to stray to Kaylene. A news alert beeped onto her phone: *Multiple shooting at Ravens Park home.* She ignored it. Just another sensational headline.

Her desk phone intercom clicked to life.

"Yes?"

"There's a Detective Gaines for you."

"Thanks." She grabbed the phone. "Thanks for getting back to me, Detective."

"Your client's name is Kaylene Adams?"

"Yes."

"She won't be meeting you at court. She's headed to the morgue, and suspected of shooting her daughters."

CHAPTER 2

The shadows lengthened outside the office as Emilie stared at the blank screen. After the Haven closed she sometimes took advantage of the quiet to get out her laptop and work at her other job: freelance investigative journalism for an online newspaper that wanted to be the next must-read. Almost no one beyond her tight circle of girlfriends understood she had dual roles, but each fed a separate part of who she was. Lately, though, the writing didn't flow. It felt stymied, and she hoped by staying late she could knock out her next article.

Instead, she kept imagining Kaylene's body covered by a sheet. Her body heaved onto a gurney. Her body thrust into the ambulance.

If only Kaylene had called her Friday rather than Saturday, so they could have gone to court immediately to file the protective order. Maybe then Kaylene would be alive. Emilie's head knew she'd had no choice but to wait, but her heart felt as though she'd betrayed her client.

The online headlines screamed that the police believed Kaylene had killed one daughter and critically wounded the other. It felt like a waking nightmare. A grainy video that appeared on a couple of the local news station websites seemed to support the theory. One viewing, and Emilie felt her stomach rebel against the lunch she'd eaten as she'd scrambled to find any explanation for the tragedy.

She'd tried to watch it a second time, but she couldn't face it.

Now she had to get this article written, but the words wouldn't come. Even terrible words would be better than none—she could always edit it later.

But the blank screen taunted her . . . the cursor blinking her failure at the top. This was not normal. Had the Muses abandoned her? She leaned across the surface of the desk. The coolness of the pressed wood felt good since the air-conditioning automatically slowed after hours.

After a moment she groaned and pushed back upright. There was no point staying any longer. She should go home, where she could at least stare at the computer screen from her bed in comfy clothes and with bare feet. The ridiculous heels she wore pinched her toes. They were a torture device, but part of her uniform and the identity she presented to clients. She wanted to remind them that they could be both strong and feminine. They could know who they were and be confident. It was possible, if one portrayed the right image. It might be an illusion, but no one else had to know. *Tell yourself that, Emilie*, she thought, wondering where her ability to help people and her words had gone.

She shoved a couple files in her bag, grabbed her car keys, and turned off the lights. The hall was quiet, the faint hum of the refrigerator whispering in the darkness as she passed the kitchen. One of the safety lights buzzed, as annoying as the mosquitoes that swarmed along the Potomac.

She felt a vibration against her side, and she stopped to rummage through her bag. How was it that the pockets always deepened when she scrambled to find a ringing cell phone? When her fingers finally clasped it, the call was gone. All that remained was the screen showing a number she didn't recognize. Oh well. If it was important they'd leave a message. She'd learned if they didn't, she shouldn't call back. No need to invite conversation with strangers who were usually telemarketers.

She jiggled the back door as she walked past. Good, it was already locked. Occasionally the cleaning crew forgot or, more likely, assumed the last staff member would lock it. So she always checked.

After that it was a quick lap through the rest of the warren of hallways to turn off lights. She loved the cheerful framed artwork, drawn by clients' children, that brightened what would otherwise be a boring beige hall. Inexpensive interior decorating with a message. It had been the receptionist's idea, when she first arrived, to soften the space and make it more inviting, but Johanna soon realized that a nonprofit's funds didn't allow for splurges. Then she landed on the idea of dollar-store frames filled with artwork children created. The result was charming and colorful. Then a donor noticed and wrote a check for larger pieces to be framed and displayed in the entry and conference rooms.

The result was unique and perfect.

Emilie stopped to examine an acrylic Kaylene's daughter Kinley had painted. The girl had been delighted to wait for her mom in the children's room, once she'd spotted the art supplies. When Emilie and Kaylene returned an hour later, Kinley hadn't heard them come in. Tongue protruding past her teeth, she was concentrating on adding a thin brush of white along a tree trunk.

Tears filled Emilie's eyes at the memory.

Kinley had glanced up. "That white edge is meant to add highlights." The words sounded so self-assured coming from a nine-year-old.

Kaylene had grinned and tugged her daughter's ponytail. "Guess all those art lessons are worth it. You've created something beautiful." As she looked down at Kinley, the worry lines seemed to fade along her eyes, and the tightness at her mouth eased. "Kaydence is our math and science gal," she'd told Emilie. "Kinley is our creative."

"And you love me for it." Kinley's grin was big enough to split the sky.

There was nothing in the child's face that day to indicate she feared her mom. Nothing at all.

Emilie walked out the front door, checking to make sure it locked behind her before proceeding down the sidewalk to the parking lot. She could have used the back door, but when she left after dusk she preferred to walk along the busy road before darting into the lot and unlocking her car at the last moment.

It might seem paranoid, but she didn't want to give anyone an opportunity to sneak up on her or into her car because she'd carelessly unlocked it while she was fifty yards away. That wasn't a good idea in her line of work.

She tried to peer into all corners of the parking lot before entering it. Even then it wasn't until she was almost to her car that she saw a person in the shadows. She hurried to unlock the car and climb inside and then quickly relocked the doors from the inside. The person stepped forward as she turned the car on and put it in reverse. Then they—she couldn't tell through the lens of the rearview mirror if it was a man or woman—let the weakened light from the street brush across their face, a safe move thanks to the hoodie that cloaked their features.

Emilie wanted to scream in frustration. Who was this person? Before she could do something, anything to fight back—but what? call the police? could they arrive in time?—the person was gone. Vanished in the shadows. If she could see who it was just once, she could do something to fix this and make them stop.

She pulled out of the parking lot and turned onto the street.

She needed to get home. Somewhere safe.

Someplace where she could pretend no one stalked her and made sure she knew it.

FIVE MONTHS EARLIER

He buttoned the top button of his tuxedo shirt, then adjusted the bow tie. Tonight's fund-raiser for the Haven would be his first step into public view since the business trades released the amount he'd been paid for InterIntell. The dollars were large enough to have those who wanted to be his friends circulate where before they hadn't acknowledged him. Tonight he simply had to smile and endure. Shake a few hands. Feign interest and leave as soon as he could.

He'd never quite fit into the social scene, a fact he

could trace to middle school when his interests diverged so completely from those of his mindless classmates.

Today would be different. He knew he could exceed expectations. A few extra zeros in his bank account helped with that.

He was no longer the skinny, nerdy kid who sat in the back row drafting code and forming ideas while the rest learned useless information like the dates of wars and theorems he'd mastered as an eight-year-old. He was the celebrated CEO of a company that revolutionized the way people lived. Where most people looked around the world and saw colors and shapes, he saw zeros and ones. He saw programs that could affect the world around him.

The fact that his dad was a high-tech exec had provided a shortcut to his own launch. He'd barely waited until high school graduation. College classes and his business kept him focused. He'd worked hundred-hour weeks, and two months ago it all paid off when he sold his business for a cool half a billion. Because of the way he'd structured the business, more than half of that landed in his own very fat bank account—a fact touted by the financial magazines and papers.

Society would see him through a very different lens now.

Money could do that. It could turn the awkward into something worthy of attention and time.

He left his bathroom and marched down the stairs and out the front door to where the Lincoln Town Car waited. He'd wear the aura of a wildly successful businessman, maybe even flaunt it a bit. All with good taste.

He slid into the backseat and ignored the driver's small talk. He needed to think about what he would do if she

was there. The woman he'd glimpsed during a tour of the
Haven. A key member of the staff, she'd be at the event
and was the reason he'd agreed to attend.

Forty minutes into the reception, each second ticking
by with excruciating slowness, he was ready to leave.
Those who knew his new situation fawned cloyingly. It
annoyed him and demeaned them. He scanned the crowd
of strangers, searching for her brilliant blonde hair, but
didn't see her.

His listened to a couple of men ten years older than he
joking about their accomplishments, though it sounded
like a string of conquests. So inappropriate in a setting
like this.

"You still listening?" A man in a polka dot bow tie,
whose name tag he hadn't bothered to read, elbowed him.

"Can't help myself."

The man seemed to think his reply was humorous.
Further proof he wasn't worth the time.

"Hey, look who's here." The man on the other side of
Mr. Bow Tie, clearly his equal in laziness and low expectations, pointed to the door. "Now there's a sight for sore eyes."

Mr. Bow Tie whistled through his teeth, a shrill and grat-
ing sound. "Mighty fine indeed. I wonder if she came alone."

Obviously she had. There was no one beside her to
remove her coat or take her arm and lead her through the
space. If she had come with him, he would proudly lean
into her every word, let her know how much he adored
her. Women liked that kind of thing . . . he'd been told.
Time hadn't allowed him to find out for himself.

But as the blonde stopped to speak to a couple of women who dripped with diamonds but hadn't aged as well as they thought, he knew he wanted to find out more than her name.

Bow Tie elbowed him again. The man really must stop that. "Wouldn't you follow her around like a puppy dog just to get her to acknowledge you?"

Bow Tie's friend, Alexander—name tags were useful for memorizing the names of people who were annoying—chortled. "Woof woof." He frowned. "But she looks like an ice queen."

"I always hated that moniker."

"Moniker?" Bow Tie leered at him. "An odd word."

"Guess money can't change everything." Then Alexander's grin faded. "Although maybe that's exactly what Miss Ice Queen wants. A man with resources."

Anger rose in him, but he decided he'd had enough of these two buffoons. He walked away, cutting through a cluster of people without noticing or caring who they were. She was there, the woman who'd entranced him with a glance. He would woo her . . . step by step.

She was talking to another woman. Her blonde hair curled around her shoulders in loose waves, so light. He wanted to touch them. Her off-the-shoulder dress revealed perfect skin, and her smile was friendly and curious. Did she know how beautiful she was compared to the hot-house flowers next to her?

Her friend noticed him first.

Then she turned, curiosity in her expression. "Hi, I'm Emilie Wesley. You are . . . ?"

CHAPTER 3

W hat did one wear to a funeral home to shop for a coffin?

When he woke up Monday morning, Reid Billings assumed the week would be like any other. Seventy hours of meetings, money, and routine. Then Monday's events happened. His boss came to him first. Social media and news websites were not the way to learn one's sister was dead and accused of taking her child's life.

Nothing could have prepared him for this.

He stood in front of his closet, numb, dreading the task before him. It shouldn't be his place to make the funeral arrangements, but Robert had refused.

Could he blame his brother-in-law? He didn't know what to think . . . His head was conflicted and his heart bruised. He rubbed his hands over his stubbled chin. He should probably shave, but he couldn't quite care.

Reid sank to the floor. In moments his world had changed, careened off its axis, and he staggered to find equilibrium. Kaylene had always been a nurturer. She'd mothered him to death, to the point his friends had called her his other mother. Though they'd drifted apart after she married, he knew she had lived for her girls. He couldn't imagine she would do a thing to hurt them, let alone try to end their lives. He'd watched the online video before his assistant Simone's warning email arrived that he shouldn't. Now he couldn't get the image of his sister holding a gun and dying out of his mind. What kind of news service allowed something like that to air where children . . . or the grieving family . . . could see it?

He rubbed his eyes, swallowing the lump that threatened to block his throat. He didn't allow emotions to touch him—that's what made him so great with finance and managing other people's money. He could distance himself from the push of the pack. While others might rush over a cliff together, he kept a distant view. It had protected his clients through the vagrancies of the markets.

But this was different from anything he'd ever dealt with. He felt paralyzed, trapped in his own body, a spectator as a great wave of emotion he didn't know how to manage washed over him.

Why, Lord? This isn't right on any level.

He knew the world was evil. Just watch the evening news or open an Internet browser, and the brokenness leapt at you. His work on the board of a children's home illustrated the fruit of broken families. But somehow he'd believed his family was immune.

His cell pulsed inside his pocket. While he wanted to ignore it, his boss didn't care if he was mourning and guilt-ridden. And if it wasn't Marvin Fletcher, it could be a response to one of the dozens of calls he'd made for the kids at Almost Home. The nonprofit needed an influx of funds quickly or two of the homes would close. He wouldn't accept defeat, not when he had clients with pockets almost as deep as Warren Buffet's.

He reached for the phone, still hesitant. It could be another person trying to ferret out information about Kaylene. The media calls had started slowly, but through the last twenty-four hours had escalated. He glanced at the screen as the phone rang again. Some of the tension leached from his neck. This was a call he'd take.

"Billings."

"You okay?" The deep voice shored him up. Brandon Lancaster had been his best friend since backing into Reid's car freshman year at Virginia. The burly defensive lineman had looked sheepish as he crawled from his truck and stuck out a hand. Before long the two were meeting for lunch most days and then rooming together junior year. After two years in the pros, Brandon now ran Almost Home, a foster child ministry for hard-to-place kids, while Reid spent his time making more money for those who already had wealth.

"No." There was no other answer to that question.

"God's still here."

"Yeah, I know." He did. His head knew. He was just having a hard time convincing his heart.

"Chinese?"

"Huh?"

"Man's gotta eat."

Not really. "Okay."

"I'll bring it at six."

That would give him time to get home from his appointment at the funeral home. "See you then."

Reid hung up and leaned his head against the closet. Man might *have* to eat, but that didn't mean he wanted to. There was no sense telling Brandon that. The guy still ate as though he were a lineman for the college football team.

All right, God. I know You're here even when I don't sense You, but I need You to show up.

'Cause otherwise, this life had gotten too hard to live.

Two hours later the private memorial ceremony was planned, the casket selected for when Kaylene's body was eventually released, instructions about buying a cemetery plot given. Reid walked to his car, loosening the tie that screamed Wall Street. The somber eggplant color had seemed right when he selected it; now it hugged his neck like a noose.

He still couldn't believe Kaylene had shot her girls and then killed herself. The problem was all indications suggested she had. The police were adamant they were right and he was wrong. And if he'd been this wrong about his sister, what else had he been wrong about?

He ground his teeth as he slowed for a light. No. He knew what he knew.

She would not have done the acts the headlines blazoned to the world.

It didn't matter how things appeared.

He knew the Kaylene of his childhood. Knew her heart. If he was honest with himself, he'd noticed rumblings of trouble in her marriage. Seen and heard enough at the occasional birthday party or rare family event to suspect there was more going on than she revealed.

He pulled into the parking garage beneath his building and then made his way to the elevator and to his floor. The condo felt small, empty. Maybe it was time to get a pet. Something that would be glad to see him when he came home. A distraction when he needed one.

Strange that the silence had never bothered him before.

He opened his Pandora app and selected a movie soundtrack station. Maybe some pulsing, dramatic music would help him reframe the terribleness of today . . . or sink into it.

He had to escape this funk before Brandon arrived. His friend would see through him in a minute.

Reid's phone buzzed again, and for two seconds he considered tossing it into his bedroom and closing the door. But what if it was related to the kids at Almost Home? He pulled it out. "Hello?"

There was silence, then a sound as if someone swallowed. He glanced at his screen, but didn't recognize the number, so he put the phone back to his ear.

"My name is Emilie Wesley. I knew your sister . . ."

Right. Everyone knew his sister now that she was infamous.

". . . And I wanted to know how Kinley is."

"I'm sorry, but you'll have to tell me who you are."

"I was her attorney."

Her words ricocheted through him. "Right. Why would Kaylene have an attorney?"

"Why would I lie?" The woman's voice was insistent, if a bit broken at the edge.

"Because you aren't the first person who's pretended to know my sister."

And who took the time to look up the relatives of someone on the front page. He was turning his phone off after this call. Frankly, he should hang up on this person, whoever she was. And he needed to check on Kinley. She was his niece, and he needed to know she would survive. The last thing he needed was more people trying to take advantage of Kaylene's death, Kinley's injuries, and his pain. It just showed how many sick and bored people there were.

What sounded like a shudder, maybe a sob, reached him. "I'm sorry to bother you, but Kaylene would want me to make sure Kinley's okay."

"What's Kinley's middle name?" he demanded. No stranger would know that.

"Rose. Robert picked her first name, but Kaylene insisted on Rose for her middle name. Kaylene said the moment she looked at Kinley she saw the sweet touch of a rose on her face."

Reid paused, shocked at her ready response.

"Kaylene's middle name is Grace," the voice continued. "And Kaydence Marie was a sweet young woman. A thought that terrified her mom."

"How did you learn those details?"

"I told you, Mr. Billings, I was her attorney. Kaylene hired me. I need . . . needed to know those details and many more."

Wouldn't he have known if his sister had needed an

attorney? Had he allowed so much distance to grow between them? He held the phone and prayed this deepening nightmare would end.

• • •

Emilie bit down on her lower lip. She shouldn't have called. It was stupid and impulsive, and that wasn't who she was. She spoke after thinking, moved after deliberation. She didn't call grieving brothers.

She hated grief. Hated the loss and emptiness it represented. The way it hollowed a soul and left a scar that time could ease but never remove. It was a photo missing a family member. The empty chair at every holiday dinner.

Emilie might not understand what had happened Monday, but she knew from all Kaylene had said—and not said—that leaving Kinley defenseless was not okay. The hospital refused to give Emilie a word of information, careful to protect the patient's medical privacy. Emilie knew that was right . . . but she also knew she had to do something for Kinley.

The silence extended so long she was sure he'd hung up. "Mr. Billings?"

"How did you get my name and number?"

"Kaylene gave it to me. She said if anything ever happened, you were the person to contact."

"I need to think about it. Do some research." His voice was firm, yet she heard an underlying fragility in it.

"Is this your cell number? I can text you the website that will confirm who I am and what I'm saying."

There was another pause, and then it was as though he had reached a conclusion. "All right. You can do that."

"Thank you. Please call me back."

The call ended, and Emilie immediately texted him her electronic business card. She held on to the phone. It wouldn't take long to confirm her identity—a simple Google search could accomplish that. Yet as the minutes passed, she concluded he had agreed to the text as a simple way to get off the phone.

She huffed out a breath and tugged her laptop close. If he wouldn't cooperate, she'd turn her attention to learning about Robert Adams.

The front door opened, and Emilie looked up to see Hayden McCarthy walk in. Her roommate's low heels clicked against the hardwood floors, and Emilie had to smile at the hot-pink blouse peeking out from beneath Hayden's suit jacket. Slowly but surely, her friend was breaking out of her navy and black wardrobe. "Get caught at the office, or did Andrew steal you for dinner?"

Hayden set down her briefcase beside the small glass table and smiled. "While I would love to spend time with your charming cousin, he's a little too wrapped up in his latest batch of new kids. And I have to make a living."

Ever since going into practice with their mentor, Savannah Daniels, Hayden had a new purpose . . . and added burdens. In some ways life as an overworked associate had been easier than it was now as an overworked attorney launching out on her own.

She stepped to the bar that separated the living area from the kitchen, then studied Emilie, who was leaning against the other side of the counter. "You okay?"

Emilie considered lying. It would be so much easier than unleashing the maelstrom of her emotions. But if Hayden caught the slightest hint that she was being less than truthful, she would dig until Emilie came clean.

"I can't get Kaylene out of my mind. I keep imagining her body on her front lawn." The newspaper articles hadn't hesitated to paint an image she could clearly see in her mind.

Hayden's eyes softened, and she reached toward Emilie, her touch gentle. "I'm so sorry."

Emilie shuddered. "I can't let it affect me like this."

"Give yourself space to grieve." Hayden set down her keys and then walked around the counter and pulled Emilie into a hug.

Emilie fought the urge to resist.

"Everything's felt off since . . ." She couldn't push the words out. Hayden understood why her home had ceased being a sanctuary. "Maybe I need to sell and start fresh somewhere."

Hayden's eyes glazed with concern. "We're okay here. You love this location."

She did. It sat within a few blocks' walk to her favorite restaurants and the Potomac as it curved south into Virginia. But at night she still had nightmares of her car careening out of control down Rock Creek Parkway the night she'd come home last spring to find that someone had broken into their condo and violated their home. She'd worked through it . . . she thought.

But Monday the fear and uncertainty had returned. She rubbed the goose bumps on her arms.

"Maybe you should take a vacation, Em. You've worked so hard . . . really ever since law school."

"It's what I'm good at."

"Sure." Hayden nodded. "But everyone needs time to refresh."

"I don't see you doing a lot of that either."

Hayden grinned even as her cheeks pinked. "Andrew's really good at making sure I take time off each week." She crossed her arms and leaned back against the counter. "You go from working for your clients to writing an article and back. You're an adrenaline junkie."

Emilie snorted. It wasn't as though she raced from tension-laced trials to pressure-packed deadlines for the thrill of it. Anytime she complained to her parents about her busyness, they just reminded her she didn't need to work. But the reality was she did. She longed for her life to matter, to do something that impacted others. She started to speak, but Hayden held up a hand.

"You know I love you, Emilie. You've had a terrible week. Give yourself grace, okay?"

Emilie nodded as she heard the wisdom in her friend's words. The question was how to actually live it.

CHAPTER 4

Emilie sat at her desk, replaying her conversation with Kaylene's brother. He hadn't known his sister had an attorney, hadn't known she'd needed one. That reinforced Emilie's impression her client had felt trapped. If Kaylene had let her brother into the depths of her problems at home, would she be alive?

The question had chased her through her restless sleep and now haunted her waking hours.

She opened the browser on her computer and clicked to a local network affiliate. Kaylene's death no longer ran as a banner at the top of the page, yet it only took a quick scroll to find the video on the side bar of the web page. She moved the mouse so the arrow hovered over the image. Was she ready to watch it again?

She clicked before she could change her mind.

The video was only thirty seconds of jerky images. Whoever shot it must have stood in a yard a couple doors down from the Adamses' home. In the distance sirens wailed, but otherwise the video was eerily quiet. It was as if everything had focused on the woman stumbling down the front steps. In her hand was a small black item. A gun? Red seeped through the side of her white blouse. Behind her a young woman fell across the steps leading to the sidewalk. Someone yelled for help. Then the video got shaky as a police car raced to a stop at the edge of the frame.

A knock on her office door yanked Emilie from the video.

Taylor stood in the doorway, dressed in a pencil skirt and cashmere sweater, the perfect look for a young professional who wanted to advance. She held up a cup of coffee with a hesitant smile. "It's your favorite."

Emilie accepted the cup and inhaled the rich brew. "Thank you. Do I look that bad?"

"Like you got as little sleep as I did." Taylor sank onto the chair in front of Emilie's slightly battered desk. "What did we do wrong?"

That was the heart of the question. If Emilie had done her job right, somehow she would have convinced Kaylene to quit delaying, and she wouldn't have been at the house when violence erupted.

"Maybe we didn't do anything wrong." The words sounded as weak as the conviction behind them. Sure, in the whispers of her heart, she knew she wasn't the only solution for her clients, but she was a large piece of the work at the Haven. The counselors helped women regain some semblance of self-worth and then Emilie helped them navigate the legal roads.

"And maybe we did." Taylor leaned forward, propping her elbows on her knees, intensity filling her gaze. "Do you still think we can make a difference? I've heard you tell people that you love this job because it allows you to save people. This week we didn't."

It was the truth. She had failed a desperate woman who had come to her. Emilie tried to force perspective . . . A woman had to truly want to flee. Kaylene had waffled back and forth. But she had walked through the door of the Haven needing help.

Emilie had failed Kaylene.

That reality had her boxed into a corner so tight she could hardly breathe, let alone do anything on the stack of files that represented other clients in various stages of longing to break free. Would she make the same missteps with the next woman?

She needed to believe it was possible to carry on. If not, her life's mission was a fraud.

She glanced down at her desk, picked up the top file. Glanced at the intake form Taylor had stapled to the inside cover. *Veronica needs us to fight for her.* Then she pulled the rest of the stack to the center of her desk and looked at her colleague.

"Each woman represented in these files needs us to work our hardest. Ultimately, each one has the choice on whether she'll find a safe place, but without us many wouldn't have the ability, means, or way to escape." Emilie could feel her passion for the work return as she spoke. "What we do is important, but we won't always succeed. This week has been a brutal reminder."

Taylor nodded, a flicker of determination lighting her gray eyes. "I want to win them all."

"Me too." The phone on her desk rang, and she glanced at the caller ID. It was the shelter's executive director, Rhoda Sterling. "I have to take this, but we can talk anytime you need."

Taylor left, and Emilie let the phone ring again as she tried to brush the darkness from her mind. The shadows lingered right at the surface of her thoughts, never more than a flicker away, ready to rear up and overtake her. But if she showed even a moment of weakness, Rhoda would fluff her short gray hair and pack Emilie off to the grief counselor she kept on speed dial.

Emilie blew out a slow breath, then picked up the phone before it rolled to voicemail. "This is Emilie."

"I was beginning to wonder if you'd done the smart thing and gone home." Rhoda's voice sounded crisp and businesslike, but Emilie knew it was the tone her boss used to maintain control.

"Too many clients need my help to leave." The words sounded brittle to her own ears, but she had to exude strength to withstand the force of her boss's personality.

"Emilie . . ."

"I'm fine, Rhoda."

"Doesn't mean I can't be concerned about you. Taylor too." Rhoda sighed, and Emilie could almost hear her reaching a decision. "While I'd like to give you the rest of the week off, I need you to meet with a new client. She'll need your best."

Whereas those words usually energized her, today Emilie felt a prick of something far different. "When is she coming?"

"Fifteen minutes."

"I'm on it." As she hung up, Emilie looked at the Monet prints decorating her office. Water lilies or no, she felt the walls pressing against her. She could barely catch her breath, and her skin felt on fire. *Get a grip,*

Emilie. She had to do this. The whole point of her life was using her skills to help women in crisis. She couldn't let the thought of meeting a new client cause her to look for a paper bag.

She leaned forward in her chair, forced her lungs to expand.

Something wasn't right; this wasn't who she was. She shook her head, trying to clear the haze that clouded her vision. Fine, she'd meet the client, follow the steps she always took. And in the routine, she'd become centered—she hoped.

Twenty minutes later Emilie's phone buzzed again. She surged toward it and pushed the button before she could lose the calm she'd just barely located.

"We're in conference room two." Rhoda's voice had the focused, compassionate edge she used with fragile clients.

"On my way." Emilie stood, grabbed a legal pad, and tucked a business card into it. As she hurried from her office, she bounced against the door and then forced her lungs to slowly release air.

She walked down one beige hall and then turned down another, this one ready for clients to see, with the kids' art hanging against the soothing beige paint. Her office's location kept her isolated from the flow of traffic, a necessity when she needed to focus on legal arguments, but as she passed a handful of offices that housed the social work staff, she noticed that an unusual number were empty. As she neared the small conference room, her steps slowed.

Normally she couldn't wait to meet the next client.

Normally she loved the challenge of figuring out how to help solve their problems and right their worlds.

Today wasn't normal.

She stopped short of the doorway and forced her shoulders back while she took two deep breaths. Then she lifted her chin and entered the room. No one in there needed to discover how her inner turmoil was bleeding into her actions—especially her boss.

Rhoda sat at the small conference table, holding a mug of steaming tea, probably Constant Comment with a squeeze of honey. She smiled, only the smallest hint of wrinkles at the corners of her gray eyes warning Emilie to tread carefully. "Emilie, I'd like you to meet Nadine Hunter. She needs our help."

A young woman with sunglasses hiding her face and a purple bruise swelling her cheek turned slowly toward Emilie. She raised her sunglasses, and her eyes held a bottomed-out look of emptiness.

Rhoda touched Nadine lightly on the arm, and the woman jumped as if she'd been shocked. "Nadine, Emilie Wesley is our staff attorney. She's very good and will be your advocate."

Emilie took another step forward, slid a chair from the table, and then forced herself to ease to the edge of it. She simply had to pretend that she was the confident litigator she had been a week ago. As she smiled, she extended her hand, but Nadine didn't take it.

Emilie kept her smile in place. "It's nice to meet you, Nadine." She kept her voice calm and soft. "Can you tell me your story?"

The young woman—she couldn't be more than

nineteen or twenty—looked everywhere but at Emilie's eyes. "My boyfriend uses me as his punching bag."

"Then let's get you out of there." Emilie pulled the legal pad in front of her and clicked on her erasable pen. "Before I begin collecting information, I want you to know something. I understand. While I was in law school, I had a boyfriend who thought he owned me, and it took a lot of work to break free. A protective order allowed us to get him into jail. It can be the first step for you too." Emilie paused until the woman met her gaze. "First I need some quick information to get started on a protective order that will provide space from him while you figure out what you want to do permanently."

The woman shook her head. "I can't do that. He has Jon, and he won't let me see him if I leave."

"Jon is . . . ?"

"My ten-month-old." A tear tracked down her cheek. "He's the reason I stay. I don't make enough to take care of us, and Reggie knows that. He's the smart one." She touched her cheek, and Emilie could feel all the self-loathing that simple gesture contained.

"We can help you, Nadine." Emilie met Rhoda's gaze, and she felt the strength of resolve rising within. Nadine needed someone who could speak for her, who could help protect her. Emilie would give her best for this woman. Today that would have to be enough.

CHAPTER 5

All night and into Friday morning, Emilie's mind was a cauldron of spinning thoughts. Nadine needed her help now, as did the other women represented by the files, but could she help anyone until she understood what had gone wrong with Kaylene? About four in the morning she sent an email requesting an all-staff early meeting, but she couldn't loosen the panic her fears wrapped around her heart.

She scanned headlines, but they were empty of any new information.

She still couldn't believe Kaylene had shot her girls. But if she hadn't, who did? As far as she knew, only family had been in the home, but just because the media hadn't mentioned another presence didn't mean there wasn't one.

When she arrived at the office, she sent an email to Taylor asking her to order the police report. After a time of staring at a file but not seeing the contents, she glanced at her watch and then gathered her notepad, pen, and phone. It was time to head to the conference room. Her fellow employees straggled in, curiosity or boredom on their faces as they took seats at the oval laminate table.

Black-and-white photos of DC landmarks softened the beige walls and carpet. It would be nice to have more color to warm the room, but the reality was the work they did at the Haven wasn't warm and fuzzy. It often had an edge of life and death and utter chaos.

Rhoda was the last to file in, a slightly impatient look on her face as she settled into her usual chair at the head of the table. "Looks like we're here. Mind telling us why you asked for this meeting?"

Taylor shifted in her seat, her coral top and bright turquoise beads a nice contrast to Rhoda's sterile suit. "I'm curious too."

Emilie launched into her theory quickly, before her boss could grow more impatient. She glanced at the people filling the chairs at the table. Several worked as caseworkers, meaning they were responsible for helping a portfolio of clients receive the support they needed. A couple filled counseling or other specialized roles like her own.

Her gaze stopped when it landed on Shannon Riaz. "I can't stop thinking about Kaylene Adams. I realized I didn't know her as well as some of you may have. Shannon and any others who worked with her, I'd like your impressions of her and her story. Did she have friends she confi—"

Rhoda interrupted her. "Why are we spending time on a woman we can't help when there are dozens in need of our assistance?"

"What if the story as we know it isn't correct?" Emilie leaned forward. "The Kaylene I knew could not have done what the police say."

Taylor nodded. "I agree. I can't imagine her with a gun."

"She could have had one." This came from Shannon, the recent graduate who filled a social worker role and had been Kaylene's caseworker. "She asked me how to get a permit and where to purchase one."

Emilie's heart sank. "Why would she ask you that?"

"She noticed the photo I have behind my desk." Shannon shifted against the chair. "I was on my college rifle team, and she was interested." She raised her hands defensively as Rhoda groaned. "What?"

"This is exactly the kind of information that cannot get out. We do not need anyone suggesting that we helped arm a murderer." Rhoda looked at each person around the table with unflinching intensity. "I am absolutely serious about this. I see this information in the news, I find out who leaked it, and you will lose your job."

Her gaze settled heavily on Emilie, as if she expected her to sprint to the *Nation's Post* with an exclusive.

"Don't worry, I'm not writing anything for anyone." Emilie jotted a note. "Okay, so she asked about a gun. Did she actually buy one?"

"We need to end this discussion right here." Rhoda leaned forward, palms pressed flat against the table. "Nothing good can come of this conversation."

"I disagree. If we can figure out whether Kaylene owned a gun, we can determine whether it was used in the shooting." Emilie kept pushing. "What if it wasn't her gun? What if she was trapped?"

"Then she should have let us help her. The video certainly makes it look like she was the one using it.

It absolutely cannot get out that we had anything to do with talking to Kaylene about a gun. Am I clear?" Rhoda made eye contact with each person at the table. "This is not a topic we should discuss with our women."

Emilie watched the others nod, even if with reluctance.

"Emilie?" Rhoda focused completely on her, steel in her eyes. "Do I have your cooperation?"

Emilie swallowed hard, feeling all moisture drain from her mouth. "I need to think about this."

"There's nothing to think about. Either you're working for the good of this agency or you're not."

Suddenly Taylor jerked as if she'd been jolted with electricity. She mouthed *sorry*, then pulled out her phone. "Emilie, we have a client emergency."

Emilie jumped up and made her way out of the conference room with a quick thanks, Taylor close on her heels.

"Who is it?"

"No one. I knew you needed an out."

Emilie stifled a smile as she hurried into her office. "You'd better create a real client emergency in case Rhoda fact-checks." She sank into her leather office chair and jiggled her mouse to wake up her computer. "Have you ever seen her like that?"

"No, but her assistant said she's been under intense pressure. It sounds like she's had to do some fancy stepping to keep key donors from bailing."

"I wonder why. No one has said Kaylene came here."

Taylor shrugged. "Who knows?"

Maybe they would never understand. Much as she wanted to plead that everyone was wrong about Kaylene,

Emilie couldn't ignore the voice in her head saying that somehow she should have prevented both deaths.

. . .

Reid did an Internet search for all articles related to his sister's death. Maybe a reporter had found someone to interview he hadn't thought of yet.

Which wouldn't be hard. He hadn't stayed in touch with Kaylene, allowing space to grow between them. He'd been focused on college and then launching his career. Finance wasn't one of those nine to five, walk-away-from-it jobs. At least not if you wanted to work for a top-notch firm, and he'd refused to settle for less.

What had that choice cost him?

He might never know, but he could do something now for Kinley. He could make sure she was safe, and maybe in doing that he could absolve his earlier selfishness.

The browser did its job too well, pulling up a long list of articles. So this was what it was like to be infamous. As he scanned the articles, he sensed a pattern to the reporting. There was the sensational element of the first days. Mother shoots her kids. Family in chaos. Scandal and abuse abound. Not the first time one of the couple had called the police or sought help.

Wait, they'd sought help? He reread the article slowly.

The reporter for this article had relied on innuendo, but had tracked down an unidentified source who suggested Kaylene had sought counseling and Robert had refused to participate. The source indicated it was a familiar story. Wife wants to save her marriage, work on serious issues, but receives no cooperation from husband.

Reid frowned. So how would that cause Kaylene to shoot her daughters? If Robert had been her problem, why wouldn't she have shot him? Assuming, of course, that killing someone had ever been her intent—a leap of logic Reid still couldn't make.

He felt his eyes cross as he read one more article. He stood and stretched, then went into his living room and sat at the baby grand. He closed his eyes and let his fingers move across the keys. The music poured from him. Fast, furious, forte.

It felt like a prayer. A demand asking God to intervene.

As tumultuous as his emotions were, he felt an odd settling peace as time slid by on a sea of notes that flowed without conscious thought. When he could keep his mind empty and open, he often heard God whisper.

Wasn't that how the best prayers developed?

By opening one's heart and mind to God, letting Him into the pain and the joy?

That was what he did in those moments at the piano.

The notes slowed as the air conditioner kicked on, sounding an accompanying hum. Reid swayed as the notes spilled from him.

Twenty minutes later the music eased to a fading note.

He opened his eyes. He hadn't received any insights, but he felt solid, no longer subject to the day's sucker punches and blows. As he went back to his tasks, he felt renewed hope that if he kept on the same path he would find truth. And if that truth were that Kaylene had shot and killed her daughters, then he would deal with it. Tragedies happened in a world broken with sin. But he also knew he didn't feel released from his burden to investigate. He would pursue this further . . . after he got through the afternoon's memorial service.

CHAPTER 6

Emilie straightened the hemline of the black, businesslike jacket she wore over a black sheath. The ensemble felt like a uniform that didn't quite fit. She should feel warm in the sweltering heat of a Washington, DC, August afternoon, but all she felt was a bone-level chill. She couldn't warm up no matter how much coffee or hot tea she drank, and she felt the circling vulture of fear colliding with her shock and grief.

She caught her heel on a step and stumbled, then Taylor stepped closer to steady her as they entered the heavy wooden front door.

Emilie grabbed Taylor's hand and squeezed tight. She would get through the next hour and then pray that the following week would bring a sea change in her rattled and battered emotions. She'd write her article over the weekend for the *Nation's Post* and return to the office Monday ready to forget this week. Then she spotted an enlarged photo of Kaylene with her precious girls, and her knees threatened to buckle. Taylor immediately tightened her hold.

"You okay?"

Emilie shook her head, unable to form words, and

then Taylor pulled her into a hug that she couldn't fight any more than she could return. And they hadn't even made it into the sanctuary. She allowed herself to soak in the comfort for a moment, then pushed back. "We should get inside."

Emilie looked around the large entry that was filled with people in small clumps. Did all these people really know Kaylene or the girls? This was supposed to be a private service, and she'd been surprised when Taylor told her they had an invitation. Was it Kaylene's brother's way of testing whether she really knew his sister? A small cluster of teenagers caught her eyes. Maybe they had been friends of Kaydence.

Taylor took the lead as they moved through the anteroom to the small sanctuary.

A man stood at the doorway shuffling his feet as he tugged at his shirt cuffs. This had to be Kaylene's brother, Reid, his face a masculine version of hers. The wariness on his face indicated his discomfort as he settled a hand on an older woman's back. Maybe a grandmother? Kaylene had mentioned being raised by her grandparents. Reid's brown eyes were so somber as his gaze briefly met Emilie's that for a moment she forgot her annoyance that the man hadn't called her back.

"Hey, girl. You ready to quit staring?" Taylor's soft words yanked Emilie from her thoughts.

"Ummm." The flush of heat that started at the base of her neck had nothing to do with the early-afternoon sunshine pouring through a window.

"Do you want to stop and talk to him? Confirm who he is?"

Standing slightly behind Reid was a bear of a man, his attention laser-focused on the people milling about. A bodyguard? She wasn't sure she wanted to find out, but she did want to meet Reid.

"We'll greet him, then find a seat." Just then a crying woman pushed in front of them and embraced the man. The last thing Emilie wanted was to enter the emotional fray of a stranger's grief. She tugged Taylor toward the sanctuary door. "Let's leave them alone. We can find him after the service."

Taylor selected a pew toward the middle, then slid in. Emilie squared her jaw. She would endure every second of the service that honored her client and friend. Her phone buzzed, and she glanced at the alert. It was a reminder that she was supposed to meet Kaylene for coffee Saturday morning. Once Robert had forced the girls to stop piano lessons, the two women had squeezed their consultations in when Kaylene was shopping, giving her plausible deniability if Robert asked where she'd been.

Emilie's eyes clouded with tears as she cleared the alert, then fixed her gaze on the pulpit. There was no casket or viewing. This was a time to remember Kaylene and start the process of letting go.

The service passed in a blur of meaningless words from a pastor who didn't know Kaylene. The man tried, Emilie had to acknowledge, but he missed the essence of what had made the woman so special. The way she'd found a courage deep inside, her all-encompassing love for her girls, the little ways she'd found to begin reclaiming her life. He was followed by two people, but she could tell they felt lost and confused. The reality of Kaylene's death overshadowed their memories of her. How could any of them match the woman they knew and loved with the reality of her death? The images they had with her were superimposed with Monday's grainy video.

The moment the service ended after a mournful song, Emilie was too glad to let Taylor drag her outside. "I think I'm going to start the weekend early." She didn't have the strength to talk to other women with struggles like Kaylene's. Not today. "I've got to write an article."

"The one that's refusing to cooperate?"

Emilie nodded, her throat constricting.

Taylor pulled her sunglasses down from her hair. "I'll check email over the weekend in case you need anything for Monday's deposition in Virginia Beach. Don't forget Tuesday's hearing. We can finish prepping for that over the phone if it helps."

"I haven't forgotten the hearing." Emilie tried to smile. "I'll get this article knocked out and then be ready to dive back in."

Emilie climbed into her car and drove home. As soon as she walked inside, she tossed her purse on the kitchen counter and poured a glass of iced mint tea. The refreshing coolness soothed her as she gulped it down. She slipped downstairs and changed into a comfortable maxi dress with a cardigan. The lower temperature of the basement should help wake her up and get her mind moving. The shadows felt deep, and even a dozen lit lavender and vanilla scented candles couldn't chase the gloom from her space. She turned on instrumental praise and worship, but it couldn't press back the weight of grief and guilt.

Before she could get down to the business of writing, she had to make sure Rhoda was okay with her spontaneous afternoon off. She went back upstairs and retrieved her purse from the kitchen, pausing to dig for her phone.

When she couldn't find it, she gave up and dumped the contents on the counter. As she reached to snag a tube of lipstick rolling toward the edge, she spied a folded piece of stiff paper. She opened it and stared.

I HAVEN'T DISAPPEARED FROM YOUR LIFE

Emilie reread the note, the block letters swimming along the page.

She flipped it over but saw nothing distinguishing about the paper, nothing to indicate where it had come from.

Was this someone's idea of a bad joke?

It must have been slipped into her purse at the memorial, since she'd cleaned out all the paper detritus before the service. Who would have done it? There were enough people present that there was no way she could know who had left the note for her. She slipped it into the junk drawer. Should she contact the police? Though the note caused her pulse to race, she knew that no one else would take such a benign message seriously. They'd discount her concerns, as they had before. She closed the drawer with a sigh and headed back downstairs.

Until last April, article ideas and the actual writing had flowed in a steady stream. Now her mind refused to cooperate. She'd turned in a few pieces, but not nearly of the quality she'd produced before, and her editor was placing enormous pressure on her to up her game. No one seemed to understand that stumbling onto a scandal like the one involving the son of a Mexican drug lord murdered at his father's order while in US custody was a once-in-a-lifetime scenario. Not to mention that she'd only gotten on to the story through Hayden's involvement in the case. How was Emilie supposed to replicate a coup like that without her own life being threatened? No one else seemed to consider that when they demanded more from her.

Each time she sat frozen at her computer, her panic grew.

Time and deadline extensions were expiring, and she didn't know how to recover.

An hour later Emilie still stared at a blank screen as her emotions roiled.

Enough.

She must write this article.

She plugged in her noise-canceling headphones and took a deep breath. Her editor expected a blazing exposé on a pork barrel bill careening through the Senate. Instead, she wanted to write an essay about how blind people were to the crisis of domestic violence. Yeah, her editor would love that.

Words had always been Emilie's strength. She could string them together in a way that changed judges' minds and congressmen's hearts. But tonight she couldn't get two words to make sense, let alone make the legislation interesting.

Nothing filled her mind but Kaylene's image.

She knew she could not write in any way about the Adams family. Rhoda had been crystal clear. It didn't matter that Emilie's thoughts were locked on the tragedy and how to avoid a repeat. If she wanted to continue to help women through the Haven, she had to focus on her clients, not the larger realm of public opinion. Her two careers had to remain separate.

If only her mind could agree.

Pushing back from her desk, Emilie stood and then took the stairs two at a time. She'd get her blood moving and then her brain would cooperate. She grabbed a pair of tennis shoes from beside the back door and dropped her cardigan. Two minutes later she was on the sidewalk, arms swinging, as she took off for the Potomac, stretching her stride against the restraint of her maxi dress. A little time outside would help.

Questions filled her mind as she walked. Where had God been when Kaylene and her girls needed Him? Wasn't He the protector of the innocent and defenseless?

When she returned to the town house after walking a couple miles, sweat pooling at the small of her back, the air-conditioning smacked her. Before she headed back downstairs, maybe she should find something enticing in the fridge. She opened the door and then stared at the containers and bottles.

While she might believe Kaylene would never try to murder her girls, long experience with her shelter clients had proven the unexpected and unthinkable could happen at any moment. People who were adamant they could never go home, did. Women who swore they'd never let an abuser near their kids, did. And the abused snapped.

She also couldn't ignore the video images. They were irrefutable, at least in the court of public opinion. Would the police talk to her? Probably not, since she was an attorney without a client. But maybe Detective Gaines would. He'd at least told her about Kaylene on Monday.

She pulled out her phone and left a message for him. Since it was already Friday afternoon, she doubted she'd hear from him over the weekend. But maybe on Monday she would. And maybe then she could accept the truth.

Emilie rubbed the back of her neck where tension had gathered. She had to do something to distract herself. As long as she stayed focused on Kaylene, she was a frozen wreck.

CHAPTER 7

The morning sun barged through the curtains Reid hadn't closed tightly the night before, blinding him like a spotlight. He'd wanted to spend the day forgetting the terrible week with a bout of sleep that blocked everything.

Instead, the sunlight sliced at his eyeballs.

He grunted and then thrust the sheet to the side and climbed from his bed. Might as well admit reality—the week had happened and he wouldn't sleep anymore today. Twenty minutes later his hair was still wet as he sat at his concrete kitchen table and drank a mug of black coffee. He'd spread the front page of the *Washington Post* in front of him but hadn't absorbed a word. He thrust the paper aside and took the last swig of coffee, grimacing at the grounds that came with it.

What should he do since he was up?

On a normal Saturday he'd spend at least half the day on work—trying to stay ahead of the curve. Too much happened over weekends not to keep a close eye on what the markets were doing around the world. Once he felt he'd spent enough time on work, he'd follow that with an hour or two at the gym and then slide into the back of a movie theater to watch a new release. Not necessarily exciting, but that kind of weekend was all his job allowed.

Managing hundreds of millions of dollars for others didn't leave time to find a soulmate.

It was on rare instances like this that he felt the lack. He missed having someone to share the horrible week with.

Busy. He needed to stay busy.

As he looked around the condo, the sun highlighted a layer of dust on every surface and a stack of junk he needed to go through. Might as well do it today, since he couldn't manage anything requiring brain cells. His mom routinely told him that a good cleaning service was worth every penny, but he didn't like the idea of a stranger digging through his things. He never wanted to worry about whether he'd left something out that could harm a client if leaked or stolen.

A knock at his door stirred him from his thoughts, and he pushed to his feet. He glanced through the door's peephole and grinned. Brandon. He wore an Indianapolis Colts cap backward on his head, workout shorts, and an Under Armour shirt.

Reid opened the door and leaned against the frame. "You take a shower before coming here?"

"That any way to talk to a friend?" Brandon lifted an arm and sniffed beneath it. "Think I put deodorant on."

Reid rolled his eyes. "I guess I'll let you in."

Brandon brushed past him, then they man-hugged with a slap or two before Reid led him into the kitchen.

"Can I get you some coffee?"

"Sure. Got any cream?"

Reid held up the coffeepot, and Brandon pulled a face at the inch of sludge at the bottom. "Maybe I'll take a pass. When will you get a Keurig? You can afford about twenty."

"I don't need one." He'd always had coffee from a pot growing up, and the one he had now had been a college graduation gift from his grandma. It still worked, so why change?

While Reid brewed a fresh pot, Brandon told him about some trouble they were having with a new family group that had been placed at Almost Home. When the coffee was ready, Reid poured a mug and set it in front of his friend along with a little carton of creamer that smelled like it was still good.

"Thanks." Brandon filled the mug with coffee and topped it with an inch of creamer, then took a sip. "Not bad. Sorry to make so much noise since I got here. I came to let you talk."

"No problem. It was nice not to be trapped in my head." Even nicer than he would have expected, to listen to someone else's concerns. Surely he could help fix this—a welcome change after his week. "Anything I can do to help with the kids?"

"Not a thing. They need time." Brandon hunched forward, the mug looking absurdly small in his beefy hands. "I've gone through this process plenty of times."

"Guess that social work degree was worth something after all."

"Yeah. Now fill me in on you."

"Nothing new to tell since the funeral yesterday. Thanks again for coming."

"Wouldn't have missed it. Really, nothing at all?"

"Nope."

Brandon leaned back, a disbelieving look on his face. "You still breathing?"

"Pretty sure."

"Then there's something going on up there. Spill."

"What are you, Dr. Phil?"

"If that's what it takes to get you to access your feelings. The service was yesterday."

Darn social work degree. "I'm not one of your kids."

"You need me more than 95 percent of them."

Reid placed a hand over his heart like he'd been wounded. "That stings. Only 5 percent of your clients are worse off than I am?"

"If the loafer fits . . ."

"Whatever." Reid stared into his mug, trying to come up with something he could do or say as a distraction. He wasn't ready to talk, despite his friend's good intentions.

Brandon let the silence lengthen, but Reid was on to his ways. It wasn't going to work this time, not if Reid could help it.

But Brandon just sat there, looking like he had nothing else to do but sit in that chair holding his empty mug.

"What do you want from me?"

"Acknowledge that your world is upside down."

"You know that. I know that. I don't need psychobabble to make it more real."

"Okay, stay in self-denial, man." Brandon lumbered to his feet. "I've got to get the cat some food before I head home or I'll never hear the end of it."

"Frodo is starving?"

"He thinks so. And he likes to remind me . . . loudly." Brandon paused at the front door. "Call if you need anything."

"I will." Not a chance. The last thing he needed was Brandon hovering.

As if reading his thoughts, his friend continued. "Better yet, meet me at the Union House at two, and we'll have a late lunch. I'm hungry for a burger."

Reid didn't want to say yes.

"A man has to eat."

"I've heard that before." Leave it to Brandon to focus on his stomach. And a big burger and stack of fries from the Old Town restaurant did sound good. "All right. I'll meet you there."

After Brandon left, Reid leaned against the door. What should he do until two? The floor looked like it hadn't been swept in days. He'd start there. Do that task. Then the next. If he did enough, he'd get to the other side of the day and eat at least one meal while he lived it.

He opened the door to the junk closet and reached for the broom. His fingers grazed the dustpan, knocking it to the floor. As he stooped to pick it up, he spotted a couple legal boxes he'd shoved under the wire shelves and forgotten. What was in those anyway? Today would be a good day to go through them and purge the junk. A mindless task that would give him a sense of progress. He set the broom back against the closet wall and squatted to tug the first box free. The lid caught on the bottom rack, so he tugged harder and then abruptly sat on the floor when the box finally came free.

He eased the box closer, and the handwriting on the top arrested him.

Kaylene's.

He remembered now. She'd brought the boxes on one of the hottest days in early July. The humidity had been brutal—the kind that had tourists diving from Smithsonian to Smithsonian, desperate for air-conditioning. She'd worn cutoffs and a T-shirt, and looked more like eighteen than thirty-eight. She'd asked him if he could store the boxes for her, but asked him not to look in them, so he'd shoved them into the bottom of the hall closet and forgotten them. At the time he'd wondered vaguely why she couldn't find room in her own house, but he hadn't questioned. Now she could never reclaim them.

He pulled the packing tape free and opened the box.

A card-sized envelope rested on top of a stack of file folders and photo albums. His name was scrawled on top in Kaylene's loopy script. He picked up the envelope and opened it. As he pulled out the card, a folded piece of paper fluttered free.

Dear Reid,

I hope you never see this letter. If we're fortunate, I'll retrieve the boxes before you have a chance to get nosy. You're good at that, you know. I wonder if that's a trait of all younger siblings.

Things are hard right now, but I'm taking steps to get the girls and myself to safety. And no, I can't ask you to help me. This is something I must do myself while minimizing the harm that can come to those

I love. When we're safe, I'll need these boxes. Right
now, I need to know you have them.

If you see this and can't talk to me, it means my
escape failed. Please promise you'll take care of my
girls. They are my greatest treasure. Promise you'll
keep them safe. Ask my attorney, Emilie Wesley, to
help. She knows the whole story—well, as much as
I've shared with anyone—and she understands why I
couldn't tell you and why I need your help now. You
can trust her—she'll be the advocate you and my
daughters need.

As I said, my greatest hope is that you'll never see
this. I'll come back, and we'll joke about the good ole
days. Or you'll tell me I was crazy not to let you know.
But some things a woman should handle on her own,
little brother. Know always that I love you, and thank
you for being a safe place for my girls if they need you.

Hugs,
Kaylene

She'd added a heart after her name, one with all the
swirls and emotion of a thirteen-year-old girl.

He reread the letter.

What had she been trying to tell him without saying
it directly? Did this mean Kinley wasn't safe with her
own father?

That was a crazy thought . . . wasn't it?

CHAPTER 8

"Y ou're coming out with us this afternoon. That's all there is to it." Hayden stood in the doorway, arms crossed, on her face a determined look Emilie had seen enough times to know protesting wouldn't accomplish a thing.

"I have to pack." A Monday-morning deposition of a client in Virginia Beach meant she would fly south Sunday afternoon, then back for a hearing first thing Tuesday morning. In the middle of all that she had to gain traction on her investigative piece for the *Nation's Post*. It felt like all the balls she juggled were one false step from crashing on her.

"It doesn't take that long to pack for an overnight business trip, and you have to eat."

Emilie knew she shouldn't argue with a fellow attorney. "I don't want to be a third wheel. You and Andrew go have a great time wherever you have plans. I'll be fine here." In her comfy yoga pants with a pint of black cherry chocolate ice cream.

"Nope. Plans changed. Jaime and Caroline are on their way to meet us at the Union House. We'll get some beer cheese and burgers, sit outside, and let the breeze from the Potomac cool us."

"You mean we'll fry in the afternoon sun."

"When winter is here and you're perpetually frozen, you'll look back on this excursion with warm memories." Hayden tugged Emilie to her feet. "Come on. It'll be good for all of us to get our weekly dose of vitamin D."

Emilie laughed as she let Hayden pull her to her closet. "You are creative."

"What?" Hayden turned to her with an innocent expression. "You didn't see that 10 percent of Americans are short on this vital nutrient?"

"All right, I'm coming. Let me change in peace."

Twenty minutes later, Emilie straightened her jean skirt and then looked in the mirror and swiped on some rosy lip gloss. She'd decided to go for an easy breezy look, pulling her hair into a small messy bun. She stepped into strappy sandals, then headed upstairs. Sunlight streamed through the gauzy curtains on the windows.

Hayden was reading in a wing chair in a puddle of light.

"You ready?" Emilie poured a glass of water and drank it while she waited for her roommate to set her Kindle aside.

"That took longer than I expected, but wow. You know we're just meeting the girls for a late lunch, right?"

"Yep. I felt the need to do more than run a brush through my hair." Her mother had taught her the importance of being ready at every moment for whomever you might run into. In this town, it could be anyone from a cabinet member to a congressman, with a few lobbyists and important bureaucrats thrown in. Emilie slipped her cross-body purse over her head. "Ready to roll."

When they stepped outside, the air-conditioned coolness gave way to the heavy warmth of DC. The messy
bun alone might not be enough to keep her hair from
escaping into reluctant coils. Humidity did not favor
those with wavy hair. Still . . . "You were right."

Hayden kept her gaze forward, but Emilie could feel
her curiosity. "About what?"

"The sunshine feels great."

"It should. I love you, Em, but sometimes that basement seems like a cave rather than the retreat you claim.
I still can't understand why you let me live on that sunny
second floor."

They'd had quite an argument when Hayden moved
in, and Emilie had given up trying to explain why she
felt so safe and secure in her little world below ground.
It also helped fend off distractions when she needed to
settle in and focus on a story or legal argument. Plug
in her headphones, light a candle or two, and all she
could see was the task in front of her. For some reason
that was easier in her basement suite than in Hayden's
upstairs area.

By the end of the few blocks' walk over to the Union
Street restaurant, sweat rolled between her shoulder blades, and Emilie was ready to chuck the dose
of Vitamin D for a tall glass of water and some air-
conditioning. "It will be good to get inside."

"We'll see." Hayden's smile was oddly mysterious. It
wasn't a look that telegraphed she was deep in thought
about a legal puzzle she needed to solve. More likely it
meant she was thinking about Andrew.

The hostess asked for their names.

"We're meeting some friends, and I see them." Hayden did her take-charge thing and swept past tables filled with guests, her shoes clicking against the dark wood floor. She reached the far side of the restaurant, where the floor changed to black-and-white tile and the walls were a stark white. It felt stiffer and less welcoming than the natural wood and brick in the main space.

Emilie, trying to keep up, suddenly stopped when a diner slid back his chair without looking to see if anyone was coming. He smiled a quick apology, and she realized it was Reid Billings—well, if she'd been right about him at the funeral. "Are you Reid?"

He looked at her, eyes narrowing before he forced a smile. "Yes."

"Emilie Wesley."

"Kaylene's attorney." He settled back. "I owe you a call."

"You do." She felt something in his gaze pull at her. Did her eyes mirror the wells of pain she saw in his? She dipped her chin to say it was all right. Hayden cleared her throat, and Emilie smiled apologetically. "I need to join my friends." She quickly closed the distance to the table where the other women waited.

"Getting run over by a chair is one way to meet a handsome guy." Caroline Bragg stood for hugs, her words thick with Southern honey. "Can you introduce us?"

Emilie looked back toward Kaylene's brother. He had a sophisticated air, but the stubble on his face lent a carelessness to his demeanor. His untucked polo and khaki cargo shorts gave him an unconcerned-about-impressions appearance. But the circles beneath his eyes suggested there was more going on. He caught her looking at him, and a slow smile creased his face.

Hayden tugged Caroline into a hug, breaking Emilie's focus. "We have got to find you a guy to call your own." She glanced back the way they'd come. "But you're right. He'd be a good candidate."

"All in due time. The judge keeps me hopping." Caroline looked ready for a pleasant afternoon outside. Her perfect sundress showed off her slim figure, and she wore a wide-brimmed hat that would shield her from any hint of sun that dared slip inside. She sank onto her chair and took a sip from a glass of iced tea that had condensation running down the outside.

Jaime Nichols, on the other hand, looked more than ready for a day far away from humid Virginia. Her black hair had corkscrewed around her head, and her glasses threatened to slip down her nose. "I'm so glad someone invented air-conditioning." She stood for quick hugs, then sat back down.

Angela Thrasher smiled from her chair. "It's good to see you, Emilie." She shifted but didn't stand, twirling a straw through the glass in front of her. She seemed distracted as she adjusted her cardigan. The thin woman was always cold.

Emilie nodded, still trying to get used to the fact that Hayden had hauled her former friendly rival at Elliott & Johnson into their circle. "Nice to see you again, Angela."

"We're almost all here." Hayden pulled another chair to their table and sank onto it.

Emilie frowned as she looked at her cadre plus one. "Who's missing?"

"Savannah. She wants to catch up with everyone, and this was the perfect time." Hayden had a self-satisfied tilt to her head. "She's scheming and wants to share something with us."

Jaime frowned, Angela looked unconcerned, and Caroline commented that it would be good to see their law school mentor. Savannah Daniels had provided a safe place for Hayden to land when her firm had unceremoniously fired her a few months before. Hayden's efforts to build her own base of clients was taking shape and turning into a success, thanks to the older woman. And from what Emilie had heard, Angela was starting to have similar success. What would it be like to have someone believe in her like Savannah believed in them?

The ambient noise of music playing in the background, along with the conversations ricocheting off the tile and wood floors, provided a noisy background that settled over her. She sank onto an empty chair. "It's good to be here."

Hayden grinned at all of them and leaned on the table. "Andrew's taking me to the Kennedy Center tomorrow night for an off-Broadway show."

"That explains why you were suddenly free today." Emilie placed her drink order and then set the white cloth napkin across her lap. It was nice to be with the girls.

"That sounds fun, Hayden. Andrew is so good to you." Caroline practically swooned in her chair.

"He is."

Jaime took a sip of her water. "How are you doing,

Emilie? What a week for you." The words were right, but her shoulders were stiff and her gaze distant.

"It wasn't my best." Emilie leaned forward, trying to meet Jaime's gaze. "Are you okay?"

"Fine. I want to know how you are."

"Not so good." Emilie was relieved when Savannah chose that moment to arrive in a swirl of skirts and energy.

Her arrival distracted everyone until new hugs had been exchanged. Then Savannah settled on the chair next to Emilie, turned toward her, and with great concern asked, "How are you?"

. . .

Reid swiped another fry through the mound of salted ketchup on his plate. So that was what Kaylene's attorney looked like. There was a vivacity to her that didn't come across in website photos. The question was whether she could help him. He pushed the thought away to consider later, when he was alone. This was the first real meal he'd had since Brandon had brought him Chinese earlier in the week, and his stomach demanded he give the food the attention it deserved. Amazing how a guy could live on Clif Bars and Powerade.

Brandon wolfed down another big bite of his double cheeseburger with extra bacon, then wiped a napkin across his face. "So, you know that woman?"

Reid paused, the fry halfway to his mouth. "What woman?"

Brandon jerked his chin toward a table by the wall.

"The one you ran over with your chair. She's focused on you."

Reid returned her stare, noting the blush that crept up her neck in response. She was cute, with her hair pulled up in a casual way, a few blonde strands escaping around her face. He looked away. Then he looked again.

A chuckle pulled his attention from her to the oaf across from him.

"Should I get her number for you?"

Reid maturely kicked him in the shin under the table. "I've already got it, actually."

Brandon looked surprised. "What will you do with it?"

"Not much. I don't have your beefy charm."

That elicited another guffaw from his friend. "It's all these leftover football muscles."

Leftover nothing. Brandon remained friendly with the local gym, a carryover from his playing days, but a discipline not all his former teammates had adopted.

"I need to tell you what I found." As they ate, Reid filled him in on the boxes and letter from Kaylene.

"So what did she mean? 'Take care of the girls'?"

"I'm not sure." Reid dipped the last fry in his ketchup. "I knew she wasn't happy, but she wouldn't talk about it. Guess it wasn't something her unmarried baby brother was supposed to understand." Except she'd written the letter—but then tucked it in a place he might not discover for a long time.

"Someone's got to know." Brandon leaned forward. "If she didn't talk to you, who would she have talked to?"

"Her attorney." Reid's gaze slipped over to the table

filled with women, who were now hugging an older woman who had just arrived.

"Kaylene had an attorney?"

"Yes. In fact, that woman I 'ran over' is her attorney."

"Then I'd go talk to her."

"She's out with friends. And I need to pray about it first. I'll call her first thing Monday." It was the weekend, after all, and while he worked crazy hours, chances were good she wouldn't get his message until then. Attorneys didn't exactly serve on call. "I'll leave a message, then head to the hospital. Robert hasn't returned my calls, but maybe he's too busy with Kinley. I want to see how she's doing. I'd like to learn when Kaydence's funeral is too."

They finished the meal with a minimum of conversation. Brandon washed down his burger with the remnants of his watery Coke. "Ready to go?"

Reid nodded and stood. With one last glance at Emilie, he followed his friend from the restaurant and back to the questions that dogged him.

CHAPTER 9

Emilie nibbled on her fingernail, a habit she thought she'd broken long ago. The stress of this week had brought it back. Was there a diplomatic way to answer Savannah's question without the meal turning into an analyze-Emilie's-emotional-state debacle? "I'm fine."

Savannah looked at her, eyebrow raised, but the server arrived to take their orders. When she left, their mentor must have decided not to pursue that line of questioning.

"Ladies, what Hayden and I are doing at the law firm is working well. Bringing in Angela has been seamless. We each have our own clients and freedom to take on who we want but share space." Savannah's warm eyes lit with passion and her hands gestured almost as fast as her words tumbled out. "There's still a lot of room in that big ol' office suite. I'd like the rest of you to consider the same setup. I know you, and you know me. We would share costs, but all your profits from your clients go to you."

Emilie wondered if such a system could work for her. Not likely, when most of her clients were trapped in domestic situations they couldn't escape in part because of a lack of resources. At least some funding would have to come from outside sources, as it did at the Haven, or she'd have to do a high volume of client work. She considered the question as their food arrived and the conversation slowed. Way too much risk for her.

Hayden leaned toward her. "You okay?"

"Sure." The work she did used to fire her zeal, with one victory fueling her for a month of tough work. Now one devastating miss had depleted her enthusiasm.

"How would it work when we're all engaged in different areas of law?" Jaime's question was a good one. "I do criminal work, and Caroline's clerkship would best translate to appellate work—"

"And I'm a nonprofit attorney." Emilie mouthed *I'm sorry* to Jaime for interrupting. Jaime merely shrugged, further evidence she wasn't herself. "I don't see how that can work in a for-profit setting."

Savannah shook her head, short hair bobbing around her face. "You might be surprised. There are things you can do to make it more cost effective, and your legal work isn't all you do."

"True." Emilie wasn't about to tell them that her town house had been a gift from her grandmother. They might assume she was a woman born with a silver spoon in her mouth; there was no need to confirm it. Some months she barely made it by with her salary from the Haven plus her freelance writing— occasionally she dipped into her trust fund to pay the bills. Without that, she couldn't afford to live inside the Beltway. She would have had to talk her way into a big firm job rather than taking the more meaningful work. But there was no need to tell the others all that . . . or how she couldn't take on more legal work without losing herself completely in her clients' stories.

She loved what she did, but the drain was real. There was an emotional cost to helping women and children in crisis. It was a cost she weighed heavily each time a new client came through the doors, yet it helped to share with them her own story. She could see the moment clients realized she understood.

The thought of taking on the added strain of making sure money was coming in to fund her work was too much. While she could use her trust fund for maintaining her lifestyle, she didn't want to use it to finance her work.

The buzz of excited conversation washed over her in a tide. Even Jaime seemed to catch Savannah's enthusiasm, though Emilie knew it wouldn't last. Jaime tended to flash hot or cold depending on the day and how her job was going. This must have been a rough week.

"I'm considering making a change," Jaime said. "But I'm not sure this is it."

Savannah eyed her with a calm knowing. "You'll need to deal with the past eventually."

Jaime stiffened. "The past is behind me." Yet the shadows in her eyes belied her words.

"Are you having nightmares again?" Emilie asked.

"I'm fine." Jaime forced a smile, but the faint tremor left Emilie wondering.

She looked across the restaurant, and her gaze met Reid Billings'. His friend sat beyond him, big and protective as he had been at the funeral, open curiosity in his expression, but he wasn't looking at her. He seemed to be captured by her table as a whole. Well, it wasn't surprising—her friends were beautiful enough to catch any man's eye. The big guy didn't seem the least bit daunted, even though, as a group, the women tended to overwhelm people with their enthusiasm. There was a certain energy to her friends' gestures and conversation. They owned their passions and wore their emotions on their sleeves, even Caroline with her strong sense of Southern propriety.

Another reason Emilie had always felt she didn't quite belong.

Hayden gently elbowed her. "So what do you think?"

Emilie rubbed the spot with a mock frown. "I'll consider it."

Savannah reached across the table and took her hand with a concerned smile. "I told you gals we'd lost her. We're thinking about seeing a movie, Em. There's a flashback release at the art theater in Shirlington. *Bringing Up Baby.* You'll laugh."

"You won't cry anyway," Jaime inserted with an eye roll.

Savannah laughed. "But we'll eat greasy theater popcorn and enjoy a gorgeous young Cary Grant."

Caroline mock-swooned. "Y'all know I'm in. You had me at Cary."

Emilie could feel her walls shifting. While there were other things she needed to do, she wanted even more to be with this group of friends who knew her and liked her anyway. She glanced at her watch and did a quick calculation. It was only an overnight trip, so packing would be quick. She'd still have time to prepare for the hearing before catching the shuttle flight to Virginia Beach Sunday afternoon. And she definitely needed the break and the chance to remember the world wasn't entirely colored in shades of tragedy.

"Okay, but no popcorn. I'm stuffed from this." She waved at the empty dishes that cluttered the table.

"Then it's settled." Hayden waved toward their server. "Let's get the bill paid and go enjoy some air-conditioning at the theater's expense."

. . .

The elevator doors opened with a *ding* that exposed the hospital's hallway. It was so white the light glared off the surfaces that smelled sterile but probably crawled with all kinds of nasty germs. Plastic flags alongside each door were flipped in different directions as visual cues to the medical staff hurrying along the floor. Reid curled his nose against the smell and wished he could be anywhere else as his stomach rebelled from the hamburger and fries he'd inhaled.

Brandon hadn't come with him—coward—but Reid couldn't blame him. One late hit early in his professional career had left his friend in the hospital long enough for a lifetime.

It was okay. Reid had faced down multibillion-dollar deals. He could handle seeing his niece. In an intensive care, private room.

But his feet stayed rooted in the elevator.

"Is it going up?" A nurse's kind voice jerked him back to the moment.

"I think so." He slid his arm through the opening to hold the door as she entered, then stepped out. The volunteer at the information desk had told him Kinley's room was in the far northwest corner. Room 436. He glanced at the signs pointing down the different hallways, then started down the correct one.

A few nurses and a technician passed him, but nobody questioned where he was headed.

Except him. Being here, in this place, was wrong.

He'd wanted to come earlier, but Robert had ordered him to wait. Now that Kaylene's service was past, maybe he could start finding some sort of footing with the man. They'd have to get along for Kinley's sake, so he was here to begin that process and see for himself how his niece was recovering.

The sound of hushed voices and the whooshing and beeping of machines filtered from the rooms that lined the hallway. In the rooms whose doors were open he saw an empty bed, then a family clustered around another bed, then a teenager lying in darkness, the multicolored light from the television keeping him company. Then he reached Kinley's door.

He paused. *Father, You have to help me.*

This was the last place Kinley should be. Yet it was better than dead.

The thought felt heavy, cold, and real.

He patted his pocket where Kaylene's letter rested against his chest. He would do this for his sister, even though he didn't understand what was behind her request. He would do this for his young niece, who had been robbed of her mother and sister. He would do this to find answers for the questions clouding his mind.

He turned the knob and pushed open the door, then stopped when he saw Robert sitting in the chair next to the bed. Kinley lay on the bed, blonde hair splayed around her on the stark-white pillow, face slack, chest bandaged. A young girl strapped to more machines than he could ever hope to understand. Her ten-year-old frame looked too small in the bed designed for an adult.

Robert stirred and looked at him with the arrogant air he always wore, as if everyone else should be honored to stand in his presence. Then a mask fell over his features, as if he remembered he played a role. A part that should be natural.

"Reid."

"Robert."

Curt words exchanged by men who even after sixteen years of Robert's marriage to Kaylene conveyed a distance that was as real as it was hard for Reid to understand.

Reid cleared his throat. "How is Kinley?"

"How does she look?" The words were as rough as the man's stubbled face. "Kaylene nearly succeeded in stealing both of my daughters from me."

"What happened?"

"You tell me. She was your sister."

Reid stepped back as if Robert had punched him. "She didn't talk to me."

"Guess that makes two of us."

"She used to talk all the time."

"Nonstop."

Reid wanted to smile, but it didn't seem that Robert was making a joke. "What are the doctors saying? About Kinley?"

"Nothing I'm sharing with you." Robert stood and seemed to puff even bigger as he moved to get between Reid and Kinley in the bed. "Your sister is the reason my little girl is here."

Reid put his hands in front of him. "I just want to know how my niece is."

"Then you can check with the nurses' desk. They might tell you, but I doubt it." Robert's gaze was intense, burning, but his voice remained calm. "I'm not prepared to have anyone from your family near my remaining child. Consider this your last look."

Reid took a step back. "I'll come back later. When things are calmer."

"You didn't listen. You're. Not. Welcome." The last word sounded like a gong in the small space.

Reid glanced around Kinley, noting that one of the monitors showed heightened activity. Was that her heartbeat? Could she hear their argument from the depths of her coma? He wouldn't risk upsetting her and worsening her condition. He'd find another way to learn how she was.

"I'll leave." He stopped in the doorway. "But remember, I'm her uncle, Robert. I love her and I will be part of her life." Kaylene's pleas echoed in his mind, and he felt the weight of her letter against his chest. What had she been afraid of, and why hadn't she said something when she could? "I'll see you at Kaydence's funeral."

"You missed the private service—it was only for close family." Robert crossed his arms and stood with his legs apart as if rooted into the floor in front of Kinley's bed. There was a tilt to his chin that dared Reid to try anything.

"But the medical examiner hasn't released their bodies." Steam filled Reid, and he could feel his anger in the pounding of his heart.

"It was a service like the one you held for her killer." The venom in Robert's gaze knocked Reid backward.

As Reid stumbled into the hallway and then walked to the nurses' station, his mind filled with images of Kaylene and Robert over the years. What had started with such joy had slowly shifted. He'd known it couldn't be all roses and candlelight, but now questions filled his mind.

He stopped at the station, a desk with more monitors on it than a trading floor.

A man in scrubs looked at him. "Can I help you?"

"Can I get an update on Kinley Adams's condition? She's my niece."

The man clicked a few keys on the keyboard in front of him, then he frowned. "I'm sorry, but we can't provide any information about her."

"I'm her uncle, and her father told me I could ask here."

The man frowned at the screen. "Sorry, but the father's instructions are clear. Any information to third parties is to go through him." He pointed down the hall. "You can find him down there."

"I already did. Thanks."

So Robert wanted to make sure he didn't know about Kinley's condition. Warning sirens blared in his head. Had Robert exercised this kind of control over Kaylene and somehow orchestrated her death? Had Kinley witnessed it? She must have, since she'd been injured in the shooting. If Robert was the only unscathed one, had he actually been the shooter? Reid scrubbed his face with his hands as he tried to wrap his head around the thought. As he made his way back to the elevator bank, he couldn't reconcile the idea of Robert as the shooter with the video of Kaylene holding a gun, just as he couldn't reconcile Kaylene as the shooter with the sister he had known and loved.

He needed to talk to someone who knew Kaylene. That meant her attorney. He pulled out his cell and texted a message to Emilie Wesley. Maybe they could discuss what he thought and see how it lined up with what she knew. He hit send and hoped she wouldn't ignore his text as he'd ignored hers. But if she did, he'd track her down.

Finding out what had really happened was too important.

CHAPTER 10

A s the taxi drove her from the hotel to the law firm where she'd rented a conference room for the day, Emilie glanced out the window toward the beach. She'd spent her time since arriving in Virginia Beach yesterday going through her notes and preparing for today's deposition and tomorrow's hearing back home. It felt right to be back at it, actively engaged in helping clients. She felt the clarion call in her soul to walk the sandy shore, but she resolutely stayed in place. There was something about the power of the waves and the tenacity of the sand that spoke to her. It whispered hope that she could withstand the waves crashing over her. God was bigger than the pressures she faced.

The entire image of the empty beach with crashing waves and soaring seagulls reinforced the image. The gospel of Matthew was clear that God cared about the detailed needs of those birds; but if that were true, why did it so often feel like He overlooked the needs of her clients? With one breath, He could fix everything that was wrong in their lives, but He didn't. She wasn't sure she could ever reconcile that with the image of a grace-filled God.

She shook her head. She needed to clear her scattered thoughts and focus on this deposition.

It hadn't been her choice to hold it so far from DC. It had been necessary to protect her client. Sandra's ex had made it clear he would do anything and everything to find her and bring her back. Taylor had created an elaborate plan to misdirect him from their client's actual location, and that misdirection had Sandra flying north from North Carolina while Emilie flew south.

Emilie prayed it worked, because if something were to happen to Sandra, it would crush her.

Sandra had worked too hard to break away from Garth.

The moment Emilie stepped from the cab, her phone rang.

"Can I come in now?" Sandra's voice was quiet, but there was a core strength that hadn't been present when she'd first met with Emilie to discuss her legal options.

Emilie looked around as the taxi pulled from the curb. "I don't see him."

"Have you checked the lobby?"

"Not yet." She waited for the doorman to open the door and then did another slow turn. "He's not here. I think you're safe."

Not a minute later a red Mustang convertible pulled to the curb. A curvy brunette slipped from the passenger side and headed toward the door. One would have to look close to see the blonde roots that hinted at a former appearance. Sandra hurried inside and offered Emilie a tentative hug before following her across the lobby.

The ride up the elevator to the sixth floor was silent as Sandra played with the strap of her designer purse. Right before the doors opened, Emilie put a hand on hers to still the movement. "It will be okay. This firm knows to be alert for trouble."

Sandra took a deep breath, held it a moment, and then nodded as the doors slid open. "I'll be fine."

As Emilie studied Sandra, she believed her. Sandra would make it. She would be fine.

The two stopped briefly at the receptionist's desk in the middle of a large lobby. A minute later a paralegal escorted them down a hallway lined with beautifully framed seascapes. Floor-to-ceiling glass sat on either side of a closed door, and sunlight poured from the room through the glass into the hallway. They stepped inside, and Emilie admired how light and open it felt even with a large table anchoring the room.

"You can help yourself to water or a soda." The young woman pointed toward a counter above the mini fridge. "There are notepads and pens there if you need them. If you need anything else, I'm at the desk around the corner."

"Thanks, I think you've provided everything."

The woman left, and Sandra sank onto a chair, then pushed a hand against her stomach. "I think I'm ready."

"You are." Emilie's gaze strayed to the hand that covered the spot where her client's child grew. "This will be over soon."

"It has to be. At this rate I won't be able to squeeze into Spanx much longer." She smiled briefly, then her face grew serious.

"I know." That knowledge weighed on Emilie. She had to force this to an end as quickly as humanly possible. The challenge was managing opposing counsel and the ex, who could never know the child was his. His abuse had already caused two miscarriages.

Twenty minutes later, when opposing counsel entered the reserved conference room, Emilie wanted to scream. Sandra's ex sauntered in as well, looking debonair and angry. "He's not supposed to be here."

Attorney Arnold Switzer sank onto a leather chair and set his briefcase on the stained mahogany table. "He has a right to hear everything she says, and I need him to assist with questioning."

Emilie turned to Sandra, expecting to see her client cowering in the chair. Unfortunately, if they called the judge, Switzer would likely win. Sandra sat with perfect posture, chin slightly tipped, gaze focused straight ahead.

"It's all right." Sandra's voice was quiet but firm, without a trace of a waver.

Emilie searched her eyes and then nodded. "All right. Let's get started."

Five hours later Emilie felt bruised but so proud of her client. The woman had gone round for round with Switzer, her gaze locked on Garth. Opposing counsel had been unable to get anything out of her that would harm her case. Instead, Emilie was confident the deposition recorded everything she needed to get the case fast-tracked to a resolution in Sandra's favor. It hadn't taken more than fifteen minutes for Garth's true colors to show as he interrupted and expounded on each of Sandra's answers. It would be a beautiful transcript to put in front of the judge.

Sandra was safely on her own flight, but Emilie's flight back to Reagan National had been delayed. The deposition had gone well, but she was ready to get to her home, take a relaxing bath, and let the stress of the day evaporate.

She sat in her tiny seat, fingers curled around the armrests as turbulence bounced the plane across the sky. She forced her fingers to uncurl. Wesleys didn't show fear. It was far too pedestrian an emotion. Her father had drilled the message into her with each scraped knee and nerves-inducing speech. She was expected to rise above all challenges.

But her mind had lost that memo, forgotten the speeches.

As the plane bounced through another change in air pressure, she twisted her grandmother's ring and hoped her nervous stomach would calm. When that failed, she reached for the nearest barf bag. It felt like she'd hopped on the wildest roller coaster and the nearest exit was three hundred miles away.

She held the wax-coated bag in her lap, praying she wouldn't need it. Was the opening big enough? She didn't want to find out. She used trembling fingers to pull the opening as wide as it would stretch.

The plane stabilized, but her fears didn't. Her mind went back to her car "accident" in April. The police had downplayed her fear. Hayden too. She'd assured Emilie that there was no way a random shot fired by an errant hunter near an expressway could have anything to do with her personally. It was easier to believe that, but while Emilie had pretended to go along, she couldn't. The police and Hayden didn't know about everything else that had happened.

Add in the note she'd found in her purse Friday, and she was ready to second-guess every assurance she'd received. Watching Sandra bravely tip her chin and answer each question as if it didn't matter that the man who terrified her sat across from her dissecting each word had only reinforced Emilie's fear.

Sandra knew who her stalker was. Emilie did not.

The person lurked in deep shadows, present but hidden.

Kaylene, the former Miss Iowa, could not have murdered one daughter and tried to kill the other. It didn't matter that the police believed the facts were clear. It shouldn't affect her that one grainy video made the public and media accept the evidence as infallible. Emilie knew it was wrong.

Just as she knew the accident in April hadn't been an accident.

As the plane made its way back to Reagan, she felt paralyzed between what she knew and what the rest of the world believed.

Would anyone believe her this time?

She didn't know, but she had to try to reach the police before the investigation into the shooting closed with a summary decision: murdering mom kills one girl and critically injures the other.

She had watched Kaylene tremble while telling her story of a love gone dreadfully wrong. She had coaxed Kaylene to believe more was possible. She had teased Kaylene into daring to dream. And then Kaylene had taken her girls and returned home. The woman had been absolutely convinced she could salvage her marriage, change her husband, pursue a real relationship. Instead, she'd gone dark.

She'd stopped returning phone calls.

Her email account disappeared.

The photos on Facebook showed a woman crawling back into her shadows rather than striding into freedom.

And Emilie had sat in her office in Arlington, Virginia, helpless to do anything until Kaylene became firm in her decision.

Wesleys didn't feel helpless, so when Kaylene had called begging for help, Emilie had leapt at the chance to get the protective order. She'd reminded Kaylene that they couldn't get to court until Monday. Kaylene had called again on Sunday, hesitant but still committed. They'd made their appointment to meet at court at noon. If she'd planned to shoot her girls, why would she have gone to that effort? It didn't make sense.

The plane reentered placid skies, but Emilie knew there was no calm in store for her. Not until she could get justice for her client. And not while she was convinced that someone was stalking her.

CHAPTER 11

The vaulted ceiling of the courtroom caused each sound to echo louder than Reid expected. This was not a setting he'd ever expected to find himself in. The cold, sterile surroundings were weighted with the proceedings that occurred day after day in this hall dedicated to justice. He rubbed a hand over his chin and clutched the papers he'd brought in his hands.

He might be comfortable in any Wall Street firm, but this setting intimidated him. What did he know about the law? Especially when it involved the fight to wrest custody from a father?

He couldn't get Robert's words and actions Saturday afternoon out of his head all weekend.

The stakes were so high, he prayed he didn't blow it. Was this even the right thing to do? He didn't know how else to find the answer other than to watch Kaylene's attorney in action and hopefully talk her into helping him. He'd tracked her here since she hadn't yet returned his text.

It couldn't take too long, right? Her assistant had made it sound like a quick hearing, and that's what he needed so he could get back to the world he knew and understood: finance.

Then the image of Kaylene's bright blue eyes pleading with him through the words in her letter to take care of her girls filled his mind. He couldn't walk away from her request.

"Sir, you need to take a seat." The burly deputy gestured to the rows of empty benches. "Otherwise you'll have to leave. No loitering allowed."

"Sure." Reid scanned the crowd of lawyers in front of the fence. One of them had to be Emilie Wesley, but from the back he couldn't identify her. So far it looked like a cattle-call of lawyers crammed together.

The bailiff took a step toward him, and Reid gestured to a vacant bench. "I'll wait there."

The man nodded, but his hand strayed to his gun.

Reid sat down on the hard wooden bench and shifted to find a comfortable position as he continued to examine the attorneys. All of them were in constant motion other than the two before the bench. A woman leaned closer to the bench, her crimson suit a burst of color against the sea of navy and black. Her blonde hair was pulled back in some kind of fancy twist, and she waved her arms as she talked, each gesture seeming to emphasize a point. She was definitely the woman he'd talked to at the restaurant Saturday.

The man standing next to her looked at her with thinly veiled disgust, his lips curled as he looked from her to the judge. Then she turned toward the man, and Reid caught the hint of a triumphant smile on her face. She said something to the judge with a little bow of her head and then strode out of the line.

Seeing her face full on, he was sure. This was Emilie

Wesley. When he'd looked her up online he'd learned that she spent her time in the courtroom tilting after windmills of abusive husbands and boyfriends. If Kaylene had hired her, it meant things had been very bad.

Watching in the courtroom only affirmed his conviction that he needed a skilled litigator to help him in his quest. A bulldog would be ideal. Could this woman who looked like she belonged on the big screen provide the help he needed?

• • •

Emilie resisted the urge to do a fist pump—just barely. The smug look on James Randolph's face when Judge Hughes took her side on the motion was perfect. The partner at Elliott & Johnson, Hayden's former place of employment, was out of his league in family law, a fact he now surely appreciated. After all the grief he'd caused her roommate, it felt great to beat him, even if the motion only meant his client had to comply with the subpoena.

Emilie scanned the room and saw that Taylor had already left. No need to waste her time in the logjam of motion hour. However, the time they'd prepped quietly while the line wound its way forward had been valuable. She'd nailed Randolph to the wall when he'd gotten cocky and proven he hadn't spent time with the subpoena or the law.

A man sitting on the aisle several rows back caught her attention. Reid Billings? Why was he in family court? He looked about as uncomfortable as her dad at a debutante ball. Well, it was none of her business.

As her phone buzzed in her pocket, she picked up her pace. Her victory would be exceptionally fleeting if Judge Hughes caught her pulling out her phone while in the courtroom.

As she hurried toward the exit, Reid got to his feet. "Emilie, could I have a moment of your time?"

The bailiff stepped forward, his hand on his gun, and she raised her hand to stop his forward progress. "It's okay, Joe." She turned to the man. "Reid? I'm surprised to see you here."

"Yes. When you didn't return my text, I thought this would be a good place to find you." She arched an eyebrow at him, and he sighed, his glance bouncing from the bailiff to her. "Actually, your assistant told me you were here. Do you have a minute to look at these?" He handed her a sheaf of papers.

"You'll have to take this outside." Joe's voice was urgent as his gaze flicked toward the front of the courtroom and back. "Judge is starting to focus on you."

"Thanks." Emilie brushed past Reid. "You can join me in the hall." She pushed through the heavy wooden doors, pausing to note whether he'd followed. She needed to get back to the office, but if he was here, she'd see what he needed. After a quick glance at her phone, she kept moving.

The man hurried after her as if he were Peter Pan's shadow trying to reattach. Once she'd found a quiet place in the hall, she stopped and turned, her nose almost hitting his chest. She took a half step back, but he stood immovable, looking lost yet determined.

"I was out of town for a deposition yesterday. What is it you think I should address today?"

"Kaylene told me to come to you."

"She did? When? How?" She wouldn't cry. Not here.

Reid fumbled through the stack of papers and pulled out a folded page. "She left me a note, but I didn't find it until Saturday."

At a glimpse of the handwriting, Emilie's heart sank. "Oh, Kaylene. Okay." She looked around the bustling hallway, noting the attorneys meeting with clients or opposing counsel. "Let's take this outside." She nodded at the people she recognized as she made her way down the marble stairs and toward the exit. Instead of taking the attorney exit, she led Reid past security, waiting long enough for him to reclaim his phone, and then led the way into the oppressive heat.

. . . .

The wind felt like a sauna, and he scanned the area. "Let's go to the coffee shop."

"Sounds good."

The walk was quiet, and he wondered if Emilie was lost in her memories of Kaylene.

He felt the weight of his sister's words and her trust in this woman. They reached the door to the coffee shop at the same time and she hesitated. What was the right thing to do? Did she want him to open the door for her, or did she expect to handle that herself? "May I get the door for you?"

"Thanks." She gave him a small smile, then entered. "Looks pretty busy. I'll snag that table over there so we have a quiet corner to talk."

He placed a hand on her arm to stall her as he glanced at the menu board and then back at her. "Would you like a coffee?"

"Extra-large white chocolate mocha iced, and ask if they can add peppermint." She lifted her gaze with a quirked smile. "Thank you."

He chuckled when he saw it was the most expensive coffee on the menu.

A few minutes later he returned with her froufrou drink and a good black coffee for himself. He set hers in front of her.

"Thanks. I usually get tea at coffee shops, but this one has the best mochas in town."

"Glad to get it." He settled at the table and sipped his coffee while trying to free his thoughts. He set his cup down and pulled the letter from his jacket pocket and slid it across the table to her. "I didn't find this until Saturday right before we ran into each other at the restaurant. Now I don't know what to do. As you can read, she asked me to fight for her girls if anything happened."

"She knew." A bleak expression settled on Emilie's face. "We tried so hard, but she knew." She paused as if rereading the card. "Wait, she brought this to you in July? She stopped coming into the Haven around that time."

"I guess so." Reid took another sip, then set down his coffee, trying to hide his unsteady hands.

Her jaw tightened. "What did he do to her? We were making such progress, then she disappeared for about a month. She called the Saturday before she died asking me to get everything ready for a protective order Monday. That's where I was when she was killed. At court waiting for her. We were that close to getting her out."

Reid felt the connection of their shared loss. "Now I have to do this for her. I don't know how to prove it, but Kaylene did not do what everyone thinks." He knew it no matter how much evidence the police said they had. They were wrong.

Emilie seemed to consider him. "Did she tell you anything when she brought you the letter?"

"No. It was in one of a couple boxes she asked me to store. She made a joke out of asking me to keep the boxes without peeking. I frankly forgot they were in my closet. And she had taped them so thoroughly I couldn't have checked the contents without her knowing."

"What was in the boxes?"

"A few files and some photo albums. I haven't dug through them yet."

"You should. Who knows what she decided needed to be safe with you." She sipped her mocha. "I wish she'd gone to live with you."

"Me too. Anything special about July that you know of?"

"No, other than she stopped coming to the Haven. As a team we'd made real progress with her. To the point she was ready to get out right then. Something changed, and she stopped coming. I can't think of anything unusual that would cause her to bring you the files." Emilie held her tall cup as if warming her hands, but she sat hunched as if she couldn't get warm. "I know this isn't the only reason you tracked me down. What do you want me to do?"

"I want you to help me fight for custody of Kinley."

CHAPTER 12

The words echoed in Emilie's mind. Surely she hadn't heard him correctly. "You want me to do what?"

"I want to fight for Kinley." He took a sip of coffee, and Emilie noted his hands trembling.

"I don't know that you can do that."

"I want to try." He set the cup down and then slipped his hands out of view. "I don't know how well you knew Kaylene."

"I thought very well."

"Then you must wonder what really happened."

"All week. The woman I knew wouldn't have done everything they say no matter what some crazy phone video shows."

"And they didn't know her." He put air quotes around *they*. "I didn't either, not like I should have. Maybe you knew her better." He sighed, a sound so deep and broken she wanted to weep for him. "I need someone who will help me fight for Kinley, help me do what Kaylene asked."

The words sounded like something Don Quixote would state with the same level of conviction. Was this a fight she could join? Was this a way to fix her failure?

Why was she even asking the question? It was her job to fight for those who were likely to lose. She relished the battles, so why did the thought cause her to duck beneath an intense wave of weariness and I-don't-want-to?

It was almost as though Reid read her thoughts as he continued. "I need someone who knew her outside the media firestorm. Someone who knew her heart. Is that you?" There was a challenge in his eyes that made something rise inside her.

"You don't know what you're asking."

"Then tell me."

She took a deep breath and quickly evaluated him. Could he handle the truth or would it scare him? While he looked shaky around the edges, if he was anything like the brother Kaylene had described, there was a core there that could see this through to completion.

"Not here." She glanced around the busy coffee shop. "If you're serious about doing this, we need to make sure our conversations are protected by attorney-client privilege. That means having them in private." Where should they go? Nowhere anyone would connect them to Kaylene. "We'll start at my house." She'd figure out where they could meet next after she knew he was committed.

He eyed her skeptically. "Why not your office?"

There was no way she could risk Rhoda seeing her with him until she had decided what she would do.

"If we're going to do this, you have to trust me. Even when it doesn't make sense."

He studied her for a minute as if testing her, then slowly nodded. "All right."

"Good. Here's the address. I'll meet you there in fifteen minutes."

. . .

Reid watched as Emilie got to her feet and reached into her attaché case. She pulled out her keys, but a piece of paper came out with them. He hadn't thought her porcelain skin could get whiter, but the color leached from her cheeks. He reached out to steady her. "Okay?"

She looked from him to the paper, then quickly dropped it back into her bag. "Fine. I'll see you at my house in fifteen minutes."

Her reaction bothered him as he followed a map app's instructions to her home. Traffic should have demanded his attention as he wound through Old Town, but he wanted to know why she'd been so rattled.

Parking was nonexistent in front of the red brick town house, so he pulled around the corner and walked back. The town house fit the style of the area: old, carefully restored, and surrounded by influential neighbors. Mere blocks from Old Town, it sat in a small section of the overgrown Virginia suburbs that still felt historic—like George Washington might exit an establishment on King Street at any moment. Being an attorney paid better than he thought if she could afford this.

He opened the gate and paused when he spotted Emilie sitting at a round wrought iron table set on a pad of red brick that matched the townhome. She nodded toward the vacant chair. "That didn't take long."

Reid closed the gate behind him and took a seat. "Nope. It's easy to find."

"Would you like a drink?" There was something hesitant, almost uncertain about her demeanor. Something very different from the controlled woman he'd seen in the courtroom. Yet she'd regained some of the color she'd lost in the coffee shop.

"I'm good. Are you all right?"

Her spine stiffened ever so slightly, and she watched him with a guarded expression. She slipped the sunglasses that had been perched on her hair back down onto her nose, effectively hiding in plain sight. "Tell me about Kaylene."

"From where I sit, you knew her better."

"How did she and Robert meet?"

Reid frowned, discomfort slithering up his back. "She was always a little oblique. Like they met, but she wasn't necessarily proud of how." This wasn't the first time he'd wondered why.

"She told me she was Miss Iowa and met him at a Miss USA event."

"Sounds about right. I never understood the pageant world or its appeal." That remark earned him a slight smile, and he wanted to figure out how to get it to return. "She enjoyed it, but I was the kid brother dragged to a couple excruciating evenings before my mom agreed I could stay home."

Her smile grew broader, so he pushed the image further. "You should have seen me in a blazer with a bow tie. I looked ridiculous and knew it." He swallowed against the sudden lump in his throat. "You should have known

Kaylene then. She was radiant. The other contestants were beautiful, but she was special. It wasn't a surprise when she won; the surprise was she didn't win it all."

"I could see hints of that." Sympathy shone from Emilie's eyes as she leaned toward him. "By the time I met her, though, most of that radiance had disappeared."

He nodded. "Sometime between the arrivals of Kaydence and Kinley, she changed. By then I was in college and pretty absorbed in landing the best internships that led to the best jobs." His early career days had demanded all his time, and when he'd resurfaced Kaylene had changed. "I guess I missed something important."

Emilie settled back against the chair. "She felt she should have been smarter. By the time she realized something was wrong, she was trapped. She had a toddler, an infant, and no job. She also had no access to their finances."

"Surely Grandma and Grandpa would have helped." He knew they would have, but wait . . .

"It was during your grandfather's illness."

He put the timeline together. "She wouldn't burden Grandma."

Emilie nodded. "She couldn't reach out to them and insisted she wouldn't burden you."

"She should have." His words were harsh, punched into the air.

"Yes."

The fact that Emilie didn't argue with him, but instead agreed with one quiet word, shook him. "Why didn't she come to me?"

"Because you were young and launching your career."

She didn't say *self-absorbed*, but he could feel the impact of the word as though she had shouted it. "I was focused completely on me."

Starting his career in the high-powered, high-octane world of finance hadn't left space for time with Kaylene and her family. He'd been in New York City, she'd been here, and it had been easy to let time stretch between calls and visits.

He slumped lower in the harsh iron chair. "She needed me, and I wasn't there beyond an occasional family event."

Emilie let the words hang in the air for a moment, then shook her head. "It's more complicated than that. It always is." She looked beyond him as if he weren't even there, sharing space with her. "By the time women come to me, they're often so lost they're not even sure who they are anymore. Some of them are so accomplished and composed in their careers, it's hard to reconcile that person with the one they become around their abusers. Our counselors work with them to help them work through the way they feel trapped, yet still love their partners deeply. Our social workers try to help them see what's possible. Kaylene knew if she could break free you would help her."

"Then why not ask me to do something?"

* * *

The pain flashing across Reid's face moved Emilie to reach out and touch his arm, anchoring him to the moment. She could sense his guilt and heaviness. "Because she needed to do this on her own. She had to know she was strong enough." Emilie bit back the words about how Kaylene had ended up being too weak to stay away. About how Robert's threats to take the girls had torn Kaylene's resolve to shreds. She couldn't withstand the threats and pressure.

"Then why were they at the house? If she wanted to leave, she should have left."

"I've had to accept that I won't always understand. It's the only way I can keep helping women like your sister." She glanced at her hands and took a steadying breath. Did she want to help him? No. Did she feel an obligation? Yes. And that was what she would have to live with if she walked away. "Let's head inside. I need something to drink, and we need to be intentional if we're taking this next step."

As he followed her inside, it felt like the town house shrank. While no one would ever call it large, she'd always thought it cozy and perfect. Now she understood why Andrew laughed over her "dinky" kitchen. There was no way the space would comfortably hold her and Reid. "I have iced tea or water."

"Tea's fine." He leaned against the doorway, and she tried not to notice how he towered over her, or how his muscles were chiseled beneath his dress shirt.

She filled a glass with ice and poured the tea over the top before handing it to him and making another for herself. She picked up a couple mint leaves from her stash, crushed them, and dropped them into the tea. "We can sit over there."

The black-and-white chair was perfect for her small frame, but the gray love seat looked undersized when he sat. "Were you a football player?" The words blurted out before she could stop them.

He looked at her, startled. Then a slow grin cracked his face, probably the first genuine one she'd seen. "No, my grandma said she fed me well."

"With a little Miracle-Gro." She muttered the words, but he still must have caught them, because his smile became even bigger.

"The question is, can you work a miracle and help me save Kinley?"

CHAPTER 13

Reid Billings didn't pull any punches, Emilie would give him that. She sketched on a legal pad as she walked him through what incredibly little he knew about his niece's status, even as she reeled internally from his blunt challenge. She forced herself to ignore the note, the one that had to have been placed either while she was in court or at the coffeehouse. Neither was a great option, because it meant whoever stalked her could blend in close enough to get right next to her and she'd never notice.

Reid's challenge rang through her. She had no options. If she didn't help him, she'd know she was a coward and always wonder if she could have done something that mattered for Kinley. If she did help him, she'd know she was a fool.

But wasting time on Reid's windmill-tilting agenda didn't solve the matter of who was stalking her and leaving little messages.

Reid cleared his throat, and she startled.

"I'll have to think about it."

"Why? I need your help because you knew Kaylene. Without us Kinley goes to her dad, and I have a bad feeling about that."

The problem was Emilie did too. What she lacked were facts to support that feeling, and she'd learned long ago that feelings didn't lead to success in a courtroom. Logic and facts would rule the day, though a little emotion and passion could be helpful. But only a little.

"What you're asking is very complicated. It will also require me to work on it in my off time."

"You can do it through the Haven."

"No." Rhoda would have a fit if she got the agency mixed up in something as messy and likely to fail as this scheme.

"What if Kinley recovers quickly and the doctors send her home tomorrow?"

"Then I can't help you." She would not let Reid make his emergency her crisis. "If we're going to do this, we have to do it deliberately."

"Let me know in the next day or two. If you won't help, I'll have to look for someone else, and they won't be as good."

Emilie knew no one else would care like she did. Someone new wouldn't know Kaylene and be vested in the outcome. Instead, they'd be swayed by everything that had happened last Monday.

Even as the two of them sat there in her living room, Emilie couldn't stop glancing out the window toward the street, watching for someone, anyone who looked out of place. Was someone watching her house even now? Should she reach out to the police again? Detective Gaines hadn't returned her call, but maybe if she called again he'd at least connect her with someone.

She doubted any other police officer would even listen to her concerns, and she couldn't stomach the thought of the condescension she'd receive if she ran to them with two anonymous notes.

Way back in March she'd first had the sense someone was watching her. It had been creepy, but something she could brush aside. After all, she lived in a major city and spent a lot of time in places filled with people. Why should a glance from a stranger as she walked down King Street bother her?

The feeling had returned with growing regularity until her car accident along Rock Creek Parkway in April. But she accepted what others said: the accident was exactly that. And the weird feeling, she told herself, was also just that . . . a feeling. Her enforced "vacation" following the accident while her shoulder healed from the accident was what she needed.

That lasted four weeks.

Then in May the sensation of being watched started again.

The first time it happened was in a crowded Metro subway. Easy to explain away. Then it occurred in Old Town at Il Porto, but no one except those she celebrated with looked familiar.

She started cataloging people everywhere she went. Seeing shadows where there weren't any. She'd called the police, and she could almost hear the officer's eyes rolling over the phone.

Was her preoccupation with the shadows the reasons she had missed signs with Kaylene?

She came back to the present and sighed. "I'll consider

this, Reid. You have to find out Kinley's status. How long will she be in the hospital? What's her diagnosis? Does she remember anything?" She paused, almost afraid to say the next words. "She's the lone eye witness other than Robert."

A seriousness weighed Reid's features. "That's exactly what concerns me. What if she remembers a key detail when she revives—a detail that implicates her father?"

"Then we make sure we're ready." Emile glanced at her notepad. No grand revelations hidden in the scrawls and swirls. "Get me what you learn, and I'll consider grounds for taking custody from a parent. We need to find something that will take our gut reactions to Kaylene's death and turn them into evidence." She pulled her gaze from the paper to Reid, and ignored the jolt it gave her. "Time's not on our side. The sooner we file the better, but right now we don't have any legal justification for advocating a change in custody."

"It sounds like you've decided to help me." His grin was mischievous, and she didn't want to look away.

"Maybe, but you need to understand I still have reservations."

"We all do." His phone buzzed, and he slipped it from his pocket. After a quick glance at the screen, he stood. "I almost forgot about this meeting. I'll work on the hospital angle. See if I can get us a timeline. Will you let me know what else you need from me?"

"Yes." Emilie placed a hand on his to stall him. "Please understand this is a long shot. I have a feeling there was a lot going on at home that Kaylene didn't tell anyone."

"We have to do this." His words left no room for disagreement.

"I agree, but we have to be realistic. Reid, there's a good chance we'll fail."

"And there's a chance we won't. In my line of work, we make our money in those slim chances. We'll get 'er done." He gave her a forced smile and then stood and walked to the door. "I'll be in touch."

She watched him open the door and walk away, noting the confidence in his movements. She would give anything to have that. Instead, as she glanced back down at her notes, all she saw were the problems.

• • •

Reid hurried to his car. He'd almost forgotten the meeting with his investor and Brandon. The investor needed a tax deduction, and Almost Home needed funding.

He wanted this meeting to solve both issues, but Jordan Westfall tended to have strong opinions he didn't make clear until everyone thought things were settled except for his signature. The two had met thanks to their mutual friend, David Evans, but Reid didn't know him well. He managed Jordan's money and that was all. He hoped that the combination of their business relationship and Almost Home's mission would open Jordan's checkbook. Brandon was great at what he did in many ways, but asking for money wasn't his strength. And the big guy didn't need false hope, so Reid would have to keep Jordan on task and engaged.

As he drove he tried again to get through to the nurses' desk on Kinley's floor. They'd stonewalled him so far, but maybe one call would reach someone helpful.

"Rogers." A harried voice suggested he not waste time.

"This is Reid Billings calling for an update on my niece, Kinley Adams." Reid could hear beeps and clicks in the background as he switched lanes.

"Reid? I'm so sorry about everything that's happened." The compassion in the woman's voice had him stretching for their connection.

"Melanie Rogers?" He placed her from a Bible study he'd attended at his church.

"Yes." She sighed. "There's not much to update, but I'll check her file."

There was a moment's hesitation, then Melanie continued. "She's still in a coma, but the doctors are optimistic."

"Do you have any estimate of when she can go home?"

"It's impossible to predict that. I would suggest you ask her father to add you to the list so we can provide you with current information."

"He told me I could ask for information from the desk."

"There's not much change to report. She's stable."

"I appreciate the update." The words felt so empty. "One last thing. Are visitors still restricted? I'd really like to see her."

"I'm sorry, Reid, but her father is adamant that no one other than medical staff have access to her."

"Thank you." He hung up and winged a quick thanks to heaven. It might not be much information, but it was all he was likely to get without Robert's permission. At least he'd learned they had some time to figure out how to gain custody.

Half an hour later he pulled into the Almost Home parking lot and slid into a slot next to a Porsche. Jordan had beaten him.

The sound of children's squeals pulled Reid's attention to the side area between the fourth boys' home and the community center. A couple basketball goals and a kickball ring were tucked into the space, and when he turned the corner he saw a dozen boys ranging in age from eight to thirteen clustered around Brandon and Jordan. Brandon had so many boys hanging off him he looked like an octopus with appendages of varying lengths.

"There he is." Brandon stomped toward him, or tried to, dragged down as he was by the kids.

"I see you found Jordan." Reid clapped Brandon on the lone free spot on his back.

Jordan gave him a self-satisfied, slightly awkward smile. "Can't come say hi with all these young men surrounding me."

"I told you there were quite a few." Reid high-fived a couple of the boys. "If you've met these great guys, you've seen all you need. Where's your checkbook?"

"I think I need a little more data."

Reid turned to the boys. "All right. We need time for a meeting." As the boys groaned and complained, he held up his hands and clicked the button on his keys.

"But if you look in my backseat you'll find something to do while we're inside."

As if he'd told them there was fresh pizza in his car, they abandoned the men in a flash and tore away. If he was lucky, the balls and Frisbees would keep them occupied without causing anyone permanent harm.

Brandon shook his head as he led the way to the community center and his office. "You shouldn't bribe them."

"It's not a big deal." Not on his salary, especially if helping here served the dual purpose of keeping clients like Jordan satisfied.

"This time." Brandon snorted and gestured toward the group of boys arguing over the sports items. "They practically expect it." They reached the door to the community center, and Brandon opened it and stepped to the side to let the other men enter first.

Reid glanced back at his car to make sure the kids had closed the doors. Jordan was already inside the building, hands shoved in his designer khakis, taking in the wide-open, homey space. Tables lined one half of the room. A couple times a week community meals were served, partly to give the houseparents a break and partly to keep sibling groups connected. Several multicolored couches were arranged around a large fireplace. Stacks of games filled a bookshelf on one side of the fireplace, and on the other books appropriate for young kids through tweens. A selection of YA books was on another, higher shelf.

"You should see this place when it's overflowing with kids . . ." Reid had been here several times during large meals, and the pandemonium was impressive.

"The noise." Brandon rubbed his head as he glanced around the space, shoulders pulled back and head high. "We've worked to make this a place the kids can hang out. It especially helps the sibling groups who may be split among houses."

Jordan frowned as he glanced at Brandon. "Does that happen often?"

"More than I'd like, but we're restricted when we have sibling groups of brothers and sisters. Currently we don't have a facility that allows us to mix genders. That's in the dream."

Reid led Jordan to Brandon's office. It was a Spartan setting; Brandon had kept the focus on the spaces the kids utilized. Reid thought that would play well with Jordan, a man who appreciated the decisive and effective use of funds.

Jordan sank onto one of the folding chairs in front of Brandon's desk, a battered metal contraption that looked like a leftover from the Cold War. "Let's get down to business. Why am I here?"

"You need some creative thinking about your finances now that you've cashed out, and this is an organization I've been involved with for years." Reid waited for Brandon to plop behind his desk and then settled on the last folding chair. "This is a project you can get behind and know your funds are making a significant impact."

Brandon launched into an explanation of the purpose and vision for Almost Home. It had started with his background as a kid who bounced through foster care until, as a teenager, he'd landed with a family that made him one of their own. That experience had changed the course of his life, and Almost Home existed to do the same for others.

As he listened to Jordan ask probing questions, Reid hoped this would be the solution to Almost Home's immediate needs. He needed one area of his life to go well as he figured out what had really happened to Kaylene and whether Kinley needed saving.

If she did, he couldn't fail.

FIVE MONTHS EARLIER

His hands shook and he couldn't stop pacing through the first floor of his home. The Georgetown town house was the one luxury he'd allowed himself. He didn't want a McMansion, but the town house spoke of wealth and history. It had been perfect for the rewriting of his story.

One look at her dressed for the formal evening, and he'd known she was perfect. He'd barely been able to tear his gaze away. It was like looking at the other part of himself. A piece that had been missing for too long. Yet her friend had stared at him, a sneer of derision on her face. Did she not understand who he was?

Confusion had filtered across Emilie's face as soft color filled her cheeks.

She didn't remember him. Well, they had only crossed paths briefly at the Haven. But he'd make sure she remembered who he was now. What he had accomplished. See that the headlines were only part of his story. When she really knew him, she would understand that their love was once in a lifetime. The kind that the great masters wrote about in plays and novels. It would be one for the ages, and he couldn't wait to build that future with her.

It wouldn't take much to learn her patterns and where she placed her affections.

People weren't any more complicated than the programs he excelled at building. Learn their routines and you learned what they valued.

If he was anything, he was an excellent chameleon. He'd learned how to become exactly what people wanted. He could do that now.

It wouldn't be a challenge. And when he finished, Emilie would understand how perfect their story would be.

He'd carefully craft a plan to woo her, full of mystery and romance. Step by step, and she'd understand what he'd known since their paths first collided. She was meant for him, and now he was ready to make her his.

CHAPTER 14

For the second time since Kaylene's and Kaydence's deaths, Reid got up early and prepared to return to work. Yesterday he'd been in and out of the office with the trip to court and the time with Emilie Wesley. Now he needed to return to work as if nothing had happened. If he stayed away from the office longer, key clients would notice. It was harsh, but there were only so many big fish out there . . . Even if they were nice about it, his clients expected him to cater to their every whim the moment they considered it. And one or two of his colleagues would use any situation to move up.

Reid had carefully cultivated his pool over the five years he'd been in DC. He'd intentionally selected his mentor to learn how to develop his own list so he wouldn't be dependent on anyone for crumbs.

Slowly, month by month, year by year, he'd done that. It wasn't the perfect portfolio, but it gave him significant sums to manage for others. Sums he didn't want to lose by disappearing, even with a justified absence.

It took a good forty minutes to commute to the downtown office in one of the high-rises off K Street.

The area was known for its power brokers: lobbyists, lawyers, and special interests. It was the perfect place to position a firm designed to service financial needs of those too busy to focus their own energy and time toward the matter. As he stepped from the subway, he felt the smack of the humid, super-heated air.

Welcome to DC in August. All the weather was good for was dashing from the car to the Metro to the building, not to emerge until it was time to leave. Let people come to him.

As a family of sweat-soaked tourists passed, he considered telling them to abandon the sweltering monuments. They should stay indoors and explore the memorials as the sun lowered its way to the horizon, cloaking the scene in a velvet color that provided a stark contrast to the white marble of the lit edifices.

He pushed through the revolving door into the building's lobby. A security guard, one he didn't recognize, sat at a desk behind a surround of Plexiglas and nodded at him. Reid wondered if the screen was bulletproof and then decided he'd watched too many Jason Bourne movies. The security was one perk of working in a building with some kind of government agency hidden in its depths. It was great until Jimmy John's couldn't deliver.

He tugged his ID and lanyard from his pocket and swiped it across the gate, then hung it around his neck. As soon as the gate opened he walked through, joining the flood of worker bees heading to the elevators for the swoosh to higher floors.

Light ricocheted off the highly polished stone floor

of the lobby as suits and professionals hurried toward the bank of elevators. A few palm trees were scattered around the space in an attempt to soften the edges, but Reid's clients didn't care one way or the other. They liked the high-security location—something many were used to in their everyday lives. The burden of having more money than Midas.

He stepped into an already-crammed elevator. It felt like they were part of a clowns-in-a-tiny-car exercise. He half expected someone to be filming the scene with a phone . . . perfect for a social media feed that would go viral.

Slowly they progressed, one halting floor at a time, one or two exiting at every floor until those remaining could breathe. Finally the doors opened on the nineteenth floor, and he slid through the stragglers and into the lobby of Fletcher & Associates, Wealth Management. Here nothing was held back to create the perfect image. A Remington sculpture sat on the large square coffee table, a row of pricey magazines on the ledge below. A chocolate-brown leather couch was offset by two deep chairs. Clients often complained about having to leave the perches for a meeting. A Persian rug of rich reds and blues lay beneath it all, the plushness quieting steps until people cleared it.

He strode across the space to the mahogany raised desk where the guardian of the inner sanctum sat. Priscilla Rand was a calm, almost boring woman in her midforties, in her prim navy suit with cream blouse, a colorful scarf with an abstract design softening her appearance slightly.

She stood as he came around and stepped toward him with arms open. He paused, knowing there was no escape.

"There are no words, Reid." She gave him a quick hug, one that felt sincere while appropriately brief. "Are you sure you should be here?"

"I was actually here a bit yesterday. Had to come in before I drove myself crazy." He covered the words with a rueful smile.

She frowned at him. "I must have been at lunch. But it's too early for you to be back."

"I need to do something."

"And the sharks are circling." She stepped back to meet his gaze. "Mr. Fletcher would hold them at bay."

"That might not be enough when there's blood in the water." The common phrase had never been so real to him. "I'll be fine."

"Well, if you need anything let me know. Simone is trying hard to keep things for you."

He nodded and then continued down the hall and up the stairs to the second floor. The double-story lobby provided a stunning visual space, but it also served as a barrier between the support staff and Marvin Fletcher and his key associates. It had taken five years for Reid to permanently ascend the stairs.

Simone Teal sat inside Reid's office, tablet and stylus poised to take notes the moment he walked in the door. He paused, then removed his jacket and hung it on the hook behind his door, striding in his shirtsleeves to his desk. If he moved fast enough she wouldn't repeat the scene with Priscilla. But the Howard University grad didn't embarrass either of them by doing that. Smart enough to be an associate in her own right, Simone insisted she wanted to learn the ropes from someone before she decided about the trajectory of her career.

Reid knew it wouldn't last, but he'd take her keen insights every moment she stayed.

"What have I missed?" She'd been out the prior day for a planned personal day, and he needed her download to get back in the flow.

With that, Simone launched into a systematic analysis of what had happened at the firm in the last week, before working him through a list of clients with immediate needs. "Mr. Devenue will require your personal assistance and assurance. He's being hesitant."

"Understood." For a man who'd minted a small fortune launching a high-tech company in the shadow of AOL, Devenue was reluctant to move forcefully with his own funds. "I'll get on the phone with him and get him on board."

Simone looked uncertain. "There's more involved this time than his usual reluctance."

"I'll handle it." Calming the nerves of the wealthy who wanted to grow their assets was what Reid did well. Very well.

"Here are my notes. I also need to update you on a few other accounts." Twenty minutes later she sat back and regarded him intently. "Are you sure there isn't anything I can do to help you with personal matters?"

"I'm trying to unravel what happened inside my sister's house. So unless you have some secret video feed that lets us know, there isn't." He tapped the stack of paper. "Thanks for all you did last week. I'll get started contacting the ones you noted."

Simone left him with a whispered, "Good luck."

As Reid glanced over her notes, he knew he wouldn't need luck. Luck had never done much for him, but hard work and prayer had. That's what he relied on.

One of her notes made him pause.

Vincent told Fletcher he'd follow up on your accounts while needed. I told him I would do that, but Vincent got to Priscilla and convinced her to route your calls to him. He charmed Mrs. Maverick, and she's considering transferring the account.

The words were practically gouged into the paper.

Vincent Ross was the type to take advantage of his absence no matter the reason. He'd proven he'd scrabble and step on anyone if they got him a rung closer to his goal. He had rushed into the small firm with a chip on his shoulder and thrust it around with everyone but clients. To them he could be as charming as the best used car salesman—no offense to those who were good at what they did. He was not. But he somehow managed to convince everyone he was by stealing other people's analyses and work.

The Maverick portfolio was worth a small fortune. Reid logged into the firm's system and started poking around. But when he tried to access the Maverick account and see what damage Vincent had done, he was blocked. He frowned and tried another avenue, with no success.

So, the man was intent on keeping him out.

He could do an end run of his own.

He picked up his phone and dialed George Maverick at his office. Odd that the call rang through to voicemail. He hung up without leaving a message and turned back to Simone's notes. Everything else looked okay. That she'd managed to contain Vincent's end run was impressive in and of itself. He made a note to give her a more visible role with select clients. She was ready, with him as her backstop, but knowing her work ethic, she wouldn't need much.

He rubbed his temples and scanned his calendar. Other than a firm meeting that afternoon, his day was impossibly clear. The hazard of coming back unexpectedly.

Good. It gave him time to research and consider new ways to reach prospective clients, and a good reason to contact his book of business. Offer to pay for coffee for clients and their interested friends. Up it to a nice lunch at Old Ebbitt or someplace similar for key individuals. Mr. Fletcher had taught him that the right amount of wining and dining was a necessary expense.

He hopped on the phone and systematically connected with each client, watching his calendar fill up as he did. There was hesitancy in some voices, but the promise of a free lunch if they brought a friend worked. No matter how rich they were, people liked a meal on his tab. Then he called Jordan Westfall.

A self-made millionaire several times over, Jordan had the look and feel of a Mark Z, genius with the savvy to get the right people around him to make his ideas succeed. He liked to tell people he still tinkered at the high-tech firm he'd sold. Anybody else would call it creating the apps they relied on to manage their lives.

"You want what?" Jordan had the slightly distracted sound that conveyed Reid had caught him in the middle of a thought.

"To take you to lunch and update you on your portfolio." He paused a moment. "We didn't get a chance to talk about that yesterday."

"That other guy's not taking my account. You can stop worrying. And I still haven't decided about Almost Home."

"Okay." Reid dragged out the word, a bit taken aback.

"Schedule time with David for basketball. I'll be there." He chuckled. "We can talk money then."

"Will do." Although they would not talk money then. Those conversations needed much more privacy than the local Y provided. And he felt awkward having business bleed into what had been a stress release for as long as he'd known David.

"See you then." And Jordan was gone.

Reid held the phone in his hand, hesitating. David Evans had been there throughout college. They'd diverged for grad school, David going to law school while Reid got his MBA with an emphasis in finance at a top New York school. They had reconnected when he first moved to Virginia, diverging again when David made Ciara Turner his bride. Marriage tended to limit those easygoing nights of playing pick-up games of basketball that left both huffing and puffing.

It would be good to try, but now that David had a newborn daughter, Reid wasn't holding his breath.

CHAPTER 15

Staring at a blank sheet of paper felt as productive as watching grass grow.

Earlier Reid had called to fill her in on what he'd learned about Kinley's status. She should research and break down the elements she would need to prove if they had even a chance of gaining custody.

But her mind was as blank as that stupid sheet of paper.

It only took seconds to dig up the relevant statutes. The language made it clear the law focused on parental relationships. The definitions recognized that other family members could have an interest, but it didn't draw a clear line for when another family member could take custody from a parent.

"The statute is the starting point, Emilie. Remember everything you learned in your legal research and writing course." The pep talk to herself didn't work as well as she'd hoped, but she started pulling up the cases that referenced the code.

As she dove into the cases, she felt a burble of hope. There were several cases talking about the primacy of the parent-child relationship, but then she found some related to attacking a parent's custody. One case even related to the death of the mother.

Her hope began to evaporate, though, when she noticed that the courts required a finding of harm to the child before a lower court judge could move to "best interests of the child." Without proof that Kinley staying with her father was harmful, this was a nonstarter. No one had witnessed what happened, so it was as likely that Kaylene had shot Kinley as it was that Robert had. She needed to contact the detective and see what he might say.

That was one thing she could jot on that blank page.

Emilie flopped back in her chair and stared at the Monet print on the wall. The soft colors and brush strokes usually gave her a deep sense of peace. It was her way to re-center in the middle of work that was often disturbing. While she tried to maintain her happy-go-lucky appearance with friends, it had gotten harder. The weight of her clients' deep needs had reached a tipping point. The peace incumbent in the painting she'd always loved had slipped away with her ability to help Kaylene.

She recalled standing in front of the original at the Nelson-Atkins Museum of Art in Kansas City. It had been part of a traveling exhibit, and the water lilies painting had filled an entire wall. She had sat in front of it for an hour, completely lost in the cascade of color and the way the brushstrokes changed based on her distance from the painting.

She'd learned a valuable lesson that day.

Her perspective on a case could change depending

on how close to its details she stood. If she stood nose to paint from it, she could lose the vast swirl of colors in the minutia. Still beautiful, she saw the individual bristles of the brush imprinted in the paint rather than the way the details merged into a kaleidoscope of color that formed the greater picture. Stand too far away and she lost the way each carefully placed stroke or glob contributed to the larger story being told.

As she stared at the print, she wished she could slip into the larger scale once again. While the Smithsonian had a lovely assortment of Monets, none on display had the sweeping scale and scope of those she'd seen in the Nelson-Atkins exhibit. And she didn't have time for a trip to Kansas City even if the exhibit was still there. She closed her eyes and forced her mind to slow, thinking about the painting in its entirety, being swept into the broadness and scale of the image.

She pulled up a search engine and searched for Kaylene. The first thing in the search was the video. She watched it again. Nothing new, but was it possible to slow it down or refine it? She buzzed Taylor. A minute later her assistant stood in the doorway.

"Come watch this." Emilie scooted her chair to the side to make room for Taylor. They watched the short video together. "Do you see anything?"

"Not that I haven't seen when watching it before."

"Do you know of a way to enhance the video? Maybe get a better handle of what's on it?"

"I can check."

"Thanks." After Taylor left, Emilie's thoughts turned to the girls. She knew Kaylene, but not the girls. What had life been like from their perspective before the tragedy?

Kaylene had been careful not to pull her girls into the drama at home. She'd done everything she could to prevent them from understanding the full flow of hate and derision. She'd told Emilie the girls should adore their dad. That it was good and right because he was a good father.

That was not the testimony the judge needed to hear.

What she needed was proof that the father had controlled their lives to the extent he had controlled Kaylene's.

How could she gain that when Kinley remained in a coma and her mother and Kaydence were dead?

What would a judge find to be persuasive evidence? That was where she needed to focus her attention.

If the video could be cleaned up, would it reveal something that might sway the court's opinion, persuade the judge there was an alternate explanation for what happened in the home that terrible day? But it still wouldn't show what had happened inside the home.

Had Kaylene ever said anything about Robert not allowing the girls to do activities? Had she ever talked about Robert threatening the girls? Emilie walked through the different conversations she could remember. The primary focus had been on how Kaylene and the girls could flee. Robert had controlled the finances to the extent that he gave Kaylene cash, but never access to the checkbook or credit cards. It had started as a way to relieve her stress as an overwhelmed young mom, but over time she realized it had trapped her. With Emilie's encouragement, she had set aside twenty or forty dollars a week from different budget items, slowly building a tiny escape fund. Something was better than nothing.

Had he done anything similar with the girls?

Kaylene hadn't said, and Emilie hadn't asked.

Someone knocked at her door, startling Emilie from her thoughts.

Rhoda strode into her office and settled on the chair in front of her desk, as if preparing to stay a while. "How are things going?"

"Fine." Emilie tried not to frown at the sudden interruption.

"Good, because I've heard nothing from you regarding Nadine Hunter, and she was in here last Thursday. That's five days ago."

As if Emilie didn't remember. She couldn't tell Rhoda that each time she opened the file to start working on Nadine's protective order, she froze. "I'll get to it."

"It's just a protective order." Rhoda leaned forward, every line of her body intense and focused. "I could have any of the secretaries complete it."

"Then let them. You don't need me to fill in the blanks."

"But Nadine needs you as her advocate."

"Maybe now isn't a good time."

"Really? This isn't a good time to do your job? Emilie, Kaylene was one of our clients. One of many. There are dozens more who still need our help and advocacy."

"That's not what I meant." Emilie bit back the desire to say it was exactly what she did mean. She needed this job. Maybe not for the income, but she needed it because it was a large part of her identity.

"Then I suggest you get on top of Nadine's case. You of all people understand the impact any delay can have." Rhoda sighed. "I'm spending time each day explaining to reporters how agencies like ours can keep events like the Adams tragedy from happening. Did you know the police might release the 911 calls?"

Emilie trembled at the thought of what those calls could contain. "I hadn't heard that. Why would they do that?"

"Sunshine requests. You'd better hope there's nothing that harms us anywhere in those calls."

"There won't be." She tried to infuse her words with certainty.

"Good, because I never want to hear the Adams name again. We are closing that file and moving forward."

"What if things aren't as the media says?"

Rhoda's blue eyes sparked with a fire that warned Emilie to back off. "It doesn't matter to us if the media got it right. I do not want to hear you have done one more thing related to that file. Do you understand?" Her posture softened. "We cannot allow a client we can no longer help to prohibit us from serving all the women we can assist."

Emilie swallowed and then nodded. Guess she'd have to move the rest of her investigating home. It might require a shift in her hours, but other than Nadine's matter, nothing was pressing at the moment.

The instant Rhoda sailed out of her office, Emilie paged Taylor. "I need you."

Her assistant hustled into Emilie's office and took the chair Emilie gestured toward.

"Can you finish Nadine's PO today?"

"No problem. I've got most of the information ready to plug in."

"Great. I'll need to spend time working from home."

"Gotcha." Taylor made a note on her ever-present legal pad. "I'll cover for you."

"Forward any calls to my cell." Emilie pulled her purse from beneath her desk. "I'm heading home now. Email the PO when it's ready."

"Will do."

Emilie followed Taylor from her office and then hurried to her car and home. She quickly changed into comfortable linen capris and a designer T-shirt before setting up her laptop on the first floor of the town house. Today she didn't want to be buried in the basement. She needed to know the sun was shining as she instigated the next layer of research. A quick Google search showed that the 911 calls hadn't hit press websites yet. She jotted a note to check a couple times a day.

Her thoughts turned back to Robert Adams. Were there activities he hadn't allowed the girls to participate in? She thought of all the things her parents had encouraged her to try. Swim team, piano, dance, youth group, and so much more. How on earth had they gotten her everywhere she'd needed to be?

As she reviewed her conversations with Kaylene, she couldn't remember a time Kaylene talked about the girls being involved in activities other than school and the piano lessons that he'd canceled. Had that been by choice? Maybe they were homebodies. Or was it a decision that had been forced on them by a strong-willed father who always knew best? How could she find out?

Her eyes popped open as she swiveled toward her computer.

If the girls had social media accounts, maybe she could learn what they did and thought.

It didn't take long to realize she might have to download Snapchat. On Instagram the accounts were private, and Kinley didn't have a Facebook account, but her sister did. Kaydence hadn't done anything to make her Facebook content private. As Emilie scrolled down, she was surprised at how much Kaydence had posted without any sort of personal filter. The young woman had a strident relationship with her father, one she didn't hide.

Had he seen the posts?

Emilie searched for Robert Adams. There were so many it would take days to locate the right one, if he was even on Facebook. It might be time worth spending if she could connect Kaydence's posts to his behavior. She'd had clients whose significant others had made frequent and repetitive threats on social media. If Robert had done the same, that would help draw the line . . . though surely he'd be smart enough not to post for the world to see.

She added the task to her to-do list. An intern or secretary could scan through the search results and narrow down the list of men named Robert Adams—if she had one. Wait a minute. She went to Kaylene's page and clicked on her friends. A quick search, and she had the right Robert. As controlling as the man had been, there was no way he would let her online without monitoring her activity.

She scrolled down his timeline. It was overwhelmed with comments of sympathy regarding the shooting. The vitriol against Kaylene was intense, with no one questioning what had happened.

It was as she finally reached posts more than two weeks old that Emilie began to get a sense of who the man was. She clicked on his photos and saw a string of images containing his girls, hunting, and other outdoor activities. A handful of photos had Kaylene in them. It was as if he had already divorced her from the family, funneling his attention to their beautiful girls.

There was nothing there that would indicate he didn't love his daughters wholeheartedly. Of course, people usually presented their best selves online. That was all a judge or jury would see. Only what Robert Adams wanted others to see.

CHAPTER 16

Her cell phone rang, and Emilie glanced at the screen. Reid? What would he be calling about? She swiped to take the call. "This is Emilie."

"Hey." His voice was casual and relaxed, but she wasn't buying it.

"Hey." She settled back and clicked to Kaydence's Facebook profile while she waited for him to talk.

"So last night I looked through the photo albums in the boxes Kaylene left."

"Find anything useful?"

"Not really. There are very few photos of the four of them together."

"And the files?"

"I haven't looked yet. Not sure what I'm looking for."

"Want help?"

"I could bring pizza and the files to your place some evening."

Emilie considered it as she scrolled down the teen's page. She looked for people who appeared in multiple photos and posts. "Did Kaydence have a boyfriend?"

Reid snorted. "Umm, I would have had to been more a part of her life to know information like that."

"I'm looking at her Facebook profile, and there's no guy listed. There's not even a guy showing up consistently in group photos." She scrolled through a few more photos. "For as beautiful as she was, with her blonde waves and bright smile, I'm surprised she didn't have one."

"She was young."

"Not that young."

"Then I'm never having kids. Or I'll arrange their marriages at six months."

"My dad always threatened that."

"I think I'd like your dad."

Emilie paused. The repartee felt so good, and the thought of Reid meeting her dad seemed almost right.

"When should I come over?"

"Let me double-check Hayden's schedule. She often has my cousin Andrew over for dinner, and I don't want to crowd the kitchen."

"Text me."

"Will do." As soon as she hung up she turned back to the photos. While there might not be a young man showing up in the posts, a couple girls showed up consistently. Emilie jotted down their names and then clicked to their profiles. Alaina Jotter looked like a typical, happy high school freshman. She was a cheerleader and active in the French club. Katie Trainer, on the other hand, didn't look quite so outgoing. Her photos and comments revealed a more creative soul who might struggle with depression. Yet the three appeared inseparable in the images they posted.

Emilie quickly compiled a list of information she hoped to learn when she contacted each girl.

What had been Kaydence's general emotional state the few weeks leading up to her murder?

Had she discussed any home problems with her friends?

If not, whom would she have shared such concerns with?

Emilie's family had been so stable and normal that it had been a sanctuary for Hayden on school breaks. It wasn't until Emilie started working with families like Kaylene's that she'd fully understood what a gift a loving mother and father and annoying siblings were. The interesting thing was that her family's money hadn't torn her parents apart as it did others. She'd seen money dissolve marriages when there wasn't enough and when there was too much. Somehow her parents had achieved a balance where it was a tool and not a divisive force. Yes, it had blessed her with experiences and things like her townhome, but at the same time her parents had fully expected her to earn scholarships and have jobs in high school and college.

It didn't look like Kaydence had worked, so that limited the places Emilie could look for confidantes. She also didn't see many photos of groups that could be a club or a youth group. Hopefully these two young women could open a window into what life had really been like at home for Kaydence and Kinley.

Without that, Emilie's chances of wresting custody from Kinley's father plummeted.

She couldn't allow that. Not when Kaylene had worked so hard, if unsuccessfully, to leave.

She quickly drafted messages to Alaina and Katie

asking them to contact her. Her email pinged just as she finished, and she opened the new message to find that Taylor had already completed Nadine's protective order motion.

Her assistant was simply too competent some days. It took only a few minutes to read the form and make sure the information was in the right places. Then she called Taylor and told her she could sign the motion for her and call Nadine to meet her at the court the next morning. They could file the motion with the judge and get the temporary order in place. That would make Rhoda happy and hopefully provide the beginnings of protection for Nadine and her son.

The front door opened as she was getting off the phone call. Hayden walked in carrying some kind of spicy, over-the-top takeout along with her attaché case and purse. She kicked the door shut behind her and then dropped her bags on the empty chair opposite Emilie. Next she kicked off her heels and then leaned down to rub her foot.

"Long day?"

"You can say that." Hayden stood up and raised the bag. "I got enough for both of us. Figured if your day was anything like mine, you didn't have time to cook."

The thought of mixing ingredients into something surprising yet yummy pulled at Emilie, but she knew her limits. "I wish, but cooking is low on my list these days."

"Exactly." Hayden took the bag to the kitchen bar. "I'll dish it out once I change. I'm ready to get into the Macy's version of what you're wearing."

Emilie grinned at her. "I've offered to take you shopping."

"Yeah, but that requires a checkbook I don't have yet."

A few minutes later Hayden was back down in shorts, a tee, and flip-flops. Then she prepared two plates with something Indian and some naan and gave one to Emilie before setting hers down. "Dig in."

Emilie savored a bite, then glanced at Hayden. "Reid Billings wanted to bring over some files that Kaylene left with him. Is there a night this week that would work on your end?"

"Do I need to be here?"

"No." Emilie felt heat climb her neck and rued her fair skin that hid nothing. "But I didn't want to step on an evening that you and Andrew have plans."

Hayden set down her fork and covered her mouth as she laughed so hard she snorted.

"What?"

"Emilie, anytime you need to use the house that you happen to own, just tell me. Even if we had plans, it's easy enough to go out rather than bring food back here."

Emilie grinned as she realized the ridiculousness of her concern. "It's your home too."

"I'm well aware of that, but don't think I miss all the nights you stay in the basement when you should be up here." Hayden tore a piece of naan and slid it through her dish. "You schedule things when it works best for you. We'll flex. Just curious, though—why don't you have him meet you at work?"

"Not this time. Rhoda made it clear today I can't do

anything related to Kaylene's case at work. She wants to pretend nothing happened, and Kaylene had nothing to do with the Haven."

"Okay. What does Reid want to do?"

"Protect Kinley. Meaning take custody. To do that we have to meet, I have to research, and we have to do things like review those files."

"Is Kinley still in intensive care?"

Emilie nodded. "There's a lot we don't understand, and I want to dig into the issue as hard as I can. Kaylene deserves that." She tapped her pen on the pad. "But I can't do that at the Haven. Kaylene is dead, so our attempts to help her are over. Rhoda assumes that Kinley's fine with her dad."

"Even though you know Kaylene tried to flee."

"Yes."

It sounded so stark and cold, but she knew that was the position Rhoda had to take. She answered to so many people who had to continue to support the Haven, or they couldn't help anyone at all.

"So what do you need?"

"A place to work." She glanced around the small living area. "I could probably do it here."

Hayden's face lit up, the look that telegraphed she'd had a brilliant idea. "What if you worked out of Daniels, McCarthy & Associates? You wouldn't have to have him come here with the files."

But Emilie kind of liked the idea of having him back here, though she wasn't ready to voice that, not even to Hayden. "I don't want to work with you, Hayden."

Her friend waved her words off as if they were

inconsequential. "I'm not worried about that. You know it's perfect. Our office is less than a mile from yours. We have extra offices just sitting empty. And Leigh could help you if Taylor can't. She complains I'm not keeping her busy enough."

"Maybe I should have Reid work with you." It sounded like Hayden could still use more clients. That was one thing Emilie didn't want . . . the scrape and scramble to keep new clients coming through the door. Anyone who said it was easy was crazy and way too extroverted. But she also didn't want to give Reid to anyone else. This one was personal, even if hard.

"No, you need to do this." Conviction shone in Hayden's eyes. "I'm busy, and you know . . . knew . . . Kaylene. You have the passion to fight this through. For me Reid would just be another client. This is one of those cases that takes someone 125 percent committed. I've had cases like that." A shadow flicked across her face, and Emilie knew she was thinking about the Rodriguez family. "But this is yours. It must be handled well, and you're the woman to do it. Let me help by providing work space."

"Thank you." Emilie cleared her throat, fighting back the sudden lump lodged firmly inside. "I need to do this. And I want to do this."

"Absolutely. You heard Savannah at the restaurant. She'll be delighted. I'll bring you a key tomorrow so you can come and go as you like."

Emilie breathed an inward sigh of relief. She didn't want to admit it to Hayden, but Bella, the receptionist at the front desk of Savannah's office, scared her more than a little. Her formidable presence could soften into immense warmth when she liked you, but Emilie wasn't convinced she fell on that side of the equation. "Thank you."

Hayden grinned at her. "Welcome."

Emilie returned her friend's smile. "Any grand ideas for proving Robert Adams was behind the shootings?"

Hayden groaned and braced her hands on the counter. "Is that all you want?"

"Yes. One bit of evidence that shows the world that Robert Adams wasn't the perfect image he presented to the world." She couldn't rely on a 911 call that had yet to be posted. Detective Gaines had yet to return a call. And the video was bitter evidence. "I'll get together with Reid as soon as possible to go through those files, but I can't rely on their holding the magic bullet. Taylor is checking on the video."

"What about the person who took the video? Have you talked to them?"

Emilie palmed her forehead. "It must be someone from the neighborhood."

"From the block."

"Probably a neighbor."

"One of them will have information."

"You're right." And now she had another excuse to spend time with the handsome and intriguing Reid.

CHAPTER 17

Sweat poured down his temples and through his shirt as Reid leaned over his exercise bike in his extra-bedroom-turned-man-cave and pedaled harder and harder. The stress of all he couldn't control was supposed to melt away with the exercise, but the knot tightening his stomach refused to budge.

He'd prayed and played the piano.

He'd read the Word.

He'd exercised.

He'd read books and financial articles late into the previous night.

None of his usual coping tools was making a dent. He'd spend another restless night if he couldn't exhaust his body and mind. His left foot slipped from the pedal, and he leaned back and gulped oxygen.

He'd invested millions of dollars for clients. He'd managed those dollars to stay ahead of a volatile market and its vagaries. None of that caused stress like this gut-level need to understand what had happened in Kaylene's family. What had been going on that she hadn't shared? And why hadn't she?

He was no longer a young kid who needed protection.

He'd never thanked her for all the times she'd stood between him and an overstressed mother who couldn't handle parenting on top of putting food on the table. By the time his mom dumped them with his grandparents, he'd been a little relieved. While he was never outright neglected, he understood all too well Brandon's kids at Almost Home and their hunger for adults who saw them as they were and loved them anyway. Fortunately, he'd had a couple teachers who cast the vision for a different future and helped him see beyond his immediate situation. Some hard-earned scholarships and a lot of study later, he'd proven his way into an entry-level job at a prestigious New York City investment firm. He'd gladly transferred to the DC office five years later to be closer to Kaylene and her family, but by then they were strangers.

He'd waited too long, and in the process failed her.

When she'd needed someone, Kaylene hadn't come to him. He wasn't even convinced she'd fully gone to her attorney.

He pulled the hand towel from the handlebars and swiped it across his forehead and around the back of his neck. Where could he start to get to know his sister and figure out what her life had been like? There were the files, but Emilie could look into those. There had to be an area that only he could explore.

After a quick shower he went to his office and pulled a box from the top shelf of the closet. It was where he kept past years' Christmas cards from key people throughout his life. Often the cards were filled with photos, and while he didn't have a family of his own, he enjoyed vicariously living through his friends. At this point in time, it was better than walking the floor all night with a colicky kid.

The cards in the box weren't organized, so it took fifteen minutes to sort through them and find the handful from his sister. He arranged the cards chronologically, and it was like a flip-book, seeing his nieces grow from infants and toddlers to young ladies.

He set the cards to the side and pinched his fingers on the bridge of his nose. It shouldn't be this hard to look at them, but it was a reminder of all he'd lost. That Kinley had lost. One day, hopefully soon, she'd comprehend the depths of it. What would that do to her?

When he'd stuffed the emotions away, he pulled the cards back over and started reading Kaylene's messages. They were mostly perfunctory holiday greetings, but a couple had longer handwritten messages. No matter how he parsed them, none indicated she needed help or had concerns. Instead, the words matched the happy family image he'd believed existed.

He'd been wrong.

And he was going to find out why. He set the photos on top of the boxes of files. He'd take those to Emilie too and get her read on them. Maybe she could intuit something in that special way women did. His phone dinged and he glanced at it.

Bring the boxes over tomorrow night? Hayden said any time will work for her.

He quickly typed a reply. Tomorrow works. Be there around seven?

Perfect!

For the first time since Kaylene had died, Reid felt the first inkling that maybe things would work out after all. That his life wasn't destined to be a tragedy.

Early the next morning Reid went through the motions of returning emails, monitoring the markets, and running a few ratios to test his gut on where to invest while his mind wondered what they'd find in Kaylene's files. Then he listened in on an investors' call with the CEO and CFO of a Fortune 100 company, making notes but not truly hearing anything. It was as if his brain knew what to do from a position of autopilot. He was present, he was working, but he wasn't really engaged.

At nine o'clock he moved to a coffee shop, hoping the change of venue would help. Common Grounds was a quaint little shop right off the main strip in Old Town Alexandria. It had an artsy vibe that usually motivated him to do some of his best work, but he was still flailing as he took his Americano to a small table.

He was hunched over his laptop trying to force work when he heard a familiar voice.

"White mocha cappuccino with skim, please."

When he glanced toward the order counter, his pulse paused for an instant before roaring to life. Standing at the counter in black slacks and a red blouse with a funky scarf draped around her shoulders was Emilie Wesley. She looked perfectly put together, her blonde hair coiled into a prim yet loose twist of some sort. She was all edgy, but with bright pops of color. Not the way he presumed an attorney would dress, based on those he'd known.

But from the moment they'd met, she hadn't been what he expected.

She moved to the side and did something on her phone while she waited for her name to be called. She was self-contained like an island, then she glanced up and joked with the barista as if they were old friends.

The woman intrigued him.

She held herself separate. Alone.

And it seemed it was by choice.

He leaned forward, watching her carefully.

The barista handed her the tall drink with a smile, and she said something back, the words too soft to catch. Then she turned and started slightly when she spotted him. Her eyes widened, and she took a step toward him, a slow smile forming on her face.

He spoke first. "Hello."

He started to get up, but she motioned him to stay. She cocked her head to the side and studied him. "I don't think I've seen you here before."

"We've missed each other then. It's one of my favorite coffee spots." If he could figure out her regular time, he'd change his schedule to match hers.

Emilie blew across the tiny opening in the lid, holding the to-go cup as if it would protect her from something. Surely not him. He'd done nothing to make her defensive. At least not that he could remember. He tried to make his expression more open and welcoming.

She giggled, actually giggled, and then shook her head. "You don't have to try so hard, Reid. I don't think you'll bite."

"Ah, good." He paused, feeling a bit awkward. "Well

then. What are you working on?" Drat. Wrong thing to ask. He didn't need her thinking he was asking about his sister's case.

This time she burst out laughing. "I really make you uncomfortable, don't I?" She took a deep breath and met his gaze. "I don't usually have that effect on people."

"That's understandable." Her eyebrow arched, and he began to backpedal. "What I meant is you give this aura of being above everything. Like a goddess or something."

"That is definitely not my life."

He suddenly realized that he was still sitting like a lout while she continued to stand. He quickly rose and half pulled out a chair. "Would you join me?"

She studied him a moment, then she glanced at her watch. "I can for a few minutes."

Reid sank onto his chair and scooted his laptop and coffee to one side of the table to make more room for her. She sat on the edge of the chair and continued to hold her cup. What was a safe, neutral topic that would help him get to know her?

"So tell me why you chose law school."

A ghost of a smile tweaked her lips. "I think it chose me."

He cocked his head, intrigued. "There's a story here."

"I'll share, but only if you tell me more of yours."

"Easy enough." He settled back and crossed his feet, being careful to keep his legs out of her way. "Why law school?"

"Because it was a way to magnify my voice and make people notice what I said." There was a quiet conviction underlying her words. As if each was tied to a memory that remained in living color. She took a sip as she considered him, then continued. "Words are my superpower. When I use them, things happen and events change."

"Always?"

She quirked an eyebrow. "Usually." She set her cup down. "What's your superpower?"

He laughed. Superpowers were for the Avengers, not mere mortals. "Those are reserved for exceptional people."

"You don't think you're one?"

Her words wrapped around him, fitting much better than he cared to admit.

CHAPTER 18

Should she snatch those words back, erase them from the space between them? No man wanted to be told he didn't see himself as amazing and light-years beyond competent. Justin, her law school boyfriend, had taught her that principle. It was his guiding light: she existed to stroke his ego and remind him how incredibly amazing he was. When she hadn't done that, he'd made sure she suffered.

Their lives had been so intertwined that to this day Emilie struggled to have normal interactions with men. Justin had made sure she would always be an idiot around men who intrigued her.

"I'm sorry. You can ignore what I said."

"No." The word shot from him. "It's hard to imagine I'm anything but average when I think about where I've come from."

"Where are you from?"

"Baltimore."

"That's a fine place to grow up."

"Sure. But it's the events of my childhood that I was thinking about."

"Okay." Everyone had things they didn't love about

their growing-up years, but as she watched his jaw clench and release, she realized his might be deeper than she would have guessed. "I really need to get back to work, so forget I asked anything."

He put a hand on her wrist, freezing her in place. "Maybe this will help you understand Kaylene. We were abandoned when I was about five. Mom left us with our grandparents, but they weren't thrilled to have a teen and a youngster around the house. Their idea of retirement had been long trips in their Winnebago."

"That must have been hard for all of you." She tried to imagine her grandparents raising her. They were wonderful, but they weren't her parents.

"We worked it out. Kaylene took care of me a lot, even after we settled into a rhythm with Grandma and Grandpa. They did the best they could, but she still took a lot on herself while trying to finish high school. The fact that Mom bopped in and out of our lives didn't help."

"And their vision of retirement didn't fit with kids who needed to be in school."

He shook his head. "After a few months they adapted. It might have taken me longer. While many kids talk about what they want to be when they grow up, I was focused on making it through the day. Grandma insisted on college, so I went. It was there that I realized I intuited the way numbers and ratios work." He shrugged. "I guess I was hardwired to manage money."

"That's definitely not my skill set."

He took a sip of his drink. "I'm afraid it's not much of one."

"You should see my checkbook."

"You still have one of those?"

"If I didn't I'd never know whether I had money." She didn't tell him that her trust fund ensured she'd never run out. That was information she didn't lead with. Ever. It was better, more real, if guys never realized she was one of *those* Wesleys.

"There's a story there." He arched a look at her.

She couldn't help smiling. This could be extremely dangerous. She should get up and leave. Before she could decide he was as wonderful as he seemed. But somehow she couldn't manage to leverage herself out of her chair and away from this conversation.

"Did I mention I'm a reporter? Couple that with my legal skills, and it's all about the words. You're the numbers wizard."

He laughed, a sound rich and real that rolled over her. "I like that. I'm pretty sure no one's ever called me a wizard of anything."

"I'm glad to be the first."

He smiled at her, and it threatened to vacuum the air from her lungs. Yet instead of feeling terrified, she was drawn into the deliciousness of the moment. Tonight could be trouble if a few minutes over coffee could do this. She blew out what was left of her oxygen and then drew it in slowly, forced a small smile, and lurched to her feet. "I really have to get going. Put that superpower to work."

He stood, but the look in his eyes telegraphed he wasn't the least bit thrown off by her words. He knew she was running.

"All right." His gaze locked on hers, and she felt warmth fill her. "Let me know if you think of anything else. Otherwise I'll see you tonight."

"I will." He took a half step closer and reached toward her, then stopped. What had he been about to do? "Italian good?"

"Surprise me."

He nodded, but seemed to see through her into her heart. "You don't need to hide, Emilie."

She bit her lower lip and nodded, then turned abruptly away. She'd slipped out of Common Grounds before she realized she'd left her half-finished cup of white chocolate decadence behind. Reid had rattled her with his ability to see through her defenses. The question was, what did he see?

Emilie had left the all-staff meeting the week before with an unsettled feeling, a feeling that had been needling her ever since. She'd been out of town Monday, in and out of the office Tuesday, and Wednesday had evaporated. It wasn't until this moment, driving back to the office after her unexpected encounter with Reid, that it hit her.

Even if Shannon had told Kaylene about guns, that didn't explain where her client had obtained one. Emilie needed to talk to Shannon and learn more when Rhoda wasn't there to manhandle the conversation.

She'd need ammunition of her own to get Shannon to talk, so she stopped at Sugar Shack Donuts. With an apple cake doughnut for Shannon and a mixed selection for the rest of the staff, she'd have the perfect excuse to head to Shannon's desk for a late-morning coffee break. She'd also ask her for background on Nadine Hunter.

But first, doughnuts . . .

When Emilie reached Shannon's office, the young woman was seated at her desk, a massive Styrofoam cup of soda on her desk.

Emilie rapped on her doorframe and then held up the bag with its lone apple cake doughnut. "I got something for you."

Shannon looked up from her computer screen, a dazed expression on her face. She reached for the bag. "You think the Mountain Dew doesn't give me enough of a sugar buzz?" She tugged the doughnut free. "Thanks! I haven't had one of these in a while." She set it on top of the bag on her desk and then licked her fingers. "What can I do for you?"

"Do you have a minute to talk about Kaylene? Then I need to connect about another client."

"Nadine?" At Emilie's nod, Shannon sighed and her mouth drooped. "There's not much to say there other than good luck. But what I can tell you about Kaylene?"

"There's something about the way everything unfolded that doesn't make sense."

"You can't sleep either?" Shannon leaned back, the doughnut forgotten on her desk.

"Kaylene loved her daughters."

Shannon nodded. "They were her life." She paused and broke a crumb from the side of the doughnut. "But she was changing in those last months."

"What do you mean?"

"She'd started to lose hope. Her whole tone shifted from *When I get out of here* to *How do I get the girls free?* I had hoped she'd escape when she started working with you, but then she quit coming."

"It was hard for her to get here."

"No, it was impossible. But she'd done it for a while, tying her appointments to the girls' piano lessons." Shannon shook her head. "Something changed, and she wouldn't explain. It was almost like she could sniff freedom, and it scared her."

"But she asked you about guns?"

"In a way." Shannon reached for a photo on the credenza behind her desk that showed her holding a ribbon and a rifle. "She saw this and asked me if shooting was hard. I joked if I could do it anyone could." She frowned at the image. "I had no idea she'd actually buy a gun and get good enough to hurt someone."

"What if she wasn't the one who did the shooting?"

"Then the video of her with the gun wouldn't have been all over the Internet." Shannon leaned across her desk, and Emilie sank to a seat. "I've gone on a few crime video sites to see if I could find anything else. So far nothing."

"There are such sites?" The thought sickened Emilie.

"Sure. Everyone has a cell phone and thinks they should share." Shannon leaned back with a shrug. "There are some twisted individuals who believe the whole world should know what they've done."

"Robert Adams wouldn't do something like that."

"I don't know. If he was as controlling as Kaylene indicated, he might have posted something if he was part of

the killing. Think about it . . . controlling whether someone lives or dies is the ultimate act of authority." Shannon
paused, and Emilie felt horror rush through her.

"He could do something like that." The question
was how to find it if he did. "Have you watched the outside video?"

"Yeah. The images are so jerky and chaotic. I felt like
I was on a roller coaster." She clicked a few keys and
pulled it up. Together the women watched the jerky
images of grass, trees, cars.

Then a body, a young woman's. Slouched on her
side. Face away from the camera. A red stain spreading.

A woman stumbled down the stairs, holding something. A gun. A man followed her out, baseball cap
pulled low, and she stumbled as he yanked her arm.
Then she folded to the ground as sirens roared closer.

Then lights, blue and red. Swirling around.

Adding to the insanity.

"Can you believe she was shot inside and made her
way outside where she died?" Shannon's shoulders
slumped, and she fingered the napkin she'd set the
doughnut on. "If Kaylene wasn't the shooter, somehow
she got the gun in her hand."

Emilie nodded, the information backing up what
she knew. Like everything else, she'd begun to doubt
her perceptions were true.

The image jerked again, and the camera went up,
catching the side image of a hand mirroring the motion.

"So whoever shot the video had to cooperate with
the police when they arrived." Emilie mulled that over.
"A neighbor would do that, right?"

"Maybe. But I got the sense they weren't close to their neighbors."

"Well, I need to find this neighbor and talk to them." It wouldn't be a bad idea to spend an afternoon doing exactly that.

"Would you run into the middle of gunfire?"

"I don't know. I'd want to be brave enough to stop it."

"But you're not good friends with these people. You wave when you see each other, but don't cross the street with cookies at Christmas or share cookouts in the summer. Robert kept Kaylene and the girls isolated and unknown." Shannon crumbled more of the doughnut where it sat on its napkin. "In that kind of environment, would you run into the chaos, or would you call 911 and tell yourself you'd done your civic duty?"

"That's really disturbing. Yet entirely possible." In law school they'd studied the case of Kitty Genovese. No one had helped her in the sixties in a busy New York City neighborhood, no matter how much she called out. Everyone safe in their apartments had relied on someone else to call the police or intervene. And the woman had bled to death on her stoop. Scholars had studied the situation to learn why so many people ignored her pleas and learned there were too many people around. Everyone assumed someone else would act.

"Too possible. We deal with those situations every day. People know abuse is happening, but rarely intervene. It's a sad reality." Shannon's eyes widened as she glanced behind Emilie, and she quickly turned the screen back toward her.

Emilie shifted to look over her shoulder.

Rhoda stood there, a tight smile pasted on.

"Do you need me?" Emilie asked.

"No, just checking in with everyone. What are you two working on?"

Shannon sputtered, but Emilie hurried to speak over her. "I was asking Shannon for more information about Nadine Hunter. I want to make sure I'm taking the right steps to help her."

"You haven't filed the motion for a PO?"

"Not yet. The draft is complete, but Nadine hasn't returned our call to schedule a time to meet at court. She may not be ready to file."

"See what you can do to encourage her. We need to get her little family to safety."

Emilie nodded, glad it was Rhoda's responsibility to find them a place to live. Her job was to get them the order the police could enforce when her ex showed up.

Rhoda turned her attention to Shannon. "Don't forget we have the case conference for Tina at one."

"Got it on my calendar."

"See you then." Rhoda stood in the door another minute before nodding and stepping away.

Emilie rubbed her neck and met Shannon's troubled gaze. "What am I missing?"

"I'm not sure." Shannon shifted and scooted her chair across the mat. She grabbed a thin file and slid it across the desk. "Here's everything I have on Nadine. She doesn't talk a lot, since her self-worth is in the basement. Good luck."

"One last question. Any idea where Kaylene would have bought a gun?"

"None." Shannon pressed her lips together as if to keep words from escaping.

Emilie took the file and stood. "Thanks. If you think of anything . . ."

"I'll let you know. But, Emilie . . . you can't get your hopes up. The reality is Kaylene and Kaydence are gone. Kinley's all that's left."

The remnant of the doughnut was now a pile of shredded crumbs. They might taste as good as when it had been a doughnut, but the form had been forever changed.

Just like the Adams family.

One event had shredded it, completely changing its character even if it still bore the same name.

CHAPTER 19

Emilie left the rest of the doughnuts in the staff room for whoever wanted a sweet treat. Her own appetite had evaporated to the point the yeasty aroma left her feeling sick.

She found Taylor waiting outside her office. Emilie flopped into her chair. "Can I see the Hunter PO?"

"Sorry I couldn't reach her yesterday. After you left, Rhoda had an emergency for me, so I could only call once."

"That's okay." Emilie handed Taylor the file Shannon had given her. "Here's Shannon's file. See if there's anything useable in it. We might as well add it while I talk Nadine into filing."

Taylor took the Hunter folder, then slipped another envelope across the desk toward her.

"This came for you this morning. It's marked personal."

"Thanks." It was all Emilie could do to force out the word. "Let me know when the PO's ready."

As Taylor left the room, Emilie stared at the familiar handwriting. Her stalker hadn't forgotten her. As if the notes slipped into her purse and briefcase weren't enough, he had decided to mail her a letter.

She opened the envelope and read the words, written as usual in block letters:

YOU ARE MORE MYSELF THAN I AM. WHATEVER OUR SOULS ARE MADE OF, YOURS AND MINE ARE THE SAME.

Emilie read it again. The message sounded old-fashioned and almost poetic even as it disturbed her. Was it a quotation? She typed the words into Google . . . *Wuthering Heights*? Whoever was stalking her read the classics?

Who was this person, and what did he want from her? The quote was more than weird, it was frightening.

She picked up the phone and placed another call to Detective Gaines. Maybe he could help her connect with an officer who'd take these threats seriously. As she left a voicemail, she didn't feel much hope. She slid the letter into a folder and tried to work, but when she'd read a statute four times without the words making sense, she gave up. Maybe moving would help. She stood up, twisted a few times, then plopped back down. She pulled up a different file and tried to focus on where this client was in the process. Soon the morning had disappeared, followed by lunch. She settled back to work, but fifteen minutes later she was still staring into space, so she pulled up the draft of her article. The very rough draft that was more white space than words.

What she'd bragged was her superpower now seemed dimmed by some form of kryptonite, one that left her paralyzed.

The right words eluded her.

She was writing with the sophistication of a second grader. Her editor would spew the article back at her in an instant if she submitted it.

Would her words disappear in the courtroom as well as at her computer?

It had been false bravado to promise Reid this was who she was, because right now her gift had all but abandoned her, leaving her stripped and empty. She groaned and leaned against her chair, grateful Rhoda had told her she could work on her writing when she had no pressing items at the Haven.

Who was she without words?

Did she want to find out?

Could she afford to learn the truth?

Her phone jolted to life on the desk, and Emilie scrabbled to grab it as it danced across the clear surface.

"This is Emilie."

"Hi." The voice was young and hesitant. "I'm Alaina Jotter. You messaged me."

Emilie lurched forward in her chair and then reached in a drawer for a pen and pad of paper. "Thank you so much for calling me. This won't take long, but I really need your help. More important, Kinley Adams needs your help."

"What do you mean?" Her voice was small, like an unsure little girl.

"I need information on Kaydence."

"You and everyone else. She's dead, and now everyone wants to know how wonderful she was. What good does it do?"

Was it bitterness or grief Emilie heard in the girl's voice?

She took a breath. "What I'm wondering, Alaina, is how things were at Kaydence's home. Really were, not some perfect social media version."

"Why?" There was a quiet caution in the teen's voice.

"Because I need to decide what to do for Kinley. I worked for Kaydence's mom, and she asked me to help the girls if anything happened to her."

"Then she shouldn't have murdered her own daughter!" The words were sharp and brittle.

"I don't think she did. Not the Kaylene I knew."

"Maybe none of us knew her." The girl's voice broke. "I keep waiting to wake up and find out this was a bad dream."

"Me too, Alaina." More than this girl could know.

"I always thought Kaydence had a great relationship with her mom. She was always nice when we were over, but Kaydence wouldn't let us come unless her dad was out of town."

Emilie jotted a quick note. "Why do you think that was?"

"Kaydence never said, but he was really strict with her. He liked to tell her what to do. But my dad makes me feel that way sometimes."

"Most dads do. Did she say anything to you that made you think there was more going on?"

"Not really."

"Would you think about it and call again if anything comes to you?"

"I guess."

"This is important, Alaina. I'm trying to figure out what happened."

"Why?"

"Because a judge will need to know. Because I need to understand how I could have missed this."

Alaina was quiet a moment. "I Googled you."

Emilie laughed, though she shouldn't have been surprised. "What did you find out?"

"You're a reporter, but you're also an attorney. Which one are you right now?"

"I'm Kaylene's friend trying to figure out what happened and how to best help Kinley."

"I'll think about it."

That was all Emilie could ask. "Thank you."

After the girl hung up, Emilie sat writing notes about the call. She sensed that Alaina knew more than she was saying, but the girl had to decide whether she trusted Emilie. This was one of those times when wearing two hats didn't necessarily help.

Maybe Katie, Kaydence's other friend, would contact her as well. Between the two, Emilie might form a real picture of what Kaydence had thought about her family.

She went back to work, and after a few hours she realized she'd accomplished as much as she could, and the office had quieted. When she glanced at the time on her computer, she realized why. It was after six. Time to head home if she wanted to beat Reid to her door.

As she stepped out of the office, the sun peeked from a cloud long enough to slice across her eyes. The brick town house was a warren inside, but it had a peaceful, nonchalant exterior. Cheerful red geraniums drooped in the end-of-day heat from the flower boxes hanging from the windows. The large planters on either side of the front steps were filled with pansies that could use an extra drink too. The colors were a little faded, as if the August days had taken their toll on the heels of a July that had experienced record highs. Emilie felt as wilted as the flowers.

She took the time to pour water on each grouping before tucking the watering can back behind a planter and heading to her car.

As she walked she felt a presence. The kind that made her stop, turn a slow circle, and question her judgment. She saw nothing.

But she felt it.

Was someone watching her in the slowly forming shadows leaning from a row house? Or was her mind still preoccupied by the lingering fear she'd been unable to shake since receiving the letter?

Her mind wouldn't accept that the crash along the Rock Creek Parkway had been the result of a hunter not paying enough attention. There was nothing simple about shooting a car and causing the driver to crash. Her shoulder was still sore, and all the recovery and physical therapy hadn't been enough to get her back to normal.

Her physical therapist told her to accept a new normal.

That was something she didn't want to suffer easily.

There had to be a way to get back to one hundred percent physically and without constantly looking over her good shoulder. She squinted, trying to see through the shadows and under the bushes and ornamental trees that framed the front steps up and down the block.

There was no one there, nothing to see, just the ghosts in her mind.

She tightened her grip on her computer bag and pulled her keys from her pocket. Then she stepped onto the sidewalk and around the building to the parking lot. It wasn't large, but it also didn't have much overhead lighting. Maybe she should ask Rhoda to expand the motion-sensing light so that it gave more protection. Not just for her—it wasn't unusual for clients to come in for meetings at all hours from early morning until eight or nine in the evening. The women they served had to slip away when they could, when it was safe to disappear. At least she was leaving tonight before the sun disappeared behind the surrounding buildings.

Emilie clicked the lock button on her key fob, and the lights flashed on and off, accompanied by the annoying horn beep. She'd traded in her Mazda for a sporty MINI Cooper, deciding she needed something new that didn't have crash memories associated with it. While the Coop didn't disappear into a crowd, it also wasn't as eye-catching as the red Mustang convertible she'd had her eye on. But it got her around and allowed her to park in any slot the DC area could throw her way.

She opened the door and slipped into the car. After one more scan, she shifted into reverse and slid from the lot. But the feeling that someone was watching chased her from the parking lot all the way home.

CHAPTER 20

The oversized envelope that held the old Christmas cards slipped as Reid carried the two file boxes up the steps to Emilie's front door. He adjusted his hold to get the Italian takeout back in the center of the top box. He lightly tapped the door with his foot as he tried to keep the envelope from sliding off. A moment later she opened the door, and he stood dumbfounded. Her hair was down and it waved around her shoulders. Her face looked bare of all makeup except maybe a little lipstick. And she wore a skirt with a sparkly T-shirt. Over all, the effect was that he was expected but not prepared for. That he was seeing an unvarnished version of Emilie Wesley, and he liked what he saw. She'd been so flashy in court and the times he'd seen her during the workday that this was unanticipated.

"Come in." She smiled at him, then scooped the envelope and takeout from the top of his pile. "You can set those on the coffee table."

He stepped inside and eased them onto the white fabric surface. "Do you want to eat first or start on the boxes?"

"Let's eat while it's warm. It smells great. What did you get?"

"Lasagna, chicken alfredo, a carbonara, with salad and breadsticks. There should be a couple slices of cheesecake for dessert."

"That sounds perfect, and like you expect someone to join us."

"Just wasn't sure what you'd prefer." He noted the soft strains of instrumental music playing, the backdrop adding a note of peace to the home.

Emilie set the over-the-top bag on the counter, then stepped into the kitchen. "Would you like some iced tea?"

"Is it sweet?"

"Of course. This is the South, you know."

"I'll try some then." There was no way he was going to tell her he preferred his tea the way God made it—without all the sugar. But as long as a spoon wouldn't stand in it, he could drink it.

"I thought we'd eat on the patio if it's all right with you."

They carried everything out through sliding glass doors and set the food on a small glass-topped table. It looked delicate enough to tip if he placed an elbow on it. "Sounds good. We can enjoy some sunlight before getting to work."

Her grin warmed him more than the sun's rays. "When the humidity isn't 100 percent I like to sit outside a bit in the evenings. Otherwise it's easy to spend my waking hours in front of a computer."

The conversation flowed between them as they enjoyed the food. He noted that she sampled each dish but loaded up on the salad. Next time he'd grab an assortment of salads and pastries from Panera. They returned to the galley kitchen for the cheesecake and coffee.

As they waited for the coffee to steep in a French press, Emilie studied him. "How do you want to approach this?"

"Each of us could take a box."

"True." She pushed down the plunger in the press, then poured them each a mug. After she'd doctored hers with a cinnamon creamer, she carried her mug and plate of cheesecake into the living area. "There isn't a lot of extra space, but I think it will work if we flip through the files while they're in the boxes."

"Sure." He took a bite and enjoyed the creamy cheesecake perfection. "The boxes aren't overloaded, so it shouldn't take all night."

"It's all right if it does." Emilie sipped her coffee and sighed. "I love tea, but coffee is what's called for with dessert." After she'd eaten half her slice, she set the plate on the counter behind her and then turned to the box nearest her. She yanked off the lid and glanced through the files. "She didn't label these?"

"Not that I could tell. We may not find anything worthwhile in here."

"Or we could find the perfect item. Hayden would say this is document review and a rite of passage for attorneys."

The front door opened and her roommate appeared.

Emilie gestured toward Reid. "Hayden, this is Reid Billings. Reid, this is my roommate, Hayden McCarthy."

"Nice to meet you, Reid." She studied him, and he

hoped she liked whatever it was she saw. "I'm going to head upstairs as soon as I grab a drink."

"There's no need to run away. We'll stay quiet." He gave her his most charming smile.

She returned it, then gave Emilie her attention. "If I can do anything, just holler."

Once Hayden had climbed upstairs, Emilie tugged a stack of files into her lap. "I think this is a case where we'll know what we're looking for when we see it. Try to go through the files carefully, but don't get bogged down in those that don't have anything related to her marriage or don't look helpful in some way."

Reid pulled a small stack of files from his box and opened the first one. A collection of receipts. He flipped through the first few but couldn't note any sort of pattern to them. Something to look through more closely at another time. The next file had a collection of programs from various events. Why had Kaylene thought these were worth taking to him for safekeeping?

He tugged out the next group. The first folder had nothing helpful, but the next held a stack of loose-leaf notebook paper covered in Kaylene's handwriting; he saw a date at the top of the first page. He quickly scanned the first page, and his breath caught.

"This is a journal of sorts."

Emilie glanced up from her box. "What do you mean?"

He handed her the paper. "Have a look."

A small V appeared across the top of her nose as she read. "It's a record of threats he made."

He flipped through the pages in his hand. "It covers a six-month period. There must be twenty entries."

"I wonder if she did this at Shannon's request. Our case workers tell clients to start a contemporaneous journal of violence or verbal threats to help build a foundation for a protective order. She never called to say she wanted these boxes back?"

"No." If only she had.

"This can be helpful, but I'm not sure we'll be able to get it admitted as evidence. We might be able to since she's dead and can't testify for herself. We'll just need to establish that this is her handwriting."

"I have the Christmas cards and the letter I showed you before."

"Great. Set that file to the side so I can find it again easily." She offered the page back to him. "I was beginning to think we wouldn't find anything helpful."

"I'd had the same thought." He studied the pile of useless files. "What if all of those were a cover for the important items like this journal?"

"It's possible. Let's see what else we can find."

Soon it was nine o'clock and he hadn't found anything else that at a quick glance appeared helpful. He was opening the last file when Emilie pumped her fist. "What did you find?"

"There's something in this padded envelope." She eased open the flap and turned the envelope upside down over her open palm. Several small, clear items fell out, one landing in her hand and the others bouncing onto the padded coffee table and on the floor. "What on earth?"

"Is that . . ."

"A diamond." She looked at him, wonder in her eyes. "This must be a couple carats." She clamped her hand around it and dropped to her knees. "We have to find the others."

He snagged the one from the coffee table, then joined her searching the floor. "Where would she get diamonds?"

"Found it." Emilie sat and held up another diamond. "She needed money to escape."

"So she what? Took the diamonds out of her wedding ring? Robert would have noticed."

"Not if she replaced them with fakes."

"I don't have her ring, so we can't check."

"But we can make sure these are real. If so, we now know what she planned to use as restarting money." Emilie shook her head as she stared at the glittering diamonds. "A stone like these can be worth $10,000 or more, depending on the cut and color."

She slid the diamonds back into the envelope, then handed it to Reid. He shook his head. "I can't believe she found a way to do this."

"She was determined."

"I wish I'd been around to help."

"But you are now when Kinley needs you." She started piling files back in the boxes. "Leave these here and I'll go through them again later. I have a feeling we found the reasons Kaylene left them with you. You provided a safe place for her journal and her escape money. You were exactly what she needed to make her plan work."

"Now I just need to be that for Kinley."

"We're well on our way."

As he looked at her, Reid hoped she was right. Instead, he felt time expiring, and with it his opportunity to keep Kinley safe.

CHAPTER 21

When Friday arrived, Reid continued to work at undoing the damage done to his accounts by Vince while he was gone. Calls followed calls, lunch appointments on top of each other. But slowly he could see a pending reversal. Sounded like most of his clients were committed to him. Some expressed relief to have him back; it seemed Vince had indicated he'd be gone much longer than a week.

He'd stolen the Mavericks, though, a key piece of Reid's investment strategy. They provided the bulk of the funds and had the most to gain or lose. Vince had played on that too successfully. As a result, the Mavericks weren't interested in what they called a "quick fix." They were going to let Vince prove himself, as they'd done with Reid.

It made no sense. Maybe Reid could find someone else. Someone with equal financial backing. But he'd lost too much in the last two weeks. He had to get them back.

"Mr. Fletcher wants to see you. Five minutes." Priscilla disappeared as quietly as she had arrived.

Reid stared after her. Why would she come to

his office rather than page him or send an email? A moment later Simone wandered in with a tall coffee, black the way he liked. She set it in front of him, her tablet in her other hand.

"What's the priority for today, boss?"

"Do you know why Fletcher wants to see me?"

"Rumor is he's got a new client coming on board. Big enough to replace the Mavericks, maybe more. He's going to set up a competition for who manages it."

"Great." Fletcher liked to make his associates prove they were hungry. Good thing Reid was. Especially if he wanted to add caring for his niece and her unknown needs to his plate. "That must be what the meeting is about."

"I think so." Simone studied him. "You still aren't sleeping." It was a statement, and one that didn't require a response. "I'll have Fletcher's assistant let me know when the meeting ends, and I'll be here when you come out."

"Thanks." Reid sat back as she left. What kind of contest would Fletcher have up his sleeve this time? Whatever it was, it would force Vincent and Reid onto opposite sides, with a little healthy competition from the newer associates. The last time the boss had concocted such a scheme, it had sucked up every moment of Reid's time for two weeks. At the end of it he'd had a stable of committed clients—committed until he had to leave for a family crisis.

Time to find out. He grabbed his iPad and the cup of coffee and headed to the conference room attached to Fletcher's office. Another Remington statue sat in the middle of a battered table made from old railroad ties.

The table was an intriguing blend of rustic and sophistication; the worn sides of the rails were polished to a high sheen and shellacked to a rich beauty. The carpenter had actually built the table in the room, and a hole would have to be punched around the door to make space to haul it out someday. An assortment of antique chairs resided around the table. One had to arrive early to snag a well-padded one.

Fortunately, Reid had timed it right.

He sank onto the extra padding of a Queen Anne chair, one of the few with arms. The others straggled in, and Reid saw Vince frown. He liked to think the Queen Anne was his personal chair. Last time Reid had checked his name wasn't emblazoned on it.

Fletcher came in with a strut of ego. The short man had a Napoleon complex; Reid had noticed that some of his shoes could almost be called platforms. He was always in a three-piece suit, buttoned even on the hottest, most humid days. Today it was blue seersucker. He looked like he'd stepped out of a photo from the thirties. He settled into the chair at the head of the table and slowly surveyed everyone.

"I've got an interesting challenge for you." His words were slow, distinct, precise. Nothing wasted. "Over the last month I have developed a new stable of prospective clients. They are prepared to sign, but want to know the next generation that will actively manage their money. I've told them about each of you. They want more, so I created this test. If you pass, you'll add them to your list and be set up for a lucrative future. Fail, and I'll wonder whether you belong here."

Priscilla stepped up and passed out a folder to each person.

"Inside that folder is your group of prospects. There is overlap among some. Others are uniquely yours to gain or lose." Fletcher steepled his fingers in front of him. "You may want to work together, but it is your choice. Good luck."

He stood and left the room. Vince waited long enough to not run over the man, then bolted from the room, his purple tie flapping. Reid opened his folder and saw dossiers on four people. He glanced around the table and saw his remaining colleagues surveying theirs.

One looked at him. "What's our strategy?"

"If you want to work together, then we need to share who we have." The others nodded, and he felt the weight of their trust. "If there's overlap, that will help shape our steps."

Slowly the folders slid toward him. As he fanned out the dossiers, careful to keep each in its home folder, he noted a few duplicates. Some were trust fund kids. Others old money, made and managed the hard way, over time. Most were from Virginia and the surrounding area. Strategies formed even as he felt the gaze of those at the table.

This was when he loved his job. When the pressure coincided with the knowledge it would take a bit of work and he'd have the prospect of real success . . . perfection.

He looked up to gauge the people sitting at the table. Simone had slipped in at some point, as if she'd received a text he hadn't sent. Next to her sat Luke Langford, a second-year guy out of Virginia, every bit as smart as Reid, if a little awkward. Across from Luke sat Annabelle Lotus, who had the mind of Scarlett O'Hara and the style of a Southern belle. She constantly saw angles and possibilities others didn't, but Fletcher and Vince didn't see that secret strength in her. She was living with Matt Arch, who'd joined the firm the same year as Reid but didn't have the drive to make it to the top rung. In fact, he seemed quite content managing a small book of clients, a task he did very well.

If they acted like a team, Reid felt certain they'd succeed. They'd just need to dig.

"All right." Reid handed the folders to Simone, who quickly pulled out her phone and took photos of the dossiers. "Let's get started."

His computer continued to ding, alerting him to emails from the team. Annabelle's had details about the prospects' backgrounds that suggested she had sources who knew them personally. Not for the first time he wondered how she'd landed at the firm. After speed-reading her email, he forwarded it to Simone, who would compile the information in a book they would use as they met the different individuals.

Then he turned to the emails from Matt. He'd given Matt the task of determining the best strategy for investing the infusion of assets. Part of that would be affected by the clients' desires and interests, but for the team to succeed they needed the outlines of a plan they could sell. Matt could synthesize vast amounts of data, and Annabelle would funnel information to him as quickly as she uncovered it.

So far there was nothing from Luke, and they needed his best guesses on who Vince might have in his dossier. Since Vince had shown a willingness to go after clients that weren't his, Reid was determined to stay ahead of him on this project. As far as he could tell, Vince would work alone. That would make the task more daunting and increase the chances the man couldn't get everything done in a timely fashion.

At noon Fletcher had sent an email with more details. They had one week to develop and submit a strategy to the boss. At the same time, they must compile a thorough dossier on each prospect, expanding the information they had received with significant details. He wanted a strategy that would be unique to the interests of each while addressing the weaknesses in their current portfolios.

While that task seemed impossible, it meant the information was available somewhere in the public realm. Reid's team simply had to access it. Annabelle's list of boards and work histories for each was a start, but there were gaps. Those gaps could contain key information that would affect their success.

He pushed back in his chair, considering the next steps. How to find the missing information?

Simone.

He needed her brainstorming with him. Together they'd see more than either would separately.

He buzzed her desk, and a minute later she walked in with a mug of tea and her faithful tablet. After she settled in a chair and set her mug on the stone coaster he pushed toward her, he leaned forward. "What do you think?"

She clicked her stylus on her tablet and then turned it to him. She'd already created a spreadsheet with graphs. "Here are my initial thoughts."

He scanned it. "You've got some good work here. Walk me through it."

She spent the next fifteen minutes giving her synthesis of what they'd learned during the day, then she clicked another series of buttons. "Here's a punch list of what we're missing. It'll keep the three musketeers busy over the weekend."

He scanned the list. It was thorough and contained almost everything he'd thought to include. "I have a couple things to add, but this is good work, Simone."

She studied him as if waiting.

"There's no *but*. Good job." His desk phone rang, and she stood.

"I'll wait for your additions and then get the gang back to work."

"Thanks." He grabbed the receiver as she exited his office and closed the door behind her. "Billings here."

"So I've got a friend here who tells me you've asked about Kinley."

Reid sank against the back of his chair as he took in Robert Adams's dull voice. "I'm concerned about her, and you told me I could ask."

"Then call me."

"You made it clear that wasn't a good idea."

"Keep harassing the hospital, and you'll never see

her again." His brother-in-law's voice was as cold as it was firm. There was no heightened emotion, just a hard certainty.

"I care about Kinley."

"I'm her father. You're only her uncle, who came around once a year. Guess who will win."

Reid pushed back the guilt Robert's words resurrected. "This isn't about winning or losing."

"That's where you're wrong. It's always about winning. I will always win with my daughter. It's what fathers do."

Reid wished he'd recorded the conversation. Anything to capture the man's flat words and hard edges. The ones he carefully hid in public where others would notice. "All right. When can I come see her?"

"She's still unconscious."

"Then it's a perfect time. She won't know I'm there, but I can be assured she's getting good care."

"Maybe. I'll call you." Then the man hung up.

Had he been played or was Robert serious about letting him see his niece? Could he have figured out that Reid was exploring more permanent options?

CHAPTER 22

After a fitful night spent chasing shadows that loomed in her dreams, Emilie arrived at her desk at the Haven an hour before the office officially opened. A quick glance showed that there was no protective order waiting on her desk. Maybe she'd have to pull up the file and finish it herself. First she had to find Shannon's file and Taylor's notes. A quick look on Taylor's desk didn't reveal them. Then she placed a call to Nadine, but it went to voicemail, so she left an innocuous message as if they were friends planning to meet for coffee. A quick conversation would let her know Nadine's state of mind. This had to be handled carefully so Nadine could leave with her son before her boyfriend knew what she planned.

Since she couldn't sleep or write and was on hold with the protective order, was there something she could do to help Kinley? She couldn't check on the diamonds or talk to the Adamses' neighbors at this early hour. Her cell phone rang, and she picked it up. She didn't recognize the number. Who would call at this hour of the morning? "This is Emilie."

"Detective Gaines returning your call."

"Thank you." She scrambled to pull her notes from one of her in-boxes.

"I've only got a few minutes. Crazy weekend working homicides."

"Have you watched the video from Kaylene's death?"

"The one the media has?"

"Yes. I wondered if you have a cleaned-up version." It sounded so crazy to voice the question, but she had to know if the police had analyzed it.

"We're working on it. The case is pretty open and shut." He didn't say not a top priority, but she could hear it.

"What if Kaylene didn't do this?"

"It's unlikely."

"I don't think so." She blew out a breath. "I had worked with her for several months. She was a mother intent on saving her girls. That woman would not kill them."

"Unless she felt something had changed. It happens." His voice was firm, but not unkind.

"Will you let me know when it's cleaned up? I'd like to see it."

"You could do the same thing yourself."

"Not without something better than what's online." The quality was so bad, she didn't see how it could be improved. "If you have another minute, I have a quick question."

"Keep it brief."

"Yes, sir. Can you recommend an officer I can talk to? I have a personal situation."

"Related to a crime?" His words were alert and sharp.

"I think I'm being stalked." She couldn't believe she'd just blurted out the words.

"Officer Miranda Roberts. She's the liaison for your agency and a good detective. Do you have her number?"

"I do, and I'll contact her. Thank you."

Detective Gaines clicked off. Emilie's fingers hesitated over the phone. Could she risk asking Officer Roberts for help? The woman was tough as nails with a soft exterior when dealing with their clients. Would she exhibit the same sympathy with Emilie? Emilie didn't need that; she needed someone to be aware of what was happening. She placed the call and left a message.

While she worked to discover what had happened in the Adamses' household, she could also review old client files. Chances were her stalker lurked somewhere in those. Maybe she'd identify whether a shadow existed in her life or if she'd overreacted in her own small version of PTSD. That's what her primary care doctor had suggested, even after she'd found a stuffed elephant peeking out of a gift bag on the hood of her car last April. That was hardly a figment of her imagination, but the doctor told her it was likely a coincidence. She hadn't wanted to believe him, but maybe she needed to . . . After she did more digging, that is. Something attorneys were trained to do that effectively, and she was nothing if not effective.

She'd been the one to piece all the information together to break the Rodriguez drug cartel, and she did not believe they'd been after her. Her article had posted the same day she was shot.

"Good morning." Taylor entered the office, looking sharp yet feminine. "I grabbed a black coffee and muffin. I suspected you needed the caffeine more than you needed the cream."

Emilie accepted the to-go mug with a grateful smile, feeling the warmth from the cup seep into her hands but not reach the chill that clung to her. "How are you?"

"Fine." She set her tea on the corner of Emilie's desk. "Couldn't sleep again?"

"Not well, so instead of lying there and getting frustrated, I'm here." Emilie brushed back a lock of hair. "I tried to reach Nadine, but nothing."

"We'll reach her." Taylor plopped onto a chair. Then she grabbed her tea and gestured to the muffin. "You'd better take a bite before I change my mind about the diet I'm on. Those are decadent."

"And 100 percent good for me."

"Sure." Taylor waggled her eyebrows mischievously, then took a sip of her tea. "So how can I help?"

"That personal letter I received yesterday? It has me spooked. It makes me think my shadow is back." She couldn't say *stalker* to Taylor. Not yet. "Have you thought of any clients or significant others I should add to my list?"

In June, as soon as Emilie had returned to the Haven, she'd asked Taylor to pull together a list of potential clients who were angry or frustrated with her. The list had been short—a half dozen jotted down in Taylor's distinctive swirls. None had seemed the right person for the scrutiny she felt. The clients had moved and the exes had disappeared.

"Not since you asked a couple months ago. Are you sure it's necessary?"

"Maybe not, but that letter feels like a change. Last night I thought someone was lurking out of sight when I walked into the parking lot. I hate that feeling." Emilie held her coffee, consciously forcing her hold to relax so she didn't crush the cup and spill the steaming hot beverage. "I want to be strong enough to walk to my car without wondering who is waiting where I can't see them."

Taylor gave a slight shrug. "You can't control everything, even your emotions and fears."

"But that's it. I don't like fear. I've never lived that way." Not really.

"Do you want me to pull the files again?"

"Yes."

"Have you contacted the police?"

"I left Miranda Roberts a message, but I don't want the word to spread here." Not until she had a better understanding of what she faced.

"Understood." Taylor stood and turned to leave, but not before Emilie noted a flash of sympathy.

The young woman was too astute for her own good. She intuited emotions and layers to situations that most would never identify. It's what made her excellent in her job working with at-risk women. But Emilie didn't like it when that same empathetic magic was directed toward her.

She didn't need anyone's pity.

For goodness' sake, she was a young woman of privilege, part of a loving family. Graduate of a top law school and using her education to help those in need fix their problems. All of that should allow her to sleep like a baby. Instead, she'd awoken last night in a cold sweat, the accident playing through her mind like the chaotic footage of a movie, camera shots in juxtaposition to each other in a dizzying kaleidoscope that left her breathless, heart pounding, and awake. Very awake.

She returned to the old list Taylor had given her months earlier. Plugged the first name into the search engine. Waded through page after page of returned links. Wasted her time, even as it felt like it was all she could control.

The phone on her desk rang and Emilie hit the intercom button. "Yes?"

"Your editor's on line 3."

"Thanks, Taylor." Emilie blew out a breath. She was now a week late turning in her latest article. Surely Olivia understood. She clicked on the line and took a breath. "This is Emilie."

"The woman I've been looking for."

"I know I owe you an article."

"Yes, you do, but that's not the reason I'm calling."

It wasn't? Now Emilie was confused . . . and the butterflies in her stomach took flight.

"Can you meet me at Lady Camellia's for tea? Say, four o'clock?"

"Okay." Emilie jotted down the address and then returned to work.

While Georgetown wasn't that far from Old Town, it took time to drive across the Potomac and to the right neighborhood. Finding parking took even more time. By the time Emilie climbed from her car, she risked being late.

The building was brick painted mint green with a couple tables set outside the front door. Fortunately, Olivia wasn't waiting there or they'd melt in the heat. Emilie stepped inside and found the tearoom charming. Why hadn't she heard of it before? It looked like the perfect place to schedule a high tea with the girls. From the brick exterior of the row house to the blanched yellow wallpaper with pink figures to the clean, white tablecloths and elegant chairs to the empty gold picture frames decorating the wall, it was a place one would raise a pinky while sipping exotic teas and nibbling tasty macaroons. She looked up and saw elegant white chandeliers braced on the ceiling by an ornate bronze swirl of metal.

"Emilie."

She pulled her gaze from the ceiling and found her editor gesturing her over. Olivia Lanning was a buttoned-down woman who wore her explosion of auburn hair in a tight French braid that few curls escaped. Her horn-framed glasses were perched on her nose as she set down the menu and gestured toward the chair on the other side of the table.

Emilie squared her shoulders and pushed a smile on as she walked to the table. "What a charming place."

Olivia nodded as Emilie sat. "I thought you'd like it. Something of a hidden gem. It will also afford us privacy."

That didn't sound good.

"We need to talk about the trajectory of your career."

"Oh." That was not what Emilie had expected. "I know my article is late, but I promise I'll submit one."

Olivia tapped the menu in front of Emilie. "First tea. I recommend the Savory. It comes with a few sweets and a couple sandwiches. The perfect complement to a pot of tea."

Emilie doubted she'd eat if the conversation took the turn Olivia's tone suggested. In spite of her mother's careful schooling, Emilie could barely focus on Olivia's words as her thoughts returned to the real reason the woman had invited her.

Finally Olivia brushed her cloth napkin gently across her lips. "Now that we've enjoyed that, we need to talk about you." She slid her small plate to the side, placed her elbows on the table, and leaned forward. "Part of my job as editor at the *Nation's Post* is to keep all our content going by having the correct writers in place."

"Yes."

"Since your Rodriguez exposé, you've been flat. Nothing of note written. Filler pieces."

"It's not every day a Pulitzer-worthy piece falls in my lap."

"That's my point. Lightning won't strike twice unless you're out there with your kite and key. What are you doing to find your next exposé everyone will talk about?"

Emilie's throat suddenly felt brick dry. She picked up the delicate china cup and took a quick sip of the soothing English Breakfast. "I haven't found inspiration, nor have you funneled many ideas my way."

"Yes . . ."

"So there isn't much."

"And that's a problem." Olivia's gaze bored into her. "Do you know how many articles we publish a day?"

"No."

"If you came to staff meetings, you would. More than fifty."

"But it's online. We can go down and no one notices."

"Au contraire. The publisher, investors, and advertisers notice. And they're asking about you. It's been more than two weeks since your last article, and that one wasn't up to your usual caliber."

"This is the first deadline I've missed. Every writer hits a slump."

"Yes, but there are a thousand aspiring opinion changers in this town who want to take your place. Each assures me they will get every piece in on time, if not early."

There was nothing she could say . . . unless she had the story of the year. Her thoughts flitted to Kaylene's death. Maybe she did . . . but not quite yet.

Olivia read her silence with a sigh. "I see. Well, I'm afraid I have to replace you."

"Could I take a leave of absence?" Emilie couldn't let go of everything she had worked so long and hard to build. "I have a track record of stellar pieces, and often more than you requested."

"It's not how we do things."

Emilie's heart stuttered. She couldn't let go of reporting, not when she loved it. "As you mentioned, we won't know if my Rodriguez report finaled or won the Pulitzer for months. Letting me take a vacation while keeping my allegiances tied to you is in your best interests."

Olivia pushed her glasses up her nose. "I'll ask, but I still need your article."

"Thank you." Emilie wouldn't beg for her job, especially not when she was struggling to string words together. However, she'd invested years into building her right to speak on relevant issues, and she valued the forum it gave her. "I'll find something."

"Quickly, I hope. Even if I can talk the publisher into this scheme, there are no guarantees how long we can hold a slot. The pressure is intense for an article now."

"Understood."

Olivia waved for the check, and within a matter of minutes Emilie found herself on the street. It was a slow walk to her car, and she allowed her thoughts to wander.

Was it time to give up writing?

Most thought it was a side hobby for her, the identity she'd built as E. M. Wesley. That she had an online, go-to political news source to display her investigations had been a side benefit. While not *HuffPost* or *The Federalist*, it aspired to be and got closer each month.

Now it was slipping from her fingers. Of course she could hope to transition her writing to another news source, but she didn't want to start at the bottom again unless she had no choice.

In many ways she'd dabbled in writing and the law to have a fallback when she decided she didn't like one or it decided it was done with her. But it was supposed to be on her terms.

Now both endeavors that brought her such joy felt threatened.

If only she could go back to before Kaylene died.

CHAPTER 23

Her phone dinged as she climbed into her super-heated car. A text from Taylor told her to call Detective Gaines ASAP and listed a new number for him. Emilie groaned as she leaned against the hot seat of her little Coop. What could he have learned since this morning? She wasn't sure she could handle one more blow in an already rough week. It had to be five o'clock somewhere. Surely she could call it a week.

The responsible part of her dialed his number and waited for him to pick up. When he did, they agreed to a time and place to meet. He hadn't wanted to meet at the police station, but had been willing to see her that evening. She'd have just enough time to get to the designated park in Fort Ward if rush hour cooperated.

The location seemed a little cloak-and-dagger, so she called Hayden so someone would know where to find her if she disappeared—admitting to herself she'd read too many thrillers. On her way she detoured to a gas station and bought two bottles of ice-cold water, then pulled into the parking lot.

When she reached the small bandstand in the park, she found the detective sitting on a bench, wearing a basic navy suit and watching peoples' comings and goings. There was a studied relaxation to his stance that telegraphed how alert he was—was he expecting her to do something crazy?

She sighed and adjusted her purse strap on her shoulder, then lifted her chin and marched to him. No way would she allow him to know she was anything less than perfectly comfortable.

When she sank onto his bench and pulled two bottles of water from her bag, his eyebrows spiked. "It's a warm enough day. I thought you'd like a cool drink."

"Thanks." He took the bottle and downed half of it in one swig. "I had one of the techs take a quick stab at cleaning up the video."

"That was fast. Thank you." She set her purse beside her on the bench. "Did it change anything?"

"Maybe."

Her pulse spiked at the word, but he moved his hands up and down in a placating gesture. "There's nothing clear, just an impression it gives me that she's uncomfortable with the gun. It also looks like she's looking for help. It could mean she's a good actress."

"Or that she knew she was dying."

"Or that her girls needed assistance." He looked at her, gray gaze boring through her. "What are the odds an argument got out of control?"

"Definitely possible." Emilie took a sip of the cool water as she thought about what Kaylene had told her in their appointments. "Robert wasn't often physically violent, maybe only one time. But he used his words like fists. It sounded like he could shred people in an instant and turn any conversation into a heated argument."

"So how would a gun get involved?"

"I'm not certain." She studied her hands, then decided to trust him. "She may have explored getting a gun."

"She had a concealed carry. But we can't tell whose gun she had when she died because the serial number was filed off."

"So it could have been Robert's."

"Or one either of them bought off a dealer. We'll never know."

"If she had a concealed carry permit, wouldn't she have to have a gun?"

He shook his head. "Not necessarily. Some people get them in the event they ever get a gun."

Emilie thought about that, but nothing about Kaylene having a gun or a permit to carry one made sense. "Unless she needed it to feel safe when they left."

Detective Gaines looked at her with a question in his eyes. "I'm not following."

"Kaylene wanted to get away from violence, not create it. The only way her having a gun makes sense is if she was convinced she had to have one to successfully escape."

"She thought her husband would follow her."

"Exactly. And he would have tried." That would explain the diamonds as relatively ready cash. She still had to check on the stones to see if they were real.

"Unfortunately, none of this changes the reality that she killed her kid." Detective Gaines leaned forward. "Look, I know you want to believe your client was set up. That's impossible. Hers are the lone, clear prints on the gun, and they're where we would expect them to be for someone who shot it."

"What do you mean the only clear prints?"

"There were smudges of overlapping fingerprints, but nothing we could run."

Emilie let the idea run through her mind. "Then how are hers usable?"

"She fired the gun."

"But Kaylene was shot. Someone else used the gun, if you're sure she was shot with it."

"Ballistics confirms it. Shot with her own gun."

"There must have been a struggle." She could imagine the fear and adrenaline Kaylene had experienced. "She must have been so scared and in pain."

"Probably." He didn't say anything else.

All right. She'd brainstorm as if he were cooperating. Maybe plant an idea in his mind. "What if her husband wore gloves?"

"Then we would have found the gloves. We didn't."

"Did you search him?"

"As soon as the scene was contained. Officer safety came first."

"Okay." She thought through her questions. "What did you see when you arrived?"

"Two girls shot, one dead. A mother who died on the scene clutching the gun used in the shooting. A father deep in shock who insisted it couldn't have happened."

"Did you interview him?"

"Yes." Detective Gaines stood and his jaw locked. "He was as you'd expect. He didn't know what had happened or why. He insisted it was a quiet day. Kept coming back to the fact that they were going school shopping."

"And for no reason at all Kaylene grabbed a gun and started shooting."

"Yes."

That was less believable than the idea that she had premeditated the series of events. "Have you talked to any of her friends?"

"Her husband says she kept to herself."

"Because he made her."

"That's your opinion." He glanced at his watch. "Send in a formal request, and I'll send you the cleaned-up footage."

"Before you leave, could I ask your opinion on another matter?"

"Quickly."

She told him about the notes she'd received and the shadows. "I'm going through files and trying to connect with Officer Roberts as you suggested. Is there anything else you'd recommend?"

"Try to minimize handling of any notes."

"I have, and I'm keeping them in a folder."

"Good. If you don't hear from Officer Roberts by Monday, let me know. She's the best at these sorts of cases."

"Yes, sir."

He turned toward her, seriousness cloaking his rugged features. "Don't minimize this situation. If it escalates, let me know immediately."

Emilie's thoughts returned to Kaylene. "Was anyone else in the Adamses' house?"

"Her husband says no, and we didn't find evidence of anyone."

"Okay. Maybe he's hiding something." He had to

be, because otherwise she might have to accept that Kaylene had done the unthinkable.

"Maybe, but the evidence won't change because she's dead. And her husband is incredibly consistent in his story."

Her interest was piqued. "Incredibly?"

"Yes. Almost word-for-word repetitive."

"Interesting."

"Yes. But there's nothing you can do with that. If I could, I would."

It was a slim opening, but it was an opening. "Can I get a copy of your report and notes?"

"If you go through the proper channels."

"We've tried."

"Give the desk sergeant a call." He gave her a name and number. "He should help."

She nodded. It was something. "Thank you. I'll follow up on that."

"Good luck." He paused a moment. "I wish your version of events was right. It's horrifying to think a mom would do this, but unfortunately it happens. Often for no easy-to-understand reason. We may never know why she snapped."

"Kinley's the only eyewitness."

He paused. "What do you mean?"

"What if she knows something she's not supposed to?"

"We won't know unless she wakes up." He rubbed a hand along his jaw. "We've talked about the possibility."

"She might need a safe place to land."

"Then I suggest you have one ready. But you'll have an uphill road to get a judge on board."

She didn't need him reminding her of that.

The detective went on his way, moving in a remarkably stealthy manner for such a tall man. As she followed his progress, she noted someone in a hooded sweatshirt watching her from the edge of the trees. How long had he been there?

She had to leave while Detective Gaines was still near and before the shadow approached. Emilie suddenly felt vulnerable and exposed. She swallowed, stood, and then gathered her purse and tried to walk without breaking into a panic-stricken run.

Still, once she reached the top of the hill, she looked back to see if she could make out any details of the hooded man. He was gone. Disappeared as much like a ghost as he'd been every other time she'd spotted him.

In spite of the warmth, she felt chilled to the bone and exposed.

CHAPTER 24

Saturday morning Emilie stopped at Alexandria Heirlooms and Jewels in Old Town on her way to work. She stepped into the shop off King Street, her bag tucked firmly against her side. She may not know the exact worth of the stones she carried, but she had a feeling they were real and valuable.

A man with gray hair and glasses perched on a beak-like nose stepped from a back room. "Can I help you?"

"I wondered if there was someone here who could appraise a few diamonds for me."

"I can do that." He rattled off a list of letters that she supposed were designed to tell her he was qualified. "I can examine them right here and give you a loose estimate. Then you can leave them for a more careful inspection."

"Let's start with the quick one."

"Come over here and have a seat while I test the stones."

She sank onto a stool that was set in front of a bank of glass display cases. He pulled a small instrument from beneath the case.

"This is a diamond tester that will send heat through your stones to test whether they are diamonds."

She pulled the padded envelope from her bag and carefully opened it, shaking the diamonds into her palm. He pulled out a velvet pad, and she set the gems on it.

"Let's see what we have." He picked up the largest diamond with a pair of tweezers and carried it to a microscope. "The clarity and color are very nice. Looks to be 2.5 carats." He replaced the stone and then repeated the process with the others. "These are nice stones."

"Approximately how much are they worth?"

"Based on this quick survey, for insurance purposes I'd say $50,000. For sale, probably five to ten thousand, less if you need the cash quickly."

Emilie considered how far Kaylene could have taken the girls on the lesser amount. "Thank you."

"Do you want to sell them?"

"Not today." She replaced the diamonds in the envelope and then in her purse. "I'll need to think about it. Thanks for your help."

She let the numbers bounce around her mind as she went to work to get ready for Monday's hearing. That amount could have bought time for Kaylene to get a job and start taking care of the girls on her own. If only they'd been able to leave.

Taylor had gotten Nadine's motion for a protective order on file with the court. Now it was time for a phone call with Nadine to prep her for the hearing. While the woman would have to testify, she would rely on Emilie to convince the judge that the PO was necessary to protect Nadine and her little guy, Jonathan.

Nadine's first question was focused. "Please tell me he won't be there."

"I don't know. Usually respondents don't show up for preliminary hearings. Most don't have any idea that a motion is pending. That's why it starts as a fifteen-day order."

"I can't do this." There was a hoarse note to Nadine's voice. "He'll kill me when he finds out."

"If we don't do this, you'll never escape. And the judge won't issue the order without testimony from you." Emilie spoke in a softer tone. "I'll be there to guide you."

"I don't like talking to strangers."

"Judge Monica Bell is a woman you will feel comfortable talking to." Some of her clients had frozen the moment they were called in front of the bench and couldn't provide one word of testimony. In many ways that was worse than never filing if the abuser found out. "I won't lie to you and say it's a sure thing, Nadine, but I will do all I can to ensure you and Jonathan are protected." She couldn't let Nadine's hopes rise only to have her shell-shocked and traumatized if her boyfriend appeared.

Those were moments she hated her job. She wanted to keep the world safe and contained for Nadine, but that was beyond her power. Nadine reluctantly agreed, and Emilie let her know what kind of information the judge would need. "See you Monday morning at eleven."

Emilie signed off and sank back into her chair.

But there were so many more times she'd come through and saved her clients.

Was it really you?

The voice startled her.

Taylor hurried into her office. "Did you need something?"

Emilie shook off the voice. "What are you doing here? It's Saturday, get out and enjoy."

"I'm doing what you are, getting things ready for next week. But I'm leaving in a minute. Do you need anything before I go?"

"No." Other than another rush of adrenaline. Her heart had responded to the whisper by taking off. She could practically feel it beating against her rib cage. "Nadine's prepared for the hearing."

"Great. I hope it goes well."

"Me too." Emilie pressed a hand against her heart as Taylor left.

Don't underestimate My presence in your success, child.

Emilie lurched to her feet, her chair scraping behind her. "Father?" Her whisper seemed to echo in the room. "I need to get out of here."

Emilie grabbed her purse and keys and bolted from her office. In no time, she had gotten into her car and driven back to her town house. A quick change later, and she was headed back out in workout clothes with a bottle of water, careful to take roads that had lots of foot traffic.

She fast-walked toward Tide Lock Park, seeking a moment of peace and clarity. There was something about the sliver of green next to the Potomac that gave her a sense of time and space. It had been part of the lock system to move boats along the river until it flooded in the 1820s. If this thin slice of beauty could bring peace, surely there was a similar slice in her life that could do the same.

She sank onto the steps and listened to the quiet waterfall as it splashed between two eyes and then down to a pool filled with freestanding sculptures of eyes and mouths and other broken pieces of white stone. It felt like the arrow piercing one of the white blocks of marble had pierced her own heart.

She was hemorrhaging inside from the pain of years of client experiences, Kaylene being the ultimate catalyst for her crisis. Her capacity to feel and care was emptied. She'd seen too much, heard too much, experienced too much. Her heart had cracked along fault lines, and she couldn't process the borrowed pain or her inability to truly help her clients.

Don't abandon Me, because I will never abandon you.

The words whispered in her mind like the mist from the waterfall brushing her face.

The words insisted they should be understood and remembered, but they felt devoid of any true, compelling meaning.

I am still here.

She closed her eyes against the emotion the words released.

How did God know she felt so alone? She had friends. Good ones. She lived with one of her best friends. Yet lately it felt she sat somehow separate and apart. She could be with them, yet feel no connection at the soul level.

As she sat there she watched a steady stream of joggers pound by, some with leashed dogs, others pushing strollers, more with headphones, sweat pouring down their faces and backs. She kept an eye on them, but no one paid attention to her where she sat in the fog of humidity by the waterfall. If she squinted it seemed she could see someone in the mist, much as it seemed her heart could hear that still, small voice.

Oh, she wanted to believe God was still there and saw her. But if it were so, wouldn't He have kept Kaylene and Kaydence safe? Would Kinley be lingering in ICU betwixt and between?

Why did He remain in the shadows when she needed Him most?

Emilie stepped through the back door and took off her shoes. Hayden was cleaning the kitchen, a diffuser releasing a citrusy smell in the air as Young & Free played from her phone. Emilie could feel the energy flow around her. She crossed the floor to drop her empty water bottle into the kitchen sink.

"Hey. Can't you see I'm cleaning?" Hayden's dark shoulder-length hair was pulled in a messy bun that looked perfect, and she was dressed for a night out.

"That's why I knew you wouldn't mind one more." Emilie slid past her to the fridge. "What's with the deep-clean?" While the roommates usually kept the space neat, this went well beyond wiping the counter with a Lysol wipe and putting dishes away.

"Andrew's coming for dinner. I hope that's all right."

"Considering I introduced y'all over a pan of my lasagna, how can I say no?" Emilie forced a bright smile. She had known Hayden and Andrew were perfect for each other and ready to risk their individual fears for love. She hadn't thought through how it would make her an occasional outsider in her home.

"You're welcome to join us."

"Third wheel alert."

"Emilie, you know that's not true."

"Who am I to get in the way of you staring into the dreamy eyes of the most eligible bachelor in DC?"

"We'll move gazing to the patio."

There'd be more than gazing, and they both knew it. Emilie was happy for them. Which was why she could force the smiles her cousin and best friend expected even as she asked God if it would ever be her turn.

She was a mess. One minute she couldn't stand the thought of a man because she was so weighed down by her clients' experiences and collective baggage; the next she whined about the fact that her man hadn't appeared yet.

Hayden laughed and then wiped the counter down one more time. "You've got that look again."

"Which one is that?"

"The one you used to get in property when Prof Dinkens asked you to explain which parcel of land was subservient in the easement scenario."

"Don't remind me." She'd had nightmares of drawing and redrawing lines for hours that month. "You know what the best part of law school was?"

"The day we graduated."

"Yep." Although she wouldn't trade the friendships she'd made, she hadn't been cut out for it like her friends. She'd fought hard to eke her way into honors. But she'd had a good time even if that had meant participating in a few mandatory rituals like being called on by professors and that ridiculous Moot Court competition. She'd loved other aspects, such as Inn of Court and writing for a journal.

"Where'd you go?"

Emilie jerked from her thoughts and found Hayden's concerned gaze on her. "Sorry."

"You okay?"

"Sure." Emilie pulled a glass from the cabinet and filled it with water. She took a long drink to buy time for Hayden to jump in before she had to continue. "How are your cases? The judges keeping you busy?"

"Busy enough. Have you thought about Savannah's offer? I can't help thinking you'd be happier working on another kind of law."

"Like what? This is all I've done." Emilie had known the big firms weren't for her as much as they'd known she wasn't for them.

"You're always haunted. And you haven't relaxed since the accident in April. I'm ready to rent a cabin on some quiet place like St. Simon's Island and send you there to recover."

"While that sounds lovely . . ." Well, not really. The thought of being so far from people she knew sounded lonely. "I can't leave. Besides, you can't afford to rent a cabin."

"I didn't say how nice the cabin would be." Hayden chuckled, but when Emilie didn't join her, her roommate folded her arms. "I'm worried about you."

"I'll be okay." *I will be, won't I, God?* Somehow she'd fix this fear-laden malaise even if it meant forcing an act she didn't feel. *Fake it till you make it worked, right?* "There's no reason to abandon my job until I see you make it work."

"So now it's on me to get you over there?"

"Absolutely." Emilie grinned at her roommate, a grin she felt all the way to her toes. "You're setting the tone and expectation for me. If you can make this work, cobbling together court-appointed cases . . ."

"Don't forget I do have a few cases, thanks to the Rodriguez matter."

"Yeah, the Department of Justice is quaking in its boots." Hayden quirked a face, and Emilie laughed. "I appreciate the thought, Hayden, I really do."

"But . . ."

"But there's too much I don't know right now." Where she fit was a big question. Especially as a knock rapped against the front door, and a huge smile erupted on Hayden's face. She needed to know God had a place for her. If the Haven wasn't it, she didn't want to rush into another almost, but not quite right position. The emotional cost was too high. She wanted to find that place where her passions matched her talents and she didn't feel like she was ready to fall into fear.

She gazed at her roommate who, looking gorgeous, knowing her man was on the other side, unlocked the door. Emilie waited in the kitchen to give them a moment alone and felt the weight of her personal torment.

She needed a change, a fresh start. But she wasn't convinced that taking a risky job on her own was the way to get the change she needed. That wouldn't address the change it might take to shake her stalker either. At the same time, as she watched her cousin kiss her roommate, she felt the need to be far away from her home.

CHAPTER 25

Her cell phone rang next to her on the chintz couch in the basement. Hayden and Andrew were upstairs, and while they'd invited her to join them, she'd opted to watch a movie in the basement and give them space.

She flicked a finger across the screen. "This is Emilie."

For a moment there was complete silence, then she heard slow, deep breathing.

"Who is this?"

"No one important. You made sure of that." The voice was muffled, indistinguishable.

"You don't scare me." Emilie's mind raced as she scrambled to grab a pen and slide a pad of paper in front of her. She quickly jotted down what little the person had said and then glanced at the display for the phone number. Unlisted. Of course.

"You heard me." More heavy breathing as Emilie tried to ignore the slight tremble in her fingers. "But you won't forever."

"I don't understand." Her words were halted by the buzz of a dead line. She glanced at the phone, then hung it up. Her mind raced as she jotted down the last words and then read them all.

She hit *69, but the call didn't go through.

What did the caller mean that she'd made sure he wasn't important? She hurriedly dialed Miranda Roberts's number and left another message. There was little the officer could do to help, but Emilie wanted the woman to have a record that her stalker had escalated to calling her . . . though there had been no other mysterious gifts left on her car.

She rubbed her forehead as she leaned against her desk and reread the words. The call had been short, less than twenty seconds. Not long enough to identify who it was or understand the meaning behind the call.

This month had been too much, and she was over it.

She pulled up the soundtrack to the *Chronicles of Narnia* on her phone and closed her eyes as the sweeping music built to a crescendo before cascading down to a trickle. The swell and diminuendo formed perfect counterbalances, holding her attention as she relaxed.

After the forced period of relaxation, it was time for action. She collected a notebook, her appointment calendar, and a stack of notes from a side table. She grabbed her sleeve of multicolored erasable pens, since it was easier to write down what she needed to do if it was in pretty colors and any mistakes could be easily swept from the page. Then she sank onto her love seat with a sigh.

Where to start?

January wasn't too far back.

She flipped to the beginning of the year and quickly scanned week by week. In January she hadn't noted anything unusual. February looked equally normal. It was in March that she'd made her first notation about something odd. It was something she'd learned to do her first year at Mason when a boyfriend had transferred his anger to her after she'd had a protective order filed against him. A week with a detective coaching her, and she'd gathered sufficient evidence to have the man arrested with certainty of a conviction. That experience had made the Haven the perfect job for her. She understood what these women experienced and could walk them to the other side of their stories as the detective had helped her.

The March entry looked innocuous enough. *Thought someone followed me as I walked home. Probably my imagination. It's been a long week.*

As she examined the spread for that week, it came back to her with startling clarity. She'd had two short divorce trials. In both the husband had been angry about custody, insisting the children should be with him. But she'd had the expert testimony to show the damage that had been done to the kids, physical in one case and psychological in the other. The guardians ad litem had sided with her, as had both judges.

It had been a case of what needed to happen being clear, but the men hadn't agreed.

Could either of them have followed her?

The week had ended with the Haven's annual banquet. Such an exhausting night.

In April she'd had a series of hang-ups, enough that she'd changed her number and immediately placed it on all the do-not-call lists. That had ended the phone calls.

But as she scanned the calendar more closely she noted that she'd made one other entry about a package that arrived. It had ticked after delivery, as if on a timer. Johanna, the receptionist, had immediately put the package out back and called the police. Because of their clients, the Alexandria City police had an officer there in minutes. He'd called in the bomb squad, but after a thorough inspection the squad had opened it to find a ticking clock and a few sticks that were supposed to look like dynamite. Scary but not dangerous. Emilie hadn't mentioned the incident to Hayden, because her roommate had been in the middle of a massive trial for one of her court-appointed clients, a trial she had gone on to win decisively with a little of her sleight-of-hand legal magic.

The incident had moved to the back of her mind then, because Hayden became embroiled in the Rodriguez case, which bled over to Emilie's life. Add in working a little romance wonder for Andrew and Hayden, and then the car accident on Rock Creek Parkway.

The car accident had left Emilie shaken and convinced that someone was out to get her. The park service had been thinning the deer population, and it really could be that a hunter had hit her car by mistake. But the person must have been a terrible shot.

She'd tried hard to believe it was a case of wrong place wrong time. Those sorts of things happened all the time. The split-second decision that changed a person's life.

But the truth was she wouldn't have headed toward the parkway if she hadn't received a text from a client requesting help. By the time she'd remembered that detail, the woman was gone. Off to South Carolina to stay with a relative, as Rhoda had encouraged. Emilie mentioned the text to the police officer, but he was more consumed with the spiraling drug case spreading around Hayden.

So she'd let it go.

What else could she do without losing her mind?

She'd watched.

Distance had crept in. She removed herself from the closeness of friendships. To protect them. To protect her.

Emilie tried to pull her thoughts free, but as she tapped the pen against her lips, she felt lost. Encircled with fears. What if someone wanted to do more than scare her?

Perfect love casts out fear. She knew that, but the truth barely dented her fears. She reached for her Bible on the small table next to the couch. Maybe if she saw those words in context she'd push the knowledge past her stubborn mind to her heart. She turned to 1 John chapter 4 and read:

God is love. When we take up permanent residence in a life of love, we live in God and God lives in us. This way, love has the run of the house, becomes at home and mature in us, so that we're free of worry on Judgment Day—our standing in the world is identical with Christ's. There is no room in love for fear. Well-formed love banishes fear. Since fear is crippling, a fearful life—fear of death, fear of judgment—is one not yet fully formed in love.

What did well-formed love look like? She worked with women who needed to know that. They needed kindness and patience as they worked their way to freedom. But had that purpose somehow become corrupted as she worked with more women? Was it a combination of the 1 Corinthian 13 attributes read at every wedding, or did it look like the fruit of the Spirit? Either list seemed unattainable. On her best day she didn't live half of either.

Or was her focus off, and she was just supposed to love God well? Was that the beginning and end?

She didn't think so, since Jesus had clearly answered the religious leaders that the greatest command was to love God, and the second to love one's neighbor as oneself. That's what she was trying to do at the Haven. Love her neighbors, those who needed help because they were the least of these in many ways.

Then why did she feel overwhelmed, afraid, and alone all at the same time?

. . .

The sky darkened beyond his windows at Fletcher & Associates as Reid pushed back from his desk and rubbed his eyes. The research was coming together, but they'd need to do more to win the competition. Vince could replicate what they'd accomplished with a little hard work of his own, or by helping himself to information left carelessly on a desk. They needed appointments with the prospective clients to learn the details good research couldn't always find. The personal stories and motivations that formed the foundation for long-term relationships.

He pulled the first file to the center of his desk and then picked up his desk phone. But instead of dialing his client, he found himself calling Emilie. It wouldn't hurt to get an update from her. See if she'd found a way to protect Kinley while they figured out what had happened.

"Hello?" The voice was small, almost emotionless. A stark contrast to her usual enthusiasm.

"You all right, Emilie?"

"Sure." She cleared her throat, and he bet if he were in the room with her, he would observe a startling transformation. "What's up?"

"Thought I'd see if you'd learned anything today."

"The diamonds are real. Probably worth thirty thousand as fast cash, maybe more."

"Those were her running funds."

"As soon as she sold them, she would have had time to hide and rebuild with the girls."

"Okay." He let that reality sink in. "She was getting ready."

"Yes." She cleared her throat again. "Maybe we should go talk to her neighbors tomorrow. They might be home since it's a Sunday."

"That would work. I could get you around two."

"That sounds good." She paused, then hurried forward. "Why'd you call? Really?"

Could she see through him so easily? The thought didn't leave him feeling exposed but relieved, like someone might care to get to know him. It would be easy to say the call was just about his concern for Kinley, but that wasn't the whole truth.

"Reid?"

"Want to go to dinner with me tonight?" There was a pause. "If you have other plans, I understand. This is rather spontaneous."

"Did you say 'rather'?" She laughed, and there was delight in her voice. "I think I'd like that. Especially if it means you might say things like that again. Can you pick me up at seven?"

He glanced at his clock. That gave him forty-five minutes to get home, clean up, and drive to her place. "Make it seven thirty, and I'll be there. I know the perfect place."

"There you go again."

"What do you mean?"

"Sounding like you've got a script right out of Hollywood. I don't need anything fancy. You'd better let me go, or I'll be wearing yoga pants when you arrive."

"Yoga pants are fine."

"Not this time." He could hear the smile in her voice. "See you at seven thirty."

Reid started powering down his computer, ensuring it would require a password to restart. No way would he make it easy for Vince to steal his work. But tonight he would forget work for a while and get better acquainted with an interesting lady.

CHAPTER 26

Clothes still on hangers were strewn across Emilie's bed, and she worried her thumbnail as she pondered which outfit was perfect for a spontaneous date/non-date. She didn't mind the interruption to her useless worrying. She hadn't come any closer to determining who it was that lurked in her shadows.

As she touched the soft cotton blend of a white, one-shouldered sundress that was covered with large cornflower-blue flowers, she decided that was the one. She wanted Reid to look at her tonight and see a woman, not an attorney.

What would it be like to have him look at her the way Andrew gazed at Hayden? Sure, Hayden made it easy, since she practically glowed with love.

That wasn't in Emilie's immediate future, but for a few hours she could hope to attract a handsome man's attention and forget all the noise happening in her life.

One night of escape.

That wasn't too much to ask, was it?

They'd share a good meal with some perfect Southern sweet tea. A bit of conversation on a restaurant's patio while the humidity blanketing the air reminded her they

were in Virginia. A few minutes of learning about someone else and discovering why he did the things he did.

That's all she wanted.

She hurried through a shower, then slipped on the
dress and some sparkly silver sandals poised on the
kind of heels that made her feel like a queen. It was hard
not to feel gorgeous when wearing strappy stilettos.
Hayden said they made her wobble and feel anything
but regal, but Emilie was fine as long as she didn't walk
across cobblestones.

She twisted her damp blonde waves into a French
twist and teased a few tendrils to ring her face. Then
she swiped on the perfect amount of makeup to show
she'd tried without caking it into a mask. It would melt
off the moment she stepped outside anyway. A swipe
of pale-pink lip gloss, and she was close to Audrey
Hepburn's relaxed elegance, without the I-spent-hours-
preparing look.

She slipped her phone and a twenty as well as a
credit card and the lip gloss into a pretty blue clutch
and headed to the basement stairs. A glance at her
pearl-banded watch confirmed she'd gotten ready with
fifteen minutes to spare.

Perfect.

Now he'd wonder at her speed and femininity. It
would add to her appeal . . . she hoped.

Hayden looked up from the wing chair where she
was flipping through a magazine. "Wow. Where are you
headed?"

"On a spontaneous dinner date. Where's Andrew?"

"Grabbing his car to take me out for ice cream. Said

he had to park a couple blocks away and doesn't want me to melt."

"Awww."

"Don't think you can distract me that easily." Hayden swung her legs around and leaned forward. "Who's the lucky man?"

"Reid Billings."

Hayden frowned as she set the magazine aside. "But isn't he a client, Em?"

"Not tonight he isn't, and we haven't formalized any sort of attorney-client relationship." It wasn't like she had a signed engagement letter. "We're two people who met because of our mutual love for Kaylene."

"Be careful."

"I always am."

"Yes, you are. But that is not the appearance of a woman who is out to enjoy a casual meal with a friend." Hayden gestured toward her with a sweeping up-and-down motion.

"Maybe I wanted to dress up."

"Maybe. But, Em, you haven't done anything like this in months."

Those words pointed straight back to when the trouble had begun. Emilie had seen each prospective man as the one silhouetted in shadows. It hadn't been worth the risk. "I'm safe with Reid."

"Of course you are." Hayden frowned, concern putting a V between her eyebrows. "Why wouldn't you be?"

"No reason." She twirled a bit, showing off her shoes. "Want to borrow these beauties the next time you and Andrew go out?"

"That would be a no. I'd fall off them."

A knock at the door sent Emilie's heart racing in the best possible way. She felt a wave of giddiness rise inside as if this really were a date that she could let her heart sink into. For tonight she would forget any potential issues and simply enjoy. She took a step forward and teetered, then glanced at Hayden with a faux frown. "You were saying?"

"Oh, stay there." Hayden stood with a laugh. "You can pose for him while I get the door."

. . .

The door opened, but it was Emilie's roommate who welcomed him.

"Hi, Reid. Come on in." She stepped to the side, but Reid couldn't have moved if his life depended on it.

Emilie stood against the white half wall topped with a black countertop. Her dress was an interesting off-the-shoulder thing that hit right above her knees, showing off shapely calves and sparkly death traps on her feet. How did women manage those? She looked all feminine and soft, without the hard edges or the sweetly Southern sarcastic tone she sometimes used as a shield.

"You might want to raise your chin." So much for the slight snark being softened.

"I wouldn't want to deny you the reaction you worked for."

Hayden snorted and stepped against the wall. "Let me make space for your verbal sparring."

Emilie didn't seem to hear her. "Worked for? This is au naturel, honey."

Honey. No one called him that except his grandmother, but it sounded very different coming from Emilie. Not sure he'd choose that term of endearment, but . . . "You can call me honey anytime you like."

Yep, he was right. A soft color slid up her neck into her cheeks. She'd expected him to be annoyed at the term. He'd have to remember to stay in the unexpected zone.

Emilie tilted her chin, still not coming anywhere near to matching his height, even on those stilts.

"Are you ready?"

The roommate snorted. "You've met your match, Em."

Em. He liked the sound of that. It suited her. He turned to the roommate. "I'll have her home before she turns into a pumpkin."

Hayden grinned. "Have a fun dinner."

"I'm counting on it." Reid swept his arm toward the door in what he hoped was a gallant gesture. "Ready, milady?"

Emilie rolled her green eyes, the emeralds burning bright. "Whatever." She turned to Hayden. "If you don't hear from me in three hours . . ."

"I won't send the cavalry. Have a good time, kids." Then she shoved Emilie toward him, and the breathtaking woman tottered a moment on her heels before regaining the grace she wore like a garment.

Emilie slipped around him, her full skirt barely brushing his side. "Where are we off to?"

"While I'm tempted to keep it a surprise"—she spun

toward him—"I won't. Do you mind walking the few blocks to Old Town?"

"As long as we avoid cobblestones."

He glanced down at her shoes, trying not to be arrested by the shapely image of her legs. "We'll drive."

A man passed them as they went down the sidewalk, blond and looking a bit like Emilie. His gaze assessed Reid in a way that felt very protective. Big brotherish. Guess he hadn't asked Em about her family. Yep, he definitely liked the sound of that name.

"Emilie?"

At the question in the man's tone, Emilie slowed down a fraction. "Hi, Andrew. I'd stop to introduce you, but I believe Hayden is eager for her treat. An ice cream date? Really?" Her face contained an amused smirk. "I thought I'd trained you better than that."

"Guess not." The man took her kidding in stride and stuck out a hand. "I'm Andrew Wesley, Emilie's cousin. And you are?"

"Reid Billings. Nice to meet you."

"Take good care of her." The *or else* was left unsaid but noted just the same . . .

He guided Em down the sidewalk and toward his Lexus. He held the door as she slid in.

She touched the seat, and her face softened. "Do you take this good of care of your house?"

"It's a fairly bare-bones condo, but yeah." He closed her door, then walked around the car and slid inside. "This was a bit of a splurge. Living here, I never know when traffic will get bad and I'll want something nice and comfortable to be stuck in." He pulled onto

St. Asaph, and a few minutes later pulled into a parking garage. "The restaurant is just across the street."

He slid a hand to her back and guided her across the crosswalk and then down the brick sidewalk to the Taverna Cretekou. Above the yellow awning three flags flapped in a light breeze. A small line of people waited at the hostess stand. Good thing he'd called ahead for a reservation. Most tourists would opt for the air-conditioned inside, not knowing that a few feet away a beautiful patio space waited. Last time he'd been here he'd had to shift his chair to avoid being tickled by a flowering something or other all night.

He gave the host his name, and a minute later they wound their way through the dining room with its exposed brick and whitewashed stucco and around tables and chairs to the patio door. "I hope you don't mind that I asked for the patio."

Emilie shook her head, then sank onto a seat at the table the host had guided them to. "You won't believe that I've never eaten here."

"It's just a few blocks from your town house."

"I guess I do what most do and have a few favorites I return to." She picked up the menu and scanned it. "This looks good."

"I've enjoyed everything I've tried." They settled on a combination platter and salads. There was something intimate about knowing they would share the meal, even if he knew from experience it was too much for two people to eat.

Overhead fans on the ceiling of the pergola kept the air circulating, and they sipped iced tea while they waited for their food. It was a comfortable conversation that ebbed and flowed. Emilie wasn't bothered by silence. In fact, she seemed to appreciate pauses and a slow pace. When the platter arrived, she leaned forward and let him explain each dish.

"I'll claim the spinach and feta filo." She tapped her fork against the item.

"Sold. I'll stick to the meat dishes." He stabbed his fork in some ziti.

She took hold of the conversation. "Tell me more about your path to a career in finance. Was it something your grandparents pushed you toward?"

"My grandpa wanted me to be a doctor. My grandmother thought I should be a priest."

She quirked an eyebrow at him. "Horrors."

"To hear Grandma tell it, I was the worst sort of disappointment. Too bad she didn't ask what I wanted before telling all her friends I was destined for a life in a collar." He tugged lightly at his button-down. "Too bad this collar doesn't work for her. She's coming around."

"My dad wanted me to be a lawyer with the Department of Justice, to defend freedom from tyranny. He's not sure what I do qualifies."

"You're doing exactly that, on an individual basis."

"True, but it's not quite as brag worthy." She shrugged lightly. "So you've found what you want to be when you grow up?"

"So we're on to deep questions. All right." He took a sip from his tea as he considered. "I don't really think about that. I guess I'm more focused on today."

"And all I think about is the future."

He could hear an unspoken *and the past.* "That's quite a burden to carry."

FOUR MONTHS EARLIER

Maybe if she saw him protecting her, she would become aware of how perfect they were for each other. He glanced around his man cave and drummed his fingers on the leather couch. He needed to show her quickly, while he had freedom from work, how he could be all she needed. Already new ideas for technology innovations were crowding his mind, but he wanted to finish things with Emilie first.

Maybe if he went to the office for a couple hours first, then he could focus on her and show her how he protected her.

He grabbed the keys to his sports car and then froze.

Wait. He didn't have an office anymore.

He needed someone to help him enjoy the riches he had earned.

He needed Emilie.

Just as she needed him. Today she would start to understand.

How best to show her?

A note on her car? That sounded so junior high, but he also liked the mystery of it. Would she?

Yes, the idea grew on him. She needed him. He could help her see that. It would be easy to do with his resources. And once she'd benefited from all he had to offer, there would be no going back.

Quickly he pulled together what he needed and grabbed the addresses his investigator had provided. Amazing how money could obtain the impossible so readily. He drove through the back roads across the bridge into Arlington and then wove through Rosslyn, Courthouse, into Clarendon, and across to King Street. Then past the high school and the George Washington Masonic Temple into Old Town. He circled the block around her office, looking for her car. It wasn't as flashy as the one he would give her, but her George Mason Law School bumper sticker confirmed he'd found the right one. He drove down a block and parked. She would have no reason to know what he drove, but he didn't want to take chances.

He grabbed the gift bag and got out of the car. After locking his BMW, he walked the block back to the Haven. What a ridiculous name. Like a location could give anyone security and peace. Still, he supposed they did good work, and if it mattered to her then he'd make it matter to him.

His check to the Haven showed how much he wanted to support what she valued.

Had she noticed?

It didn't matter. She wouldn't be able to miss this. Women liked cute things.

He double-checked the parking lot. No one was around, so he walked in, careful to keep his back to the light that looked like it hid a security camera. He wanted her to discover that the gift came from him without cheating by looking at a video. This was a slow wooing. A drawing her attention to him in a way that would bind her to him.

The driver's door of her car was locked. He sighed in frustration, even as he knew it was the smart action for a beautiful young woman who worked at a place like this. He'd have to talk to her about allowing herself to be in

danger by working with women who had crazy husbands
and boyfriends. There were other ways she could use her
talents to help people.

He placed his gift on her hood against the windshield,
then slipped into the shadow of the bushes to wait for her
to appear.

CHAPTER 27

As they'd walked back to his car and his arm had brushed hers, Emilie fought how he affected her. She'd been comfortable talking with Reid over dinner, as though they'd known one another for years. He'd heard everything, even the words she hadn't spoken.

She didn't let men close, but as he'd taken her hand to ease her into his car she wanted to ignore her rule.

He sank onto the driver's seat and turned to her. "Want to take a drive along the parkway?"

She bit her lower lip as she considered. Noting his gaze straying to her lips, she quickly released it. "Okay."

It was okay. He was no threat to her; in fact, she felt safe with him.

She didn't know what to do with that.

Should she sink into it? Or should she turn and run, mindful that it could all be a mistake and she had somehow allowed herself to be deluded into thinking he wasn't dangerous? The miles slid by as they traveled along the George Washington Memorial Parkway headed south. When they reached Mount Vernon, Reid turned around and drove back north. He parked when they reached Jones Point Park, and Emilie didn't mind that he hadn't consulted her.

They walked along the piers that poked into the Potomac River, her strappy sandals dangling from her fingers, her hands clasped behind her back so their fingers couldn't brush unintentionally. She felt the pull to him more than she wanted to admit. She had to rein in it. She had to.

The sound of water lapping at the shoreline was overlaid with the sound of cicadas. Reid led her to the end of one of the piers, and she sank to the planks carefully, adjusting her sundress skirt beneath her. He eased down beside her. The moon was silhouetted against the river with the soundtrack of nature. The silence felt good and comfortable, right.

Then Reid asked a question and soon they were talking about nothing and everything, careful not to let their voices carry.

A vibration in her handbag made her reach for her phone.

It's almost midnight. I'm headed to bed. You okay?

"Everything all right?"

Emilie checked the time and then shook her head. "Just my roommate checking on me. I can't believe it's already midnight."

"Are you the cinder girl?"

There was teasing in his tone, but she needed to end this magical evening. "I really should get home before I lose a slipper." Magical as it had been, nothing could come of it. Not while he was technically a client . . . and would remain one until they learned if they could get custody of Kinley changed. "Besides, I'll see you in a few hours when we head to Kaylene's neighborhood."

"All right." He climbed to his feet, then reached down to help her up. "Thanks for agreeing to dinner."

She nodded, fighting the grin that wanted to consume her as he led her to the car, a grin she couldn't allow. When they reached the house, he kept a bit of space between them, enough to keep her wondering . . . would he lean down? Now that her shoes were back on, it wasn't that far.

"Good night, Em. Thanks for a spontaneous evening."

She loved his use of her nickname.

"You're welcome." She unlocked the front door and slipped inside, grateful Hayden wasn't waiting up. This was an evening she wanted to think about before she shared it.

The next afternoon the clouds drifted across the sky threatening a rainstorm as Reid picked her up. "We'll have to make quick work of this."

"I hope it doesn't chase everyone inside." She settled against the seat, then smiled as he handed her a to-go cup.

"I got you an iced tea."

"Thank you." She didn't even care if it was sweet or not, but as she took a sip, she knew he had studied her.

He grinned at her before pulling onto the road. "I don't know how you can drink it that sweet."

"Nectar of the gods." She took a sip and enjoyed the icy sweetness.

The drive to the suburb took half an hour, during which she asked him if anything had changed with

Kinley. She didn't ask if he thought Robert would be home. The thought unsettled her. Maybe she should have come to do this alone, because the man would have no reason to know who she was but would recognize Reid in an instant. They discussed how they'd handle anyone who came to the door, but the primary focus would be the young man who took the video posted around the world.

"I wouldn't be surprised if someone else was home and saw something." Emilie tried to calm the butterflies filling her stomach by praying for peace and direction.

Reid reached over at a red light and took her hand. "All we can do is try. The police have already talked to everyone."

Something she'd confirm as soon as she followed up with the desk sergeant on Monday. "We're trying to fill in everything we don't know."

An hour later, Emilie felt the tension cording across her neck as they knocked on the door of the last house on the cul-de-sac. A young mom hadn't been able to tell them much, and the young man who posted the video knew less than nothing. Reid rapped on the screen door, and Emilie shifted as they waited. A middle-aged woman came to the door, a concerned frown marring her expression.

"Yes?"

"Hello, I'm Emilie Wesley."

"Tell me you're not another one of those reporters." The woman peered through her glasses. "Wait, I recognize you."

Emilie touched her chest. "Me?"

"Yes. Don't you write for the *Nation's Post*? Your picture is always by your byline. But I haven't seen anything by you in a while. Did you stop writing?"

"Just between assignments." Emilie refused to meet Reid's gaze. "Do you have time for a couple quick questions?"

"Is this about what happened across the street?"

Reid nodded. "My sister was killed in the shooting."

The woman's mouth opened, then shut. "You're Kaylene's brother?" She squinted like it was time to get her prescription updated. "You look a bit like her. She mentioned you once or twice. Said you were a good brother."

Reid swallowed and glanced away. "Not good enough."

"Don't believe that lie for a minute. She knew you were there if she needed you. Come on in." She stepped back from the door, then led them into a comfortable living area. "My name's Amelia Ford. I don't know how I can help, but I'll tell you what I told everyone else who's asked. Kaylene did not kill her girls. She loved them too much, and I don't care what the papers say."

Emilie took the seat Amelia gestured to, Reid a step behind her. "Did she ever talk about her marriage?"

"Only every week when she came over for Bible study. It was Wednesday mornings while he was at work." Amelia sank onto a wingback chair. "She had to be so careful. Told me she wanted to leave but didn't know how."

"I was helping her with that." Emilie swallowed against the knot of tears that surfaced.

"She needed more than any one person could give her. It was something she had to address herself. She was days from leaving. Planned to pick the girls up from school for a family emergency and then disappear." Amelia looked past Emilie's shoulder, clearly seeing something in her mind. "She was so ready to be free of the fighting and intimidation."

"Did she tell you anything that would help us prove she didn't do this?"

"If you really knew her, then you know it wasn't possible." She met Emilie's gaze. "You don't know how much I wish I could tell you something tangible. He kept the fights inside and out of public view. He's smart, but I have to believe all that inflated idea of how much smarter he is than everyone else will be his downfall."

The ride back to Emilie's townhome was quiet. She didn't know what to do other than be grateful Robert hadn't been home and seen them—as far as they knew.

Reid double-parked in front of her home, then hurried around to let her out. "Thanks for going with me."

"I wish we'd learned something helpful."

"We aren't done."

But she knew he felt time running out as much as she did. Having the diamonds helped explain how Kaylene would have financed a disappearance. Talking to Amelia reinforced what they already knew: Kaylene had been poised to leave. But none of it proved Kaylene hadn't been the one to shoot Kinley. It was the impossibility of proving a negative.

"I'll call you if I hear anything."

She nodded at Reid's quiet words, said good-bye, and then walked to the front door. She pulled out her keys, but the door slid open before she put the key in the lock.

"There you are." Caroline squealed as she pulled Emilie inside and gave her an enthusiastic hug. "We've been waiting hours."

"Try fifteen minutes." Jaime was slouched in one of the armchairs, a relaxed and content expression on her face.

"What did I forget?" For the life of her Emilie couldn't think why her friends were there. "Where's Hayden?"

"She thought we needed food, and you weren't here to whip up magic for us." Caroline grinned, a few summer freckles moving on her nose. "I told her that's why there's delivery."

"Actually, that was me." Jaime waved her iPhone. "I was in the middle of placing an order when Hayden jetted out. Guess she had better ideas."

Emilie shook her head at the banter. "Let me take my purse downstairs, and I'll be back in a minute."

She slipped down the stairs to her basement suite. Still not clear on why her friends were upstairs, she freshened up in the bathroom before slipping into a comfortable sundress. She did a quick spot check in the mirror. *All right. That's as good as it gets. Now to see what they want.*

Normally the gang got together once a month, but then it was on her calendar, not a drop-by. The faint *ding* of the doorbell hurried her up the steps.

"I've got it, Emilie." Jaime's take-charge voice didn't slow Emilie's steps one bit.

She reached the kitchen in time to see Jaime stepping back to allow Savannah Daniels to enter. There was something about Savannah's presence that was a balm even as it confirmed Emilie's suspicion something was up.

Savannah held up a bag as soon as she saw Emilie. "Can you slide these into your freezer?"

"Sure." Emilie took the bag, then peeked in to see two quarts of Ben & Jerry's colorful ice cream containers facing her. "You're spoiling us."

"It's the kind of weather that demands ice cream." Savannah slid her purse off her shoulder and set it on the table. "Besides, we need brain power as we generate ideas."

Emilie secured the ice cream and then turned back to the group. "Who wants to fill me in on the purpose of this gathering?"

"I will." Savannah pulled a sheaf of papers from her oversized bag, then sorted them. "We've got to figure out Daniels, McCarthy & Associates."

"Last time I checked there's only one associate."

"Not many clients either." Jaime rolled her eyes as Caroline batted her in the shoulder. "Come on, Caroline. You've got to admit it's true."

"Sure, but you don't say those things out loud."

"Keep 'em bottled up, and I'd be trapped working for a judge five years later too."

"First, you have to have the brains to get a clerkship."

Jaime's jaw dropped, and Emilie felt hers do the same. "Caroline?"

Savannah moved between the two. "That's enough,

ladies. I don't know what's going on, but it's time to back off."

"She insulted my mind," Jaime sputtered.

"And you insulted her job." Savannah looked between the two as the front door opened and Hayden entered, carrying two large bags. She set them on the kitchen island and glanced around. "What did I miss?"

"Caroline and Jaime acting out of character." Savannah shook her head. "Maybe they aren't ready."

A sweet and spicy aroma wafted from the bags as Hayden opened them. "They didn't kill each other in law school. This too shall pass. I seem to remember a certain mentor reminding us of that . . ."

"About once a week." Emilie well remembered all the times she'd stopped by Savannah's office desperate for a reminder she could finish law school.

"Try once a day." Caroline glanced around, then raised her hands defensively. "What? Some of us needed more encouragement than others."

Now Emilie laughed. "You are the Southern queen of comfort. Remember all the sweet tea and scones you brought to study groups."

"Well, some of us pretend better than others." Caroline reached for a paper plate. "Can we eat, please? I think I'm just hangry. Let's do something productive."

"How about a movie then?" Jaime glanced around. "Oh yeah, the TV's downstairs."

Hayden and Emilie had intentionally kept the small first floor clean and light. There wasn't room for a couch and entertainment center if they wanted it to feel open. Hayden rarely watched TV anyway, and Emilie had created a comfortable arrangement in the basement that worked well when she watched a classic movie.

"We can go down there. We could even pop in something like *White Christmas*—maybe that will cool us off from this crazy heat." Maybe watching a movie would distract her friends and keep them from pecking at each other. Hangry or not, something was definitely up.

"After we brainstorm. I promise it won't take long." Savannah gestured toward the counter.

The spicy, salty smell of Chinese takeout wafted from the containers, and Emilie's mouth watered. "Tell me you have some sweet and sour chicken."

"And a spring roll, both with your name on them." Hayden began to pull takeout boxes and tubs from the two bags. "Caroline, here's your vegetables and rice. Jaime, they were out of beef and broccoli, so I got you the beef and veggies." She handed over the containers and packets of chopsticks, while Emilie slid behind her and grabbed plates. Then Hayden tugged out a flat container. "Here's your shrimp lo mein, Savannah. And a garlic chicken for me."

Emilie handed out plates and then pulled two folding chairs from the small hall closet. After she filled her plate with food, she sank onto one of the folding chairs next to Hayden. She leaned closer and whispered, "What's going on?"

"You might call it an intervention."

Savannah blessed the food and silence descended as they ate, Jaime the only one brave enough to use the chopsticks rather than opting for a fork and knife.

Emilie wiped her mouth with a paper napkin and then

leaned forward, trying to catch Savannah's gaze. "I feel at a distinct disadvantage. What are we brainstorming?"

"Jaime."

Jaime started as Savannah said her name. "Now wait a minute. I am not in the mood for an intervention or whatever you want to call this. I thought this was about your firm."

Hayden set her plate to the side.

Uh-oh. This was going to get serious fast if Hayden needed her hands to talk. Jaime seemed to know it too, as she straightened in her chair.

"Relax, Jaime," Hayden said. "This is really about all of us."

Jaime didn't relax, but she didn't bolt.

Hayden continued. "Savannah and I have put together a tentative plan to expand the firm. I'm finding a niche with the court-appointed work I've taken to get things going."

"I've got my nice stable of small business clients." Savannah smiled at them. "But there are more who need our help."

"I really want to get out of criminal defending, though it is paying the bills." Hayden glanced at Jaime, who was pushing rice around her plate. "I'm much more comfortable and adept at plaintiff's litigation."

"Those clients not following you?" Caroline crossed her legs at the ankles as she leaned back.

"Slowly, but it will take time and effort to build, not something I can do while running around with these court appointments."

"Those pay your bills." Jaime's tone sounded a little

hurt, and her face was shadowed. "Though some of the clients aren't great. Still, someone has to provide that defense."

Emilie tried to think of a way to lighten the mood, get everyone off their defensive positions and back in accord. The women assembled in this room were her lifeline, the people she would trust with her life and do anything for. As she looked from face to face, she knew Caroline was stuck in her job, in a rut she couldn't see her way free from. Despite her words, Jaime had been miserable for almost as many days as she'd worked there. She refused to admit defeat and instead sank her teeth into it like a dog with lockjaw. Hayden was enjoying the bloom of a new way of practicing, but one that didn't quite fit, and Savannah sat there as if seeing what could be, but not wanting to pressure her children. Then she handed out the paperwork, and Emilie revised her opinion.

"This is a flow chart. With all of our names on it."

What were they thinking? She'd never leave her job, especially when it was one she did well most days. And she wanted to do it with excellence once she'd overcome her fear another client would die on her watch.

Savannah flipped to the second page. "If you'll look here, you'll see Hayden and I have developed a prospective timeline and range of business for each of you. We can't pay much yet, but I believe the six of us could create a dynamic firm."

"So Angela is staying?" Caroline's words were quiet, her gaze focused as she read.

"Yes. The plan is she will continue taking court

appointments, but also build her network." Hayden shrugged. "We need her for drafting and arguing motions. We'll still need an appellate attorney."

"I'm not scared of a courtroom." The words were right, but Caroline's voice indicated she was quite content on the judge's side of the bench.

"With this we can each practice to our strengths. We'll all develop client lists, but if we're together we'll be something unique. A firm of women."

What would it be like to work with her friends? Emily had loved it in law school, but could they keep their friendship if they all worked together day in and out?

As the debate continued around her, she wanted to believe it was possible . . . but she wasn't ready to take the risk.

CHAPTER 28

Monday morning Emilie woke to her phone vibrating across her nightstand.

"Hello." Didn't the caller know she didn't want to leave the dream world where Reid was close and the air crackled with the possibility he would lean closer?

"I still need your article." The crisp voice belonged to Olivia. Her editor.

"It's only Monday. We just met Friday." Emilie rubbed her eyes and yawned.

"Didn't think I'd interrupt your beauty sleep at eight o'clock."

"Eight?" She bolted upright, then swung her feet around and over the edge. "Leaping lizards."

"Reverting to childhood?" Olivia's tone was sarcastic.

"I have a protective order hearing at nine."

"And an assignment I can give you eight more days to submit. I need an exposé as big as your Rodriguez article."

The article that had almost gotten her killed? No thanks. Emilie was ready to be done with that kind. On the other hand, if the subject didn't matter, her mind wasn't interested. "Olivia, I don't have anything."

"I had a feeling you'd say that, so I'm sending you a list with twenty potential topics. Let's get you that Pulitzer."

She groaned as her phone buzzed with a message before she'd even set it down. Olivia was as serious about wanting an article as Emilie was that words had abandoned her.

Thirty minutes later she flew from her house to work to pick up the file before hurrying across Old Town to the Juvenile and Domestic Relations Court. It was a good thing the court was a few blocks from her town house, because Nadine Hunter was already pacing outside the metal detector. As soon as she spotted Emilie, she hurried over. "Reggie's here. I thought you said he wouldn't come."

"It's his hearing too." Emilie readjusted her hot-pink court bag on her shoulder, then showed her ID to the guard. "Remember, the judge, the bailiff, and I are there to protect you."

"Right now. But you won't be later."

It was true, and Emilie refused to make promises she couldn't keep. The guard waved them through. When she stepped next to Emilie, the young woman was trembling. Emilie stopped and placed her hands on Nadine's arms.

"Nadine, look at me." The woman's gaze skittered everywhere but at Emilie, until she repeated her words. "We won't let anything happen. I promise. Once we have the protective order, he can't come near you or the police will take him to jail."

"How do you know?"

"Because this isn't the first time I've helped someone. I needed one too, and it worked. It'll be okay." She infused passion into her words. "Let's get up to the courtroom."

Judge Monica Bell sat at the bench, black robe billowing around her as she leaned forward, a hand over her microphone as she listened to two attorneys argue.

Nadine looked overwhelmed by the room and the atmosphere. Emilie tried to see it through the eyes of a first timer instead of someone who appeared in this room in front of this judge multiple times a month. While not as formal as some, there was still a seriousness and heaviness to the room. A clear sense that decisions issued here affected lives long-term.

The court reporter was positioned next to the judge, as was a bailiff. The line was short, and if everything went well, they'd be in front of the judge in ten or fifteen minutes. Emilie used that time to quietly remind Nadine what to expect. "It's most important to look at the judge and ignore Reggie when you're explaining why you need the protective order. I'll make sure you explain why Jonathan must be included."

"If he isn't, I can't have the protective order. Reggie will already punish me, but if Jonathan stays with him, I'll never see my son again." Nadine's voice rose, and Emilie placed a calming hand on her.

"I won't let that happen." Emilie kept an eye on the comings and goings, wondering who Reggie had hired to be his attorney. That person could wait until the hearing to file their appearance, keeping her in the dark. Some lawyers found a strategic advantage to the surprise, but the reality was Emilie's approach to the hearing remained unchanged. She asked the same questions and advised her client in the same way. It was simply a courtesy to be alerted ahead of time and know whether an agreement was possible.

Reggie stood by himself, a tall and thin man built like a runner. Based on what Nadine had told her, Emilie was careful not to underestimate his strength. He spent a lot of time in a gym, but had a metabolism that didn't let anything he consumed stick around.

"Miss Wesley." Judge Bell's voice pulled her from her thoughts.

She startled as she realized the other attorneys were done and had moved aside with their clients. "Your Honor?"

"We're ready for you. Is your client with you?"

"Yes."

"How about her boyfriend?"

She glanced to where he'd waited. "He was against the wall over there."

"Do you see him now?"

"No, Your Honor."

"Take a moment and look for him while I work with the court reporter to wrap up my order from the previous hearing."

"Yes, Your Honor." She turned to Nadine. "Stay right here. You'll be safe with the bailiff in here." Emilie moved past the bar and into the gallery. A moment later she pushed through the door and into the hallway. He wasn't waiting there.

Where had Reggie gone?

She described him to the deputy waiting in the hallway, but he didn't remember seeing a man of that description. She then walked to the metal detector and asked the deputies stationed there if they remembered seeing him. As she expected, they didn't remember him either. After one more pass through the hallways, she returned to the courtroom. A pulse of fear began to build. "Nadine, where's Jonathan?"

"With my friend Amy."

"Is she someone Reggie would expect to watch your boy?"

"No. I don't think he knows who she is. He definitely doesn't know where she lives. She moved a week ago."

"Did you text her about it or communicate in any way that he could read?"

"Nope. Just calls."

"Okay." Emilie turned to the judge. "I couldn't find him anywhere, and none of the deputies remember seeing him."

"All right." The judge opened a file, then flipped through the pages. "Are you ready to proceed?"

"Yes, Your Honor. Could I let Nadine call her friend and warn her that Reggie has left? I would feel better if she was alerted to keep Jonathan close."

"You may have a minute to make the call." The judge nodded to Nadine, and she quickly took out her phone and placed the call. After she hung up, the judge looked at Emilie with the faintest hint of a smile. "Ready?"

"Yes, Your Honor." Emilie quickly walked Nadine through the questions. The judge asked a few of her own and then granted the motion.

"Go check on your boy, and be sure to check with the police in a couple days to determine whether the order has been served on the defendant." She stamped a sheet and handed it to the clerk. "Because he was here and then left as I called the hearing, I will make this a permanent two-year order with the caveat that he can petition for a hearing at any point. Good luck to you, Miss Hunter."

"Thank you."

Emilie echoed with her own, "Thank you." After they were in the hallway, she turned to Nadine. "Any questions?"

"So I need to ask the police about the protection order?"

"To ensure it's been served. That's technically when it becomes effective. Also, keep a copy with you always. Put one in the diaper bag, one in your purse, and one in your car."

"I won't have a car now."

"That's okay, keep it with you, so it's always available if you need to show it to police." She led Nadine back to the front door. "Do you have a way to get to Jonathan?"

"I'll take the bus."

"No, I'll take you. Let's go make sure your little guy is okay."

CHAPTER 29

"The doctor anticipates Kinley will be released from the hospital within four or five days." Nurse Rogers's words should have been welcome, but when Reid considered how far they were from stopping Robert from taking her home, he couldn't help being alarmed.

"Thank you for the update." He glanced at his calendar, noting all the appointments and meetings filling it. "How long are you on the floor?" He noted the time. Somehow he'd get over there, even if it meant Simone had to cover a meeting. "I'll come by before you leave."

After she hung up, Reid sat there, mind whirling. This was the word he'd waited to receive. Time was slipping away, and he was no closer to doing what Kaylene had asked. How could he wrest custody from Kinley's father? He hadn't been an eyewitness to the burgeoning disaster.

There was someone that Kaylene might have confided in that he hadn't considered: Grandma. A spry ninety, maybe she'd been invited to their home more regularly. Maybe she'd seen or heard something that could help. He picked up his phone and called.

"Hello?" Grandma's voice had a tremulous quality to it, the lone sign age was catching up to her.

"Hey, Grandma."

"Reid." Her voice brightened, a reminder he should call more often.

"I've been thinking about Kaylene."

"It's all so terrible."

"Yes." Grief filled the silence, thick and heavy. He cleared his throat. "I just wondered . . . You've been with their family more often than I have the past few years. Did you have any idea there was trouble?"

"I don't know . . . it seemed okay." She sighed, a wealth of unsaid words. "I guess I didn't really know anything. The Kaylene I raised never would have done the terrible things the news says."

"How did she and Robert get along?"

"Fair enough." She clicked her tongue. "My generation tends to leave well enough alone, and Kaylene never complained."

"Maybe she should have."

"Maybe. But if someone doesn't say there's a problem, how are we to know?"

"I wonder what we missed."

"We can torment ourselves or accept the fact there's nothing we can do."

That's what dogged him. He could still do something for Kinley. "She asked me to care for her girls."

"When did she do that?"

"In a letter I found this week. She wrote it a couple months ago."

Grandma snorted, actually snorted. "Then you don't know if she still meant it."

"Maybe, but what if she did? She left it with me last

month, but it was sealed in a box of her stuff. I've learned that the doctors expect to release Kinley this week. Why would Kaylene ask me to protect her girls if they didn't need it?"

"Because she had a bad day or a bad week." Grandma sighed. "You wouldn't understand, never having married, but even the best marriage has seasons where the partners can't stand each other."

"Not you and Grandpa."

She snorted again. Grandma was getting sassy. "You know better than that. You lived with us long enough to see good and bad."

It had never seemed that bad to him . . . though there were the early days when the addition of two grandchildren to their household had added layers of stress. Even as a six-year-old, he'd noticed that. But once they reached a détente—an acceptance of their new reality—it had seemed good. "It only seemed that way when you taught me piano in the camper."

"That was crazy." She sighed. "We were careful to explain to Kaylene when she married that we aren't a place to complain. We'll pray with you. We'll encourage you. We will not allow bad-mouthing of your spouse. Your grandpa was firm on this and I agreed." She sighed again. "Your grandpa had such wisdom. Said it was important to remind young married folks that once they were married they're a unit and need to make their marriage covenant inviolable."

"But what if Kaylene needed us?"

"Then she needed to ask."

"As long as it wasn't to complain about Robert?"

"That's about the scope of it. However, I made it clear to her if he ever hit her, she was to come immediately. I don't care what your grandpa said, some things are never acceptable."

Reid rubbed his forehead as he considered what she'd said. While it made sense, he wondered if somehow Kaylene had become isolated and believed she couldn't ask even family for help. That was a situation that shouldn't have existed. "You never noticed anything?"

"Well, I didn't like the way Robert always talked down to your sister. She couldn't do much right in his eyes. Kaylene was brilliant, top of her class in college, and then she married him and it was like all her oomph disappeared. He doted on those girls though. They hung the moon as far as he was concerned."

"So you were never worried?"

"No." She was silent a moment. "Now, before you depress me completely, tell me about your world."

Reid told her a few stories about Brandon's kids and his work. Then she filled him in on the latest high school musical she and a girlfriend had attended. The call reminded him how unique his grandma was. He hoped to be as active and independent at her age.

He promised to touch base with her before too much time passed and then hung up, tapping his phone against his chin.

Grandma hadn't had the information he'd hoped for, but maybe the call would get her thinking and prompt long-forgotten memories to surface.

He was too much younger than Kaylene to know her friends, but maybe he could figure out who she talked to. He pulled Emilie's information up on his phone, then pressed send, while he ignored the voice telling him it was just an excuse to contact her. At least he hadn't called her as often as she entered his thoughts.

"Hello?" Her voice brought a warmth that was unexplainable and unexpected.

"Hey, this is Reid."

He heard a rustling, like she was settling back. "What's up?"

"I got a call from my friend at the hospital, and Kinley could be released this week."

Emilie blew out a breath. "We expected it to come." She paused. "So, as early as Friday. We don't have enough evidence."

"Is there anything we can do to stop her release?"

"I'm reaching out to some of Kaydence's friends from social media, but the girl I've talked with wouldn't tell me anything helpful. The investigating detective didn't have what I wanted either, though the police report is here now." She sighed and he could hear pages rustling. "There's not much here we didn't already know."

"That's a lot that isn't what we need. Have you seen the 911 calls anywhere?"

"Not yet. I keep checking, but I'm almost afraid of what could be recorded."

It could help them or prove what the police believed. "Do you think the police would give them to me?"

"I don't know, but it's worth asking. I'm still working on tracking down where she got the gun, and we could try to talk to her counselor. It might work better if you contacted her, since you're a relative. She'd probably require me to get a subpoena, unless Kaylene went with one from our list of recommendations." He could hear tapping on a keyboard. "I sent a request to Shannon. I'll see what she knows."

"Sounds like you're keeping busy, Em."

"As much as I can do from here and stay under the radar."

"I talked to my grandma. I hoped she knew something that I missed. She didn't."

"We just keep digging. If Robert did anything to Kaylene or the girls, someone knew. We have to find them."

Reid stared at his feet thrust out in front of him. A toe was starting to poke through a hole in one sock. "I'm not so sure. My grandma is a great woman, but she made it clear that she and Grandpa told Kaylene not to come to them with problems in her marriage. What if everyone she tried to talk to had the same attitude? It wouldn't take long before she'd stop trying."

"But she didn't. She came to me professionally, and she wrote a letter to you."

"Sure, but she didn't give me the letter when I could do anything about it. And she didn't let you actually help her."

There was a sharp intake of breath. "That's not true, Reid. I was waiting at court for her." Her words tumbled out in a rush. "She was trying to get help when the shooting occurred. That's why I'll never believe she gave up and took matters into her own hands. She was ready to do what was necessary to break free."

"Maybe Robert found out."

"He must have."

"Grandma did say Robert liked to belittle Kaylene. Maybe he couldn't stand the thought of her living on her own. If he belittled her in public, what did he do in private?"

"It was verbal with some physical violence. I had one case this spring where the man got terribly physical and in my face at a hearing. I'd never had a deputy escort me to my car before, and I hope it's never repeated. There are men who don't like the idea of losing the control they believe is their right."

Reid thought over his interactions with Robert. At the hospital, the man had exercised absolute control over the room. No one could go in or out without his approval. And that was an environment in which he should have little power. What had he been like at home?

"We should talk to people who worked with him."

"That's a good idea." Emilie drew the sentence out. "I wish we could locate some of Kaylene's friends. If she had any."

"What do you mean 'if she had any'?"

"It's not unusual for the dominant partner to limit interactions the other can have. He may have tightly controlled who she could see and talk to and how often she could do that. He might have viewed it as an effective way to punish her for perceived violations. Her social media wasn't helpful, and his was innocuous, other than ignoring her."

"Couldn't we reach out to the people listed as her friends?"

"We could, but it will take a long time to contact each one individually."

"Time we don't have."

"Exactly."

"What do you recommend?"

"Let me talk to my colleagues again. That might save us some wasted effort." She paused, and he leaned back and pinched the bridge of his nose. Her next words made it seem she could read his mind.

"Don't give up hope, Reid. We'll do all we can, but don't forget the power of asking God for help. He already knows who we need to talk to." She paused again and then plunged ahead, her words tumbling over each other as if she had to speak them before she lost courage. "Maybe Kaylene was wrong. Maybe her letter was old. Maybe Kinley doesn't need protection from her father. We may have to accept the fact she's okay where she is."

Reid felt the pressure build up behind his eyes. He couldn't accept her words, no matter how much truth might be buried in them. "Someone murdered Kaydence."

"Ye-ess." She dragged the word out, as if she wondered what he meant.

"Kaylene and Kinley were shot before the police arrived."

"Yes."

"That means someone killed my niece, and if it wasn't Kaylene, the person will get away with murder. If that person is my brother-in-law and we don't fight for Kinley, we're letting her go home with her sister's killer."

CHAPTER 30

The lights in the parking lot flickered to life, casting halos around the cars beneath them as Reid pulled into a slot. He was arriving much later than he'd hoped. An emergency meeting had erupted after he talked to Emilie, but at least his team had landed one major prospect. That certainly helped his odds of beating Vincent at this game.

As he'd headed to his car, Rogers, the nurse, had called again to say he needed to get there immediately because Kinley was beginning to twitch. It sounded like that was a much better sign than it had been when he was a kid who struggled to sit still through long school days. In first grade, it had been a sign of weakness, but tonight he prayed Kinley would twitch to life. The days had been long and worry filled as he'd waited.

The unknown was whether Robert would be in her room and, if so, what would he do about Reid's arrival?

Reid needed to believe they could serve Kinley's best interests. Robert had done nothing to bring Reid into the information loop or indicate his initial harsh stance would adjust even marginally. Letting Reid become part of Kinley's life would be akin to admitting he had erred by cutting Reid out of the process.

That wouldn't happen.

Maybe now that Kinley was making her way back, Robert would ignore the previous conversation.

Reid pushed from his car and slowly walked across the lot to the hospital entrance. He'd go in and match Robert at his own game. He'd take control before Robert could. Walk in like he belonged, like being that little girl's uncle gave him every right to be there, because it did.

The bright lights of the lobby made him blink as he strode past the information desk to the bank of elevators just out of view. The off-beige walls did little to soften the glare from the fluorescent lights. The squeak of rubber-soled shoes against the tile blended with the antiseptic smell that nothing could soften. A tech of some sort wheeled an empty gurney by, barely missing Reid's shoe. He stepped back and bumped against a wheelchair, one in a row lining the wall.

He pushed out another breath and headed into the elevator bank, pushed the button, and waited for the doors to open.

He waited for an orderly to push a gurney in before entering the car. The ride up seemed too long and too short at the same time. He needed to steel himself for meeting Robert, but the cowardly part wanted nothing at all to do with his brother-in-law.

He wasn't a weakling. He stood up to threats when they came. So why did Robert generate this flight effect rather than a fight one?

The doors opened and Reid stepped off. The antiseptic smell slapped him in the face, and he had to force his steps down the hall. The quiet beep of machines and the hum and multicolored light of TVs swooshed from some of the rooms he passed, curtains around the beds pulled against prying eyes. Other rooms were empty. A woman walked toward him in hot-pink scrubs, slowing as they passed. "Can I help you?"

"I'm visiting my niece. She's in room 418."

The woman frowned and studied him closer. He wouldn't be surprised if she asked to see his ID. "Melanie mentioned you. I would hurry, as her father isn't there right now."

"Thank you."

An alarm sounded behind him, and she nodded before sweeping past him in a rush.

When he reached Kinley's room, he heard muffled voices. With a quick rap on the doorframe, he walked in.

He stilled when a doctor and nurse looked up from their huddle at the computer docked in her room. The doctor looked like he should still be in undergrad, and the nurse had the wizened look of a woman who had seen much and been bothered by little. Their conversation halted, and the doctor stared at Reid.

"Who are you?" His intonation was perfect for the smoking caterpillar in *Alice in Wonderland*.

"Reid Billings. I'm Kinley's uncle, here to see how she's doing."

"Are you cleared to be here?" The doctor turned to the nurse. "Is he? Her father is very strict about who has access."

"He's on limited admit."

Reid's gaze raked over Kinley's small frame. She

looked thinner than ever. Her fingers twitched where they lay inside the nurse's light grip.

"Is the twitching a good sign?"

The doctor followed his gaze. "Yes, it indicates there's brain activity, as if she is awakening from a deep sleep. That's exactly what we want to see happen. It's no guarantee of a full recovery, but it's a hopeful first step. We were about ready to ask her to respond again."

The nurse leaned close to Kinley's ear. "Sweetie, I want you to try to squeeze my hand." She waited a moment. "That's it. Good girl. Now try to open your eyes."

Kinley's lashes fluttered but her eyes didn't quite open.

"Good try." The doctor smiled as he patted her shoulder lightly. "Now rest, and we'll try again tomorrow."

"This is good?" Reid felt so out of his element.

"Everybody is unique in how their bodies respond to trauma. Kinley has taken a while because we had her in a drug-induced coma last week to give her body the best chance of healing. Now we're asking her to come out of it."

As the doctor answered his questions, Reid sensed that Kinley had received good care even if he wasn't sure what all the terms meant. "Is there anything else I should know about her status? When she'll wake up?"

"That is totally up to this young lady."

The nurse leaned closer and brushed a greasy strand of hair out of his niece's face. "That's right, Kinley. It's time to wake up, sweetie. We're ready for you to work."

Kinley's thin fingers twitched, and Reid watched, willing her to do more. To open her eyes. To wake and tell him everything she'd seen that terrible morning. But nothing more happened.

He slumped. "Is it all right if I sit with her?"

The nurse nodded, her mousy hair bobbing around her face. "I'll help watch."

He didn't ask what she'd watch for, just settled into the chair. His eyes skimmed the computer printouts. All the readings were gobbledygook to him, and the beeps made him jump. "Come on, Kinley. We need you."

"And I need you to leave." Robert's voice stabbed through Reid.

Reid straightened. "Robert."

Robert strode to the side of Kinley's bed. "You must leave."

"Not this time." Reid refused to flinch from Robert's intense stare. "I'm glad Kinley's starting to respond."

"Take one last good look. As soon as she's out of here, you'll never see her again."

"Don't be so sure." Reid set his jaw. "My attorney will change that."

"No attorney can make that happen."

"Mine can."

"You'll only waste your money. I'm Kinley's father."

Reid fisted his hands and blew out a breath. "My attorney is good at this."

Robert snorted. "The little girl from the Haven? You'll have to do better than that. Now leave before I call hospital security."

He knew about Emilie? Reid swallowed hard and then nodded. "I'll leave, but this isn't over."

As he left, he heard Robert sneer, "Yes, it is."

CHAPTER 31

With a long list of people to contact related to Kinley's case, Emilie started her day at Daniels, McCarthy & Associates. Rhoda remained adamant that nothing related to Kaylene's death be investigated from the Haven. After a quick hello to Bella Stoller that turned into a warm chat with the motherly reception-ist, Emilie hurried down the hall to the empty office Savannah had opened to her. She'd make her calls and get out before anyone else derailed her with a need to talk. So far, Rhoda hadn't noticed when she arrived late at the Haven or took a long lunch on occasion, but at some point, she'd ask questions.

Emilie started with a call to Allison Carruthurs, the counselor Kaylene had seen. The woman wouldn't tell her much in the moment other than she'd had no indication Kaylene planned to use any kind of violence against Robert or the girls.

"Every conversation I had with her was about her strength and how she could escape with the girls. After she told me about how Robert monitored her move-ments, I knew she must find that strength."

Emilie paused in her note taking. "What do you mean 'monitored her movements'?"

"He logged her mileage and matched it against her errands, let her know when she'd gone too many miles. He only gave her the keys when she'd been good. She even told me he seemed to have some way of knowing where she went."

"You mean following her movements through credit card use?"

"Oh no. That would have required him to trust her with finances. She got cash only if he deemed she'd behaved." The woman paused. "I don't want to say too much until I've looked at her file, but she commented that he knew her route and where she'd gone."

"As if he tracked her?"

"Exactly. Might be why he gave her a smart phone."

Emilie was still thinking about that conversation when her cell phone rang. A minute later she was embroiled in a conversation with Officer Roberts.

"Sorry for the delay returning your call. How can I help you?" The woman's voice was crisp and focused.

"I wanted some advice." Emilie quickly filled her in on what had been happening.

There was a moment of silence, then Officer Roberts sighed. "You're in that place where there's not enough information for us to act on, but I want you to take precautions." The woman proceeded to give her the kind of advice Emilie would give her clients. "If you have more incidents be sure to let me know. Keep a running record too. We'll need that to build a case if this escalates."

"I'd like to keep that from happening."

"So would I. Keep me posted."

Emilie rubbed her temple where tension coiled. "I will. Thank you."

By the time she reached the Haven around ten, she was ready to call it a day. Taylor followed her into her office, a legal pad at the ready. "A man came in for you and hovered in the lobby for an hour."

Emilie frowned. "Did he say who he was?"

"No. He unnerved Johanna though."

The receptionist was usually unshakeable, a requirement for being the guard. "When was he here?"

"She said from nine fifteen to tenish."

"Okay, I'll follow up with her." Was it her stalker or Nadine's ex haunting the office? Sometimes people got the most twisted ideas about what was an effective use of their time. Emilie tapped the Hunter file where it sat on her desk. "Can you follow up with your police contact to emphasize that this PO has to be served ASAP?"

"Sure. A friend got me a copy of Kaylene's concealed carry, by the way. It's on your desk."

"Okay, I'll look at it next." Emilie paused. "Let me know if you need anything else."

"Rhoda asked me to send you to her right away."

"Any idea why?"

"None."

Emilie rubbed her forehead. This was going to be one of those days, the ones that left her wishing for a quiet afternoon in front of an air conditioner with a glass of iced tea, soft music playing in the background while she read a book by a favorite author. Instead, today she'd slog through, searching for any iota of control she could wrest while she was carried along in a river that thrust her where it chose.

Emilie's cell vibrated and shimmied across her desk. She grabbed it and glanced at the number. Reid. The river eddied her around another blind bend. "I'll take his call, then head to Rhoda's office."

Taylor shook her head, her shoulder-length curls swaying. "I wouldn't. Rhoda really wanted to see you now."

"Okay." She tapped a text to Reid. Call you in 15? If she was lucky, Rhoda wouldn't need much from her. "Thanks."

Taylor nodded and stepped from her office. Emilie collected her thoughts while grabbing a legal pad, but she froze as her office phone rang. The number was one she didn't recognize, so she took the call.

"Hi, this is Katie Trainer. You left a message?" The girl's voice was hesitant, but mature.

"Thanks for getting back to me." Emilie sat in her chair and grabbed a pen.

"Alaina said you wanted to talk about Kaydence?"

"Yes."

"She said it was okay to talk with you."

"I knew Kaydence's mom and am trying to learn more about their family and what happened."

"It's still hard to believe she's gone." The girl's voice wavered.

"I know. Did you know Kaydence well?"

"The three of us did everything together. Sometimes the friends you were close with in elementary and middle school fade in high school, but we didn't let that happen."

Emilie well remembered those days and the preciousness of friends who stuck with you through the awkward tween days. "Did you know her mom?"

"Sure. We spent the night at Kaydence's house a few times, and I saw her at events. She seemed like such a nice lady." There was a pause and then the girl blew out a breath. "Do you think she killed Kaydence?"

"No."

"But if she didn't . . ."

"That's part of what I'm trying to figure out."

"You're the only one who's asked about Kaydence. I wish the police cared."

"They do. They're busy with so many cases, it can be enticing to accept the easy answer, but I want to make sure it's the right answer." Emilie considered where to take the conversation. "Did Kaydence get along with her mom?"

"Better than I do with mine. It felt like it was them against her dad."

"Why?"

"He was so strict, and it drove Kaydence crazy. There was this nice guy from my youth group that she liked, and her dad wouldn't even let her go on a group date. He wanted to keep her little, but she was headed to college in a couple years. What would he do then?"

"A good question. Did she ever say he hurt her?"

"No, but I wouldn't be surprised if he did something to Mrs. Adams."

"Really? Why?"

"There was a time when she dropped Kaydence off, but had a sprained ankle. Another time she had bruises on her arm, but Kaydence said her mom was clumsy."

"Maybe she was."

"Maybe, but there was something about the way Kaydence said it that made me think she was reading a script, you know?"

"I do." She'd seen it before. Clients who had said something so many times, they parroted it even when they knew they could be honest. Kaydence might have wanted to share what happened at home with her friends, but it sounded like she hadn't. Who provided the script? Mom or Dad? "What was Kaydence like?"

"Smart and quick with words. She always knew what to say. She knew how to get the teachers to love her and how to put a classmate in their place without crossing the line to cruel."

There was a knock at her door, and Emilie looked up to see Johanna standing there holding a huge bouquet of multicolored roses exploding from a crystal vase. Her jaw dropped and she gestured toward the corner of her desk. "That's interesting. Why do you think that was?"

"Because it was the only way to survive at home."

Emilie let the silence build as she waited for Katie to continue. Johanna set the flowers down and then slipped from the office, the scent of roses soon filling the small room.

"You have to understand—Kaydence never said anything that I can point to as proof her dad abused them. But there was always this cloud on her face when she talked about him. It evaporated the moment she'd talk about her mom or Kinley." There was a loud noise in the background. "I have to go, Miss Wesley."

"Can I call if I have other questions?"

"Sure. Leave a message, and I'll get back to you when I can."

"Thank you."

After she hung up, Emilie took a moment to collect her thoughts and jot them down while Katie's comments were fresh. There was something about what she'd said—the young woman intuited something more happened behind closed doors, but it wasn't enough evidence to convince a judge Kinley needed to go home with her uncle. For that to happen, she needed appeal-proof verification that Kinley's best interests would be harmed if she went home.

And that substantiation seemed impossible.

She tugged the small card from the flowers and opened it. *For the loveliest woman of all.*

Of course it was unsigned. Could Reid have sent them? She snapped a photo and sent it to Reid with a quick thank you. The bouquet was a little over the top, but beautiful.

Her phone dinged with a text. Robert knows about you.

Reid's message made no sense. How?

Not sure.

Emilie gathered her legal pad and pen and wove her way through the office maze to Rhoda's office. The executive director's office had a bank of windows that were filled with bulletproof glass . . . just in case. The sad thing was those precautions were needed. One corner of one pane had a feathering that marred the

do to change his mind, I would, but I've about exhausted my grand ideas. I'm open to thoughts."

"Is this our major funder?"

"Yes."

The reply left no room for caveats or wondering. Something more had to be behind this than the Adamses. "Can you tell me anything more?"

"I've already said too much. If you come up with ideas or arguments, let me know." The phone on her desk rang, and Rhoda reached for it. "Sorry to have such bad news."

As Rhoda picked up the phone, Emilie nodded and then stood, a plan already forming.

CHAPTER 32

The team sat around the same conference table where the client competition launched Friday. Simone handed out Excel spreadsheets with updated information on who had contacted each person and the status of research about the prospects. Luke, Annabelle, and Matt took a moment to read the information while Reid scanned it one more time. He was feeling good about where they stood. Of the twenty potential clients they'd been assigned, his team had made initial contact with half, not bad considering the layers it took to reach some.

"What's next?" Reid punted the question out there to see how everyone would respond. If they'd think creatively, this competition was theirs.

Annabelle glanced at him, then at Matt.

"Annabelle?" She had to learn to speak for herself, but he'd prompt her if it helped.

"What if we got them all on the phone—"

Luke snorted. "We've already done that. We can't contact them too frequently."

"If you'd let me finish . . ." There was a spark in her eyes that made Reid bite back a smile. Good, she needed to stand up for her ideas. "Let's invite them to a reception where we give them the full experience of what Fletcher & Associates provides."

"A party?" Matt grinned and then reached over and patted her hand as if she were someone to be mollified. "These are wealthy people who won't want crackers and cheese."

"Where will the funds come from?" Luke jumped back in with a curl to his lip.

"If we pooled our marketing budgets, we could have the event as early as Friday. Make it an after-work mixer. An intimate experience in which we introduce them to the *team*." She emphasized the word and then focused on Reid. "We'd build their personal connection with the firm. They're already interested, so if we make the calls with the right script, it'll work."

"I like it." He turned to Simone. "Can we pull it off?"

"Absolutely." She jotted a few notes on her iPad. "Frankly, it's brilliant, because it pulls them into the setting. The office is impressive. And sometimes last-minute events work best."

"Let's do it." Reid turned to the men for their ideas, but other than ongoing research, he didn't hear anything fresh. "All right. We'll split the list for personal invites. I'd also like one hand-delivered to each prospect by tomorrow at lunch. Up the personal touch. I'll work on the presentation aspect. Let me know what you think the top three needs or interests of your prospects are, so I can focus on the right areas. Set the time for an hour. We'll mix for thirty minutes, present for fifteen, and then back to mixing."

"I'll make sure Mr. Fletcher can attend," Annabelle put in, and Reid nodded. She was the one to ask.

"I'll ensure we have the right mix of hors d'oeuvres and drinks. No more than forty attendees, correct?" Simone glanced at him.

"Right. Let's do this." As he left the room, things were headed in the right direction. Now to find the proper angle in the presentation to win the business. As he walked to his office, he sidestepped Vincent, who'd been near the door. "Listening for ideas?"

"I don't need yours. I've got plenty of my own." The man thrust back his shoulders and walked away, but not before Reid caught the dark circles beneath his eyes. Working solo created a burden that teamwork shared.

Did he have a big enough team to save Kinley? He hoped so, but hope might not be enough. His phone buzzed, a reminder about a basketball game Brandon had set up for tomorrow night. Exercise sounded perfect. He needed the release and hopefully the clear mind that came on the other side.

• • •

Emilie's list of potential stalkers had shrunk as she clicked through one Google search after another. The list of names wasn't narrowed enough to produce results that meant anything.

A knock at her door brought her head up from the computer screen. Rhoda stepped in with a dark-haired man behind her. Emilie smiled as she recognized him from the newspapers a year ago and the annual fund-raiser in March. He had that slightly awkward, movie-star look. Hair spiked to roughly nuanced perfection and a tailored look the pressed khakis and button-down didn't relax.

"I don't think you've met Jordan Westfall." Rhoda waved a hand toward him. "He's here for an update on our efforts."

Emilie pushed back her chair and then stood. "Actually, we met at the fund-raiser last spring."

"You remembered." He held her hand for a moment.

Heat built in her face. "Of course." His gaze was focused and intense. She refused to squirm beneath the scrutiny. "What brings you to the Haven?"

Rhoda stepped slightly between them. "Emilie is our attorney. At some point, with the right funding, I'd love to either make her full time or hire a second attorney."

"Why not do both? Though it doesn't appear she's busy currently." He studied her desk, which held the stack of files, and she nudged the computer monitor out of his view, just in case he was looking.

"You caught me right after I organized."

He gave her a slow smile. "Of course."

"It's the nature of our work. We move from crisis to crisis." Rhoda headed toward the door. "Well, let's continue the tour and let Emilie get back to work. At any moment we could need an emergency petition or defense. Thanks for letting us interrupt."

"Nice to see you again, Mr. Westfall." She met his gaze as he continued to study her.

"Likewise." His gaze locked with hers intensely, and after a moment he pivoted and followed Rhoda on the tour. Emilie sat frozen, her mind blank. What was that about? She shook her head and then looked at her screen. What had she been doing? Oh yeah, looking through clients. She typed the next name from her list into the firm's document retrieval program.

Chris Marville. She remembered him, since she'd handled the case from protective order to completed divorce. Chris had been an odd ex rather than a scary one. It had been the way he stared first at his ex-wife and then, over the course of the two-day custody battle, had transferred that energy to her. It had been dialed in with a focus she'd felt even as she forced herself to ignore him. But he'd never said or done anything more than stare. In and of itself, that wasn't enough to make a man dangerous. Was it?

She entered the next name. Randy Sheets seemed a more likely candidate. Until she'd seen the pictures of the marital home destroyed after her client and the kids left, she'd believed him coldly controlling, one of those men who focused on himself and his needs and wants. This burst of violence at the house had utterly obliterated walls, torn out cabinets and sinks, and ruined flooring. It had been enough to cause her to watch him warily through the final mediation, but the pictures had also been enough to prompt him to finally settle minutes before the trial began. He might be a narcissistic controller, but he hadn't turned his violence on a person . . . yet.

That *yet* left Emilie cold.

The last ex was a boyfriend, a man who'd never agreed to commitment, something that should make her client eternally grateful. They'd had no kids, so once she gathered the courage to make her plan and leave, the client escaped. Then the ex started appearing at her job, her new apartment, restaurants. Only a protective order that threatened his top-secret clearance—and by extension his livelihood—made him leave. She'd explained to his attorney that without a clear demonstration that his behavior had changed permanently, this young man would have the protective order slapped on him with all that it meant. Bill Hutchins finally received the message when she filed the preliminary paperwork.

She leaned back and rubbed her eyes. Staring at the computer screen with such focused attention was making her eyes cross. She hadn't found anything that seemed likely to make a client's partner turn her direction with the threat of violence. While Randy had been violent to his home, he hadn't been to his wife or kids.

Her stalker was a shadow, not bothering to communicate much, but ensuring she felt his or her presence.

Emilie paused.

Her?

Could it be an actual client who wasn't happy with how her legal matter had concluded?

She didn't want to think someone she'd helped would turn on her. She mentally ran through her cases and clients from the past year. None seemed a strong candidate for someone who would terrorize her from a distance. They were women who had themselves been bullied and intimidated.

She'd ask for Taylor's opinion. Her assistant heard and saw things Emilie didn't. Taylor saw them when they arrived and was often the contact in an emergency. In that space between lawyer and client, paralegals often spent more time on the phone with the clients, hearing their everyday issues and concerns. It was a service the attorneys could provide but really shouldn't. It wasn't an effective use of their time, but it also wasn't something all clients understood. They'd hired the attorney, not the paralegals, and the realities of the legal profession didn't always match expectations. Especially if you weren't familiar with how the law worked.

Who could understand before being forced to confront the legal system? TV and books didn't give an accurate picture. Things had to be shifted and adjusted for the story. The result was unrealistic expectations. Could such expectations lead someone to feel aggrieved and focus on Emilie?

Emilie rubbed her left shoulder where the tension had parked. She could feel the knot and knew it was something even a visit to her chiropractor wouldn't release.

If she could convince herself the feeling was the work of an overtired, overstressed mind, then she could release this belief that someone lurked in the shadows everywhere she went. She called Taylor in and shared her latest idea.

Taylor's brows furrowed, and her head cocked to the side. "You really think that could happen?" She frowned and twirled a pencil through her fingers. "No one comes to mind."

"Would you consider it? Look through client files from the last two years as you have time." Emilie hoped

Taylor heard the tone that said she knew her idea was crazy.

Taylor gave a quick downward motion of her chin. "I can do that." The pencil stopped twirling, and she stood. "I hope you're wrong."

"Me too." Emilie sagged against her chair. She wanted Taylor to prove she had an overactive imagination. Then she could laugh as she blamed her fears, and in a few months or a year this season would be nothing more than a time she remembered with a feeling of foolishness.

She pulled up a copy of the spreadsheet she'd compiled with each of her clients from the last three years. After hitting print, she watched as the pages spilled from the printer. The list was longer than she'd expected. Amazing how the clients blurred together even as each name brought a specific set of facts and a face to mind.

Some might believe it was only a list.

But she knew differently.

She picked up a pen and went to work. Before she left, she'd have notes beside all the names, notes that hit the key points of their cases and stories. Then when Taylor was done with her list, they'd compare.

CHAPTER 33

The squeak of rubber against waxed wood ricocheted off the walls and high ceilings as Reid walked into the YMCA gymnasium. He tossed his bag onto the bleachers and sat to change into his basketball shoes. A hand clapped on his back, and he jerked forward, almost eating his knees. He finished tying his shoe as he wrenched to see who had tried to knock his teeth out.

Brandon stood there, cocky grin in place, looking too tall and broad for a basketball court. He belonged on the much bigger football field. "Pretty absorbed in those shoes. Forget how to tie?"

"Ha-ha." Reid stood so Brandon didn't feel so dominating. "How long you been here?"

"Long enough to get us on the list for a court."

"Thanks. Everyone still coming?"

"David texted that he's on his way."

He clapped Brandon on the shoulder. "Good to see you."

"I know. The game wouldn't be the same without me. How are you doing?"

"I still feel discombobulated."

"Probably will for a while. These traumatic events. They take time, and it's different with each."

Reid nodded as he let the words slide around him. He didn't want more psychoanalyzing by a friend. What he needed was the physical outlet of a friendly game that would turn fiercely competitive. In the end he'd be bruised, sore, and, he hoped, ready to sleep soundly for the first time since Kaylene died.

David strode through the door and tossed his duffel on the floor, where it slid into Reid. He pulled Reid over for a quick man hug. "Sorry about your sister and niece."

"Thanks." What else could he say? He vaguely remembered David and Ciara attending the service. Much of that day was shadows, nothing concrete and solid. As David stepped aside, Reid saw Ciara coming, toting baby Amber in a carrier thingy that looked like a torture implement for the mom. Then he froze. Beside Ciara, lugging what had to be the mother ship of all diaper bags, was Emilie Wesley.

She wore a flowing top and a pair of skinny jeans that fit just right, and he had to remind his lungs to do their job. She glanced at him and a shy smile tipped her lips. He took a step toward her, but David intercepted him.

"She's a special friend, Reid."

"Okay." It wasn't like his friend to warn him off. "You know we've been on a date, right?"

"Yep, and I'm serious. I'm watching closely. Ciara is very protective of Emilie."

Reid held up his hands and took a step back. "Noted."

. . .

"I'm so glad you came tonight. You work entirely too hard."

Ciara's words circled around Emilie as she set the monstrous bag on a bleacher bench. How much stuff did a two-month-old need? Even in her most must-be-prepared-for-any-situation days in college, her backpack had never been this stuffed. She was scared to unzip the bag and peek in, for fear the slightest movement would cause the contents to explode like a demented jack-in-the-box.

First-time parents.

She couldn't ignore the joy looking into Amber's clear blue eyes brought. Recently it felt all she experienced was an overwhelming exhaustion and fear that she couldn't perform up to some elusive standard she'd set for herself. She was disappointing everyone— herself most of all.

It was a rock that threatened to sink her beneath the waves, and she wasn't strong enough to swim back to the surface.

"You okay?" Ciara's words brought her back to the moment, and Emilie forced a smile.

"I'm good." She glanced around the battered gym. "Why do you come to these again?"

"When you're married, it means you go to smelly, noisy places because it's what your husband likes." She unfastened a couple of the bizarre collection of buckles strapping Amber to her seat. "David likes to show off for me, and it gives him time with his friends when he doesn't feel he's cheating us of time." She shrugged and glanced at Emilie. "It's a small enough thing."

Her words conveyed a message that love comprised a series of small sacrifices that built over time to a lasting relationship.

Emilie sensed the wisdom embedded in the words. When would she find the man with whom she could build a lasting love? Ciara had found hers with David. And Hayden looked to be building her happily-ever-after with Andrew. What held her back from finding the man who could love her truly, deeply, and with that everlasting, all-consuming love—but wouldn't burn into the unbridled need for control, as the women who came to the Haven had experienced?

Emilie wanted to be loved.

She didn't want to disappear into someone else's control.

The possibility terrified her.

"You still with us?" Ciara's words snapped Emilie back to the moment.

"Yeah. Got lost for a second."

"You could say that." Ciara shifted the now freed Amber in her arms and then nudged her chin toward the basketball court. "I see you've captured the attention of David's friend Reid."

Emilie felt heat crawl up her neck. "I'm not looking for attention."

"So says my friend who is desperate to be loved."

Ouch. "Who gave you the crystal ball into my soul?"

"God can whisper the truth even through little ole me."

Emilie's gaze trailed to the court, where David and Reid had been joined by the hulking guy she'd seen at the funeral and again in the restaurant. He was tall and probably had a hundred pounds on her, but not one was fat. He screamed athlete—a different look from Reid, who wasn't muscle-bound. Yet Reid had an intelligence and spark that drew her.

There was a flurry of activity at the doorway, and she turned to see another man walk in, flanked by a man and a woman. She recognized him at once. "Does that guy have security?"

Ciara turned from digging through the bottomless bag. "Jordan? It might be overkill, but he must have needed them for something earlier today."

"Seriously?" The woman never stopped scanning the room as she moved ahead of the men to take a loop of the court. "That's intense."

The guys greeted each other, a standoffish vibe coming from the latest entrant, as if he wanted to enter in but couldn't quite let himself.

"You don't know who he is?" Humor tinted Ciara's words.

"Oh yeah, I do. He was at the Haven yesterday, and I met him at a fund-raiser before that. Jordan Westfall, the uber-wealthy former CEO of InterIntell. How does David know him?"

"Jordan's not a core part of the group, but David grew up near his family."

As she watched the men team up, Emilie's gaze kept returning to Reid. "Do they play often?"

"It depends. Jordan is a new addition, but the other three try based on their schedules."

Brandon and Reid were paired, while David and Jordan hustled back and forth as a team. Jordan was awkward as he moved around the court. Reid kept a steady stream of talk going as they moved. He did a spin move as he went up, and Jordan groaned as the ball danced around the rim before bouncing out.

"You don't get extra points for style." David chuckled as he leaned over with his hands on his thighs. "Especially when it doesn't go in."

"Let's take a quick break." Before waiting to hear what the others said, Jordan stalked to his male body-guard and returned with bottles of a sports drink for the guys. He sat on the bottom seat of the bleachers, back ramrod straight.

"He doesn't know how to relax." Reid's voice pulled Emilie around. He stood a couple feet away and put up a hand. "I didn't want to get too close."

The faint odor emanating from him suggested he was still a little too close, but she didn't say so. He pulled a hand towel from a navy duffel at his feet and wiped his face and neck. Emilie couldn't tear her gaze from him and he seemed to know it.

"I didn't expect to see you here tonight," he said.

"Would it have changed anything?" The words popped out.

"Quite possibly." He grinned at her. "I would have worn stronger deodorant."

The words surprised a laugh from her. "I'm not sure it would matter."

Brandon walked by and moved toward the court. "Come on, you softies. We ain't got all night."

Reid lurched to his feet, then turned toward her. "Go out with me tonight?"

She wrinkled her nose, knowing she should say no but wanting to say yes. "Not without a shower."

He pulled his sweaty T-shirt from his chest and grinned. "What? This isn't good enough for you?"

"Umm . . . no."

"You're on. One shower in exchange for one date."

"Coffee."

"Sure, Em." He saluted her as he trotted backward to the court.

As she watched him go she couldn't help wondering what he thought she'd agreed to.

Jordan stopped a few feet from her and waited.

"Hi, Jordan. Nice to see you again."

"Good to see you. Join me after the game?"

"She just agreed to coffee with Reid." Ciara jiggled Amber as she watched the two.

"She can speak for herself."

Emilie puffed out a breath. "I'm sorry, Jordan, but Ciara's right."

"Maybe this weekend."

"Maybe." She watched him stalk to the court and then turned to Ciara. "What was that?"

"I'm not sure." She slipped the pacifier into Amber's mouth and then handed the little bundle to Emilie. "Jordan's sometimes a little awkward."

Emilie snuggled the baby closer, suddenly wishing she was anywhere but there. Still, her gaze strayed to the man pulling his sweaty shirt out, revealing carefully sculpted muscles. She could lose herself in that heart-stopping grin of his if she allowed herself.

CHAPTER 34

As the boys moved up and down the court sweating and throwing insults at each other, Emilie and Ciara talked, but Emilie was grateful her friend didn't press for details about her relationship with Reid. The elephant might linger in the room, but apparently Ciara was comfortable letting it be . . . for the moment.

But Emilie couldn't help herself. "What do you know about Reid?" The question popped out before she could stop it.

Ciara paused in the middle of changing Amber's diaper. How she got the tiny thing to go around right, Emilie hadn't a clue. Ciara fastened the Velcro and then snapped the baby's onesie in place. She gave Emilie a smug smile. "Why do you ask?"

Emilie glanced at the court and saw Reid and Jordan collide. Jordan ricocheted off Reid, sliding across the floor a few feet as his bodyguards stood, ready to intervene. What had them worked up? Jordan waved them back, and they eased to their positions as Reid helped Jordan up.

Emilie reached for little Amber, enjoying the warmth of the tiny girl and feeling the smallest hesitation at the idea that she could one day have children. She didn't want to risk having any child of her own experiencing even a sliver of what she'd seen and heard. There were stories that haunted her dreams and shadowed her days.

She tried to gather her thoughts. "He intrigues me, that's all."

"You like him." Ciara leaned forward, propping her elbows on her knees and her chin in a palm. "Someone has finally piqued your interest."

Emilie felt that darned heat that came with fair skin begin to burn up her neck. "Yes, but I have to know more before I trust myself."

"You mean trust him."

"No, trust me." Emilie sighed and shifted the baby in her arms. "Ciara, the stories I've heard."

"And things you've seen." Ciara cocked her head and studied Emilie. "You have to trust God's story for you."

Emilie breathed in Amber's sweetness and innocence and contrasted it with what she had seen. "Someone has to help these women, and right now that's me."

Sometimes she wondered if she could keep it up, or if she would reach a point where her mind filled with so many stories and clients she would cease sleeping in exchange for worrying. She had to find a way to release that need to fix it all herself, but even with the circumstances surrounding Kaylene's death, Emilie felt the struggle to hold on tightly. She knew this wasn't God's best for her, but how did she balance that with the way He'd created her to see a need and address it?

Ciara reached over and touched her knee. "I'll pray God gives you strength."

Should she tell her friend about the notes? That some-one was shadowing her? Had possibly done that since her accident in April? Before she could decide, Ciara continued.

"Reid is complicated. He's a financial whiz who doesn't trust how good he really is. If you give him a hundred dollars, he'll give you back a hundred twenty. His clients give him much more. He sees patterns others don't and uses that for his clients. He doesn't come from wealth, but he moves among the wealthy with ease." She leaned back and placed her elbows on the seat behind her. "He takes a while to get to know. I was engaged to David before I peeled back his layers. He helps Brandon with his foster home, a weight he's voluntarily taken—like someone else I know." She gave Emilie a meaningful look.

Amber gave a little sigh, and when Emilie glanced down, the little thing was asleep. She'd curled right in and trusted Emilie to keep her safe. It felt like both a burden and a benediction. "He sounds interesting."

Ciara grinned at her. "We've already established that." She opened her mouth to say more, but closed it as the men came off the court.

• • •

Whatever the women had talked about looked serious, based on Emilie's expression. What had brought that concerned hint of wrinkles to her face? He wanted to know so he could smooth them away. He thought about asking, then caught a whiff of his scent as he pulled his Dri-FIT shirt collar up to wipe his forehead. "Wait for me?"

She glanced at him and then nodded. At least she hadn't changed her mind.

Reid hurried through good-byes with the guys, then grabbed his duffel and ran to the locker room. He hadn't planned to go anywhere but home at the end of the game, but he had a fresh change of clothes in his locker. Ten minutes later he toweled his hair and then pulled on street shoes.

When he got back to the basketball court, Ciara and David had left, but Jordan sat there with Emilie, his entourage lurking behind, while Brandon shot a few more hoops. His buddy pulled the ball in, then jogged toward Reid. "I stayed to chaperone."

Jordan said something to Emilie that made her laugh. Her cheeks were flushed, and she looked at Jordan in a way that made a fist tighten in Reid's chest. She hadn't ever looked at him that way. What would it take—other than a few million dollars—to get that same attention? He swallowed back the thought. He needed to get a grip, especially when Brandon stood there watching him with a knowing grin.

"I'm sure he's keeping her company for me."

Brandon raised his eyebrows and dipped his chin in a disbelieving look. "Are you seeing the same thing I am? 'Cause right now I think you're delusional."

"Thanks." Reid rubbed a hand over the stubble that dotted his face. He hadn't taken the time to shave, and now it looked like it would have been wasted anyway. He couldn't compete with a multimillionaire. He pushed his shoulders back. "Good game tonight. You should ask Jordan for a donation for Almost Home."

Brandon frowned and fisted his hands on his hips. "I don't take advantage of people I've played basketball with."

"Almost Home is a good investment for him. We'll get him to see that." He thumped Brandon on the shoulder. "I'm rescuing the woman over there. See you later." He forced a cocky grin in place and strutted toward the duo. "Ready, Emilie?"

She looked up at him, and her eyes sparkled like the softest emeralds, true green but not cold. "Sure." She turned to Jordan and extended her hand. "I enjoyed chatting, Mr. Westfall. I'll be in touch." Her chin came around in a little circle that looked like flirting as she stood.

Jordan met his gaze with a challenge embedded. What was Reid going to do about him moving in on Reid's territory? At least Em had called him *Mr. Westfall*. That was formal . . . and distant.

How did the guy instinctively know Reid wanted to claim her? Jordan had Spidey senses like no one Reid knew. It was enough to make the guy unlikeable, but David kept bringing him, and Reid valued David's friendship too much to let one guy who let him manage millions of dollars get in the way of that.

Reid extended his elbow for Emilie. "Did you drive yourself?"

"No, I caught a ride with David and Ciara, but they left. They assured me you'd be a gentleman." Her eyes sparkled as she gazed at him.

"Absolutely. What would you like?"

"Coffee."

"Coffee," he acknowledged. "I thought we could hit Common Grounds, since it's close to your home."

"Of course." She nodded, but he felt her fingers tremble as she placed them on his arm.

Interesting. He tried to help her relax by chatting as he led her to his Lexus, but she remained curiously tense. He'd have to ask about that, because it hadn't been present the other night.

"Thanks again for the roses. They were extravagant, but beautiful. My office smelled wonderful."

"Roses?"

"The ones I texted you about."

"I wish I could take the credit." Wished he'd had the thought.

The tremble intensified. "They weren't from you?"

"Unfortunately, no."

"Hmm."

He glanced at her and noticed her cheeks had colored as bright as a pink rose. Great, now he'd embarrassed her, but he couldn't take credit for someone else's great idea. "No card?"

"Not signed."

"Too bad I didn't know that when you asked."

She stopped and looked at him with her mouth open. "You mean you'd take credit for someone else's idea?"

He met her gaze, noting the laughter in her eyes. "Only when it's one I wish I'd had."

"Oh." Her gaze dropped, but he could see she was pleased.

After a few minutes' drive and another five of circling

for a parking place, he opened the car door and tried not to notice her legs as she slid out. She was slender, yet had curves that were rather distracting. She had been quiet on the way, seemingly content in the silence, which was probably a relief after the pounding balls and squeaking shoes at the court.

He opened the door to Common Grounds, and a moment later they stood in front of the menu board. All he wanted was a black decaf, but she ordered something that would taste impossibly sweet, just like last time. At least she was consistent. She added a slice of lemon pound cake, and he decided on an M&M cookie.

A small table in the corner was the perfect spot to talk without the distraction of people coming in and out to satisfy their caffeine addictions. He set his mug and cookie on the table, then pulled out a chair for her. She eased onto it with a ballerina's grace.

"That move amazes me."

She glanced at him, startled. "What move?"

"The one where you slide onto the chair so elegantly. There must be a secret class teenage girls take that men are excluded from."

"Oh, it's top secret. If I told you . . ."

She winked, and Reid almost spit out his sip of coffee. She was surprising in her silence and in her words. About the moment he thought he understood her, she would do something that left him convinced he was deluding himself.

There were depths to Emilie Wesley that were unexplainable, but depths he was determined to plumb. She would be worth the effort.

for a riveting phone call operator the car, and then the to home, but she it as she out. She list bewter and had slowly in the rain, which with the which was perhaps the person after the petarating car, and then the none of the contract.

The opens the door to Carmen's rounded an adjourned suit. They stood in front of the them hurt while Carmen was tales, dear, but she needs sometime and prelim as.

CHAPTER 35

Thursday morning images from the basketball game and coffee date warred for attention with the latest stack of legal motions Emilie needed to review. She'd worked her way through half of the stack when a distraction came in a call from Jordan Westfall. She sent it to voicemail, a remarkably easy way to avoid someone. There was no reason for him to call her.

At eleven Taylor entered Emilie's office overloaded with a mug of coffee for each of them and a stack of folders under her arm. She sidled up to Emilie's desk, and Emilie grabbed a mug as Taylor edged the folders onto the desk. "I've got a stack of filings you can take with you when we're done."

"Great." Taylor sank onto a chair and then reached for the files. "Do you care how we go through these?"

"Not at all."

"Okay." Taylor took a sip from her mug, then set it on the edge of Emilie's desk. "Let's start with Benson."

The first five old client files contained no surprises. Taylor had noticed the same things Emilie had that might make a client want to take action against Emilie. A comment here, a disgruntled phone call there, but nothing that seemed to rise to the standard necessary to cause someone to move to harassment. Especially when some of the cases had ended more than two years earlier.

While Emilie had full custody hearings or divorce trials for some clients, the majority were a contested protective order. Relatively quick and to the point. Evidence presented, a decision rendered, police enforcement to follow. There wasn't much about the process that Emilie controlled in a way that a client could blame her.

"Do you want to continue?" There was an upswing in Taylor's voice, and the pencil ceased moving around her fingers as if she hoped Emilie would stop the waste of time.

"There has to be something." The last files might have something she could track to her shadow.

"All right." Taylor sighed. "Then let's look at Raleigh Hardin. Her boyfriend was the one who showed up at her job, the daycare, everywhere. We got her the protective order, but it didn't accomplish much. The man didn't care that he had an order to stay clear. He reminded Raleigh she was his every chance he could."

"I remember. Why do you think Raleigh would blame me?"

"I don't." Taylor frowned, and the pen took up motion again. "I think more likely it's him. The police finally got it across that the PO was serious by putting him in jail the fifth time he violated. And . . ." She paused. "He was released on parole at the end of March."

"Where's Raleigh?"

"Left the state. Moved home to Georgia, so if he

can't go to her because of the conditions of parole, maybe he'd shift focus to you."

Emilie nodded, then jotted a note. "Reasonable assumption. Any indication of violence?"

"Other than hounding Raleigh? An assault and battery in college. Got a slap on the wrist. That's it."

"Okay. The timing fits. It would take him a while to figure out Raleigh was out of reach."

"Exactly. Then he'd turn to someone he could touch."

Emilie steepled her fingers. "Remind me of his name."

"Marcus Wilcott."

"Right." His image and behavior flooded her mind. He never bothered to charm the judge. His demeanor was hard enough to make someone step across the street if he approached. Some people couldn't be convinced they were wrong. Stubbornness was a trait they valued.

"I'll see if I can find his parole officer, learn more about where he is and what he's up to." Emilie jotted a note. A quick call would take care of him.

Taylor nodded, then shuffled that file to the bottom. "The best bet for a client is Maddy Shift. She called several times after her case was resolved."

Emilie scanned her notes and frowned. "Why didn't I know?"

"There was no point. I thought she just needed to vent." She leaned forward and met Emilie's gaze.

"What bothered her?"

"She was convinced the dream she had would never come true."

"What dream was that?"

"That's why I didn't mention it, it sounded so crazy."

She grimaced and shifted against the seat. "I was sure she would come to her senses. She didn't do anything while we worked with her that indicated she would suddenly dream about you and think you were behind her current woes."

"Which were?"

"She lost her job and ended up in transitional housing while she struggled to find work. It wasn't good, but there wasn't anything you could do about it."

"Unless she was wrongfully discharged."

Taylor nodded. "But that's not the kind of law we do. I told her Legal Aid was her best bet, even though they don't like run-of-the-mill discharges."

It was true. The employee side of discharges could be tricky. She remembered one of her professors talking about how easy it could be to get someone fired and how hard it was to prove discrimination had occurred. The professor had been clear that didn't mean you shouldn't file a claim, but it was hard to make a living on that side of the case.

"Did she call again?"

"A couple times." Taylor shrugged. "Each time she'd talk for ten minutes. Tell me she'd dreamed you were the answer to her situation. I'd eventually end the call, and she wouldn't call again for months."

Emilie considered the information. If she'd been in Taylor's shoes, she would have handled it the same way. "When was the last time she called?"

"I double-checked before putting her on the list. It was April 1. I almost thought it was a joke." Taylor ran a finger along the edge of the top folder.

The pause lengthened, so Emilie leaned forward. "And . . ."

"She didn't have a reason. Said it was the last time she'd call. She was tired of us not helping and didn't need us anymore." Taylor's finger slid up and down the file so quickly Emilie expected her to get a paper cut.

"Odd, but doesn't mean she's fixated."

"True, but this does." Taylor slipped the top sheet from the folder and handed it to Emilie.

It was an ordinary sheet of white paper, and the message looked like it had been typed on a typewriter rather than run through a printer.

Dear Ms. Wesley,

   I've tried to reach you for help. My life has fallen apart and all I needed was a little assistance. I thought it reasonable to seek it from you, my attorney, but clearly I was mistaken. I have learned the hard way not to rely on others. First my husband, now you. It is a lesson learned after great hurt and trouble, but one I have learned well. Do not worry. I will never bother you again, at least not that you know.

There was a handwritten signature at the bottom.

"No one would be crazy enough to sign their name to something like this." Emilie let the letter fall to the top of her desk and then reread it.

Could this woman have decided Emilie was to blame for everything?

Maddy Shift. Emilie let the name roll around her mind, recalling everything she could of the woman and her story. She'd married young to flee an abusive home life, only to find a husband identical to her father. What followed was typical, except she hadn't had a child. The divorce should have meant a clean break, especially when her ex found someone else to control.

But it hadn't.

Maddy had followed another pattern. There were two. Women who could find a support network and the inner strength to back away, and those who immediately found another man like their first.

The man Maddy fell for next had quickly accelerated to physical abuse, the stage where she left her first husband. This time she didn't have the strength to believe she was worth more. When Emilie offered to help with a protective order, Maddy had been reluctant to agree. It had taken several calls and one meeting, a meeting Emilie wouldn't let her leave until after they'd walked over to court, the makeup failing to hide the purple and green circles that darkened Maddy's left eye and her jawline.

It was after the protective order that Emilie had ended the client relationship. There were too many clients and potential clients who needed her help to escape their situations. She couldn't continue to pour time into someone who didn't desire change. Emilie had made sure Taylor understood that as they sent the closing letter. No wonder Taylor had shielded her from Maddy's ongoing calls.

"I'll do some checking, because unfortunately it makes sense." Emilie jotted a note at the bottom of her list. "Any indication when she talked to you that either her husband or her boyfriend was back?"

"No. Sounded like she'd moved on." Taylor's shoulders slumped and her fingers stopped moving along the files.

"Don't forget all the women we've helped to rebuild their lives."

"Maddy wasn't one."

"No."

That one word summed up the work they did. What they achieved. And what they couldn't.

"That's all I have, except for a lead on Kaylene's gun." Taylor handed her another sheet of paper and then grabbed the stack of filings with Emilie's notes. "I'll get started on these."

"Thanks."

Taylor left, and Emilie scanned the sheet of paper. Then she grabbed her phone and hit speed dial. "What are you doing for lunch?"

CHAPTER 36

W hen she'd called him about lunch, Reid had harbored the hope that Emilie was ready to continue their date from last night.

Not exactly.

Tactical Precision loomed on the left side of Jeff Davis Highway as Reid followed his GPS. "I've never noticed this place before." It blended in with the other slightly industrial-looking businesses on the right as they headed south.

"I can't say I have either." Emilie's voice hesitated as she looked through the windshield. "Here's hoping we learn what we need."

"You take the lead, and I'll be your protector." He'd meant the words as a joke, but something about them caused Emilie to stiffen.

"This feels so off." Emilie sighed. "I can understand Kaylene thinking she needed protection, but she told me one reason she was afraid of Robert was his gun arsenal. How would one handgun counteract that?"

"There's a lot about my sister I didn't know."

Emilie shook her head. "Let's see what we can learn." She reached for the door handle as soon as he pulled into a parking space, and pushed open the door before he could come around to help her. "We'll see if they're helpful. The police probably talked to them and spooked the owner."

"Then you'll lay the Southern charm on nice and thick."

She shook her head. "I don't like to if I can avoid it."

When they entered, a few customers were looking into display cases as employees pulled out guns one by one and explained the virtues of each. They were careful to return one gun before pulling out the next.

A tall man, his posture screaming ex-military, stepped from a back room and eyed them carefully. "How can I help you?"

Emilie stepped closer to the counter and turned on a full-watt smile. Did she understand how breathtaking she was when she did that?

"Hi, I'm Emilie, and this is my friend Reid. His sister bought a gun here about six weeks ago and then got some training. We wondered if we could talk to whoever helped her."

The man's stance didn't relax one iota, and his frown seemed to intensify. "We don't release information like that."

"I had a feeling you'd say that." She chewed on her bottom lip, taking the role of a weak Southern belle so completely that Reid almost did a double take. It was scary how easily she slid into a role that was not her. "I'm her attorney, and we're trying to prove she didn't use the gun to kill her daughter."

The man's brows knit together in a way that would

be scary if there weren't a solid glass counter between them. "Then I suggest you get a subpoena."

"I'd like to avoid that if we can." She sighed and played with a strand of her hair. Reid watched the man follow the gesture. "She tried to leave her abusive husband and was desperate to take the girls with her. I know she would never hurt them." She looked at the man with an intensity that would have made Reid step back if she'd settled that look on him. "But I can't prove it . . . yet."

"I fail to see what that has to do with us."

"That's the great thing. If you help me, I won't get a judge involved, but if I do her husband will know who to talk to here. He's not a nice man."

The man crossed his arms, and his biceps bulged. "That doesn't scare me."

"It should." She leaned over the counter. "Because I believe he used her gun to kill one daughter, critically injure the other, and frame my client. And he's going to get away with it if I don't get some information."

The man finally looked at Reid. "Is she always this intense?"

"Every time I see her." It was one of the things he appreciated about Em. She threw herself in with whole-hearted fierceness.

"What's the name of the customer?"

"Kaylene Adams."

His shoulders shifted. "I have nothing to say about her."

"Then her husband will get away with two murders. I won't let that happen." She dug in with a determination that made Reid want to cheer.

"Lady, do you have any idea how many people have pestered us about her? The police. ATF. Journalists sniffing around. Why should I help you?"

"Because if this had happened to your sister or wife, you'd want me bulldogging for her." Emilie met the man stare for stare, and Reid knew the guy was a goner.

"Give me a minute. I can't do this without my partner's approval." He stepped into the back room, and they could hear a muffled conversation before he returned with a petite woman who looked like she could match Emilie spunky pound for pound.

"Gerry tells me y'all want info on Kaylene?" At Emilie's nod, she studied them before reaching a decision. "All right. It's about time someone cared about that poor woman." She turned to Gerry. "Let's bring them back."

The next hour passed quickly with the woman, Lindsey, giving them all the information she had. "Normally I wouldn't do this, but it can't hurt her now that she's gone." She sighed and rubbed at her neck. "She was committed to getting out. It was easy to tell she didn't like guns. At all. If she'd felt there were another way, she wouldn't have bought that little one. I gave her lessons and made sure she knew how to use it."

Gerry nodded from his seat on a folding chair. "She held it like it was a dead mouse the first time. I've rarely seen anyone so uncomfortable."

"But she was adamant she needed one to stay safe when she and the girls left." Lindsey looked Emilie dead in the eyes. "When I saw the headlines, I knew the police had it wrong, but they didn't listen. Had their notions of how the event occurred, and nothing I said made them waver in their determination."

Reid pushed from the wall and began pacing. "Why couldn't anyone stop this?"

Emilie placed a hand on his arm, but he brushed past her. "Reid, it's a process. Kaylene was doing what she could."

"But you were helping." He turned and pointed at Lindsey. "So was she. The one person she didn't turn to for help was me. That's wrong. I'm her brother." His voice rose with each word until he was almost yelling. He wanted to pick up something and hurl it. The sound of something breaking couldn't begin to replicate the fragments he felt shredding him. "She should have come to me."

"You were her baby brother. She was protecting you." Emilie's words grated rather than calmed.

The truth seared him.

"And she asked you to protect her most precious possessions. That's why we're fighting for Kinley." Emilie reached out cautiously. "We'll protect her while we can."

"Em, it's not good enough."

"It's all we can do."

The truth slammed into him like a physical punch.

Lindsey stood and looked at Gerry. "I'll copy what we have. You can subpoena it later, but this will get you started."

Ten minutes later she returned with a stack of paper. Emilie flipped through it, then handed it to Reid. The first few pages looked routine. The application to purchase the gun and then the concealed carry paperwork they already had. It was the next few pages that grabbed him around the throat and squeezed until he could barely breathe. Each page represented one of Kaylene's meetings with Lindsey. In addition to the record of what Lindsey had coached her on were lines of observations. Snippets of their conversations. It was almost like Lindsey had known she'd need a contemporaneous account.

"I do this for certain clients. The ones who are fighting harder to escape. Most of the time these notes are never needed, but if they'll assist you now, it's worth the record-keeping."

Emilie nodded. "Thank you. This will be very helpful. I may call you to testify."

"I'll do whatever I can."

Reid nodded, but as he followed Emilie from the back, he felt the impact of what Kaylene had done, and the burden to do the impossible and rescue Kinley.

"Have you heard anything more from the hospital?" Emilie's question reminded him how short their time was.

"Not yet. I'll call again, see if I can catch Melanie Rogers." He wanted the nurse to say there'd been a problem and that Kinley couldn't come home yet. He held the door for Emilie as they left the gun shop.

"Call from here." Emilie nibbled on a thumbnail as she watched him pull out his phone. "I need to know how much time we have."

A minute later he hung up. "Looks like Monday or Tuesday."

"Okay." Emilie turned around, her hands in her jeans

back pockets. Did she understand how fetching she looked? He tore his gaze from where it shouldn't be back to her hair. Today it was hanging loose and he wanted to run his hands through it. See if it felt as soft as it looked. Grrr. He needed to focus on Kinley and what she needed, not the amazing woman who watched passing traffic on the highway. "Take me to the office, and I'll flesh out what we have and what we need."

"What can I do?"

She turned around, a determined set to her jaw. "I need to convince the judge you're ready to provide a safe place for Kinley. Does your apartment have space for her?"

His thoughts scrambled as he ran through his rooms in his mind. "Sure. I'll move my workout room." That wouldn't be a massive project . . .

Who was he kidding? It'd take at least the weekend to get it whipped into shape. "How does one make a space girl-ready?"

"Paint the walls Pepto-Bismol pink." He blanched, and she started to laugh. "Kidding. How about you clean it out, and I'll get paint. We can get that taken care of in a few hours."

"I can do that."

"Great." She headed toward his Lexus. "Better drop me at Daniels, McCarthy & Associates and I'll figure out how we'll save your niece."

CHAPTER 37

Simone hurried after Reid as he jetted through the office, up the stairs, and down the hall before plowing into his office. "A box was delivered for you. COD."

"Really? I didn't know people still did that."

"It's on your desk. Mr. Fletcher will want you to reimburse the firm or he'll have the costs taken from your next check."

"Fine. I wonder what it is." Reid strode into his office, already focused on the file-sized box perched on his desk.

"Good question, but one that will have to wait until you tell me why it was so important I meet you at the elevator." She plopped in a chair and crossed her legs.

"I need your help."

"Does it relate to tomorrow's reception?"

"No."

"Then it should wait." She studied him carefully with her dark eyes. "You do understand I'm pulling together a critically important client event on mere days' notice."

"I think I remember that."

She didn't laugh as he'd expected. Instead, she leaned back. "What do you need?"

"I need you to figure out everything a ten-year-old girl needs to feel at home and order it for me."

"All right, but remember this when I ask for a raise."

The moment Simone left, Reid picked up the box and looked for the sender. Robert Adams. Inside he found a stack of planners that must go back several years. The only other items were a few books including a Bible. He set the box aside as Simone buzzed him with a question. He'd have to give the box's contents attention when he was done here.

The afternoon passed in a rush of preparing the draft slides for tomorrow's presentation and jotting down the notes he would memorize in the next twenty-four hours. Then he headed home with the box, his mind already focused on how he was supposed to get his man cave ready for Kinley. Simone had shown him something on Pinterest that only stressed him out more.

He unlocked his door and walked past the grand piano, pausing to play a chord on his way through the room. When he reached Kinley's space, he set the box down and sank to the floor. Once he got his workout equipment and oversized chair out of there, the room would feel bigger. He leaned against the wall and thought for the thousandth time about his sister's last request. She had left him a burden he feared he couldn't carry.

Please promise you'll take care of my girls . . . Promise me you'll keep them safe always.

He hadn't had the opportunity to protect Kaydence, and he was failing Kinley. From Emilie's words, she thought they had something to go on, but they lacked clear proof Robert was involved—proof that would convince a judge Kinley should be with him instead.

He didn't mind the expense, though Emilie hadn't mentioned a bill. He'd spend thousands to honor his sister's request and protect his niece. He knocked his head back lightly against the wall. There had to be something they hadn't considered. How could two smart people have such awful luck at finding a voice for Kinley?

Could the planners in the box contain more than daily records of where the girls needed to be when? Could Kaylene have inserted some sort of code or information about what her day-to-day life was like?

God, You've got to help us.

Robert would not have sent anything that contained a shred of evidence against him. But what if Kaylene had been smarter than both of them?

Her decision to flee wasn't spur of the moment. She'd had a counselor, changed out her diamonds, worked with the Haven, and bought a gun and learned how to use it. But the clerk's conviction that she'd bought it solely for self-defense wouldn't stand if ballistics proved her gun was used to shoot Kaydence and Kinley.

For each sliver of evidence they had, there were four people ready to discount it. Even Kaydence's friends' testimony wouldn't go far unless the judge was lenient. That would only buy a reprieve before appeal. Reid wasn't a lawyer, but he knew allowing them to testify would be risky at best. At worst, it could turn Robert's attention to them, and Reid hesitated to do that.

He pulled out Kaylene's planners that went back

three years. He selected the most recent and flipped slowly through the pages, scanning for anything that would indicate something other than routine. His sister's neat handwriting swirled in colors. She'd used purple for Kinley and orange for Kaydence. Both girls took piano. What had they liked to play, and who were their favorite composers?

He should have known what his nieces loved without having to scan an old calendar. Why hadn't he been invited to their recitals?

He kept flipping, and a pattern emerged. One where Kaylene scheduled an appointment at *the H* every time the girls were at piano.

The Haven? There was one easy way to find out if she'd had weekly appointments there.

He pulled his cell phone from his jeans pocket and dialed Emilie.

"Hey. I'm going through a box Robert sent to work today."

"Does it have anything we can use?" There was a lilt of hope to Emilie's voice.

"Planners, her Bible, and a few other books. I noticed something in one of the calendars."

"Yes?"

"Every time the girls had piano lessons, Kaylene has a note for an appointment at 'the H.' Is that the Haven?"

"Probably. How often were the piano lessons?"

"Once a week during the school year."

"I didn't see her that often. But I know many of her appointments were tied to the girls' activities."

Reid had the feeling he got when he knew a stock was

the right investment. Sometimes there wasn't a solid field of evidence to support his gut, but he'd learned to trust it, and that had made his clients a lot of money. He would do the same now. "I think this is important."

"We've known all along she's been at the Haven." There was a pause. "Sorry, Jordan was calling again."

"Jordan? What does he want?"

"He's left a dozen messages since last night asking me to dinner. He's got me ready to say yes to a date just to make him leave me alone."

"Wait a minute. How will saying yes get him to do that?"

"I'll be the most boring date in history. Won't take long for him to regret asking."

"How'd that work for the gal in *How to Lose a Guy in 10 Days*?"

"Terribly, but she doesn't have my finesse and experience at pushing men away."

He didn't like the sound of that, didn't like it one bit. "And if I asked you?"

"Asked me what?"

"If I asked you out? Would you say yes?"

"I already have." She sighed, and he gave her a moment to think. "You know, it's really not a good idea for me to go out with a client."

"I'm not your client yet."

"But you will be the moment we file for custody of Kinley."

"I won't give up so easily, Em."

"I didn't think you would." She paused again. "I don't want you to either."

"Good." He didn't fight the grin that came at her quiet admission. "We're going to see if there's anything between us, Emilie Wesley. I promise you that."

After he hung up, he went back to the journals. If there was something there, he'd find it. He owed that to Kaylene. And then he'd explore what the future might hold with his favorite attorney.

CHAPTER 38

The phone on Emilie's desk rang, but she ignored it as she scrolled through the guts of her legal argument. She'd made good progress outlining the need for a temporary change in custody and an emergency protective order. She still didn't have the 911 call, and left a message for Detective Gaines asking if he could let her listen to it.

If she could get that call, it might give life to the story. The judge had to see the Adams family as Emilie and Reid had understood them. But without Kaylene and Kaydence here to testify, all she had was hearsay. Robert's attorney would have a fit and raise all kinds of arguments about the unfairness of allowing testimony that couldn't be rebutted. Then the attorney would launch into arguments where Robert could testify. But if Emilie had the call, she might not need Kinley to testify.

The thought stopped her cold as her phone started ringing again.

Would she really consider putting a ten-year-old on the stand? There had to be a better way.

The phone continued to ring, stopped, and then started again.

"Fine." Emilie turned toward her door. "Taylor, do you know who's calling?"

Her assistant came to stand in the doorway. "Sorry, the calls aren't coming through me."

"Can you grab it?"

"Every time I pick up, whoever it is hangs up."

Emilie twisted her grandmother's ring around her finger, then puffed out a sigh as the phone started again. "All right. Let's see who's so determined."

After the next ring, Emilie picked up the phone and hit the line. "Emilie Wesley."

There was silence, and she took a deep breath as her right hand fisted on top of the desk. Something clicked inside. She was tired of feeling on edge all the time. Tired of the sense someone was always watching but never talking.

"Hello? You have one second to talk or I'm hanging up."

"Really, Miss Wesley?"

"Who is this?"

"Darlene Wright. Robert Adams has hired me as his attorney. We've filed an emergency motion that should be waiting on your fax machine. The judge wants to see us in an hour."

Emilie's thoughts scrambled. What kind of motion could the attorney be referencing? "I don't understand. Why would you contact me about something related to Mr. Adams?"

"Have your assistant check the fax. See you in an hour."

The phone clicked in her ear, and Emilie hung up as her spine slackened. "Taylor, can you check the fax?"

"Everything okay?"

"I don't know, but supposedly the judge wants to see me in an hour." Sweat trickled down the small of her back and the room felt overly warm.

Taylor scurried from the doorway and returned a couple minutes later, scanning as she walked. "You're not going to like this."

"The bullet's coming from Wright—of course I'm not going to like it."

"Here." Taylor handed over a thin stack of paper, then turned to the set she retained. Emilie sped-read as Taylor continued. "She's requesting a protective order against you."

Emilie reread the language. "A protective order for harassment? Against me? That's crazy!"

"And brilliant. If she wins, you have to leave Robert Adams alone, which means he gets Kinley, no questions."

"Or Reid finds a different attorney." It was breathtaking legal finagling. She'd almost gotten the protective order against him filed, but not in time to save Kaylene. Now it felt poetically wrong for Darlene Wright to use that strategy against her. How had they known today was the perfect day to file, and how had they known to file against her?

Emilie turned to Taylor. "Call the court and see what the clerk can tell you."

"On it." Taylor spun out of the doorway, and in a few minutes Emilie could hear her quietly talking.

Emilie turned her attention back to the petition for a protective order, something niggling at her mind as she read it more slowly, without the shock of being its target. She knew this law as well as anyone. As she read the facts, she knew the order wouldn't be granted.

There was no way Robert Adams could effectively argue she had done anything involving an act of violent force or threat that resulted in an injury to him. Neither could he have a fear that she would do something leading to death or bodily injury.

That was the legal standard. Why file a petition destined to fail?

She glanced at the calendar, tried to think like Wright. Darlene was a good attorney. One who had earned her bulldog reputation. What was Wright really trying to accomplish by filing this? Wright wouldn't risk angering the judge by wasting her time if there wasn't a goal to be achieved. What was it?

Emilie leaned back and closed her eyes.

She didn't have time to waste. Not if there really was a hearing in forty-five minutes.

"The clerk says the judge isn't happy, but there is a hearing."

Emilie sat up and looked at Taylor. "Why not wait for motion hour?"

"Wright pushed hard for an emergency."

"What's the emergency? What's happening that I'm missing?" Her thoughts raced as she tried to focus them.

Taylor sank onto the edge of a chair. "What's happening with Kinley?"

"Haven't heard from Reid today." Emilie reached for the phone and a minute later had Reid. "Anything changed with Kinley?"

"The doctors are getting ready to step her out of

intensive care with the goal of getting her home early next week. What Melanie Rogers told me yesterday is holding." His rich voice brought her comfort. "Why?"

"Adams has an attorney, a good one, who is trying some tricks. Did you say anything to Robert that would alert him to our plans?"

"No." His answer was immediate. "But he may have mentioned you."

Emilie pinched the bridge of her nose. "Okay. How did you learn about the step down?"

"Rogers called me an hour ago with the update."

"Good to know." She thought a moment. "Have you talked to Robert?"

"Not since the last time he kicked me out of her room and threatened me. Do you want me to try?"

"No, but I need you to meet me at Alexandria District Court in thirty minutes."

"It'll be close, but I'll do my best."

"Thanks." Emilie hung up, surprised he hadn't asked any questions. Would he really try to come, or was he just telling her what he thought she wanted to hear? She had to keep plowing forward. She turned to Taylor. "I need a copy of the protective order statute. I think I know what Wright is up to."

AUGUST

She was being difficult, and his patience was wearing thin.

Why hadn't she acknowledged his care and attention? He'd taken the time to learn what she liked.

The flowers had been extravagant, but something he

wanted to give her. They were impossible to ignore, just as his love for her should be impossible to miss.

She had to know who it was who watched her, had kept her safe when that man threatened her. Was she blind or did she willfully choose not to see?

Neither was acceptable.

It was time to force her to decide. Reid Billings couldn't provide for or protect her the way he could. He was a nice enough guy, but he needed to be reminded of his place. He was a servant, nothing more. And once Emilie understood what he could provide that Billings couldn't, her affections would settle on him where they belonged.

He picked up his phone. Time to call her again. Maybe this time he could talk to her. With one word, he knew she'd ease the tightness in his chest. She'd free his mind to explore and create, something that had been derailed. She was the key to his returning to the truest form of himself. She would see. He'd make sure of that.

CHAPTER 39

Reid shifted against the stone bench, wondering for the hundredth time why Emilie needed him in court on such short notice. He'd ordered his assistant to reschedule his afternoon meetings, but Simone had been livid to see him leave. *You know you must be back by four at the latest.* He'd assured her he would, because his presentation was almost ready, but he could use more prep time.

He'd rushed from his downtown DC office to the court in Old Town, only to find he'd beaten Emilie.

A few minutes later he heard Emilie. There was a distinctive sound to her pace, a percussion that telegraphed her determination. She sank onto the bench next to him.

"Hey."

He glanced at her and stilled. The word had been casual, but the look in her eyes wasn't. "Fill me in on why we're here."

"I got a surprise filing from Robert's attorney." She exhaled, blowing a stray strand of hair off her face.

He wanted to lean forward and see if she'd let him tuck it back in place, but instead ran a finger under his tie, loosening the suddenly tight noose.

"A protective order against me."

"What? Shouldn't they file against me?"

"Yes." She turned to him. "That's why I wanted you here. There must be another point to this motion, because as it is, it's a waste of the court's time and resources. Robert is no more terrified of me than he is of a bee sting."

"Unless he's allergic." That earned him a small smile. "Maybe it's a distraction. Keep you busy until it's too late."

"Possibly. I was in the middle of preparing our motions when I got the petition." She rubbed the top of the ring she wore on her ring finger. "I don't know if you'll testify, but let's ferret out their strategy."

"All right. I trust you."

Those simple words drew her startled gaze to his. It was then he noticed how pale she looked. As if she'd been dealt a blow and was waiting for the next to fall, not knowing when it would come or where it would land, just that it was imminent.

He met her gaze and held it. "I'll do whatever you need."

"Right now let's get through this hearing and show the judge how ridiculous this petition is. If she gets annoyed, then we'll be in a better position." She sighed as she started toward the door. "It's possible we'll be back in front of Judge Robinson for our motion."

As he followed her into the courtroom, her words rolled around his head. The more he learned about his brother-in-law, the more it seemed like a plot twist the man would generate. Robert liked the unexpected. To drive people to places they hadn't considered. And this move came right at a point when they needed Emilie's focus on getting Kinley to his apartment when the hospital released her.

"Here we go." Emilie's quiet sentence as she stood yanked him from his thoughts.

He glanced to the front of the courtroom, noticed the small woman moving behind the bench, her black gown billowing around her. Had the bailiff said, "All rise," while he'd been lost in thought?

Reid hesitated as Emilie moved forward, opening the small gate. She didn't glance back, so he waited where he was.

· · ·

Emilie walked toward Judge Robinson, feeling her red sheath with floral jacket become her armor. Her clients had often commented that her statement necklaces and flair were a bright light in the tension of the courtroom. Right now she wished it worked that way for her. The tension in her shoulders made it feel like she'd crack with little provocation.

As Darlene Wright approached, Emilie had all the incitement she needed. The woman wore her dyed black hair in a bob that looked more like a helmet than a hairstyle. Her black suit, hose, and heels made her look like the Black Widow next to Emilie's colorful uniform. Emilie could imagine how Judge Robinson saw them.

The judge had blazed a unique path in the late nineties and risen to the court at a relatively young age. She didn't seem interested in moving to a higher court, instead enjoying the swordplay of words and strategy in the district court. She glanced over her rhinestone-rimmed reading glasses at them. "All right, counselors, I've got to say this is a unique hearing." She focused on Wright. "Are you sure this is what you want to pursue, Darlene?"

"Absolutely. My client and I believe we have standing to pursue this protective order to forestall Ms. Wesley's aggressive tactics."

Emilie felt heat climb her neck and she bit back the urge to plow right in. One thing she had learned in moot court was to hold her tongue until addressed. That advice had served her well in her legal career.

Judge Robinson jotted a note, then flipped a page on the petition. "Explain your legal position."

Wright stood taller, looking even more like a tin soldier. "Ms. Wesley is aggressively pursuing my client during his personal tragedy to the point of harassment."

"How is that grounds for a protective order?"

"Without this order, he fears he will be harassed and pursued until she ultimately wins. He knows that as the former attorney for his wife, she has an agenda."

"I fail to see how that rises to the standard of the law."

"We believe it does, Your Honor."

"Where is the violence, force, or threat of bodily injury?"

"My client believes he shouldn't have to wait until it rises to that level."

"Great for him, but I am bound by the constraints of the laws as passed by the Commonwealth." Judge

Robinson looked around the courtroom, then used her reading glasses to point. "Is your client that gentleman?"

Emilie turned to follow the judge's gesture and then bit back a smile at the realization that the woman pointed at Reid. "That's my client, Your Honor."

"And why is he here?"

"I asked him to come in case I needed to present testimony. He is aware of everything that has happened, since I am acting at his request."

"Good." The judge nodded with an efficiency of movement, replaced her glasses, and turned to Wright. "And your client?"

"Is unavailable, Your Honor."

"I'm to believe he wants this protective order enough to waste this court's time, but not enough to appear, while Ms. Wesley's client appeared on extremely short notice."

Emilie felt hope lift inside her. The judge was making her arguments without requiring her to speak. Keeping her mouth shut was the best course.

Darlene Wright opened her mouth, but the judge held up her hand. "I've heard enough to make my decision. If your client doesn't care enough to testify, then I'm denying the protective order."

"He believes I'm sufficient to advocate on his behalf."

"Then you may inform your client he is wrong. To bring such allegations against a member of the bar is unheard of." Again Wright started to speak, but Judge Robinson cut her off. "I am not finished. If anything changes and you have facts to support the petition, at that time you may refile. In addition, if opposing counsel does anything that may violate the rules of professional conduct, you may pursue those with the Virginia State Bar. However, if your client attempts to file another motion that is unsubstantiated, you may forewarn him I would consider requests for attorney's fees and sanctions. Am I clear?"

The judge's gaze cut like a knife into Wright, and Emilie shifted back, wanting to avoid their power struggle.

"Yes, Your Honor." Wright spat the words between clenched jaws. "If that's all?"

At the judge's nod, the attorney spun on her spiky black heel and paced from the bench.

"Thank you, Your Honor."

The judge pulled her reading glasses down and studied Emilie. "You're welcome, Ms. Wesley. Be careful in everything you do on this one. You're under scrutiny, and I may not intervene with the constraints placed on me by my role."

"Yes, ma'am. I understand."

"Good job getting your client here so quickly. That helped me make a record."

"Thank you." Emilie blew out a slow breath, and at Judge Robinson's nod left the bench.

Reid slowly stood as she approached, pulling his shirt sleeves down by the cufflinks. The small monogram on the cuff peeked out, and Emilie smiled at the thought that her father would approve.

"Everything good?"

His gaze searched her face, and she allowed herself to meet it. "I didn't need to say much."

"I noticed. That good or bad?"

"Depends on the hearing, but today it was good."

He smiled slowly, and she felt the warmth of it wrap around her. If one of the sheriff's deputies hadn't cleared his throat to get her to step aside, she would have stood in that moment too long.

Instead, she grinned at Reid. "Let's get out of here."

As she walked out of the courtroom with Reid beside her, she felt the stare at her back. She whipped around, but didn't see anyone who looked out of place.

"You okay?" Reid studied her with a curious air.

"Sure." She couldn't let him see how spooked she was by ghosts.

"If you need help, you can tell me."

"I'm fine." She pushed out a breath and turned to him. "Here's the thing. Sometimes I see someone watching from a parking lot. And I find anonymous notes in my purse or bag."

"Or flowers sent without a signature."

She nodded. "That's only happened once, and my office still smells good." She broke from his intense focus. "Then I sense someone watching me everywhere."

"Should I go get the bailiff?"

"No." The word came out more forceful than she'd intended, and she sighed. "There's nothing to tell him."

• • •

Reid quickly changed his clothes and ran through his notes one more time. When he reached Fletcher & Associates, the lobby had been transformed with soft lighting and a string quartet posted at the top of the stairs. Mr. Fletcher paced in front of them, looking like a penguin in a tuxedo.

"I feel overdressed, Mr. Billings."

"You look great." Reid bit back a nervous chuckle. His solid navy suit suddenly looked two steps too casual. "Have you seen Simone?"

"I'm over here." She waved as she stepped from beside the stairs, a roll of duct tape slipped onto her wrist like an oversized bracelet. "Everything's taped down. The caterer is about set up. And the quartet has warmed up. All I need is your presentation and the guests."

"I'll have the first for you in five." Reid hurried down the hall to his office and quickly finished the slide deck. It might not be perfect, but it was the best he could do. He prayed it would be enough.

Annabelle stopped at his door, looking killer in a navy dress that hugged her form and had threads of glimmer to it. "Are you ready?"

"Yes. How about the guys?"

"Headed downstairs as we speak. Time to wow the prospects." She sashayed away as he put on his suitcoat and turned off his office lights.

The night was a blur of glad-handing those who came, talking about their unique circumstances, and addressing the ways the firm could help each. Then Reid made the short presentation, answering the questions that flew at him, energized by the back and forth nature of the exchange.

As the evening wrapped, Mr. Fletcher found him. "Very well done. I had two sign agreements tonight. Many others mentioned how impressed they were."

"Thank you, but it wasn't my idea. My team came together and made this happen."

"I like the way you say that." Mr. Fletcher patted his shoulder with a glint in his eye. "A team is almost always more effective. I'd say you have a lock on this competition."

Reid let the words settle on him. "Thank you."

"I see someone else to get on contract. See you Monday." With that Fletcher walked across the lobby to one of the key prospects. The man had asked intelligent questions and seemed pleased by Reid's responses. That was the best he could hope for.

After the last prospect left, the caterer had wrapped the last leftover veggie platter, and the band was gone, Reid called everyone together. "Great work. I think we can call this a success. Thanks to Annabelle for the idea and Simone for the implementation. We did our job, and Mr. Fletcher was pleased."

As they high-fived and fist-bumped, Reid let the satisfaction soak through him. Now to bring Kinley home.

CHAPTER 40

The doorman gave her an inquiring once-over as she approached the door to Reid's building, burdened with paint and supplies.

"Miss?" His high tone would have made her laugh if she hadn't had so many butterflies raging in their chaotic circus act. While Reid had come to her townhome, this was her first foray to his place. A part of her still screamed she shouldn't be here, that there was too much temptation to fall headlong for the man. The other part justified it, arguing that Kinley had to have a place to come home to. Emilie was choosing to listen to that part.

"I'm here to see Reid Billings."

His eyebrows rose, and Emilie resisted the urge to thrust her hands on her hips and stick out her tongue, a feat that was impossible while holding a gallon of paint and bags of brushes and drop cloths. Reid hadn't warned her there was a guard dog at the entrance. As she glanced through the plate glass windows on either side of the door she wanted to groan. There was a security desk inside too.

The doorman looked past her as if listening to some

voice. Only then did she notice the thin, curly cord coming down from his ear. That tight of security? Really? Even her family didn't have that in her dad's most paranoid moments. She hadn't realized Reid operated in this space. Though if they could get Kinley home with Reid, these extra layers would be a good idea. Robert Adams seemed the type to push his way into control anywhere he went, but the doorman would disabuse him of that.

"All right, miss. Charlie will clear you through the lobby." He opened the door for her with a slight bow of his shoulders and chin. It made her wonder if he'd been a fan of *Downton Abbey*.

"Thank you." She tried to glide through with the haughty air Lady Mary had worn, but knew she probably looked ridiculous.

Five minutes later she stepped from the elevator onto the fourth floor. Four doors spun out from the short hallway, and she quickly gained her bearings. She juggled the bags, then rang the doorbell on a plain door, the only one without a posted number.

A moment later she heard footsteps, and she stepped slightly back, wondering in a crazy way if there might be a butler on the way.

The door opened, and Reid appeared with a lazy grin on his face. Gosh, he looked . . . perfect . . . even though he wore ratty khaki shorts and an old DC Talk T-shirt that had to have been washed a hundred times. There was something about how comfortable he was in his skin that made her want to melt. He ran a hand through his hair, causing it to curl on top.

"You came."

"I told you I would."

"It involves paint and work. Maybe a little sweat." His eyes dared her to tell him what she was thinking, but she wouldn't.

Some thoughts weren't meant to be shared. Not yet.

Especially when the thoughts whispered a forever call she'd steeled her heart against. She needed to remember how undependable men were, but as she looked at Reid she wanted to chuck that conviction to the side and run straight into the arms that were crossed so casually over his chest. She had no doubt he would catch her.

The silence stretched, and she cleared her throat before holding up her bags and paint can. "I brought paintbrushes and snacks."

He quirked an eyebrow. "Snacks?"

"One can't work without proper sustenance."

"And that is . . ."

"Double Stuf Oreos and gummy bears." She grinned.

"Of course. I have mint tea in the fridge. Should be the perfect accompaniment to a gourmet array like that." He reached for the paint. "Let me take that for you."

"Well, if you don't have milk, mint tea will do." Still her heart sang. How many guys would notice a woman's taste in tea? And go out of his way to provide it? She felt her heart expand. "Can I come in, or are we going to stand in the hallway flirting all afternoon?"

He snorted and then stepped back with a sweep of his arm. "Welcome to my abode."

That he could live in this building in this zip code told her a lot about his net worth, but the way he furnished it said Pottery Barn simple. The lines were clean with lots of dark wood and beige upholstery. The wood flooring had a slight reddish tinge to it, enough to warm up the space. And the white walls had a swig of yellow to keep them from glaring.

They took another step forward, and her jaw dropped. The focal point of the living room was a highly polished baby grand.

"Do you play that?"

"I do. My grandma taught me in an RV when we traveled. It kept me busy. Now it's therapy."

She turned and studied the way the art was arranged on the walls.

"Approve?" His hand landed at the small of her back as he guided her down the hallway past the living area toward the small galley kitchen.

"It's . . ." She let him wonder as he leaned closer, and her breath caught. "Nice."

"Nice?" His eyebrows shot up. "All right. I can live with nice." He stopped next to the kitchen island. "Set your bag here, and I'll show you Kinley's room. Then you can decide how we start."

"All right." That should be interesting, if she could quit staring at him and feeling her heart lurch about her chest.

. . .

It was crazy watching Emilie take in his home. She didn't gush the way some women did. Neither did she seem overwhelmed by the over-the-top security. When he'd found the apartment, he'd liked the location more than the protection. Now that he hoped to bring Kinley here, it seemed like all the wisdom in the world to have the double layer. If you got past the doormen and the security guard to the elevator, chances were good you were supposed to be there.

Emilie's eyes widened as she spotted the Remington model on the table against the wall.

"That's not real, is it?"

"No. Just an excellent reproduction."

"Well, that's good news."

"Why?"

"Because my dad owns the original. At least that's what everyone's told him."

Her words startled a laugh from him. "Your dad owns an original Remington?"

She shrugged. "He liked it, so Mom bought it for their thirtieth anniversary."

"That's quite a gift."

"You should see what he got her."

So she was one of *those* Wesleys. Interesting. He'd resisted doing research, instead wanting to learn her story naturally. He waited for her to continue, but she took a short promenade around the room. "All right, I'll bite. What did he get her?"

"A vacuum."

"Really?" What would pop out of her mouth next? "Did it compare well?"

"Yep. It was the one time she allowed him to buy something that plugged in as a gift." She glanced at him, eyes dancing with joy. What he wouldn't give to bottle that up and diffuse it around the town that took itself too seriously.

"What?" The joy slowly leeched from her eyes. "Do I have something on my face?"

He leaned toward her and touched her cheek. She stilled, and he felt time stop as her lips parted, whether in surprise or agreement, he wasn't sure. "It looks perfect from here." Her eyes invited him closer, and he took a half step. "Emilie, I'd like nothing more than to—"

Her phone rang, some princess-sounding ditty, and she jerked back from him. "I'd better make sure that's not a client."

Reid nodded, inwardly cursing the call, even though it had saved him from going somewhere neither of them was ready to head.

"Jordan? Oh, hi."

Jordan? Not Jordan Westfall, the guy who could own two dozen Remingtons, real ones. When she hung up and turned back to him, her professional mask was in place. The one that would treat him kindly but maintain a clear do-not-cross line.

"Where's her room?"

"Right. Down this way." He guided her down the hall, but it didn't feel the same. The electricity between them had vanished with the call.

Reid had closed the door to his room and now steered her to what had been his man cave. What would Emilie think of the room? It had the required four walls, a door that locked, and a closet big enough to hold clothes for a small village. It also had an adjoining private bathroom. What more could a girl want?

That was just it—he didn't know. But Emilie would. He slanted a glance at her as she walked into the room; it felt small with all the furniture pulled toward the center, away from the walls. He'd ask Brandon to help move it to storage and his exercise equipment to the corner of his own bedroom. Then he'd get a bed and other furniture for Kinley. Or maybe he should wait until he knew if she'd need a special hospital bed for a while. The thought made his heart freeze. The journey she'd experienced was one no one should experience, and he wanted to protect her.

"Hey, none of that." Emilie must have read the anxiety in his face. "She'll be okay, and we'll get her here." There was oomph to her words, yet as she showed him the pale lavender shade she'd selected he wondered if she believed her brave words. They had a long road to complete while the clock ran faster all the time.

He shook the can of paint while she applied painter's tape around the baseboards. "How many cans do you have?"

"Just the one. I hope it'll be enough." She sat back on her heels and studied the walls. "I didn't want to buy too much, but covering this brown might take an extra coat." She kept taping from a position that looked like some funky yoga pose.

He checked the gallon. "You got the paint with primer, so we should be fine. It goes on thicker." He pulled out his phone and piped music through a speaker, then placed tarps over the carpet while she prepped the paintbrushes. "Sure you don't want to roll?"

"Oh no." Her voice was adamant. "The last time I

did that I had speckles all over my clothes and hands. Maybe my face too."

He laughed at the image. "I can picture that."

"I looked like I was trying to be a Smurf or had blue chicken pox. Not my finest hour." She held up a brush with a sharp angle. "I'll use this to edge."

The time passed quickly as they worked around the room, making easy conversation.

Her intrigue factor escalated as he learned her favorite movies (chick flicks with a fair mix of epic movies), favorite novels (*Pride and Prejudice* and *To Kill a Mockingbird*), and favorite vacation destination (mountains every time). It would take time to piece together what all of this revealed, but he wanted to peel back more layers in the pursuit of her heart.

He'd never considered pursuing a woman's heart before. Any dates he'd had might be enjoyable, but he'd never seen any type of long-term future . . . until Emilie. And it felt too new to allow his thoughts to travel that direction. If their legal pursuit was successful, he'd also be extremely busy with Kinley. He'd never had a child, let alone a ten-year-old.

As the paint went on the wall, the color had a richness that paled as it dried into a color that reminded him of fields of lavender he'd seen in southern France. "I hope Kinley likes it."

He didn't voice the hope that she'd even get to see it.

Emilie set the brush down in the tray, stood, and then slowly arched her back and twisted her neck from side to side. "This is a tween's dream room. Wait until we get it decorated."

Should he mention the streak of paint on her cheek? Nah. He kind of liked the soft, vulnerable look it gave her. Like she was little more than a kid herself. But as she came to stand next to him and leaned her head against his shoulder to admire the room, he knew she wasn't a kid. She was all woman. A rare breed of professional and caring. Sweet and spicy. Engaging and contained. And as she offered him a Double Stuf Oreo, utterly adorable.

CHAPTER 41

There was one thing Emilie would never admit to another soul. Clothes scared her. Hayden would never believe it, choosing instead to accept the carefully crafted image Emilie had created. If her best friend didn't understand this intimate detail about her, then Emilie knew she was destined to be misunderstood.

Strangely, that idea didn't bother her, except today.

Now that she needed to dress for an evening with Jordan, she felt ill equipped. He was far wealthier than her family, and if she were honest, that intimidated her. She also felt weird about accepting his invitation. He'd caught her on the phone at Reid's, and rather than get into an awkward conversation Reid could hear, she'd said yes. Now she had to honor that promise, even though she wanted nothing more than a night at home in yoga pants and a tee. Muscles in her arms and back ached from her full afternoon of painting the day before.

Her phone beeped an alert. She had fifteen minutes to get ready for a "mystery date." Jordan had been oblique about plans, telling her to be hungry and ready for entertainment.

She chewed her lower lip as she considered her wardrobe. Without knowing more, she could opt for overdressed or not. Her mother insisted one should strive to be the best dressed woman in a room. The advice usually served her well, so she flicked through her closet, bypassing dress after dress until her gaze landed on a black number she'd picked up at a Nordstrom Rack sale at least a year ago. She tugged it out and grinned.

Black silk with a hint of lace along the bodice, with a full skirt that hit above her knee in a flow of fabric. It was perfectly feminine, summery, and with a pashmina scarf would work about anywhere he took her. And if he took her canoeing, he deserved to paddle away all by his lonesome.

Her phone dinged at her again, and she jumped. She'd wasted ten minutes trying to decide what to wear. She flew through changing, teasing her hair into loose beach waves and swiping on enough makeup to give her eyes a sultry look.

She was slipping on her Kate Spade polka dot kitten heels when she heard a sharp knock at the front door. She grabbed her silver shawl and hurried up the stairs across the floor to open the door, stopping in her tracks when she spotted the black Lincoln Town Car waiting at the curb. It was a good thing she could slip out without Hayden seeing and teasing her about the ride.

One of the bodyguards from the basketball game stood outside the car, dressed in a black shirt and slacks. He opened the back door, and she peered into the interior.

Jordan grinned at her from the backseat, looking

like an excited boy band singer. There was an enthusiasm in his expression that tugged an answering smile from her. He reached toward her, and she let him pull her lightly down beside him. "You look stunning."

Warmth traveled up Emilie's neck, and she wished the sunlight didn't reveal everything. "Thank you."

"I hope you're ready for a night that will live up to you."

"Where are you taking me?" Maybe she was beyond crazy to get into a car with a man she barely knew. No, he was the crazy one for chasing her.

"Some things are more enjoyable as surprises."

"Hmm." She settled back against the cool black leather, tugging the shawl around her shoulders to protect her skin from the shock.

He tugged the shawl down along her left arm, and she fought the shiver he'd released. "John, can you turn up the temperature? The princess is cold." There was a teasing quality to his voice, teasing yet . . .

No, she was crazy. She couldn't see a stalker behind every man, every shadow.

Dinner was an intimate corner table at Georgia Brown's, the gold art scrolling along the ceiling twinkling in the light of the tea lights that matched the gold velvet of their booth. Emilie felt a tad overdressed, but kept her chin up as Jordan ordered for her, an act that left her wanting to protest she was more than up to the task.

However, as the fried green tomatoes arrived, followed by entrées of low-country shrimp for her and ribs for him, she couldn't complain. Her companion kept up a charming stream of conversation, leaving small pauses for eating.

"Dessert?" The waiter stood expectantly, as if sure she couldn't turn down any of the delectable offerings.

She placed a hand on her stomach and shook her head with a smile. "Not tonight. It was all so good, I forgot to save room." She glanced at Jordan and was surprised to find a scowl on his face. "I'm happy to wait while you have something."

He glared at her, then scrubbed the expression from his face and turned a charming smile on the young waitress. "I'll take the check. We'll return another time for your cobbler and homemade ice cream."

"All right, sir." The waitress scurried off, and five minutes later they stood on the sidewalk as the Town Car pulled to the curb. Soon they were gliding along Vermont Avenue and then, after a couple turns, on 15th Street. The Washington Monument pointed above the trees, and to the right the grass and park area led to the White House.

"Where are we headed?" There was something about the way Jordan was releasing information that struck Emilie as controlling rather than romantic. If it had been Reid, it would have seemed different, and she wondered if she was being fair. Maybe Jordan was one of those wealthy men who had created their fortune but didn't have all the social graces to accompany it.

"To an experience I doubt you've had before."

"Oh?" She slipped toward the door and angled toward him to cover the motion. "I've lived in the DC area for years."

"True, but there's a reason we say people are never tourists in their own backyard."

The car turned along Constitution in the direction of Georgetown, slowly passing the monuments as it went. The sight of them reminded her how privileged she was to live in this great city. The monuments anchored her to the experience and reminded her that many issues bigger than those she managed were decided here.

"Do you remember the first time we met?"

"You mean at the Haven?"

"No, that's not where I first saw you."

His dark eyes held her gaze with an intensity that made her want to blink, but she couldn't. It was like he mesmerized her, and she didn't understand that hold on her.

"Don't tell me you don't remember."

"Now I do." She fluttered her eyelashes at him, feeling silly and coquettish, but relieved the car was slowing to a stop at the drop-off point. "You must mean the fund-raiser."

"You were stunning, though not as beautiful as you are tonight. The emerald cocktail dress you wore made your eyes come alive. And your hair." He reached up to touch a wave, and she refused to flinch. "It was up, but loose. Elegant and casual at the same time."

She smiled but looked away. The weight of his gaze was heavy on her in the silence. "It was an amazing night." She'd been focused on the clients who had come to share their stories. It had taken true courage for those women to stand in front of strangers and recount their stories and admit the fairy tale had been a nightmare. "What did you think of the event?"

"The Haven wasn't a clear fit with my funding goals at that time."

"That's too bad, because those women's stories touched many."

He shrugged as he sank against the leather seat. "Just not me." He frowned. "Looks like we're here."

Emilie nodded, uncomfortable both with the knowledge he'd paid such attention to her back then and that he still wouldn't tell her what the night's agenda was. In another setting the surprise might be romantic, but right now it unsettled her.

That feeling built as he guided her through the crowds inside the Kennedy Center, his hand firm on her back. She had to resist the urge to shiver and step away.

They strolled through the Hall of States with its flags soaring overhead as they hung in order of admission to the Union and then through the Grand Foyer, where the view of the river across the terrace was peaceful yet compelling. They wove through those chatting in small groups or flipping through program bills. "Are we on display?"

"It's always good to be seen." Jordan nodded to several people as they passed, but didn't stop at any group.

He pulled two slim tickets from his jacket pocket and handed them to the attendant at the entrance to the Hall of Nations.

The young woman scanned the tickets. "Do you need help finding your box, sir?"

"Not tonight."

"We're in a box?"

"Of course. You're with me." He took the program the woman offered and then led Emilie to a staircase. A minute later he led her into a box that overlooked the Concert Hall from the back of the stage.

The red cushions contrasted with the gold and warm wood tones. Emilie couldn't resist leaning over the edge of the box. "I've never watched a performance from this side."

"You'll enjoy it." No question, simply a statement of fact.

CHAPTER 42

The show was a whirl of music, but no audience interaction. Emilie felt off balance as she tried to take cues from Jordan without being obvious. Once the music started he ignored her, and during intermission he disappeared, only to return with two wine flutes. She didn't know how to tell him she didn't drink, so she held it without taking a sip. He didn't seem to notice, yet she had the sense he cataloged everything she did . . . and didn't do.

As she watched him, something niggled at her mind. There was a detail she was overlooking.

He had a comfort with and knowledge of her she didn't share of him. She normally remembered people she had interacted with for any length of time. So how had this happened? Had he done intensive research? Even in this high-tech world, who would get a full background on a potential date? Then again, if she had multiple millions of dollars she might do the same.

But she didn't, and the thought that he had researched her was troubling.

When she shivered in the second movement, he took her shawl and placed it around her shoulders, a finger trailing the length of her arm. She looked at him, taken aback by the intensity in his gaze. It was as if he was hungrily looking for something in her eyes.

The ride back to her town house was quiet, but he kept her firmly at his side, then walked her to the door.

She tried to put space between them, because the thought of a good-night kiss made her feel as uncomfortable as her middle school self. Jordan was handsome, but he didn't make her feel anything . . . nothing like Reid did. She pulled out her keys. "Thank you for an enjoyable evening."

"We should do this again." There was an eagerness to his expression that made her hesitant to refuse outright.

"I don't know, Jordan."

"I'll call you, and we can set a time."

She stared at him, noting his heightened color.

"We'll be perfect together." He leaned closer to her, and her breath caught.

"I'm really busy right now." She backed into the door and felt for the doorknob. Tested it. Unlocked. She felt a release inside. "Thank you again."

"Don't make me mad, Emilie." The quietness of Jordan's words brought her up short.

"I wouldn't do that."

"Good." He nodded to her. "Good night." He pivoted on his heel and marched to his car.

Emilie watched until it pulled away, frozen in place.

Emilie woke up the next morning still feeling troubled. Before she got out of bed she Googled Jordan. He'd attended a local public high school before heading to college and his app success. She adjusted the pillows at her back while she thought about what little she'd learned. She could swear she'd never met him before the fund-raiser at the Haven. And now he was being courted as a top donor with instant access to Rhoda.

Could Jordan somehow be involved in the growing mess of her life? Even if it felt like a stretch, it was an idea she needed to pursue. The fact that the guy seemed very focused on her didn't mean anything— maybe he did that with every woman he met. He had that accomplished yet stiff air that so many smart men had in relationships. It took one conversation to know he was brilliant . . . and awkward.

And much as she wanted to deny it, she had to admit there was an appeal to his attention.

With all the beautiful women in the city, why would he focus on someone like her who didn't hit the top ten single women list?

Emilie was barely settled at her desk when Taylor appeared in her doorway, and without so much as a good morning launched into work.

"I've been thinking about your email—about Kaylene coming once a week. Social work and counseling see clients more often than we do, but every week seems extreme." She glanced down at the legal pad in her hand. "What made you ask about once a week?"

"Reid found a recurring note in Kaylene's calendar. Every Thursday afternoon from four to five the girls had piano lessons in Old Town, and she had a notation for an accompanying appointment at 'the H.' He wondered if that could be here, but I didn't see her anywhere near that often, even when we were actively engaged."

"It strikes me as too often also, even if she received career counseling. I checked our corporate calendar to see if we were offering a class during that time frame, but I didn't see anything that applied to Kaylene."

"That was a good idea." One she should have thought of. "What about job training?"

"I checked our database, and she received job-hunting and resume-building help, so that could explain some of the entries."

"Maybe there's another company or nonprofit she was going to."

"That won't be easy to determine." Taylor held up a phone book. "I've gone through this, but with the way the communities in Northern Virginia blend together, it's not a quick search."

"Based on time constraints it would have to be close to Old Town, if not right here."

"Still not easy to find."

Emilie jotted a note on her own legal pad. "I'll poke around some, but I agree that we'll start by assuming she was meeting someone here." The question remained who. She set down her pen and looked at Taylor. "New topic. What do you know about Jordan Westfall?"

"Other than he's fabulously wealthy, hot, and a little odd? Not much."

"Dig into his background for me, would you? Cautiously." Emilie did not want to send signals to the man that someone was investigating him, though it seemed fair since he'd done the same to her. "He took me out to dinner and a concert at the Kennedy Center last night. I'm not sure what to think about him, but he's an important donor. He is odd though. Something doesn't feel right."

"It never feels right to have a fabulous guy ask you on a date." Taylor rolled her eyes. "If he asked me, I'd say yes in a New York minute."

"What does that saying mean anyway? We're not from New York, so why would we care about a New York minute?"

"I don't know, but that doesn't change my answer. There's no reason to say no."

"But there isn't a reason to say yes." Not all men were created equal, a truth this job highlighted in neon colors. Men like Reid were rare, and he reminded her that she could find a man who treated her like a treasure rather than a possession.

Taylor cleared her throat, and Emilie snapped back to the present.

She needed to shake distractions—like Jordan Westfall. Time was ticking away, and unless she was successful, Kinley would be irrevocably in the custody of her father. The more time that elapsed between the tragic events and a hearing, the more difficult it would be to prove to a judge there were exigent circumstances.

What she was doing wasn't working. She had pieces of evidence, but not the key piece.

CHAPTER 43

The rest of the day passed in a blur as she finalized the motions she'd read to block Kinley's departure from the hospital. It seemed every time she hit her stride, Taylor was in her office with another urgent question. The stress showed in her assistant's hunched shoulders and tight face when she appeared again at five.

"I'm leaving if you don't need me."

"I'm good. What are you up to tonight?"

"Going swing dancing with a friend."

"Sounds like a great way to let go of stress."

Taylor's face relaxed from its tense mask. "More than you know. There's something about knowing I look like a fool out there, but not caring. My friend tells me I'm getting better each time."

Emilie matched her grin. "I'm sure you are. Maybe I'll come with you sometime. It sounds fun."

Once the office was quiet again, Emilie quickly worked through the letters and motions Taylor had prepared throughout the day. If opposing counsel would cooperate instead of delaying until Emilie's clients gave up, life would be better. Was the best lawyer the one who advocated hard for their client? Or could the best lawyer be the one who delayed? She wasn't sure, but as she watched the stack of letters and motions move from the left-hand side of her desk to the right, she knew half of the pile would evaporate if she had an attorney on the other side who cared to do an efficient job. Still, she managed to get through the urgent matters and get good, clean drafts of the documents she needed for Kinley. She'd touch base with Reid and then sign the filings tomorrow so they could get to court before the hospital released the girl. As much as she'd love to have perfect evidence, she'd have to settle for what they had.

She rolled her neck, feeling the tightness that had settled there. Time to get a massage and release the tension her shoulders held tightly like a scarf.

Since she didn't have time for that, she'd walk home and use that time when all was bright and crowds were still about to clear her head and find the equilibrium she'd need to finish preparations for filing the emergency guardianship petition in the morning.

When Emilie reached home, she could feel the sweat pooling in the small of her back. Even with tourists throughout Old Town, she'd hurried her pace, eager to get home. It had been a few days since she'd heard from her shadow. Maybe he had disappeared and she didn't need to look over her shoulder all the time. Still, the walk hadn't cleared her head as she'd hoped. Guess she'd get Hayden to drive her back to get her car, but first she'd change into something cool and sit on top of the air-conditioner vents. Then she'd have her head examined. Only someone who was incredibly distracted would think a stroll in the humidity would clear her mind.

The blast of air when she entered the town house was the cool dousing she needed. A shiver traveled up her back, and she hurried to the basement. After she set down her bag, she splashed cool water on her face and then patted a damp washcloth around her neck. Water droplets dotted the front of her crimson silk shell, and she froze. The water darkened the already rich blouse until it looked like blood.

She froze at the image, her mind moving to the pictures of Kaylene's and Kaydence's bodies covered by white sheets.

"Emilie?"

She jerked, then she reached up trembling fingers and touched the mirror.

"Emilie?" The voice was closer, and Emilie closed her eyes and whispered a prayer.

God, I can't do this anymore. I need Your help. All of my efforts are failing, and it's too easy to imagine that Kinley will join her family. How can I save her? A tear slipped down her cheek, but she ignored it. *I can't, but You can. Give me wisdom and bring the truth to light. If I can be part of that process, use me.*

When she opened her eyes, she saw the beginnings of peace reflected in her gaze.

"There you are." Hayden stepped into the thin visage of the mirror. Her navy suit was slightly wrinkled from the day, but her lipstick looked fresh. "I wanted to let you know—" She stopped and stepped closer. Her head tilted as she studied Emilie, and her brows met in the crease over her nose. "What's wrong?"

Emilie shook her head. "Nothing. Everything. But I'm praying about it."

"Okay. Is there anything I can do?"

"I don't really know. I just need to move. I think I've gotten so trapped in everything we don't know that I'm forgetting what we do have."

"Sometimes you have to put it in front of a judge."

"We're definitely there. It's got to happen tomorrow morning if we want to act before Kinley's released."

"Then you will, and knowing you, you will have a well-thought-out argument. Or a creative one."

"I'm hoping for convincing." Emilie forced a smile. "What do you need?"

"Nothing. You left the upstairs door cracked." Hayden shivered, and Emilie knew where her mind had gone. "I let that rattle me. Wanted to see you were okay."

"I am."

"Sure." There was skepticism in her voice, but Hayden took a slight step back, the signal that she would give Emilie the space she needed. It was one of her roommate's characteristics that Emilie valued . . . the willingness to wait. But in that moment, she almost wished Hayden would push.

Hayden must have read the silent plea, because she reached for Emilie. "Hey, it'll be okay."

Emilie closed her eyes, refusing to cry over a name-less fear. She blew out a slow breath, then opened her eyes and looked in the mirror. "It all became too much for a minute."

Hayden cocked a hand on her hip and made a so-what gesture. "We all have that moment some days. How can I help?"

"You could give me a ride to my car."

"Did it break down?"

"No, but I must have. I thought walking home today would clear my mind. Instead, it muddied it further."

"Of course it did. The heat index is over one hundred. I'll get you a glass of water and then change. One ride coming up."

"Thanks." Emilie forced a grin and stepped into her bedroom. Five minutes later she was dressed in a pair of white denim capris and a gauzy shirt with butterfly sleeves. As she sipped the water with cucumber slices, she could feel it flow through her. Maybe she could blame the incident in the bathroom on dehydration. That sounded better than stress.

The drive back to the office was quiet, and when Emilie climbed out, Hayden leaned out the window. "Do you want me to wait?"

"No, go ahead." If everyone was gone, she could take the opportunity to do a quick search of Rhoda's office. That wasn't something she'd tell Hayden though. "I need to do something, but I should be back in an hour or so."

"All right. I'm meeting Andrew for dinner." A soft blush colored her friend's cheeks, matching her rose T-shirt. "See you when I get home."

"I'll wait up."

Hayden rolled her eyes, then closed her window and pulled from the curb.

Emilie waited until Hayden turned, then tugged her

office keys free of her purse. As she glanced at the parking lot, she saw that her car was the last one in the lot. Still, it felt like someone was watching her. She did a slow turn but didn't see anyone. "Hello?"

She waited, though she knew her shadow wouldn't answer if he were there. Her stalker liked the act of the chase. What happened when the chase ended or she stopped playing?

Time to get inside and away from whoever's prying eyes were on her.

The key stuck in the lock as she tried to cram it in and twist. "Come on."

She felt the gaze getting closer. *You've read too much suspense, Emilie.*

No, she'd lived too many clients' stories. It took no effort for her mind to spin out what could happen if someone were watching. Finally, as she frantically twisted one last time, she felt the lock move.

She pulled the door and fell inside, letting the door fall closed beneath her weight. "Pull it together, Wesley." She listened for the click of the lock reengaging.

The office was dark, so she flipped on a light before heading through the warren, making sure no one was in a darkening office. It would be hard to explain if someone stumbled on her. She wasn't doing anything wrong . . . really. If she asked, normally Rhoda would be forthcoming. But her boss had forbidden her to pursue Kaylene's case any further, and Emilie couldn't help but feel something was going on.

She slipped through the open office door and sat at Rhoda's desk.

Where would her boss put the files that contained the information she needed? She swiveled the chair to the wall of file cabinets behind Rhoda's desk. When she handed Emilie files about various current clients, she tended to go to the cabinets immediately behind her desk. Could the files for old clients be on either side? Would she have filed Kaylene's there? Where would she store the funders' files?

It could take all night to pull each drawer and thumb through the sea of information. Emilie needed a strategy. She tugged on the first file drawer, but found it and the others locked. She turned to Rhoda's desk and pulled out the junk drawer. Instead of an assortment of pens, erasers, paper clips, and other office supplies, Rhoda's were neatly ordered to the point of compulsiveness. If she shifted the contents, Emilie had the feeling Rhoda would sense it as soon as she opened the drawer. So she settled for easing open the rest of the drawers, one at a time, and lightly fanning through the files, shifting them as little as possible.

Something was wrong with the last desk drawer. The contents didn't go low enough to hit the true bottom. She eased back on the chair. To see why there was a gap, she'd have to remove the files. What would she find, and did she want to know it?

She eased the files out, careful to keep them in orderly piles for replacing. When the last files came out, she found a legal-sized expandable folder had been placed down on its flat side, creating a cheap false bottom. Emilie pulled it out and discovered a file resting beneath it. She eased it out and opened it. Kaylene's file. She flipped through the pages and found several handwritten notes. *Kaylene is regressing. Is it something happening at home? Could it be the gun safety classes? Are the challenges of escaping too real?*

Why would Rhoda deny any knowledge of the gun if she had known all along about the classes?

Lindsey says she's making progress, but is it fast enough? Need to get her out now. The date beside that note was only two weeks before Kaylene died. Why hadn't Rhoda told her?

CHAPTER 44

Emilie heard a noise in the hallway and threw the file into her briefcase. She had to see if there was anything else in it that could help Kinley. She could come in early tomorrow to return everything. She hurriedly replaced the expandable file and then slid the other files on top, then she stood and looked around the desk and other surfaces. Everything looked as it had when she arrived.

She listened, but didn't hear anything else, so she stepped into the hallway and flipped off the office light.

"What are you doing?"

Emilie dropped her bag. "Replacing a file."

"You mean taking one." Rhoda pushed Emilie back into her office. "Why were you searching my office?"

"I'm running out of time to help Kinley and needed answers."

"And you couldn't just ask me?"

"No." Emilie winced as the light came back on. "I'm sorry, Rhoda, but I can't ignore what's happening. And neither could you." She held up her bag. "Just tell me why you were hiding files on Kaylene and not telling me the whole truth."

"You wouldn't understand." Her boss's shoulders were set, and even in a velour running suit she looked intimidating.

"I'd like to."

Rhoda gestured to a chair in front of her desk. "You might as well sit." Then she walked behind her desk and sank to the chair Emilie had vacated.

"Why did you come in?"

"I have work I need to finish tonight." She glanced around her domain. "I guess I know why you were here."

"Help me understand."

"Kaylene was a classmate of mine at Virginia."

"What?" That was the last thing Emilie had expected Rhoda to say.

Rhoda nodded and then brushed her short hair behind her ears. "I was about ten years older. It took me a while to figure out what I wanted to be when I grew up. Kaylene and I had some classes together. After we graduated and she got married, we stayed in touch. When I sensed something was wrong, I asked her to come here."

"When was this?"

"A couple years ago. This was not a new problem for her. It took time to rebuild her self-esteem, longer to form a plan." She leaned back and deflated. "It wasn't enough."

"I wish I'd known all this, Rhoda. Did she tell you details about what was happening at home?"

"Just that Robert was escalating. It was enough to make her fear he'd turn on the girls, especially since Kaydence was becoming belligerent. Kaylene knew time was running out."

"We all did."

"And we couldn't stop it." Rhoda scrubbed her face with her hands. "I've wondered what we could have done differently."

"I have too."

"I tried so hard to help her. How could she use our help to hurt the girls and kill herself?"

"She didn't." Emilie heard the certainty in her words.

"You can't know that."

"But I choose to believe it until the police can give me irrefutable evidence. They haven't."

Rhoda shook her head. "You're being stubborn." She reached for a file. "I don't know what to think, but I need to get this done tonight."

"Is it anything I can help with?"

"Not unless you have the time and interest to write a grant proposal for Jordan Westfall. He might like to see your name on it. He seems to be fascinated with you."

"I only met him briefly at the fund-raiser. I never spent any time with him until last night."

A voice spoke from the doorway. "We weren't friends."

Emilie jolted as Rhoda paled. "Jordan?"

He gave a little bow. "Here to protect you, but I guess you don't need that."

"I don't?" Emilie eyed him warily. Rhoda was shifting slightly in her chair, and Emilie worked to keep his attention on her. "How did you know I was here?"

"I always know where you are." His smile was forced. "You only go a few places. It makes it easy to find you."

"I suppose your bodyguards help."

He stepped through the doorway, hands buried in

the pockets of a hoodie that looked too warm for an August night. "Who said I need help?" He turned to Rhoda. "We meet again."

"Mr. Westfall." Her voice was hard yet not surprised, and she stilled her actions while she watched him.

"Let's come back to the idea we aren't friends." Jordan sat in the chair next to Emilie, his gaze flitting between the two of them.

Emilie's pulse pounded, but she knew she had to remain placid on the outside. Any indication she wasn't comfortable with him would backfire. "I spent time this morning learning all I could about you."

"Find it boring?" His voice sounded wounded, though his face remained a mask.

"Not at all." She schooled her voice to a gentle tone, when what she wanted to do was yell at him to get out of her life and leave her alone.

He turned to Rhoda. "Selling my business was supposed to change that." Jordan dug his fists more deeply into his pockets. Color slowly filled his face, the kind that mottled it and signaled anger.

She needed words that would calm the rising tension and buy time for her to entice Jordan to leave. "Jordan, it doesn't matter. Tell me what you need. You have so much, it must be something important."

"I want you." His words sounded like those of a young boy, one looking for reassurance.

"You've accomplished so much. A Google search shows how many people see you."

"But they don't really. They see what they need from me. Like your boss there."

"I don't need anything." Rhoda's voice was firm and her gaze direct, but Emilie noticed her hands moving along the underside of her desk.

"Oh, but you do. You want a check. All I wanted was Emilie." He looked at Rhoda and pulled a hand from his hoodie.

At a glint of metal Emilie inhaled sharply.

"Even when I came here to save your little agency."

"We will gladly accept your donation, but you need to decide what you want to do." Rhoda pursed her lips. "There are restrictions on how we can use funds."

Jordan's head jerked around, and he pointed a small gun at Rhoda. "I don't need your help."

With his attention deflected from her, Emilie tried to slide her hand into her pocket. It was too tight of a fit to slide her phone out. Darn skinny capris. Could she somehow get to the emergency screen? While Rhoda kept his attention, Emilie tried, but couldn't get room to swipe. Her hands trembled and she felt a sinking sensation.

"Jordan, your help is valuable." Rhoda's voice was firm, the one she used with clients who were losing focus. It seemed to work, because Jordan straightened. "It's the way you want to do it that needs finesse."

"I'm a successful businessman."

"You're a brilliant businessman, but that doesn't mean you know what's best for our clients. This is a specialized enterprise."

"I know that. I'm successful," he yelled.

Rhoda's eyebrows peaked in that look all mothers and women in authority had mastered, the one that warned that their baloney meter was pinging.

"Jordan, why me?" Emilie needed to buy Rhoda time. Maybe her boss would have more success reaching out for help. And if she delayed long enough, Hayden might notice she hadn't come home. "You could have anyone in the world."

"Then it's all about the money. You don't need my money. You could simply want me."

"I understand wanting to be loved for who you are."

"Exactly. But you were always unimpressed."

"It's not every day I sit in a box seat."

"But you weren't wowed."

It was true. She'd been too creeped out by his attention to relax into the experience. Out of the corner of her eye, she noticed Rhoda slip something from her desk. "What's your dream, Jordan?"

His attention whipped back to Emilie as he frowned. "What?"

"You've accomplished so much already, but what's next? What gets you up in the morning?"

"You." He lifted his gun to aim at her chest. "You're the one for me and no one else. But you never said thank you."

Okay, now she was seriously scared. Emilie raised her hands in front of her, the muscle in her shoulder throbbing as she did. "When did you decide to follow me? Was it after the fund-raiser?"

"Yes. Someone else was watching you too. I tried to take care of him, but it didn't work."

"Was that when you shot my car by accident?"

"It wasn't supposed to happen. I sent lots of flowers. Did you like them?"

"The roses? Yes, they were nice."

"No, I sent irises. A field of them."

Did he mean to the hospital? She'd received so many flowers, she'd lost track of who sent them. "Did you include a card?"

"You should have known they were from me."

She could tell he was in deadly earnest. He believed things had happened exactly as he said. There would be no convincing him otherwise. "They were beautiful."

Rhoda moved, and Jordan whipped his attention back to her. Rhoda had a small gun in her hand. Where had that been when Emilie checked the desk drawers?

Jordan pointed his gun at her again. "You didn't want to do that, Ms. Sterling."

"Oh yes, I did. You need to put that gun down and leave, Jordan." She kept her gun locked on Jordan, but her words were for Emilie. "I will protect you, Emilie, in all the ways I couldn't protect Kaylene." She tightened her grip on the gun. "You can lower that gun now or when the police arrive, the choice is yours."

Two shots rang out, a split second apart.

Emilie felt time slow.

Jordan turned to her. His gun wavered. "Help me."

She turned to Rhoda.

Saw blood gush from her neck.

Her boss gurgled, shuddered, tried to breathe.

Blood poured everywhere.

Emilie turned back to Jordan, saw the gun.

Aimed at her.

CHAPTER 45

Emilie's phone went to voicemail. If Reid wanted to reach her, he'd have to go to her. Normally he wouldn't do that so late in the evening, but the word that Kinley would be released in the morning had hit his panic button. It was time to get his niece home, and he needed Emilie to make that happen. They needed to act.

He pushed the speed limit the whole way to Old Town and double-parked in front of her town house. When he pounded on the door he half expected a neighbor to call the police, but he didn't care. He needed Emilie.

The door opened after a minute, and her roommate stood there. "Is there a reason you're pounding on my door at ten o'clock?"

"I need Emilie."

"She wasn't here when I got home a bit ago. I was about to check on her since she's not returning calls."

"That's why I'm here. My niece is supposed to be released tomorrow. We have to file first thing in the morning." He could feel the adrenaline pulsing through him. He'd been planning for this moment for two weeks, but now that it was here, he was afraid they hadn't found the key evidence necessary to do more than annoy Robert.

"I dropped her off at the Haven, so that's where I planned to check."

"I'll go."

He turned and was halfway back to his car before she replied.

He drove fast and arrived at the building within a few minutes. Emilie's car rested in the parking lot along with two others—one was Jordan's BMW roadster. Reid frowned and checked for his cell phone before climbing out. He tried Emilie again as he walked to the front door. It was locked, and the call again went to her voicemail. He slipped around to the back door and eased the unlocked door open. He didn't know if there was an alarm, but he wouldn't mind if it brought the police. Something wasn't right.

He shut the door with a soft *thud* and took a moment to get his bearings in the subdued lighting. He didn't have any idea where Emilie's office was, so he started down the hall, slowing to look inside each room. He reached one marked with her name, but it was empty.

Reid continued down the hall and around to the next. A lone office at the end of the hall had lights on. Voices filtered from inside. Though he couldn't understand the words, the tension was clear.

He had shifted closer, phone in hand, when shots were fired. He flicked the screen on his phone and hit the emergency button and then the next, then eased closer to the door.

"You don't need to do this." He felt a surge of relief at hearing Emilie's voice.

"911, please state your emergency." The garbled voice sounded so loud in the empty hallway.

"Who's there?"

Was that Jordan? His voice was reedy yet forceful.

"Come out before I shoot the beauty across from me." He cackled. "Get it. You're the beauty, Miss Wesley. I'm the beast."

"Jordan, please don't."

Reid chucked caution and closed the distance to the door. He stuck his head around the corner and quickly pulled back. A woman was dead at the desk, and Emilie and Jordan Westfall sat in chairs in front of it. Reid slipped his head back around for a quick look, and a bullet zinged past his head.

"I'd be careful if I were you, Billings. I'd like nothing more than to take your head off."

"No need to do that."

"Reid, be careful. He shot Rhoda." Emilie sounded scared, yet a cord of strength ran through her words. "I'm okay."

"911, you need to state your emergency."

Reid groaned and set the phone down. If the operator couldn't figure out a gun had been fired at his head, then he'd have to handle this alone. "I'm coming in there."

As soon as he stepped around the corner, he noted that Jordan didn't look so good. Blood streamed from a wound in the left part of his chest. It didn't look high enough to be his heart, but Reid wasn't great at anatomy. "Didn't expect to see you here, Jordan."

"I expected you." Jordan grinned wolfishly at him. "The only way to have Emilie for myself is to get you out of the way."

The guy wasn't talking sense. There was no way he could know Reid would try to reach Emilie or track her down. Emilie took a deep breath and focused on Jordan. "Let me get an ambulance for you. Maybe we can still save Rhoda and keep this from being a murder charge."

Jordan cocked his head as he studied the woman on the other side of the desk. "I think it's too late for her. You see what happens when you belittle me."

"Jordan, you don't need to listen to any of those voices."

Reid edged forward as Emilie talked.

"Don't make this worse."

. . .

"Then choose me." In his words, Emilie heard the eleven-year-old overlooked for every game. The fourteen-year-old stuffed in a locker. The twenty-eight-year-old still ignored by others except for his wealth.

"I am so sorry. Forgive me for not seeing you."

His jaw slipped open.

"I can't explain it or make it better, but I am genuinely sorry." She clasped her hands in front of her, almost begging him to stay focused on her as Reid stepped closer to his chair. Then the sound of a police siren jerked Jordan back. "Please let me get you help, Jordan. There's so much blood."

He looked down at his shirt, but his motions were so slow, as if his body couldn't quite follow instructions. "I'll be okay."

Reid caught her attention, motioned her down with his eyes, and she nodded. "Jordan, I want to help you."

"You can't." His words were slurred, and Emilie jumped from her chair as his gun hand rose, wavered, floated in response. He pulled the trigger, but Reid forced his arm up as Emilie slipped behind the desk to Rhoda.

"Rhoda, can you hear me? Stay with me." She wanted to take a pulse at her boss's neck, but there was so much blood, she reached for her arm instead. She grappled with her hand, placing two fingers along the ridge of bone, not feeling anything.

"Police! Everyone put your hands where I can see them." The officer sheltered partly behind the door, speaking into his shoulder radio as he kept his gaze on them. "Officer requesting backup."

The next minutes were a blur. More officers arrived, then paramedics, but it was too late for Rhoda. Emilie began to tremble and couldn't stop as a second team of paramedics worked on Jordan while an officer questioned Reid. An officer moved Emilie out of the way and into a vacant office. All she could do was huddle in the chair, a blanket draped around her shoulders, as an officer took her statement. She answered questions, but couldn't clear the image of Rhoda's body from her mind. She might never understand how, but she knew Jordan was her stalker. As the paramedics whisked him from the office on a gurney, she knew it would be a long time before he could harass her again . . . if he even survived.

It seemed like a lifetime passed before Reid came to her. He leaned down and pulled her close. She felt the strength of his arms and began to weep. His hand smoothed her hair and she felt a safety she'd never known. "Why did you come?"

"You needed me."

CHAPTER 46

When Emilie got home, she couldn't sit still. No matter how many cups of hot tea Hayden placed in her hands, she felt chilled to the core. "I should be okay. My stalker's gone."

Hayden sank next to her on the small love seat in her basement. "I'm so sorry."

Emilie leaned into Hayden's shoulder, feeling the warmth of sisterhood and friendship. "I'm so tired, but I know I can't sleep."

"Maybe a bath would help."

"No, Reid said Kinley's coming home tomorrow. We're out of time. I need to review the motions one more time for first thing tomorrow. I just wish . . ."

"What?"

"That we could win." The words felt so heavy, simple as they were. "I know what happened in that house, but I have no way to prove it. I didn't get to ask Rhoda why she helped Kaylene get the gun."

"Let's lay out what you do have. You've worked so hard on this case, I know there's more than you remember."

Emilie doubted it, but as she and Hayden talked through the evidence she felt a whisper of hope. "I'm going to check one more time for the 911 call. I just want one look into what happened in the house." She rubbed her temples where tension throbbed, then pulled out her phone and did another Internet search. Still nothing. But when she checked her email there was something from Detective Gaines.

> The forwarding officer forgot to include the 911 call you requested. I thought you had it last week. Sorry about that. My gut tells me there's more going on, but I can't find the thread that will pull. Let me know if you learn something.

Short and to the point, the message had a WAV file attached. "This is it." She could hardly hit the button, so much hope and adrenaline coursed through her.

"Here, I'll do it." Hayden reached over and clicked the button.

A moment later the file opened.

Operator: 911, what's the address of the emergency?
Female voice: She has a gun.
Static.
Operator: I have your location from your phone.
    Tell me what's going on.
Male voice: She has a gun.
Girl's voice: Daddy?
Woman's voice: I'll do anything. I'll say anything.
    Just put that away.
Operator: Sir, who has a gun?
Teenager's voice: Get back.

Man's voice: Calm down.

Teenager's voice: No. I'm done listening to you. Stay back.

Woman's voice: Sweetheart, what are you doing?

Teenager's voice: Ending this. He'll never hurt us again. I'm going to do what you couldn't.

Woman's voice: No. Watch out.

Shot.

Another shot.

Operator: Sir! Sir!

Man's voice: Omigod, she's shooting our daughter.

Operator: Officers are on the way and will be there any minute.

Man's voice: That's enough time.

Shot.

Operator: Sir, you need to tell me what's happened.

Shot.

Woman's voice, sobbing: What are you doing?

Man's voice: She's got the gun.

Click. End of call.

Silence settled. Emilie's thumb hovered over the play button as tears streaked her cheeks. It was surreal and painful to listen to the call. "This will help."

Hayden nodded. "But it'll still be a reach."

"With everything else I have it might be enough. 'That's enough time'?" A shiver ran through her as she recalled the cold-blooded statement.

"I'll transcribe it while you amend the motions. It won't take long at all." Hayden squeezed her. "Then we'll sleep."

The next morning Emilie called Taylor to pick up her files and bring them to Daniels, McCarthy & Associates. It would be a while before she could work from the Haven without reliving the prior night and seeing Rhoda slumped and bleeding across her desk. It only took a little time to get the motions and supporting documents finalized. At nine thirty she walked them to the General District Court and talked to the clerk.

"The hospital plans to release Kinley at noon, so I need an emergency hearing before then."

The clerk nodded as she scanned the calendar. "How soon can you have your witnesses here?"

"For the preliminary motion I was going to rely on documents and my client."

"Have him here along with anyone else in an hour." The clerk reached for the phone. "I'll call opposing counsel, and you can get the documents to her."

"Thank you." Emilie rubbed the back of her neck. The moment she left the clerk's office, she called Taylor. "Get the motions to Darlene Wright immediately."

"On my way. The copies are already faxed to the hospital."

Emilie called Reid next. "We're set for ten thirty. The hospital has our motions. I'll call the attorney there next to let him know that we have a hearing and not to release Kinley. Robert's attorney will let him know any minute."

"I'll be there." She could hear the fear and hope warring in his voice.

"Great. I need to make a couple more calls. See you

at court." Next she called Detective Gaines. "Thank you for the file."

"It was due."

"I have one more request."

He huffed out a laugh. "I thought you might."

"Could you be at Alexandria General Court at ten thirty?"

"Why?"

"I need to validate the file. Normally I wouldn't need you for a preliminary hearing, but opposing counsel has made it clear she'll fight hard." She left *and dirty* unsaid.

"I'll do my best."

After that Emilie paced the halls praying and working on her notes. At ten fifteen Taylor and Hayden accompanied her to the courtroom.

Hayden gave her a quick hug. "Hanging in there?"

"As much as I can on so little sleep."

"You'll do great. Taylor and I made sure everything you could possibly need is in this set of files. I'll sit next to you and hand things to you."

Emilie glanced between the two of them. "Thank you."

"Let's protect this little girl." Hayden gave her another quick hug, then slipped through the doors and into the courtroom, Taylor right behind her.

Emilie paced some more, watching for Reid.

When he arrived he placed his hands on her arms and stared at her. "You okay?"

"I will be once we get Kinley home." She let herself see the hope in his eyes and then led him into the courtroom.

"You can sit here." She indicated the seat on the left side of the table. She'd place herself between Reid and Robert, serve as the barrier to keep the competing men apart. Hayden sat immediately behind her, a stack of files ready on the chair next to her. Emilie set her brief-case on the table, unzipped it, and then pulled her client file and legal pads from it. Next she grabbed her blue and red erasable pens. Red to capture things opposing counsel and witnesses said that she needed to address. Blue to capture other thoughts and details. Then she zipped up her bag and set it behind her, out of the way.

Hayden leaned over and briefly explained how the files were organized.

"Thanks." Emilie puffed out a breath and braced her shoulders. She couldn't risk revealing one iota of weak-ness, not when Robert would sniff it out. The minutes ticked by as Emilie sat at the table waiting for anyone to enter. The judge wouldn't come out until the court reporter let him know all parties were accounted for. As time rolled on, Robert and his attorney were still absent. But so was Detective Gaines. She really needed him.

The door to the courtroom thundered shut behind them. Emilie about jumped out of her skin, but knew she couldn't let Robert Adams or his attorney see how rattled she was. She kept reminding herself that this was a preliminary hearing and everything didn't have to be perfect, though it would have to be practically so to convince the judge that Kinley must go home with Reid.

Her fear was the standards defaulted too much to biological parents.

She knew that most of the time that line fell in the correct place. But today she felt the inadequacy of the law. It didn't recognize that certain standards didn't always fit.

Would the 911 call be enough, when added to all the steps Kaylene had taken to prepare to leave with her girls? Would the letter from Kaylene add weight to the other evidence?

She turned and looked around the courtroom again, relieved to see Detective Gaines in a seat in the last row. He met her gaze with a nod. She released a breath and felt herself settle.

Reid seemed relaxed as he sat next to her, legs kicked out in front of him and ankles crossed. He looked every part the successful financial investor in his suit, monogrammed shirt, and classic tie. But she could sense the tension in his tightened jaw and clenched fists.

So much rode on this hearing.

She needed to use that pressure to channel her arguments, but all she felt was a stampede of fear chased by regret.

CHAPTER 47

"All rise." The bailiff's voice carried, and Emilie lurched to her feet, then urged Reid up.

Judge Robinson sailed into the courtroom with a firm set to her lips. She sat on her chair and studied them over her rhinestone-rimmed glasses. "You may be seated."

After they were all settled she read the docket number, the purpose of the hearing, and the names of those present. "I did not think I'd see you here so quickly. Mr. Adams, I'm glad you honored us with your presence today."

"Your Honor." He tipped his head but didn't look the least apologetic. His dark hair was long enough to curl at the ends, and his arms looked crammed into the button-down plaid shirt. Was he going for the Brawny man look?

The judge turned to Emilie. "I'm almost as surprised by your motion as I was by Ms. Wright's Friday."

"Yes, Your Honor." Emilie kept her gaze firmly locked on the judge. "We believe this motion is critical to the safety of a young girl."

"All right." She paused until everyone focused on

her. "We have no more than an hour for this hearing. Ms. Wesley, you may present your evidence. At that point I'll determine whether there is enough for a preliminary protective order and temporary guardianship. If there is, then, Ms. Wright, I will allow you to put on evidence. Who is your first witness?"

Emilie indicated Reid, and the judge swore him in. After he stated his name and relevant information for the record, Emilie began. She had him explain why he decided to pursue obtaining custody of Kinley. Answering her questions, he mentioned the card from Kaylene, the diamonds, her many visits to the Haven to plot her escape.

"Kaylene's letter confirmed what I already knew. That she wouldn't have murdered her daughter."

"Objection: it's a statement of opinion." Wright partially stood.

"I'll allow it since there's no jury. You may proceed."

"Thank you, Your Honor." Next Emilie walked Reid through the encounters at the hospital. "Would Robert let you see Kinley?"

"No. After my first visit, he made sure I couldn't see her unless someone was willing to look the other way. That's why I'm convinced we can't wait to protect her."

"You understand the protective order if issued today would be temporary?"

"Yes, though I hope the judge will extend it at the next hearing."

"Is there anything else you want the judge to know?"

Reid turned to the judge and met her gaze. "Kinley is the lone eyewitness other than her father to what happened in her home. If we let her go home with Robert, I am concerned she will be in grave danger if he believes she saw anything. Please give me the chance to keep her safe while we finish sorting out what really happened. The diamonds are proof Kaylene was ready to leave and make a safe life for herself and the girls."

"Thank you." The judge made a note. "Call your next witness."

Emilie looked over her shoulder, and her gaze connected with Detective Gaines at the back of the room. "I call Detective Gaines of the Alexandria PD."

After he was sworn in, she walked him through the police report. "What was the conclusion of the report?"

"That Kaylene Adams is the one who shot her children."

Emilie nodded. "Did you forward a file to me last night?"

"Yes."

"What was it?"

"A copy of the 911 call at the time of the shooting."

"Your Honor, I'd like to play it." The judge acquiesced, so she played it for all to hear.

Operator: I have your location from your phone. Tell me what's going on.
Man's voice: She has a gun.
Girl's voice: Daddy?
Woman's voice: I'll do anything. I'll say anything. Just put that away.
Operator: Sir, who has a gun?

Emilie could hardly stand listening to the call, imagining again what had happened.

Shot.

Woman's voice, sobbing: What are you doing?

Man's voice: She's got the gun.

Click. End of call.

Emilie let the silence, heavy and unshakeable, settle after the recording ended. As the judge shifted, Emilie turned back to the detective. "Is that an unaltered copy of the call?"

"Best as I can tell."

"Is there anything that makes you think it was altered?"

"No, it's the same call as the first time I heard it."

"Thank you." She glanced down at her notes. "No further questions." Emilie eased down, anticipating where Wright would take her cross.

Darlene Wright rose and straightened the bottom of her jacket. "Did the 911 call change the decision of the Alexandria police department?"

"No."

"It is still the conclusion of the police that Mrs. Adams shot her children?"

"The investigation is ongoing."

"The report states Mrs. Adams shot her children, correct?"

"Yes."

"No further questions."

"Redirect?" Judge Robinson tapped her pen against the tablet.

"Just two." Emilie stood and turned back to the detective. "Did you notice anything odd in the call?"

"Yes. Instead of urging the police to arrive, the man says, 'That's enough time.'"

"And based on your investigation, no one else was in the home? Just the four family members were there at the time of the shooting?"

"Yes." Detective Gaines's word was adamant and firm.

"Thank you." Emilie took a deep breath and looked at the judge. "That's all I have right now."

"All right." Judge Robinson pulled off her glasses and made a couple notes. Then she turned to opposing counsel. "I am undecided on the motion, but Ms. Wesley took her thirty minutes, so you may have the same amount of time. I'd like to hear your evidence."

Darlene frowned, then gathered her notes and forced a smile. "All right. My witness is Robert Adams."

The judge swore him in, and he settled against the witness chair, easily giving the basic information.

Darlene nodded toward Reid. "Has this man been actively involved with your girls?"

"No. He rarely came around."

"Because he didn't invite me," Reid muttered.

"Sh." Emilie didn't want the judge noting his interruption.

"Have you read the police report?"

"Yes."

"Is there anything you would add or change?"

"No." Robert sighed and looked appropriately broken. "It captures what happened on the day of that tragedy." He wiped under an eye, but Emilie didn't see any moisture. What an actor. "I want my little girl home with me."

Wright walked him through a few more questions and then turned him over to Emilie.

Emilie rose slowly and scanned her red notes. He was careful, but she knew him in a way he didn't appreciate. He was no different from the other men she'd come against who would do anything to maintain control. If she could push him far enough without raising Judge Robinson's ire, she knew she'd have him.

"Today, Ms. Wesley."

"Yes, Your Honor." She tapped her pad and then turned to Robert with a full-wattage smile. He leaned back and his frown intensified. "Mr. Adams, was anyone else in the home with you?"

"Objection, asked and answered."

"Ms. Wesley?"

"This is cross, but I'll withdraw it." She turned back to Robert. "You testified earlier that only you, Kaylene, and the girls were in the home, correct?"

"Yes."

"And when you called 911, shots were fired?"

"Yes."

"When the operator told you how long until the police arrived, what was your response?"

"I don't remember."

"Would you like me to replay it for the judge?" She turned back to the desk and held up her phone. "I'd be happy to do that." Very happy.

"No, that's okay." He studied her, and she could

almost see his brain spinning. "I said something about that being too long."

Emilie took the notes Hayden handed her. "I believe you said, 'That's enough time.'"

"Maybe."

"What did you mean?"

"That I hoped they'd arrive in time."

"But you actually said, 'That's enough time.'" She turned to the judge. "May I approach the witness?"

"You may."

She accepted the stack of paper Hayden offered and then walked to the witness stand. "You said, 'That's enough time.'" She handed him a copy of the call transcript Hayden had made before handing one to the judge and the last to Wright. "My question is, enough time for what?"

She turned back to him and watched his eyes dart back and forth. He was beginning to unravel.

"For the police to arrive."

"But enough time for you to do what?"

"Why would I do anything?"

"Didn't you want to finish what you'd started?"

Wright burst from her chair. "Objection. Badgering."

"Ms. Wesley?"

"You needed time. For what?" Emilie was taking a gamble by ignoring the judge, but she needed to keep the pace of the conversation going. Get Robert to forget what he was saying and to whom. He must be bursting to brag.

"None of your business."

She looked at the judge and swept her hands wide.

"But it is our business. Since the judge decides what's best for Kinley, she needs to know."

"I know what's best for Kinley," he roared.

"You do?"

"Yes, I'm her father, and I know best!"

"The court might disagree with you."

"No one will disagree with me. There is a reason she's mine."

"You don't own a child." She felt the chill of his words, but needed more. "No one owns another."

"But she will do what I say when I say it."

"Is that what Kaylene did wrong? She disobeyed?"

"That woman never knew what was best for her."

"But you did?"

"Of course. That's why she was mine."

"So you took her?"

"She was mine, and I could do anything I wanted with her."

"Even kill her."

Wright was back on her feet. "Objection, Your Honor. This is too much."

Robert bowled over her objection. "I didn't need to."

Silence fell like a blanket, Robert sitting there with a smile, arms crossed across his chest.

The judge leaned back, then looked at Emilie. "Proceed carefully."

"Thank you, Your Honor."

Robert seemed to take the words as encouragement, because he relaxed and laced his fingers over his stomach. Emilie liked the idea he was comfortable. Let him underestimate her. "What was your plan during those moments?"

"A plan is not something you make on the fly."

"No, you build it over time."

"Yes. And it was perfect."

"What about Kaydence?"

"She got what she deserved."

"Death? Really? That's what she deserved?"

"She forgot who she was."

"Along with Kaylene?"

"Too much like her mother."

"But not Kinley?"

"No." Robert leered at her. "You'll never take her."

"But you shot her too."

"No, that was her sister. Dumb girl couldn't shoot straight. I'm the better shot."

Silence fell. Emilie replayed his words in her mind, noted how his testimony deviated from what he'd offered in the report. She looked to the judge, noted Judge Robinson had caught every nuanced word. "Your Honor, I advise that you alert Mr. Adams that anything more he says could be used against him and that he has the right to an attorney."

"I'm right here, Ms. Wesley." Wright turned to the judge. "I'd ask for a recess."

"You may have that in the conference room. Bailiff, ask the sheriff's deputy to come in and escort them and keep them in that room. Then call the prosecutor. Detective, would you like to say anything?"

Detective Gaines shook his head. "You've covered it, Your Honor."

"So glad you approve." The judge turned to Reid. "I'm granting the protective order and giving you temporary custody pending the decision of the prosecutor. I am also scheduling this for a hearing two weeks from today when we'll know more about where this matter stands." She picked up her file and left the room.

Emilie leaned back and felt Reid's stare as the deputy walked Robert and his attorney from the room.

"Did that just go as well as I think?"

"Yes. We won." It was only for the moment, but it was a better start than she'd hoped.

Reid pulled her to her feet and spun her around. "I knew you could do it. Let's go get my niece."

"After we get the signed order." She grinned up at him. "Then I'm all yours."

CHAPTER 48

Reid ran his slick palms down the side of his navy khakis. He'd paired them with a collared shirt, open to reveal the neck of a T-shirt. With his loafers, he should hit the right note for an evening at Wolf Trap. Hopefully Emilie would enjoy the picnic he'd bought from the Whole Foods deli counter and the show that would follow. He had enough citronella to keep a swarm of mosquitos at bay. If the projected rain would hold off until after the show, the night would be perfect, since the seats under the covering had sold out before he had the idea. His mom had always said Wolf Trap was a romantic venue. He hoped Emilie agreed.

Kinley hobbled into the kitchen, looking alive and so good. Things weren't easy right now, but he had her with the best counselor the Haven staff recommended, and she was slowly settling in. Brandon had promised to come stay with her this evening, and Emilie had said her friend Caroline would be over as well. Like Brandon couldn't handle anything that came his way . . . but if that made Emilie comfortable leaving Kinley, it was good with him.

It would be an intimate concert.

One shared with around seven thousand.

But he hoped it would make an impression.

A knock at the door had him hurrying to it. "You ready, Kinley?"

"Sure." Her voice sounded small, but she sank onto the couch and lay down. Her little legs left plenty of room for Brandon, he hoped.

As soon as he opened the door, Brandon pushed through with a bag slung over his shoulder, holding another filled with takeout.

"Thanks for coming."

"Sure. I needed the break." There were new stress lines near his eyes. While Reid had won the contest at work, he hadn't done much to help Brandon.

"Hey. We're still going to find you the funding."

"Sure." Brandon forced a grin as he walked to the couch. "Hey there, princess. Remember me?"

She giggled. "You're Uncle Reid's friend."

"And I brought Strawberry Shortcake and American Girl DVDs."

"You're a good man, Brandon."

"Just used to working with kids."

Someone else knocked, and Reid would have sworn Brandon puffed even bigger. His little girl would be safe with him. "Calm down, big guy. I was expecting one more."

"Why?" Brandon looked around. "You think I can't handle her?"

Reid opened the door, and a cute brunette walked in. She was petite. Even shorter than Emilie, but she sparkled somehow.

"Hey, y'all. I'm Caroline Bragg." She stuck out her hand and shook his with lots of energy. "Here with my Mary Poppins bag and ready to get you out the door. You'd better scoot, man, or you will leave Em waiting. I don't recommend that." She stepped farther in, and Reid closed the door. "Who's your friend?"

Brandon looked frozen in place, like he couldn't quite take in this little fireball. Reid had to agree. She was more forceful than Emilie had described.

"Well, I know Kinley's safe with you two."

"'Course she is. Hey, sugar." Caroline sat down on the coffee table in front of Kinley. "Tonight is manicure night. Just wait until you see all the nail polish I brought. I've got rhinestones too. Everything for enough bling to blind the boys."

Kinley giggled and looked at Reid. "I like her."

"Me too." He turned to Brandon, who still looked a little starstruck. "I'll text when we leave the park, but call if anything happens."

"We're fine." Caroline's voice assured him they were. "Have a good time and get out of here."

Reid hurried from his apartment down to his Lexus and headed toward Em's town house. The streets of Old Town overflowed with the normal array of summer tourists searching for experiences that made the local history come to life. Or maybe they simply wanted a good meal or some ice cream to cool down.

He pulled into a street parking spot a few feet from her door and climbed from the car. When he knocked on the front door, he saw movement through the gauzy curtains, and a minute later she opened the door.

His lungs clenched, and he had to blink a couple times as he took in her appearance. She was wearing a sundress in bright pink with a polka dot sweater thrown over her arm. The broad-brimmed straw hat secured to her hair made her look ready for the Kentucky Derby. Between the dress and hat, he wouldn't lose her in the crowd.

"You look amazing."

A pink almost as bright as her dress crawled up her neck to her cheeks. He liked the look of softness and femininity it gave her.

"Thank you." She closed the door, then took the arm he offered and walked with him down the stairs. After he settled her in his car, she pivoted toward him. "What grand adventure are you taking me on?"

"Is a surprise good?"

She studied him a moment before nodding. "I'm not usually big on surprises, but I'll let you do it this time."

"So it'd better be a good one?"

"Yes, please."

"What's that look like?"

"Roses, good food, and sweet music."

"Hmm." He opened the dash and made a show of shoving things around as he tried to ignore the feel of her soft skin against his arm. "I'm already doomed since I forgot the roses. Any special color I should know about?"

"You'll have to surprise me." Her smile had a coquettish tinge to it, and he couldn't resist smiling back.

"We'll see if I can hit the rest of your list." He was feeling good about his chances as they drove toward Vienna and the park.

"I finally got the article turned in that my editor has been demanding. The night Kinley came home with you, the words began to flow. Olivia sounds pleased."

"Sounds like you are too."

"I'd begun to wonder if I could write again. With the Haven in such chaos, they don't need the pressure of my salary right now."

He bit back the urge to tell her he knew she didn't need the money at all, but decided that was her secret until she chose to share. As he listened, he could forget the stress of the competition at work as well as the legal wrangling with Robert. For a little while those stressors lessened their hold on him. Though from everything he was seeing, Robert would be plenty busy trying to snake his way out of the murder charges the prosecutor was pursuing. It wasn't an open and shut case, but it wouldn't be an easy escape.

As they turned into the park, Emilie started bouncing on the seat like an overexcited teenager. "Did you get tickets to the show?"

"I may have."

"Can you believe I've only been here one time, but I loved it. The setting is perfection."

He slid into a parking space, then pulled the basket and a picnic blanket from the trunk. "I have folding chairs if you'd like them."

She shook her head, and the hat miraculously stayed in place. "Leave them for now. I like the idea of enjoying a picnic on the lawn."

When they reached the grassy field leading to the amphitheater, people had set up areas for their picnics all around. The scent of rain highlighted the air, but the clouds didn't let it loose. Instead, the sun poked through, its rays warm on his face as he flipped the blanket open and let it settle to the grass.

As soon as Emilie sat down on the blanket, he opened the basket and pulled out tubs of food. In no time she was spooning dainty samples of each onto two paper plates.

"This is amazing."

"You can thank Whole Foods for that."

She leaned toward him. "I'll thank you for getting it."

A light breeze ruffled her hair, and he leaned forward to tuck a newly loosened strand behind her ear. She stilled and he didn't pull back. The sparks of electricity were almost enough to create lightning, and he knew he wanted to experience every charged moment.

. . .

Emilie hesitated, the feel of his warm touch on her cool skin electrifying.

She should lean away, break the connection, but all she wanted was for Reid to lean in and do exactly what his eyes promised. Oh, how she wanted him to kiss her. To feel his lips seal the promises his eyes were saying. Kinley was safe; surely she could now pursue her heart's desire.

He leaned a little closer, his thumb brushing her cheek in a soft stroke that had her resting against him. "May I kiss you?"

The question startled her. Had he really asked for

permission? She nodded, the words locked in her suddenly dry throat.

When his lips touched hers, it was featherlike. Then she leaned in, and he deepened the kiss. Her arm reached around his neck until she could tangle her fingers in his hair. This . . . It was even more than she'd anticipated.

"Get a room."

Emilie jerked back as the words were followed by laughter. She didn't want to scan the crowd, but instead buried her face in Reid's shoulder, her hat bobbing up as she did. His chest rumbled, and she peeked up at him. Laughter spilled from him as she met his gaze.

"I guess we made an impression."

She wanted to whisper that he had certainly made one on her. Instead, she pushed away and started fumbling with the food containers. Why wouldn't the lids fit?

"Emilie." His voice was like a caress.

She didn't deserve this. Her hands trembled and she looked for something else to do. "We should go get the chairs."

"Not yet." He took her hands, and his thumbs began to caress circles on the back of her hands. How could such a simple motion make her a ball of putty he could shape any way he wanted? Is this how her clients found themselves with the wrong man? A simple touch? Perfect words? Then their defenses crumbled like hers?

"Come on." He tugged her to her feet.

"But the food. The blanket."

"It will still be here when we get back. And if it's gone I can get more."

"All right." She chose to let go of the questions. Reid had proven himself to be the opposite of those other men. She would choose to believe in him, in the possibility of them. He was a worthy man.

He led her on a stroll away from the crowds of the amphitheater toward the woods with the smaller children's theater. Then they slowly made their way back, fingers interlocked, her heart content.

The show was magical. Reid never did go claim the chairs from his car. Instead, Emilie leaned against him, safe in the circle of his arms as the music of a string quartet wrapped magic in the evening air.

Later, as he walked her up the sidewalk to her front door, awkwardness filled her. What was she supposed to say now? Did he expect another kiss? Did she want to give him one? That was a ridiculous question; everything in her screamed yes! But was that the wise thing to do, or would this growing thing between them explode out of control?

What had happened to her firm rule about not getting involved with a client? As she looked at her fingers nestled next to his, she reminded herself the worst was over. He didn't need her lawyering as much as she needed him.

He must have read the warring thoughts on her face, because when they reached the door, he pulled her closer and leaned down. "What you do to me, Em."

She loved hearing him say her nickname that way, in that voice. "You melt me, Reid."

He leaned down and captured her lips again, this time in a sweetly passionate way. Time stopped as she let herself trust this man. When he pulled back, he leaned his forehead against hers. "You captivate me, woman."

She giggled. "I think I prefer 'Em.'"

"Duly noted." He tugged her close and sighed. She fit so well against him. Could she fit so well for the rest of her life?

"Go out with me tomorrow?"

She stepped back and laughed. "Can't get enough of me?"

"No." He grinned and took a step back. "I thought we could take Kinley to the zoo. I've got a wheelchair for her and thought the fresh air would be good for her."

"I'd love that."

"We're going to see where this leads, Em."

She couldn't contain her grin. "All right."

"Thanks for a great evening."

"It was perfect." And it was.

TWO WEEKS LATER

Emilie leaned back against her love seat. She held her laptop and felt the joy of words spilling from her. She'd talked to Olivia, and after she turned in this article she was taking a break from writing, at least for a while. Not because the words were gone. No, those had returned in a flurry of delight the week after Kinley's hearing.

With Robert under arrest for murder, thanks in no small part to Kinley's testimony, the flood had been unleashed. She hadn't let Kaylene down in the end. The story just had a different conclusion than she would have hoped.

Kinley told the judge that her father had been yelling and threatening her mother, and then Kaydence suddenly appeared with a gun and waved it at him. As their mother tried to get the gun from her, it went off and hit Kinley. And then she saw her father take the gun and shoot both her mother and her sister. What had started as a terrible accident had turned into a heinous crime.

In a week, she and Taylor would move over to Daniels, McCarthy & Associates. Emilie hadn't expected the move, but Savannah had assured her she could take the pro bono cases, and she thought she'd keep them a little more separated by not working at the agency.

With the Haven in disarray following Rhoda's death, Emilie knew she didn't want to become the executive director. She could do the job, but her heart was in helping people through the law. Until a new funding source could be found, the Haven needed the break from her salary. Jordan lingered in a coma, but the blood loss made it unlikely he'd survive if he didn't have a fortune paying to keep him alive. If he did survive, he'd spend the rest of his days in jail.

She hoped the distance from the Haven would help her hear what she was supposed to do now. She wasn't sure, but even as it unsettled her, she knew she was taking the right steps. God was the best career planner, and He would lead her.

Heavy footsteps sounded overhead, and she bit back the grin that wanted to explode across her face. Reid.

Lighter steps double-timed after his. He'd brought Kinley. Her heart felt full as they reached the stairs. He was so much more than she'd hoped for, and Kinley was an unexpected blessing. Helping her heal soothed the aching places in Emilie's heart. Kaylene and Kaydence were gone, but Kinley would recover.

Emilie hurriedly clicked a few words and then hit send on the article as the two who held her heart clomped down the stairs. She set the laptop aside just in time, because Reid hurried to her and tugged her into a hug.

"Em."

She sighed and let herself be loved. "Reid."

Kinley squeezed between them, and it became a hug of three.

Justice might have been imperfect, Kaylene and Kaydence were gone, but they had saved Kinley. In the process she'd found Reid, and he was perfect for her. Her heart was full.

ACKNOWLEDGMENTS

This book is the result of what-ifs, prayer, banging my head against the computer screen, more prayer, binge writing at a hotel in Dallas in between ACFW board meetings, and incredible edits. I pray the result is a book you will inhale and characters you'll love. I really enjoyed getting to know Emilie better and creating a suitable hero for her. I hadn't realized until this book that with *Beyond Justice* I'd created a series of heroines who are clambering for their own stories to be told, but nary a next hero in sight. Thanks to Tricia Goyer for helping me flesh out Reid. I'm already excited to have him show up in future books alongside Andrew.

Some stories grow out of experience, and this is one of those. I've had the privilege of working with women who were in the process of breaking free of situations that were intense and heartbreaking. It takes a village to help these women and men find the strength and make a plan. Locally we are blessed with agencies and leaders that come alongside them in a meaningful way. I worked with one of the best—Nora. She brings such grace to each situation and is a true help to those in need.

My prayer is that this book, while entertaining you, will also help you see the other side of relationships. People in these hard relationships need a listening ear and someone to pray with them and not judge them. No matter how much one person wants to save a marriage, some simply are unsalvageable without God's intervention.

My thanks to the Grove Girls, who make this writing journey so fun! Can't wait for our retreat! And to Colleen Coble, Robin Miller, Rachel Hauck, Tricia Goyer, and so many others who will brainstorm as soon as I email or call. My husband and daughter, Abigail, were also great brainstormers from the moment the what-if hit me at our apartment table in Siena. I never expected to get this idea while teaching a study abroad . . . You never know where that next what-if will come from.

Thanks so much to Amanda Bostic and LB Norton, my amazing editors. Thanks also to the rest of the incredible HarperCollins Christian Publishing fiction team: Paul Fisher, Jodi Hughes, Becky Monds, Kayleigh Hines, Allison Carter, Kristen Golden, and Karli Jackson. It has been a dream to work with you, and the dream-come-to-life is as wonderful as I'd hoped. Thank you for all you do to help craft my stories and then get them into the hands of readers. A book doesn't come to life before it is read, so thank you for being a key piece of breathing life into my stories.

Many thanks to Karen Solem, my amazing agent, who continues to believe in me and advocate for me.

Last but definitely not least, thanks to my family.

They have to live with me when I'm going crazy under deadline pressure. They understand the rhythms of a writer's life and believe in me when I wonder how a story will come together. This book fought me, and they kept encouraging me and putting up with a really tired mom. Love you guys!

DISCUSSION QUESTIONS

1. Emilie just wants to make a difference, but it seems her ability to do important things is slipping through her fingers. Have you had a similar desire? How did you make it come to life?

2. Reid has let the pressure to create a career replace family relationships. It's so easy to do. The urgent presses out the relationships we need and desire. Are you able to balance career and family? Service and family? How do you strike a balance? Is it even possible?

3. Emilie longs to be seen for who she is without external labels defining her. Is it possible to look past the labels to see people for who they really are? How can we do that?

4. Kinley is a little girl in need of a protector. She is truly helpless. How can you step to a place of helping those in need? How can you live Micah 6:8 (NIV)?

> He has shown you, O mortal, what is good.
>   And what does the LORD require of you?
> To act justly and to love mercy
>   and to walk humbly with your God.

5. Reid engages in a contest at work. He creates a team around him while a colleague tackles the challenge alone. How do you prefer to work? Alone or in a group? Why?

6. Reid wonders if it's time to build a family in his life. Then Kinley needs him. He's suddenly placed in a role of having a ten-year-old who needs him to protect her. What advice would you give him as he navigates that change?

7. Have you known anyone trapped in a relationship like Kaylene's? What happened?

8. What would you tell someone trapped in a dysfunctional relationship? What about someone in a domestic violence situation? How would you encourage them?

ABOUT THE AUTHOR

Cara Putman is the author of more than twenty-five legal thrillers, historical romances, and romantic suspense novels. She has won or been a finalist for honors including the ACFW Book of the Year and the Christian Retailing's BEST Award. Cara graduated high school at sixteen, college at twenty, completed her law degree at twenty-seven, and recently received her MBA. She is a practicing attorney, teaches undergraduate and graduate law courses at a Big Ten business school, and is a homeschooling mom of four. She lives with her husband and children in Indiana.

. . .

Visit her website at CaraPutman.com
Facebook: Cara.Putman
Twitter: @Cara_Putman